GIANT DAYS

VOLUME TEN

BOOM! BOX

BOOM! BOX

GIANT DAYS Volume Ten, June 2019. Published by BOOM! Box, a division of Boom Entertainment, Inc. Giant Days is ™ & © 2019 John Allison. Originally published in single magazine form as GIANT DAYS No. 37-40. ™ & © 2018 John Allison. All rights reserved. BOOM! Box™ and the BOOM! Box logo are trademarks of Boom Entertainment, Inc., registered in various countries and categories. All characters, events, and institutions depicted herein are fictional. Any similarity between any of the names, characters, persons, events, and/or institutions in this publication to actual names, characters, and persons, whether living or dead, events, and/or institutions is unintended and purely coincidental. BOOM! Box does not read or accept unsolicited submissions of ideas, stories, or artwork.

For information regarding the CPSIA on this printed material, call: (203) 595-3636 and provide reference #RICH – 840714.

BOOM! Studios, 5670 Wilshire Boulevard, Suite 400, Los Angeles, CA 90036-5679. Printed in the USA. First Printing.

ISBN: 978-1-68415-371-8, eISBN: 978-1-64144-354-8

GIANT DAYS

CREATED & WRITTEN BY
JOHN ALLISON

ILLUSTRATED BY
MAX SARIN
(CHAPTERS 37 & 40)
JULIA MADRIGAL
(CHAPTERS 38 & 39)

COLORS BY
WHITNEY COGAR

LETTERS BY
JIM CAMPBELL

COVER BY
MAX SARIN

COLLECTION DESIGNER
KARA LEOPARD

ASSOCIATE EDITOR
SOPHIE PHILIPS-ROBERTS

SERIES DESIGNERS
**MICHELLE ANKLEY
& GRACE PARK**

EDITOR
SHANNON WATTERS

CHAPTER
THIRTY SEVEN

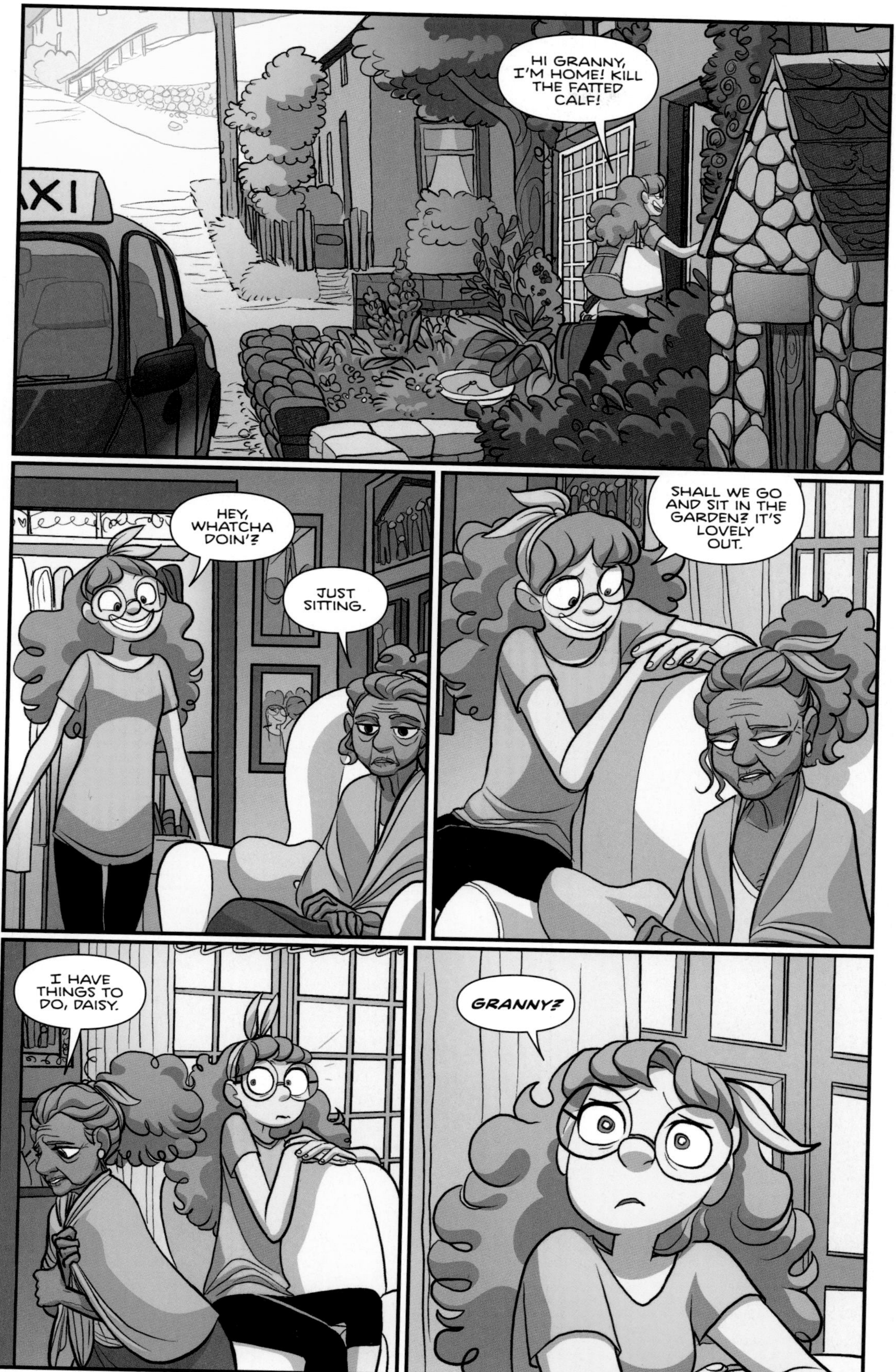
AXI
HI GRANNY, I'M HOME! KILL THE FATTED CALF!
HEY, WHATCHA DOIN'?
JUST SITTING.
SHALL WE GO AND SIT IN THE GARDEN? IT'S LOVELY OUT.
I HAVE THINGS TO DO, DAISY.
GRANNY?

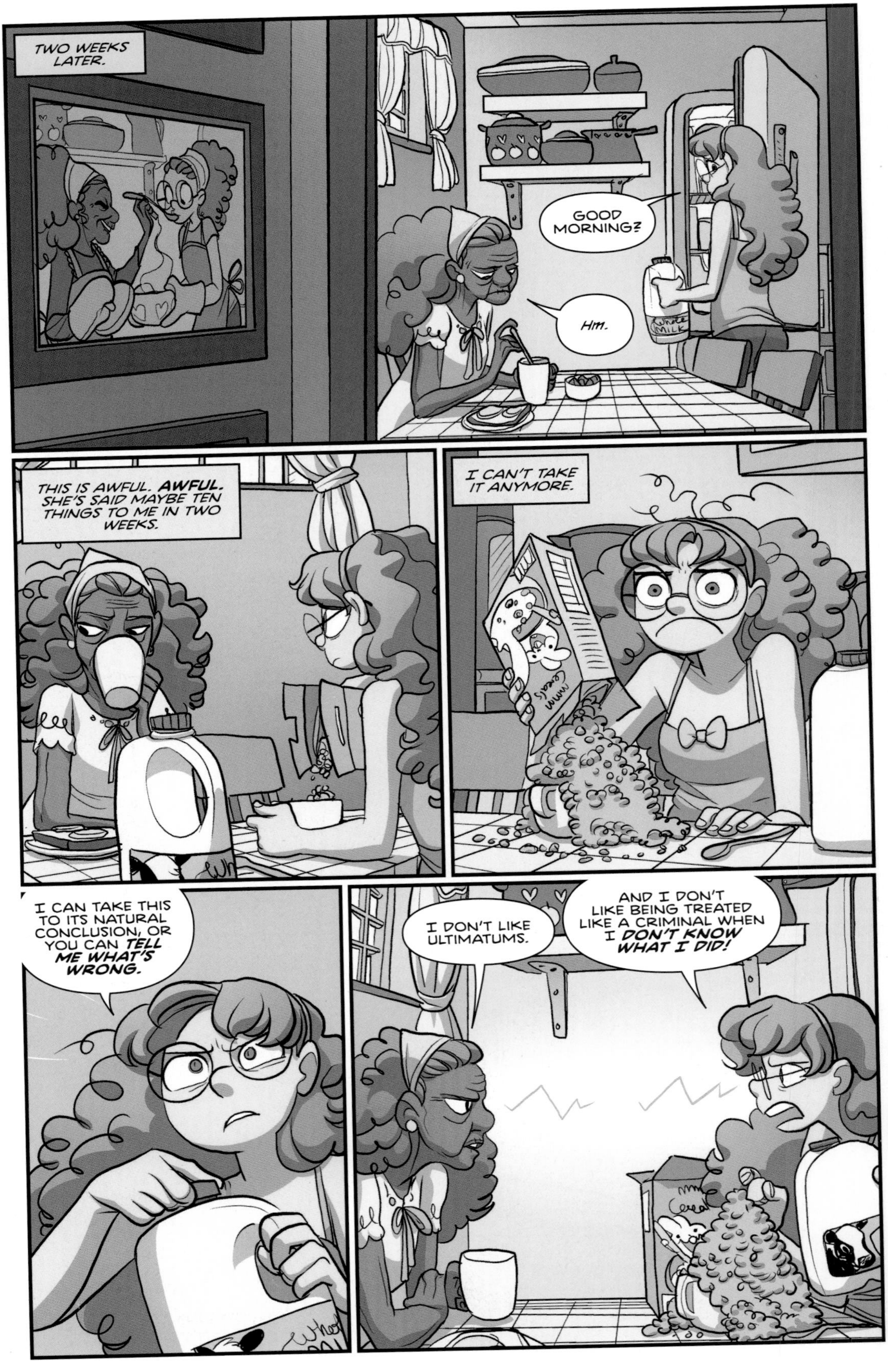
TWO WEEKS LATER.
GOOD MORNING?
Hm.
THIS IS AWFUL. AWFUL. SHE'S SAID MAYBE TEN THINGS TO ME IN TWO WEEKS.
I CAN'T TAKE IT ANYMORE.
I CAN TAKE THIS TO ITS NATURAL CONCLUSION, OR YOU CAN TELL ME WHAT'S WRONG.
I DON'T LIKE ULTIMATUMS.
AND I DON'T LIKE BEING TREATED LIKE A CRIMINAL WHEN I DON'T KNOW WHAT I DID!

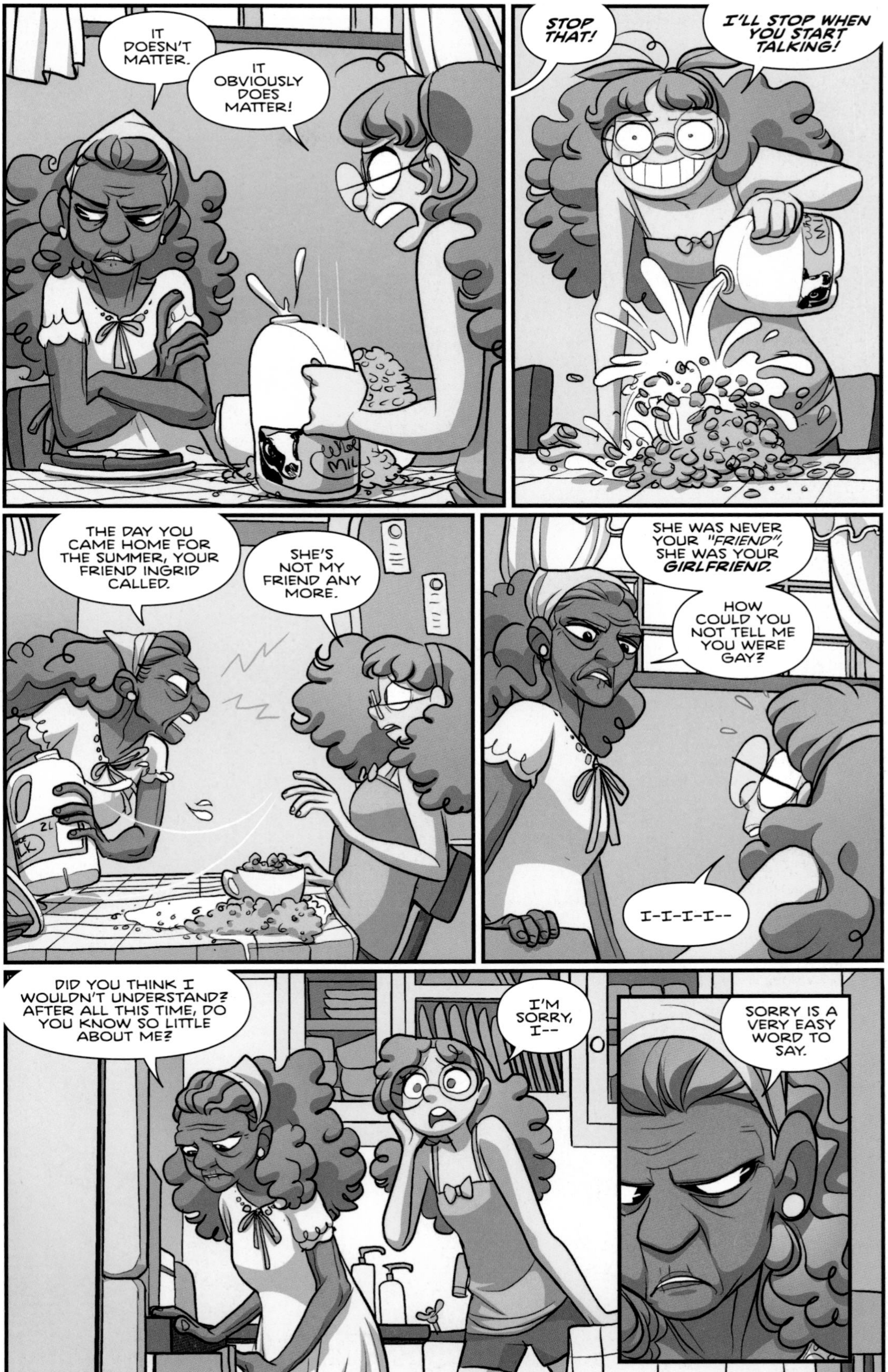

IT DOESN'T MATTER.
IT OBVIOUSLY DOES MATTER!
STOP THAT!
I'LL STOP WHEN YOU START TALKING!
THE DAY YOU CAME HOME FOR THE SUMMER, YOUR FRIEND INGRID CALLED.
SHE'S NOT MY FRIEND ANY MORE.
SHE WAS NEVER YOUR "FRIEND", SHE WAS YOUR ***GIRLFRIEND.***
HOW COULD YOU NOT TELL ME YOU WERE GAY?
I-I-I-I--
DID YOU THINK I WOULDN'T UNDERSTAND? AFTER ALL THIS TIME, DO YOU KNOW SO LITTLE ABOUT ME?
I'M SORRY, I--
SORRY IS A VERY EASY WORD TO SAY.

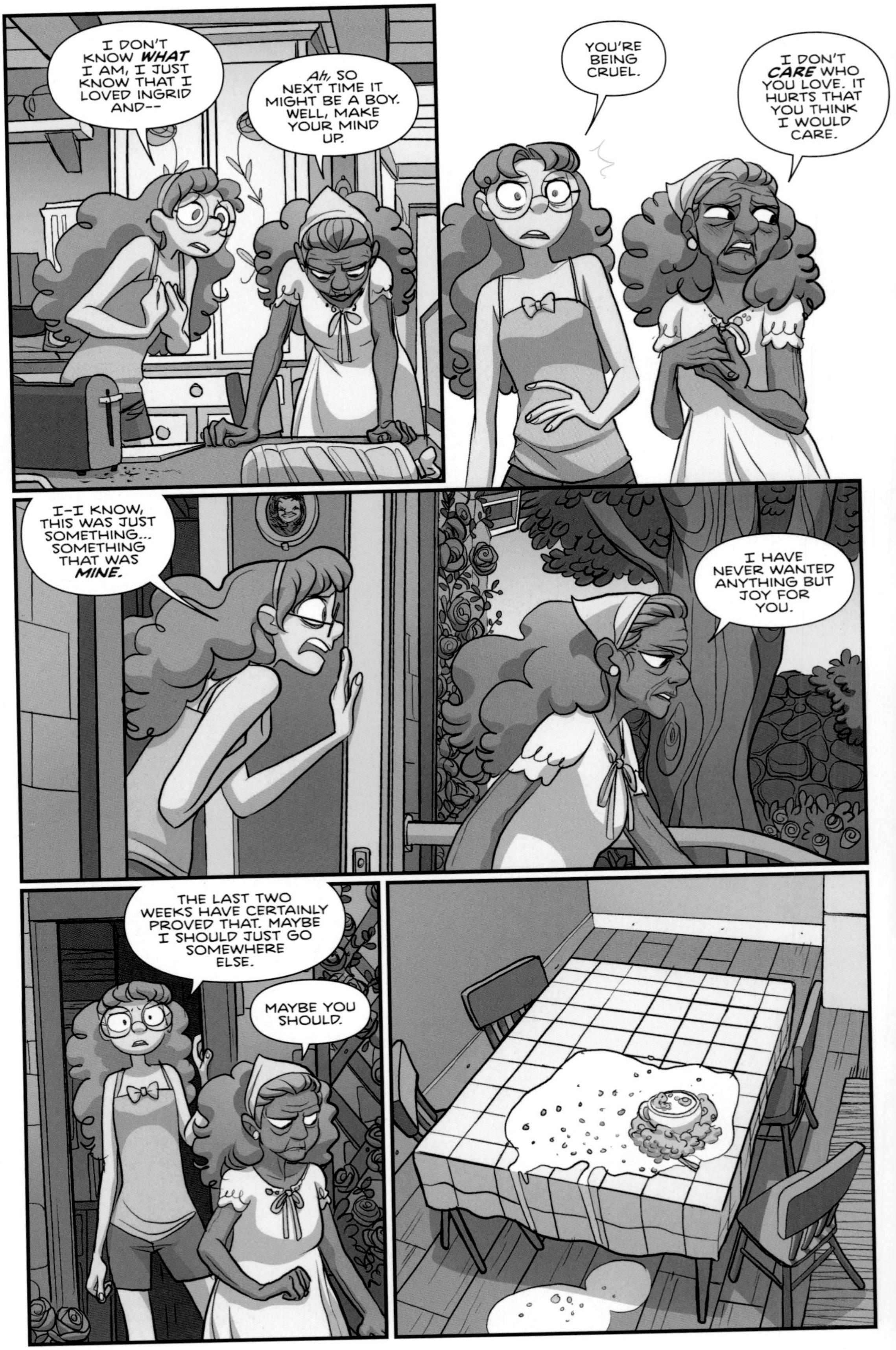
I DON'T KNOW WHAT I AM, I JUST KNOW THAT I LOVED INGRID AND--
Ah, SO NEXT TIME IT MIGHT BE A BOY. WELL, MAKE YOUR MIND UP.
YOU'RE BEING CRUEL.
I DON'T CARE WHO YOU LOVE. IT HURTS THAT YOU THINK I WOULD CARE.
I-I KNOW, THIS WAS JUST SOMETHING... SOMETHING THAT WAS MINE.
I HAVE NEVER WANTED ANYTHING BUT JOY FOR YOU.
THE LAST TWO WEEKS HAVE CERTAINLY PROVED THAT. MAYBE I SHOULD JUST GO SOMEWHERE ELSE.
MAYBE YOU SHOULD.

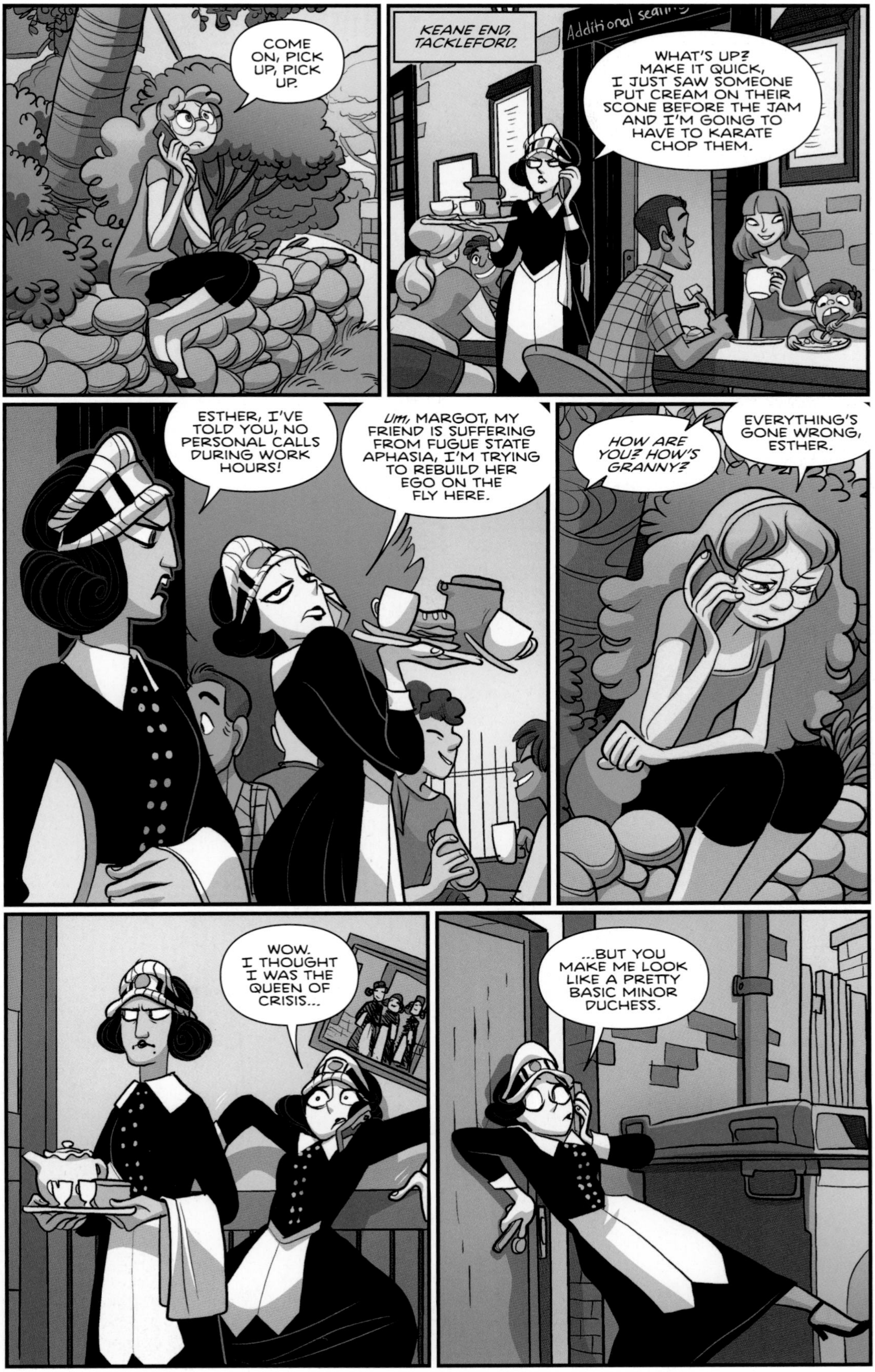
COME ON, PICK UP, PICK UP.
KEANE END, TACKLEFORD.
Additional seating
WHAT'S UP? MAKE IT QUICK, I JUST SAW SOMEONE PUT CREAM ON THEIR SCONE BEFORE THE JAM AND I'M GOING TO HAVE TO KARATE CHOP THEM.
ESTHER, I'VE TOLD YOU, NO PERSONAL CALLS DURING WORK HOURS!
UM, MARGOT, MY FRIEND IS SUFFERING FROM FUGUE STATE APHASIA, I'M TRYING TO REBUILD HER EGO ON THE FLY HERE.
HOW ARE YOU? HOW'S GRANNY?
EVERYTHING'S GONE WRONG, ESTHER.
WOW. I THOUGHT I WAS THE QUEEN OF CRISIS...
...BUT YOU MAKE ME LOOK LIKE A PRETTY BASIC MINOR DUCHESS.

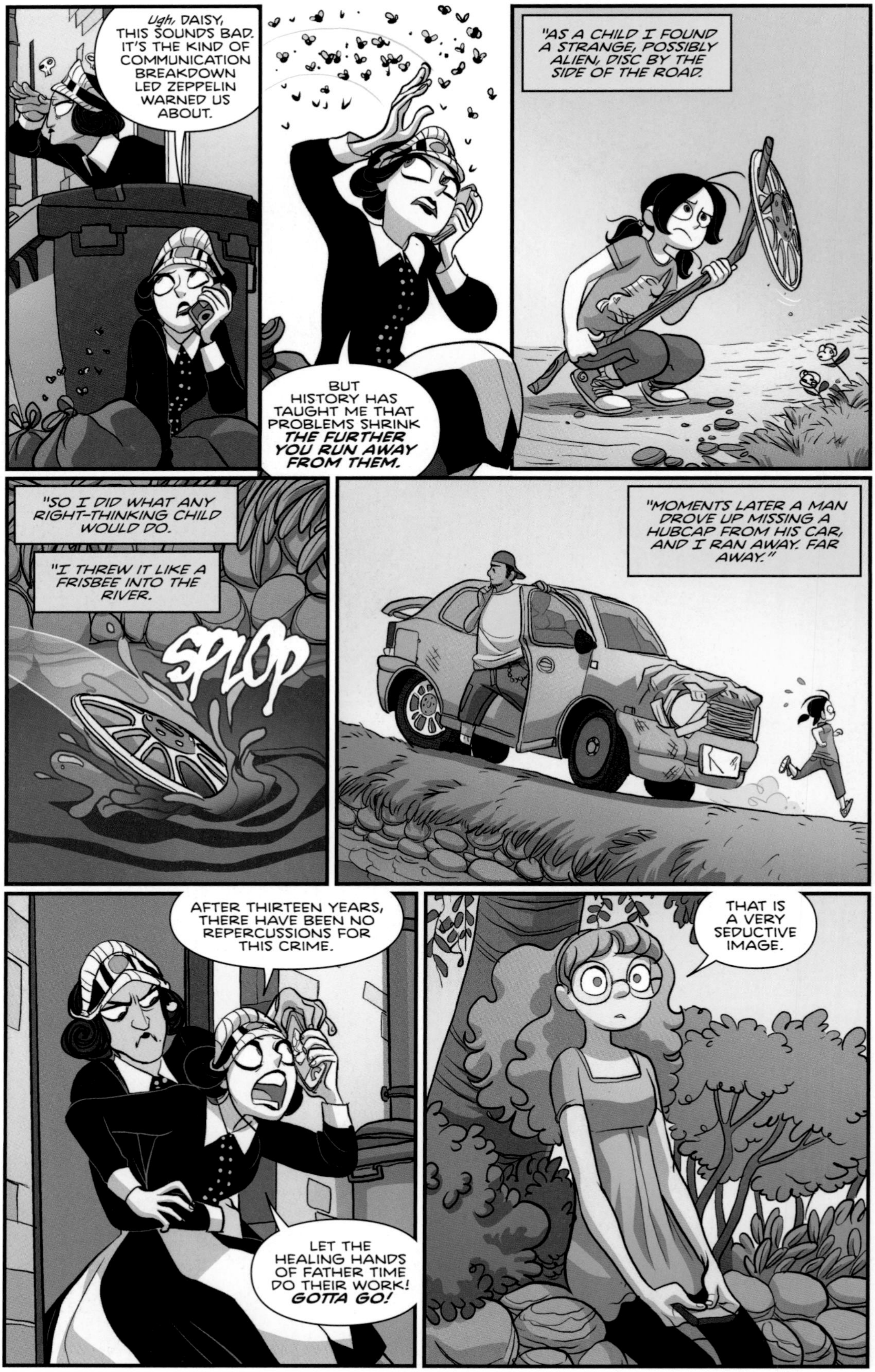
Ugh, DAISY, THIS SOUNDS BAD. IT'S THE KIND OF COMMUNICATION BREAKDOWN LED ZEPPELIN WARNED US ABOUT.
BUT HISTORY HAS TAUGHT ME THAT PROBLEMS SHRINK THE FURTHER YOU RUN AWAY FROM THEM.
"AS A CHILD I FOUND A STRANGE, POSSIBLY ALIEN, DISC BY THE SIDE OF THE ROAD.
"SO I DID WHAT ANY RIGHT-THINKING CHILD WOULD DO.
"I THREW IT LIKE A FRISBEE INTO THE RIVER.
SPLOP
"MOMENTS LATER A MAN DROVE UP MISSING A HUBCAP FROM HIS CAR, AND I RAN AWAY. FAR AWAY."
AFTER THIRTEEN YEARS, THERE HAVE BEEN NO REPERCUSSIONS FOR THIS CRIME.
LET THE HEALING HANDS OF FATHER TIME DO THEIR WORK! GOTTA GO!
THAT IS A VERY SEDUCTIVE IMAGE.

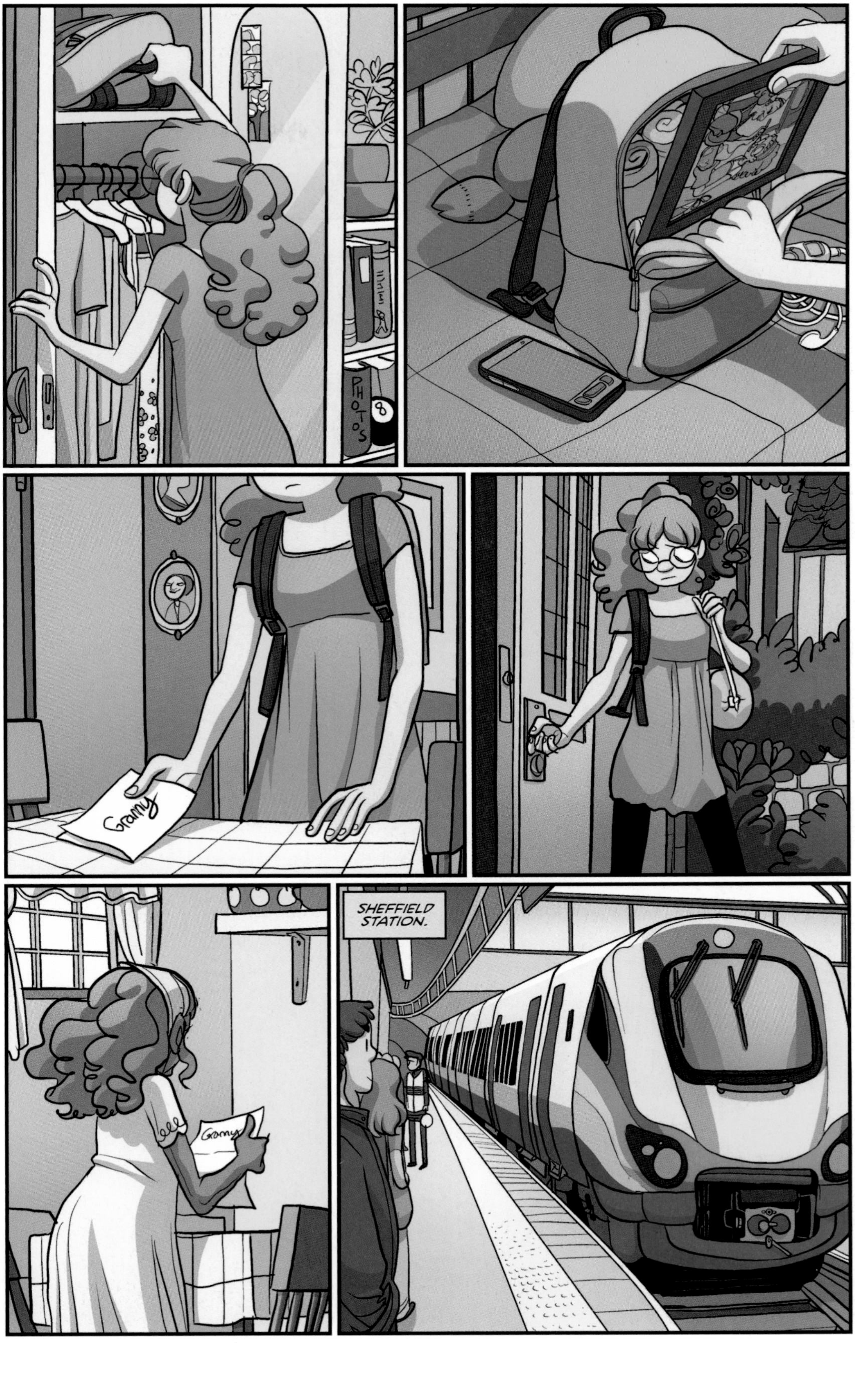
PHOTOS
Gramy
Gramy
SHEFFIELD STATION.

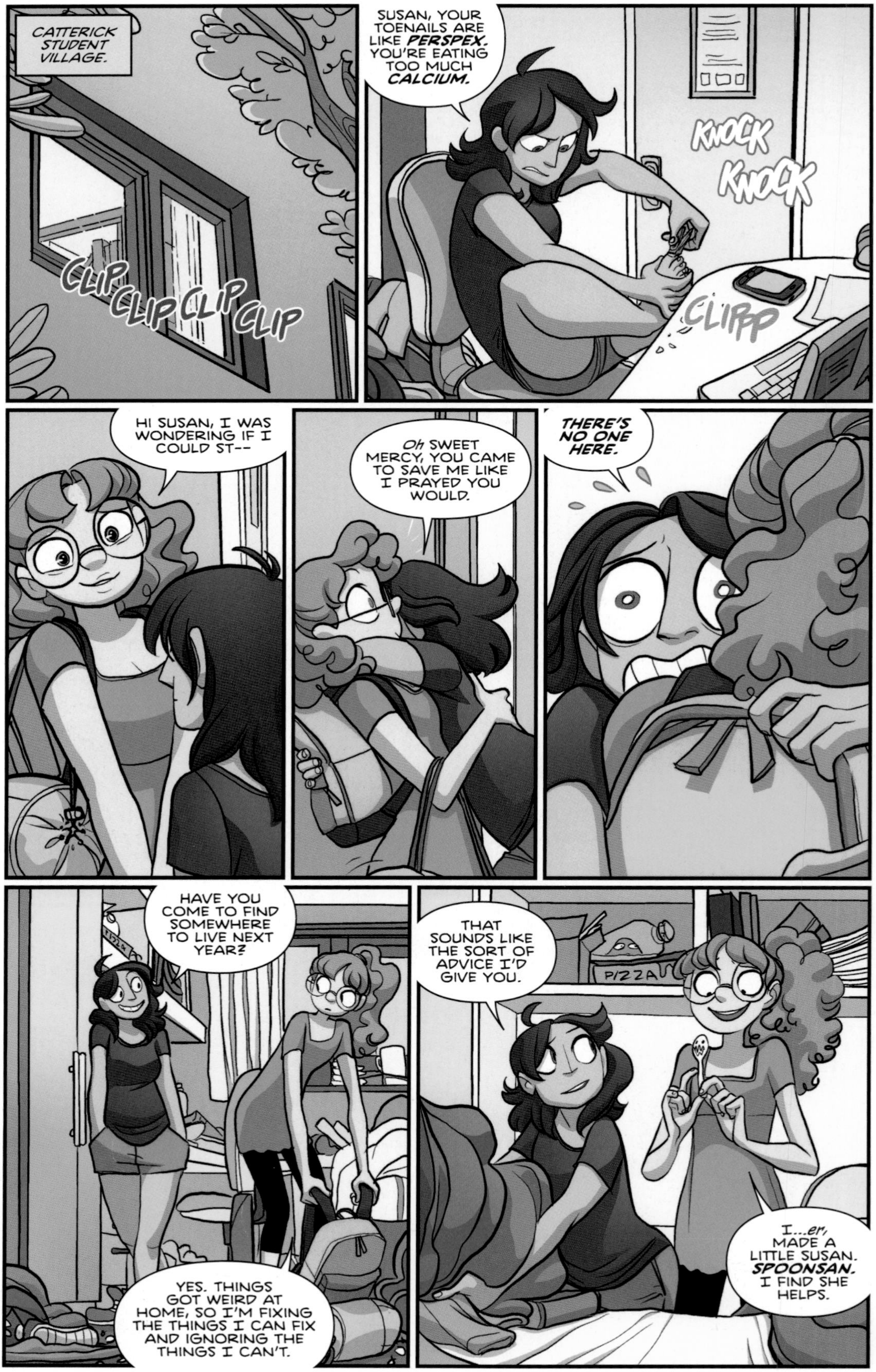
CATTERICK STUDENT VILLAGE.
CLIP CLIP CLIP CLIP
SUSAN, YOUR TOENAILS ARE LIKE *PERSPEX.* YOU'RE EATING TOO MUCH *CALCIUM.*
KNOCK KNOCK
CLIPP
HI SUSAN, I WAS WONDERING IF I COULD ST--
Oh SWEET MERCY, YOU CAME TO SAVE ME LIKE I PRAYED YOU WOULD.
THERE'S NO ONE HERE.
HAVE YOU COME TO FIND SOMEWHERE TO LIVE NEXT YEAR?
YES. THINGS GOT WEIRD AT HOME, SO I'M FIXING THE THINGS I CAN FIX AND IGNORING THE THINGS I CAN'T.
PIZZA
THAT SOUNDS LIKE THE SORT OF ADVICE I'D GIVE YOU.
I...*er,* MADE A LITTLE SUSAN. ***SPOONSAN.*** I FIND SHE HELPS.

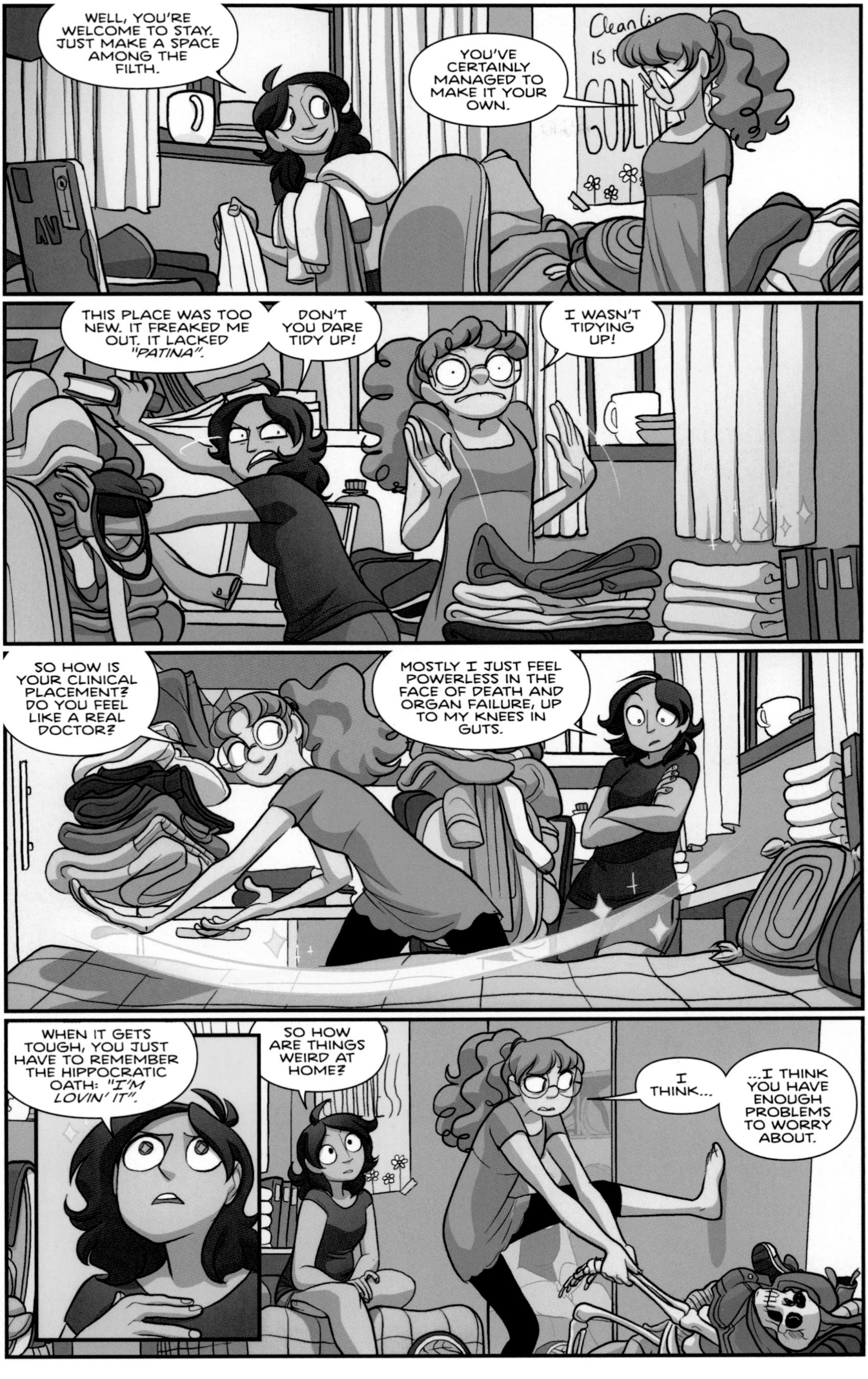

WELL, YOU'RE WELCOME TO STAY. JUST MAKE A SPACE AMONG THE FILTH.
YOU'VE CERTAINLY MANAGED TO MAKE IT YOUR OWN.
THIS PLACE WAS TOO NEW. IT FREAKED ME OUT. IT LACKED "PATINA".
DON'T YOU DARE TIDY UP!
I WASN'T TIDYING UP!
SO HOW IS YOUR CLINICAL PLACEMENT? DO YOU FEEL LIKE A REAL DOCTOR?
MOSTLY I JUST FEEL POWERLESS IN THE FACE OF DEATH AND ORGAN FAILURE, UP TO MY KNEES IN GUTS.
WHEN IT GETS TOUGH, YOU JUST HAVE TO REMEMBER THE HIPPOCRATIC OATH: "I'M LOVIN' IT".
SO HOW ARE THINGS WEIRD AT HOME?
I THINK...
...I THINK YOU HAVE ENOUGH PROBLEMS TO WORRY ABOUT.

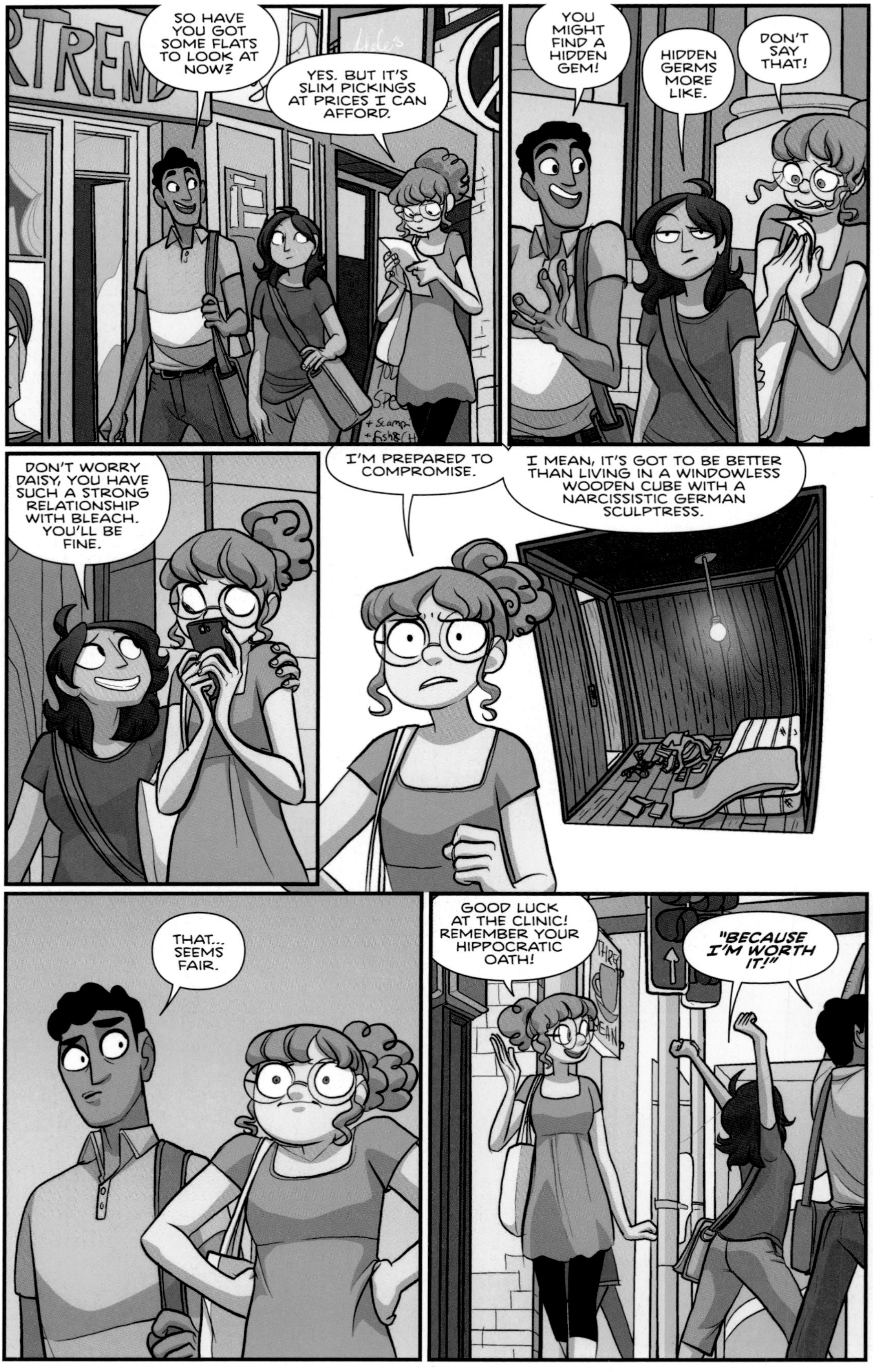
SO HAVE YOU GOT SOME FLATS TO LOOK AT NOW?
YES. BUT IT'S SLIM PICKINGS AT PRICES I CAN AFFORD.
YOU MIGHT FIND A HIDDEN GEM!
HIDDEN GERMS MORE LIKE.
DON'T SAY THAT!
DON'T WORRY DAISY, YOU HAVE SUCH A STRONG RELATIONSHIP WITH BLEACH. YOU'LL BE FINE.
I'M PREPARED TO COMPROMISE.
I MEAN, IT'S GOT TO BE BETTER THAN LIVING IN A WINDOWLESS WOODEN CUBE WITH A NARCISSISTIC GERMAN SCULPTRESS.
THAT... SEEMS FAIR.
GOOD LUCK AT THE CLINIC! REMEMBER YOUR HIPPOCRATIC OATH!
"BECAUSE I'M WORTH IT!"

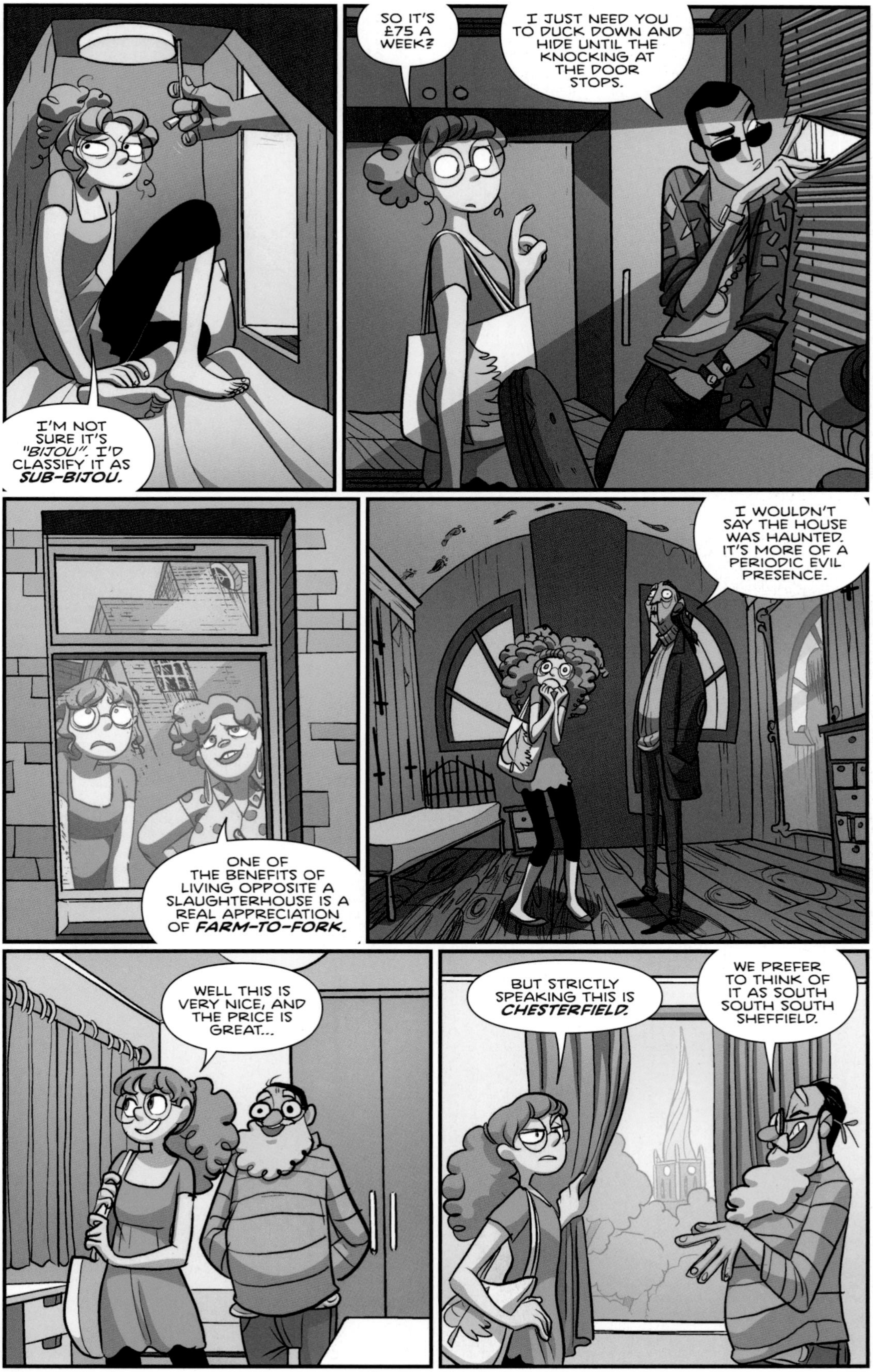
I'M NOT SURE IT'S "BIJOU". I'D CLASSIFY IT AS **SUB-BIJOU.**
SO IT'S £75 A WEEK?
I JUST NEED YOU TO DUCK DOWN AND HIDE UNTIL THE KNOCKING AT THE DOOR STOPS.
ONE OF THE BENEFITS OF LIVING OPPOSITE A SLAUGHTERHOUSE IS A REAL APPRECIATION OF **FARM-TO-FORK.**
I WOULDN'T SAY THE HOUSE WAS HAUNTED. IT'S MORE OF A PERIODIC EVIL PRESENCE.
WELL THIS IS VERY NICE, AND THE PRICE IS GREAT...
BUT STRICTLY SPEAKING THIS IS **CHESTERFIELD.**
WE PREFER TO THINK OF IT AS SOUTH SOUTH SOUTH SHEFFIELD.

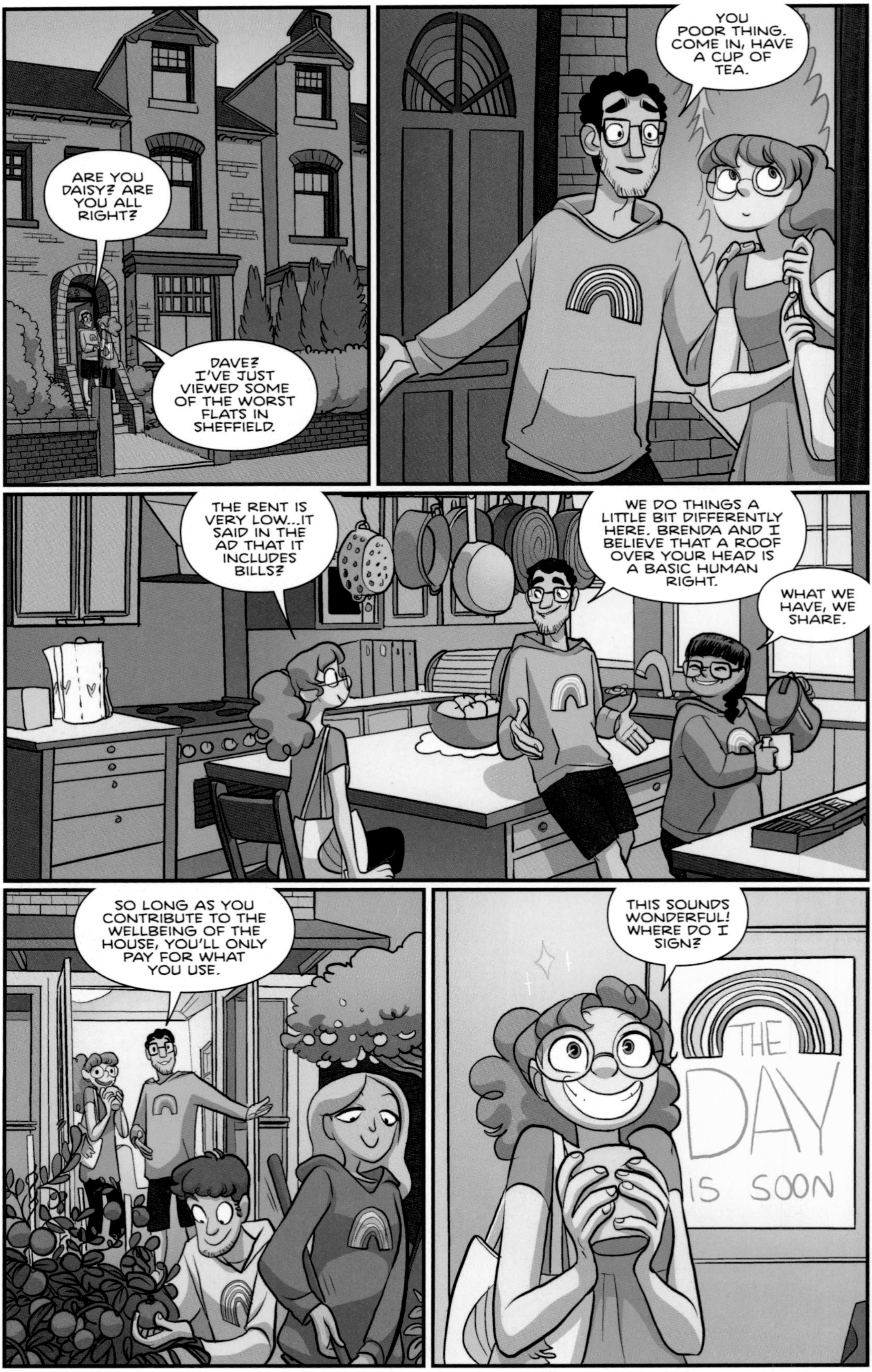
ARE YOU DAISY? ARE YOU ALL RIGHT?
DAVE? I'VE JUST VIEWED SOME OF THE WORST FLATS IN SHEFFIELD.
YOU POOR THING. COME IN, HAVE A CUP OF TEA.
THE RENT IS VERY LOW...IT SAID IN THE AD THAT IT INCLUDES BILLS?
WE DO THINGS A LITTLE BIT DIFFERENTLY HERE. BRENDA AND I BELIEVE THAT A ROOF OVER YOUR HEAD IS A BASIC HUMAN RIGHT.
WHAT WE HAVE, WE SHARE.
SO LONG AS YOU CONTRIBUTE TO THE WELLBEING OF THE HOUSE, YOU'LL ONLY PAY FOR WHAT YOU USE.
THIS SOUNDS WONDERFUL! WHERE DO I SIGN?
THE DAY IS SOON

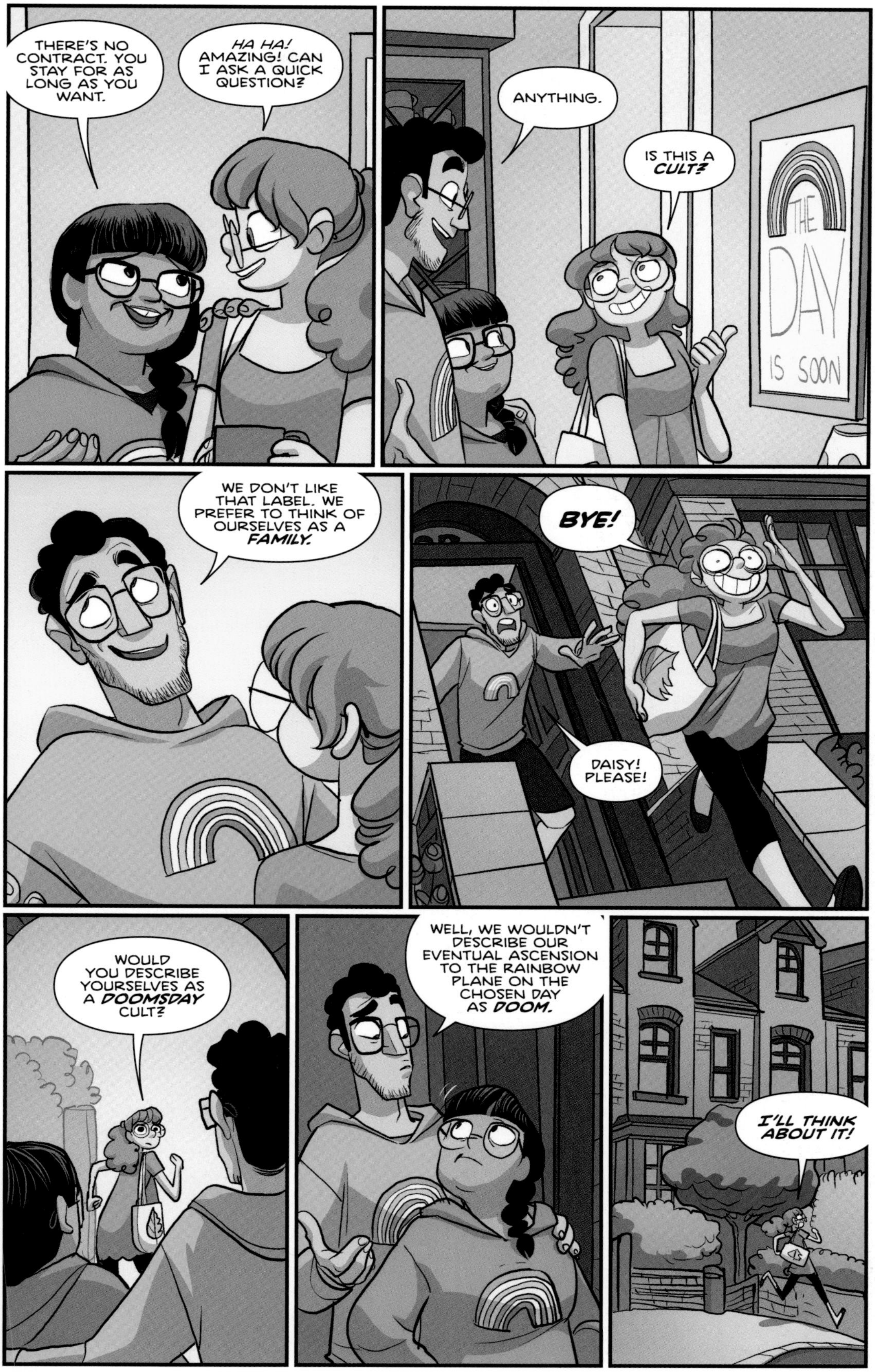
THERE'S NO CONTRACT. YOU STAY FOR AS LONG AS YOU WANT.
HA HA! AMAZING! CAN I ASK A QUICK QUESTION?
ANYTHING.
IS THIS A CULT?
THE DAY IS SOON
WE DON'T LIKE THAT LABEL. WE PREFER TO THINK OF OURSELVES AS A FAMILY.
BYE!
DAISY! PLEASE!
WOULD YOU DESCRIBE YOURSELVES AS A DOOMSDAY CULT?
WELL, WE WOULDN'T DESCRIBE OUR EVENTUAL ASCENSION TO THE RAINBOW PLANE ON THE CHOSEN DAY AS DOOM.
I'LL THINK ABOUT IT!

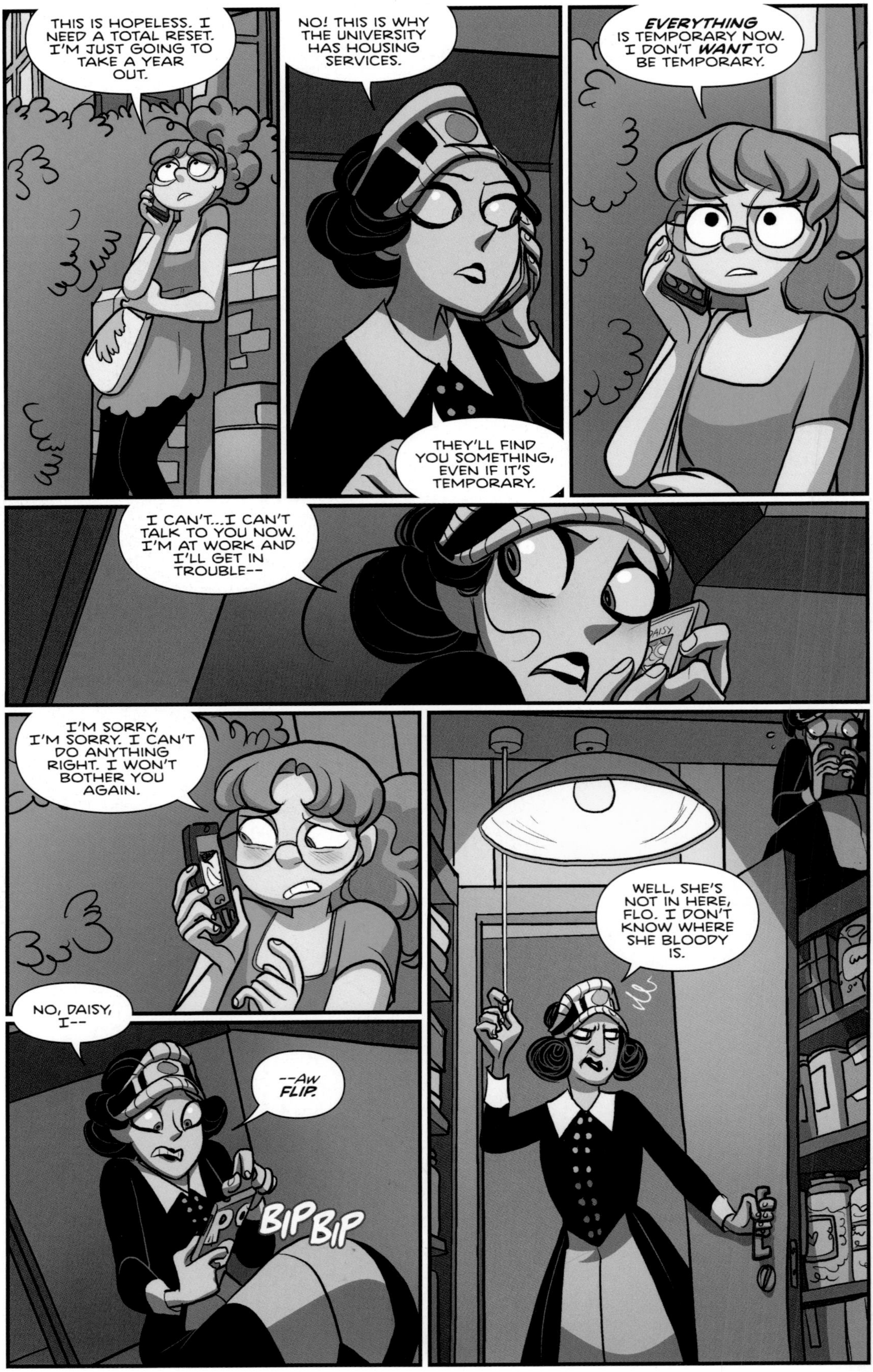
THIS IS HOPELESS. I NEED A TOTAL RESET. I'M JUST GOING TO TAKE A YEAR OUT.
NO! THIS IS WHY THE UNIVERSITY HAS HOUSING SERVICES.
THEY'LL FIND YOU SOMETHING, EVEN IF IT'S TEMPORARY.
EVERYTHING IS TEMPORARY NOW. I DON'T WANT TO BE TEMPORARY.
I CAN'T...I CAN'T TALK TO YOU NOW. I'M AT WORK AND I'LL GET IN TROUBLE--
DAISY
I'M SORRY, I'M SORRY. I CAN'T DO ANYTHING RIGHT. I WON'T BOTHER YOU AGAIN.
NO, DAISY, I--
--AW FLIP.
BIP BIP
WELL, SHE'S NOT IN HERE, FLO. I DON'T KNOW WHERE SHE BLOODY IS.

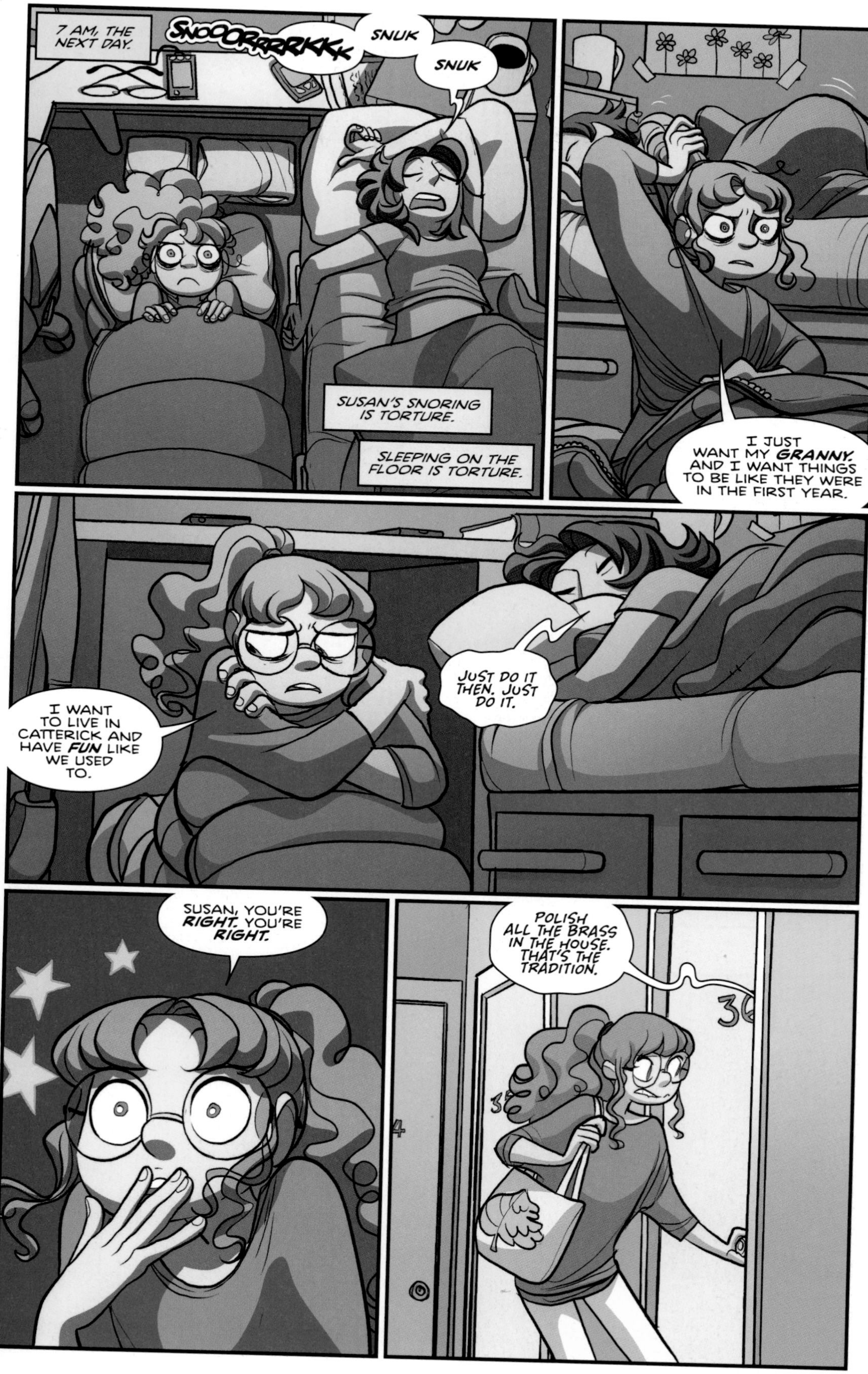

7 AM, THE NEXT DAY.
SNOOORRRRRKKKK
SNUK
SNUK
SUSAN'S SNORING IS TORTURE.
SLEEPING ON THE FLOOR IS TORTURE.
I JUST WANT MY GRANNY. AND I WANT THINGS TO BE LIKE THEY WERE IN THE FIRST YEAR.
I WANT TO LIVE IN CATTERICK AND HAVE FUN LIKE WE USED TO.
JUST DO IT THEN. JUST DO IT.
SUSAN, YOU'RE RIGHT. YOU'RE RIGHT.
POLISH ALL THE BRASS IN THE HOUSE. THAT'S THE TRADITION.

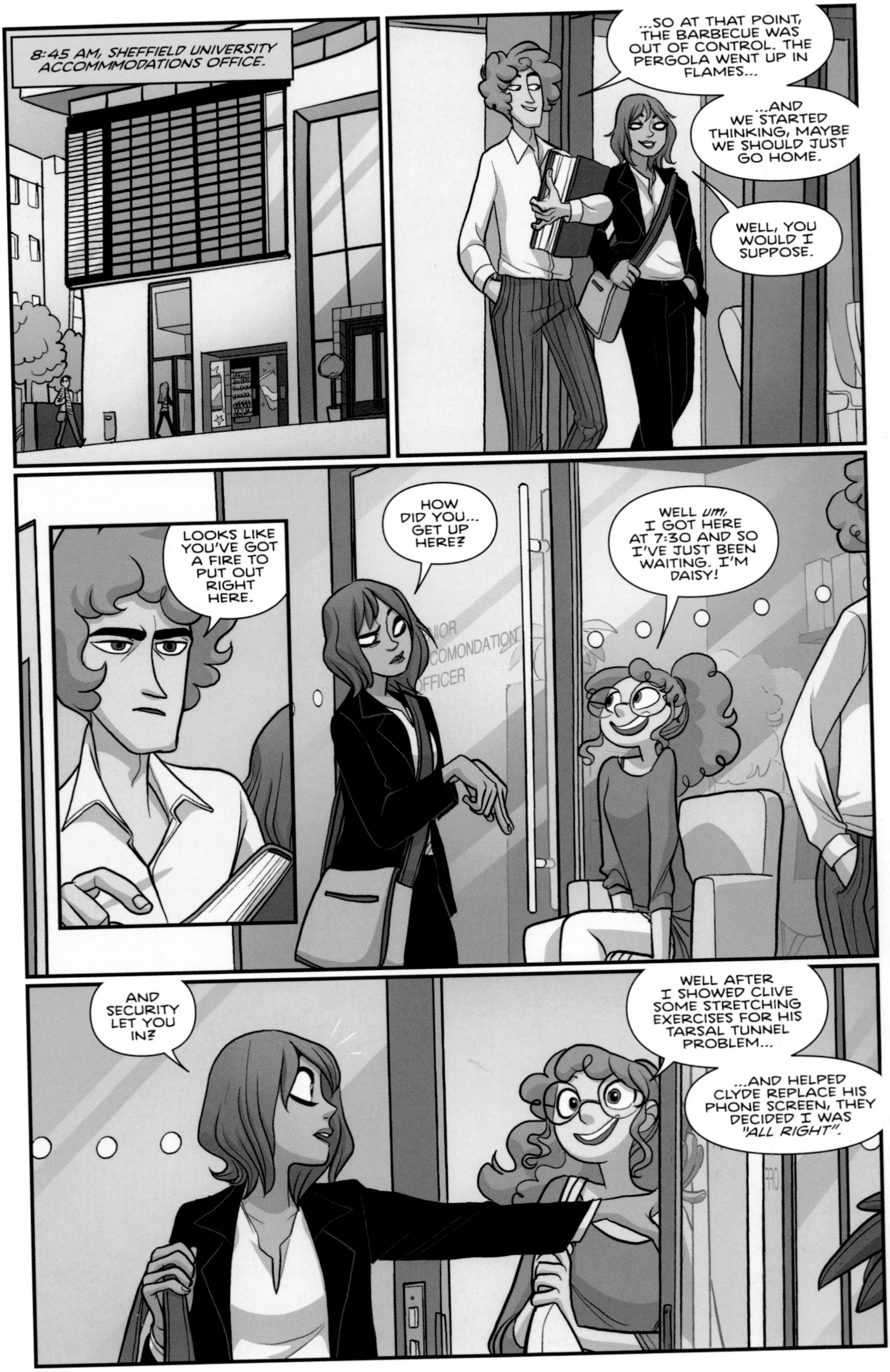
8:45 AM, SHEFFIELD UNIVERSITY ACCOMMODATIONS OFFICE.
...SO AT THAT POINT, THE BARBECUE WAS OUT OF CONTROL. THE PERGOLA WENT UP IN FLAMES...
...AND WE STARTED THINKING, MAYBE WE SHOULD JUST GO HOME.
WELL, YOU WOULD I SUPPOSE.
LOOKS LIKE YOU'VE GOT A FIRE TO PUT OUT RIGHT HERE.
HOW DID YOU... GET UP HERE?
WELL *UM*, I GOT HERE AT 7:30 AND SO I'VE JUST BEEN WAITING. I'M DAISY!
AND SECURITY LET YOU IN?
WELL AFTER I SHOWED CLIVE SOME STRETCHING EXERCISES FOR HIS TARSAL TUNNEL PROBLEM...
...AND HELPED CLYDE REPLACE HIS PHONE SCREEN, THEY DECIDED I WAS *"ALL RIGHT"*.

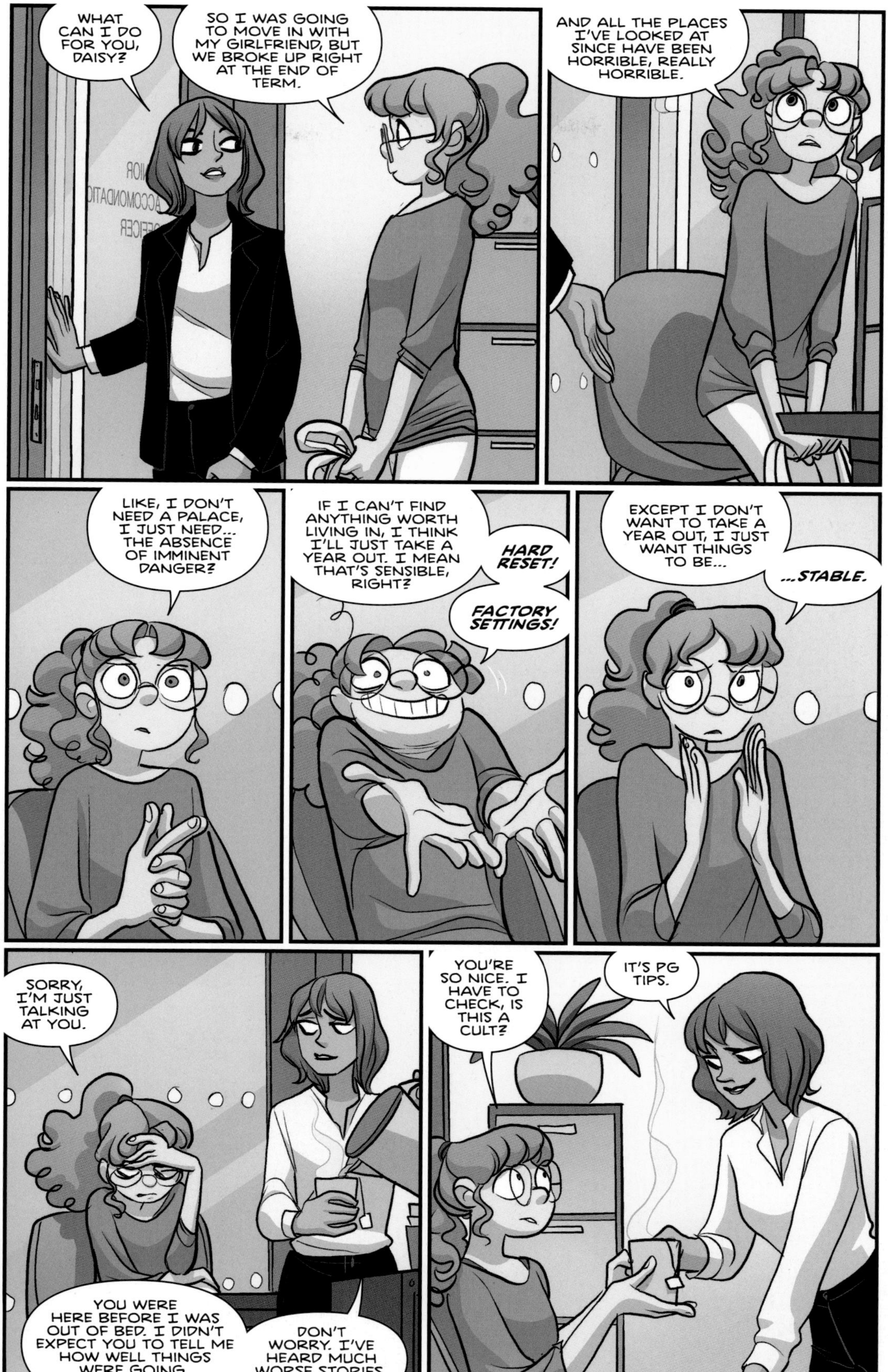
WHAT CAN I DO FOR YOU, DAISY?
SO I WAS GOING TO MOVE IN WITH MY GIRLFRIEND, BUT WE BROKE UP RIGHT AT THE END OF TERM.
AND ALL THE PLACES I'VE LOOKED AT SINCE HAVE BEEN HORRIBLE, REALLY HORRIBLE.
LIKE, I DON'T NEED A PALACE, I JUST NEED... THE ABSENCE OF IMMINENT DANGER?
IF I CAN'T FIND ANYTHING WORTH LIVING IN, I THINK I'LL JUST TAKE A YEAR OUT. I MEAN THAT'S SENSIBLE, RIGHT?
HARD RESET!
FACTORY SETTINGS!
EXCEPT I DON'T WANT TO TAKE A YEAR OUT, I JUST WANT THINGS TO BE...
...STABLE.
SORRY, I'M JUST TALKING AT YOU.
YOU WERE HERE BEFORE I WAS OUT OF BED. I DIDN'T EXPECT YOU TO TELL ME HOW WELL THINGS WERE GOING.
DON'T WORRY. I'VE HEARD MUCH WORSE STORIES.
YOU'RE SO NICE. I HAVE TO CHECK, IS THIS A CULT?
IT'S PG TIPS.

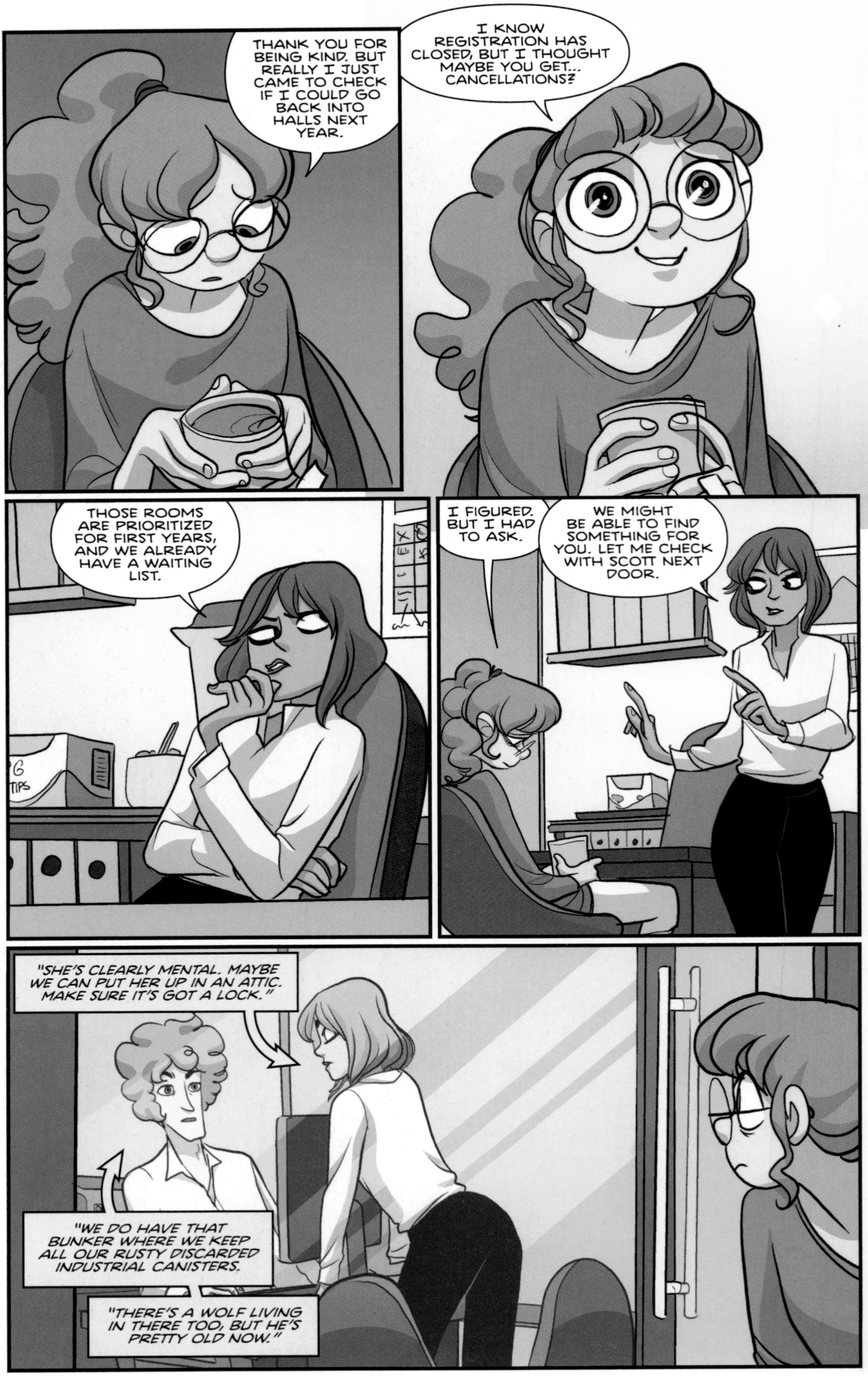
THANK YOU FOR BEING KIND. BUT REALLY I JUST CAME TO CHECK IF I COULD GO BACK INTO HALLS NEXT YEAR.
I KNOW REGISTRATION HAS CLOSED, BUT I THOUGHT MAYBE YOU GET... CANCELLATIONS?
THOSE ROOMS ARE PRIORITIZED FOR FIRST YEARS, AND WE ALREADY HAVE A WAITING LIST.
I FIGURED. BUT I HAD TO ASK.
WE MIGHT BE ABLE TO FIND SOMETHING FOR YOU. LET ME CHECK WITH SCOTT NEXT DOOR.
"SHE'S CLEARLY MENTAL. MAYBE WE CAN PUT HER UP IN AN ATTIC. MAKE SURE IT'S GOT A LOCK."
"WE DO HAVE THAT BUNKER WHERE WE KEEP ALL OUR RUSTY DISCARDED INDUSTRIAL CANISTERS.
"THERE'S A WOLF LIVING IN THERE TOO, BUT HE'S PRETTY OLD NOW."

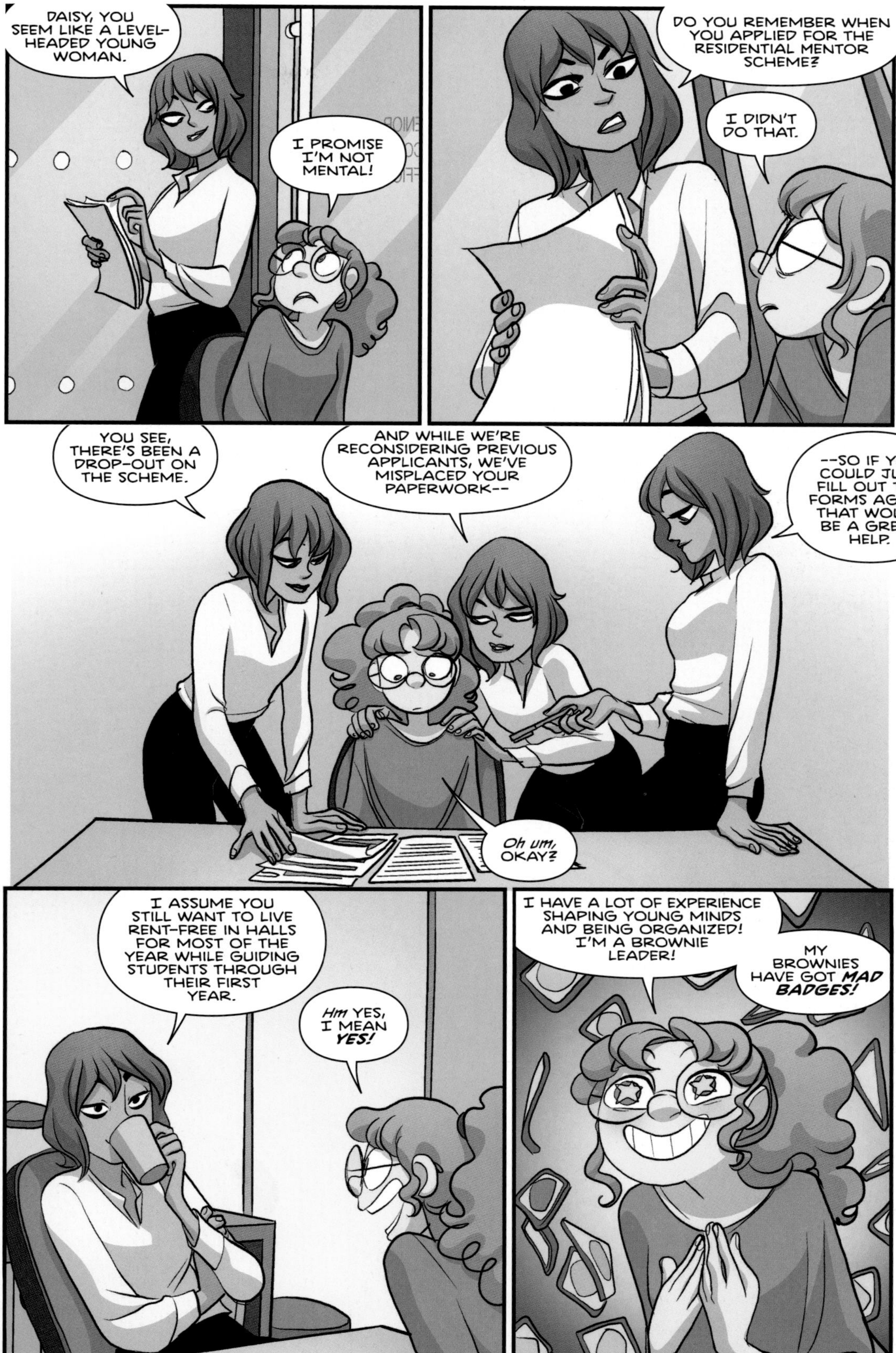
DAISY, YOU SEEM LIKE A LEVEL-HEADED YOUNG WOMAN.
I PROMISE I'M NOT MENTAL!
DO YOU REMEMBER WHEN YOU APPLIED FOR THE RESIDENTIAL MENTOR SCHEME?
I DIDN'T DO THAT.
YOU SEE, THERE'S BEEN A DROP-OUT ON THE SCHEME.
AND WHILE WE'RE RECONSIDERING PREVIOUS APPLICANTS, WE'VE MISPLACED YOUR PAPERWORK--
--SO IF YOU COULD JUST FILL OUT THE FORMS AGAIN, THAT WOULD BE A GREAT HELP.
Oh um, OKAY?
I ASSUME YOU STILL WANT TO LIVE RENT-FREE IN HALLS FOR MOST OF THE YEAR WHILE GUIDING STUDENTS THROUGH THEIR FIRST YEAR.
Hm YES, I MEAN YES!
I HAVE A LOT OF EXPERIENCE SHAPING YOUNG MINDS AND BEING ORGANIZED! I'M A BROWNIE LEADER!
MY BROWNIES HAVE GOT MAD BADGES!

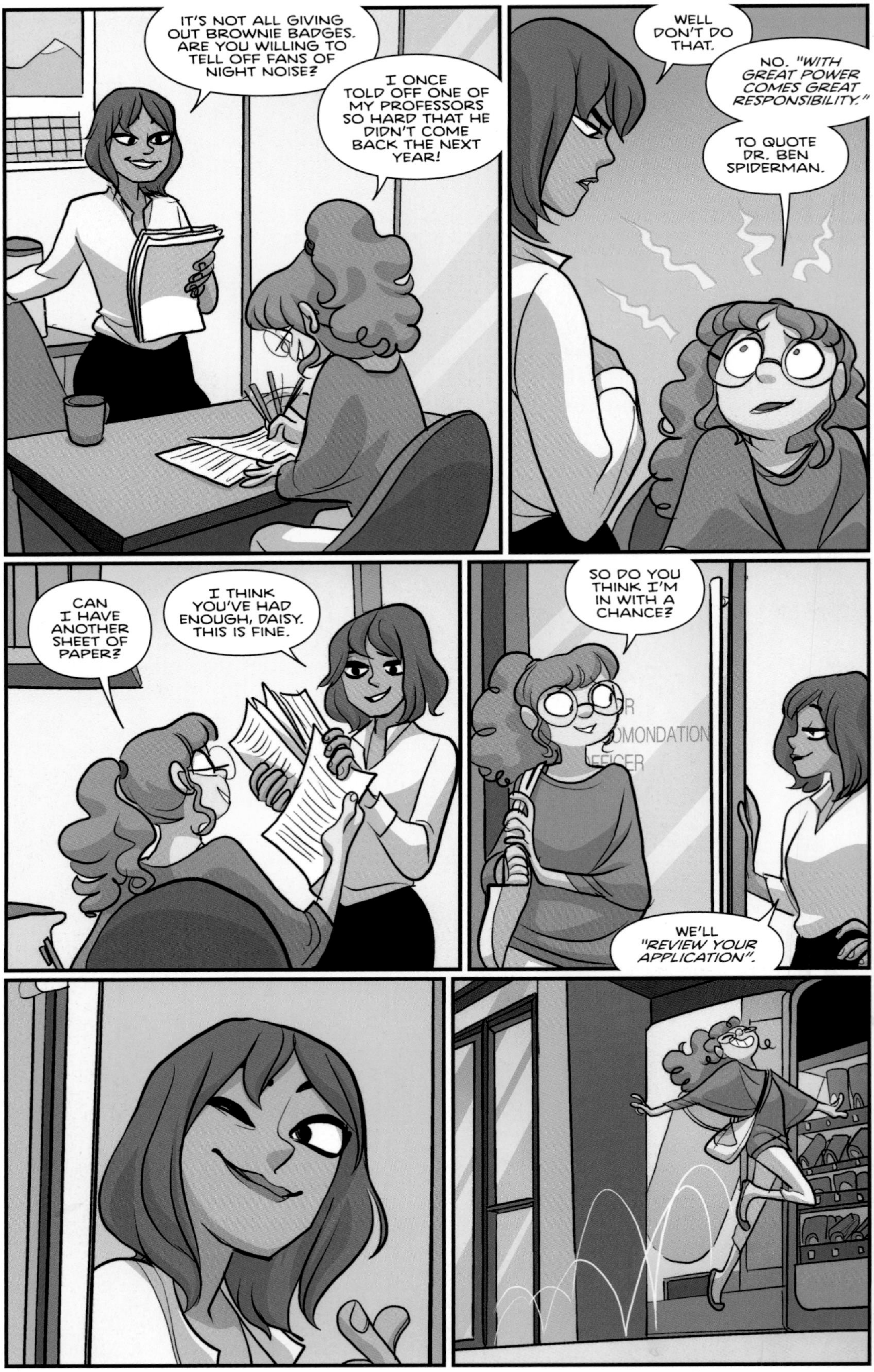
IT'S NOT ALL GIVING OUT BROWNIE BADGES. ARE YOU WILLING TO TELL OFF FANS OF NIGHT NOISE?
I ONCE TOLD OFF ONE OF MY PROFESSORS SO HARD THAT HE DIDN'T COME BACK THE NEXT YEAR!
WELL DON'T DO THAT.
NO. "WITH GREAT POWER COMES GREAT RESPONSIBILITY."
TO QUOTE DR. BEN SPIDERMAN.
CAN I HAVE ANOTHER SHEET OF PAPER?
I THINK YOU'VE HAD ENOUGH, DAISY. THIS IS FINE.
SO DO YOU THINK I'M IN WITH A CHANCE?
WE'LL "REVIEW YOUR APPLICATION".

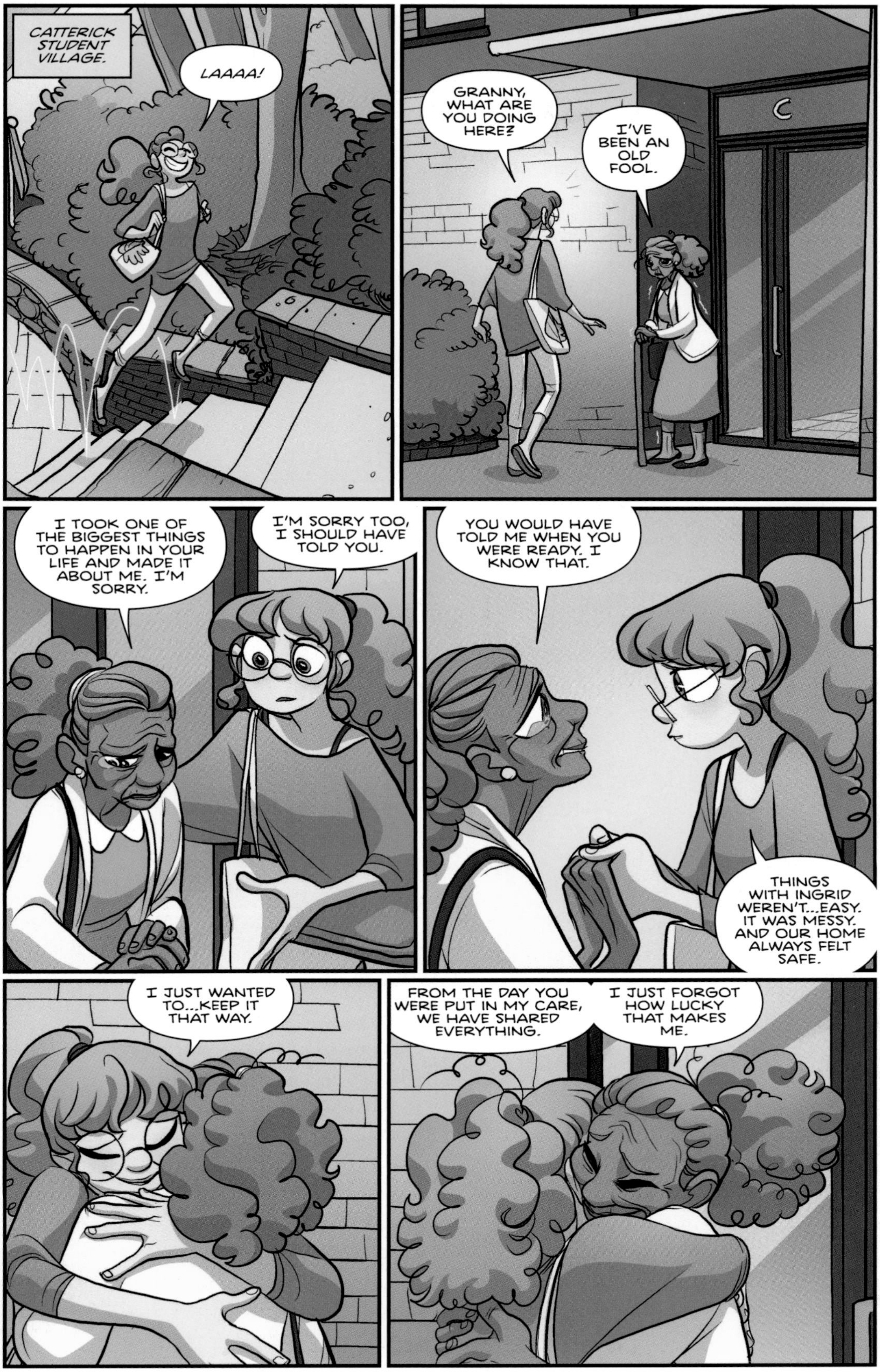
CATTERICK STUDENT VILLAGE.
LAAAA!
GRANNY, WHAT ARE YOU DOING HERE?
I'VE BEEN AN OLD FOOL.
I TOOK ONE OF THE BIGGEST THINGS TO HAPPEN IN YOUR LIFE AND MADE IT ABOUT ME. I'M SORRY.
I'M SORRY TOO, I SHOULD HAVE TOLD YOU.
YOU WOULD HAVE TOLD ME WHEN YOU WERE READY. I KNOW THAT.
THINGS WITH INGRID WEREN'T...EASY. IT WAS MESSY. AND OUR HOME ALWAYS FELT SAFE.
I JUST WANTED TO...KEEP IT THAT WAY.
FROM THE DAY YOU WERE PUT IN MY CARE, WE HAVE SHARED EVERYTHING.
I JUST FORGOT HOW LUCKY THAT MAKES ME.

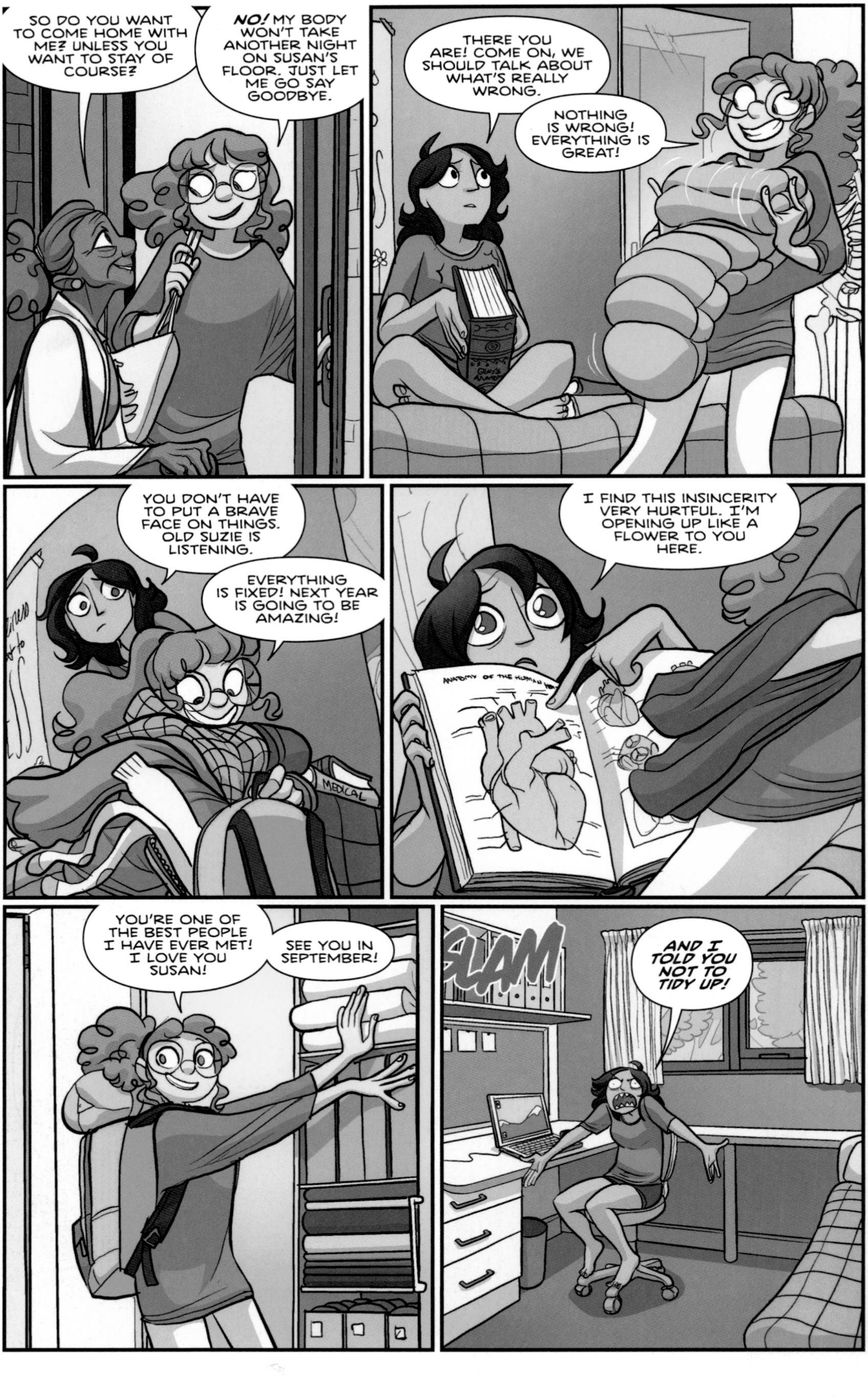
SO DO YOU WANT TO COME HOME WITH ME? UNLESS YOU WANT TO STAY OF COURSE?
NO! MY BODY WON'T TAKE ANOTHER NIGHT ON SUSAN'S FLOOR. JUST LET ME GO SAY GOODBYE.
THERE YOU ARE! COME ON, WE SHOULD TALK ABOUT WHAT'S REALLY WRONG.
NOTHING IS WRONG! EVERYTHING IS GREAT!
GRAY'S ANATOMY
YOU DON'T HAVE TO PUT A BRAVE FACE ON THINGS. OLD SUZIE IS LISTENING.
EVERYTHING IS FIXED! NEXT YEAR IS GOING TO BE AMAZING!
MEDICAL
I FIND THIS INSINCERITY VERY HURTFUL. I'M OPENING UP LIKE A FLOWER TO YOU HERE.
ANATOMY OF THE HUMAN HEART
YOU'RE ONE OF THE BEST PEOPLE I HAVE EVER MET! I LOVE YOU SUSAN!
SEE YOU IN SEPTEMBER!
SLAM
AND I TOLD YOU NOT TO TIDY UP!

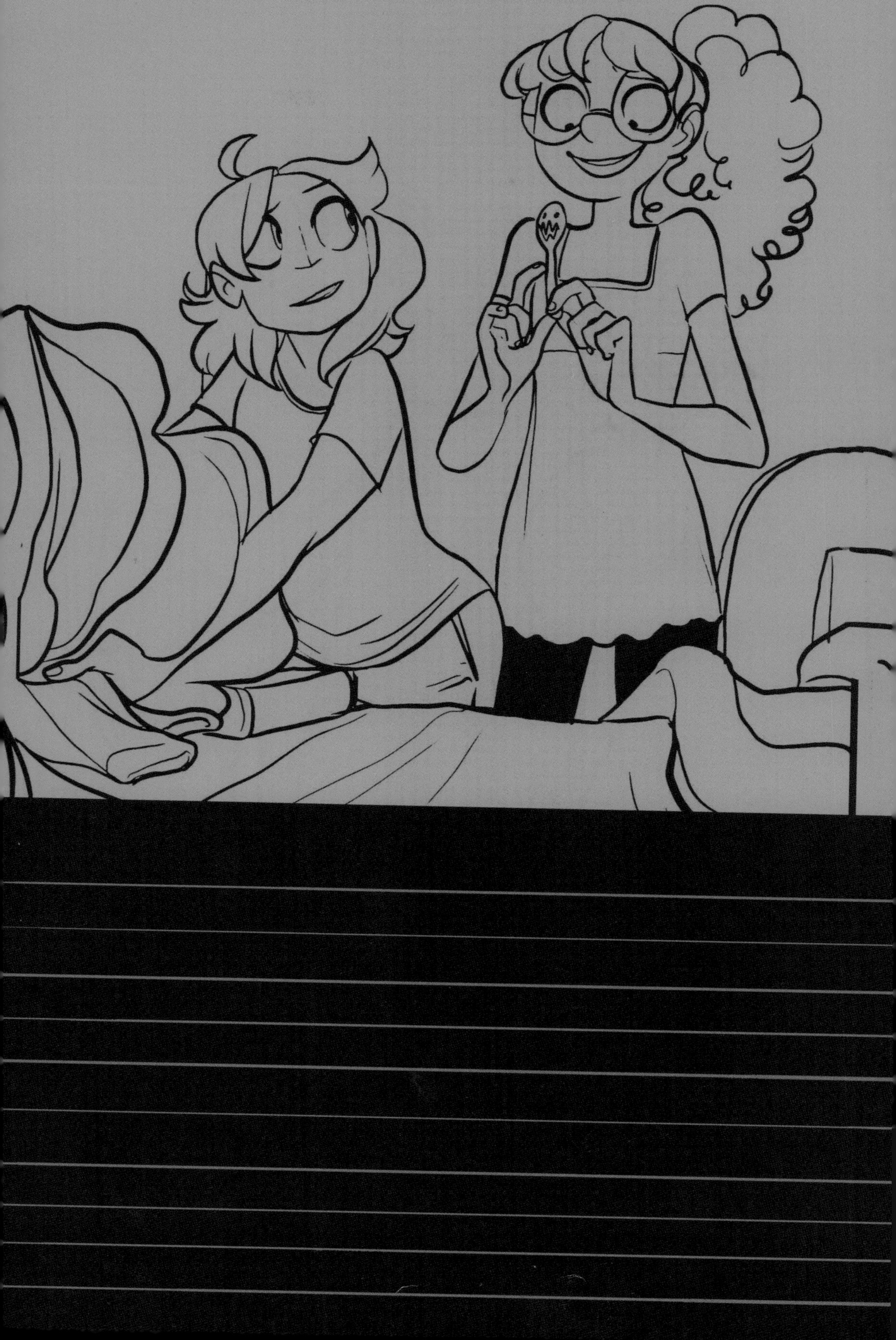

CHAPTER
THIRTY EIGHT

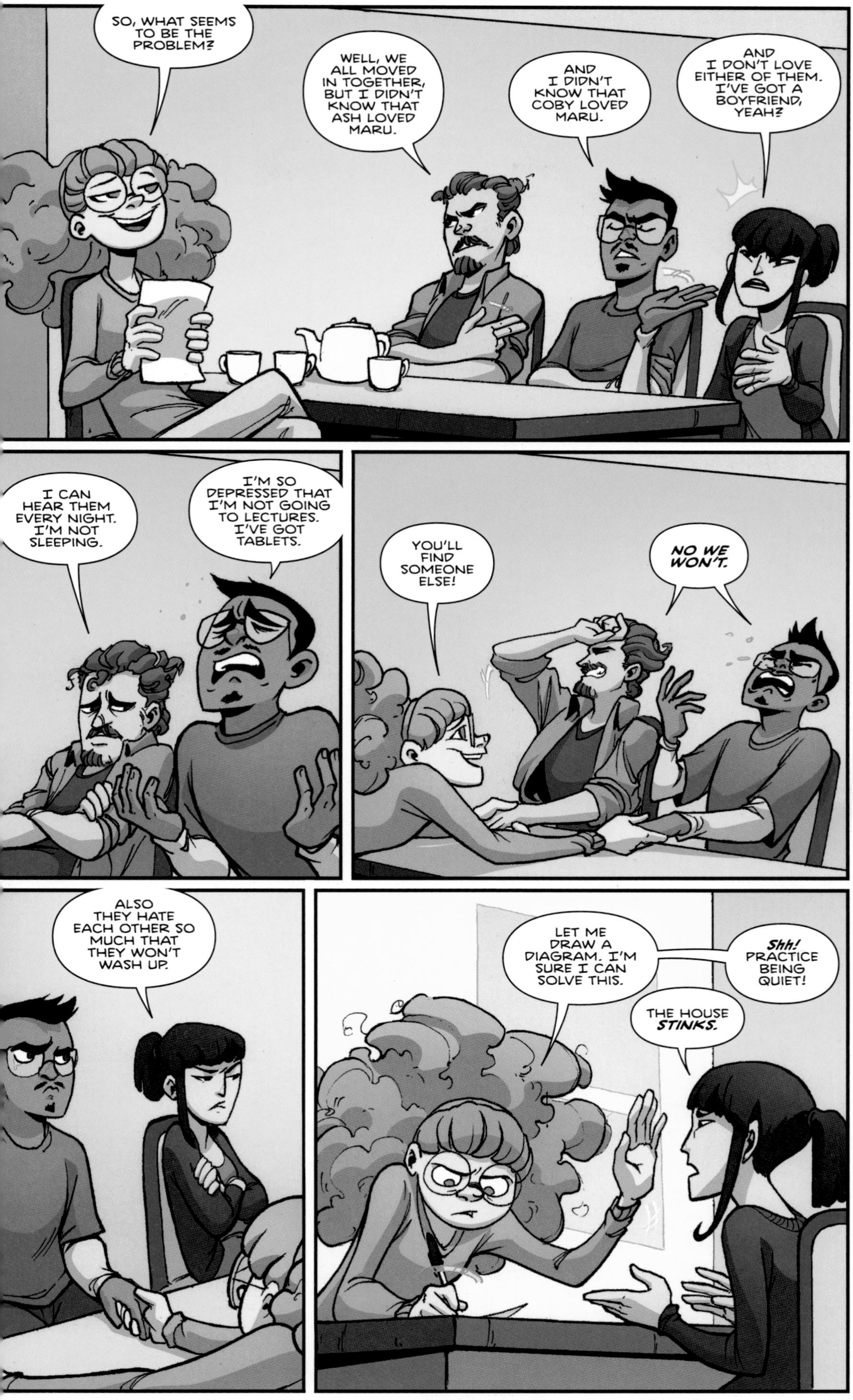
SO, WHAT SEEMS TO BE THE PROBLEM?
WELL, WE ALL MOVED IN TOGETHER, BUT I DIDN'T KNOW THAT ASH LOVED MARU.
AND I DIDN'T KNOW THAT COBY LOVED MARU.
AND I DON'T LOVE EITHER OF THEM. I'VE GOT A BOYFRIEND, YEAH?
I CAN HEAR THEM EVERY NIGHT. I'M NOT SLEEPING.
I'M SO DEPRESSED THAT I'M NOT GOING TO LECTURES. I'VE GOT TABLETS.
YOU'LL FIND SOMEONE ELSE!
NO WE WON'T.
ALSO THEY HATE EACH OTHER SO MUCH THAT THEY WON'T WASH UP.
LET ME DRAW A DIAGRAM. I'M SURE I CAN SOLVE THIS.
Shh! PRACTICE BEING QUIET!
THE HOUSE STINKS.

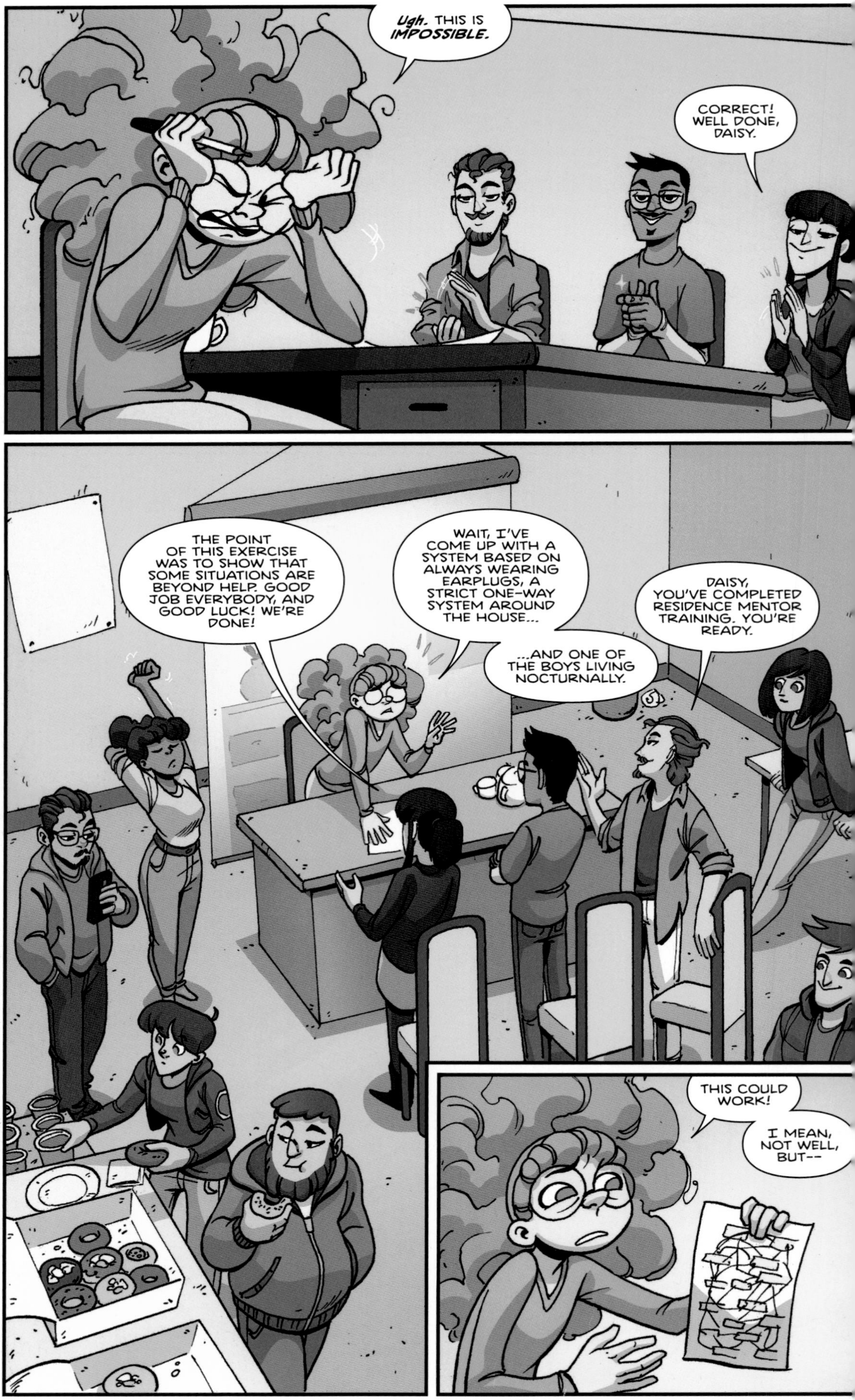
Ugh. THIS IS ***IMPOSSIBLE.***
CORRECT! WELL DONE, DAISY.
THE POINT OF THIS EXERCISE WAS TO SHOW THAT SOME SITUATIONS ARE BEYOND HELP. GOOD JOB EVERYBODY, AND GOOD LUCK! WE'RE DONE!
WAIT, I'VE COME UP WITH A SYSTEM BASED ON ALWAYS WEARING EARPLUGS, A STRICT ONE-WAY SYSTEM AROUND THE HOUSE...
...AND ONE OF THE BOYS LIVING NOCTURNALLY.
DAISY, YOU'VE COMPLETED RESIDENCE MENTOR TRAINING. YOU'RE READY.
THIS COULD WORK!
I MEAN, NOT WELL, BUT--

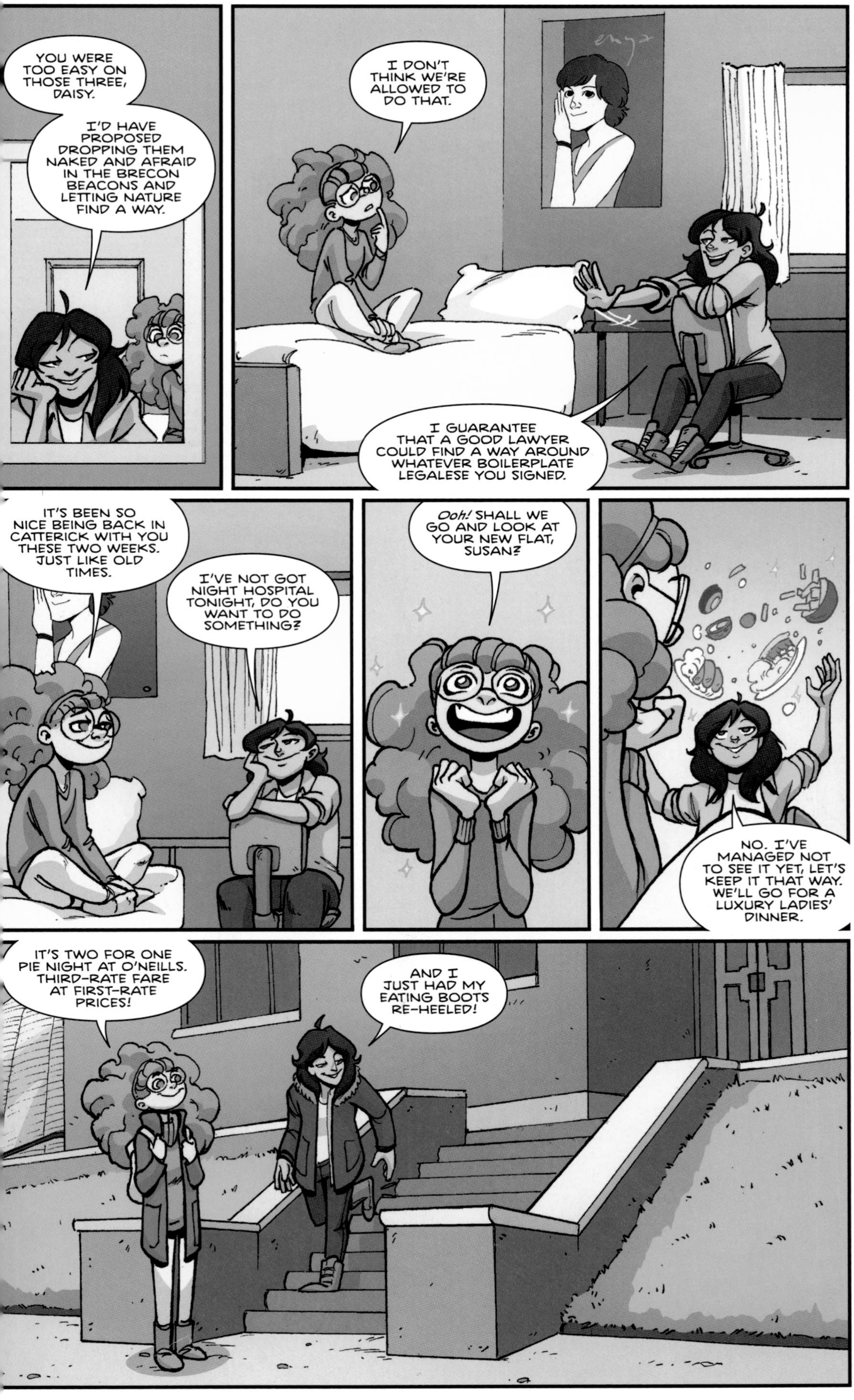
YOU WERE TOO EASY ON THOSE THREE, DAISY.
I'D HAVE PROPOSED DROPPING THEM NAKED AND AFRAID IN THE BRECON BEACONS AND LETTING NATURE FIND A WAY.
I DON'T THINK WE'RE ALLOWED TO DO THAT.
I GUARANTEE THAT A GOOD LAWYER COULD FIND A WAY AROUND WHATEVER BOILERPLATE LEGALESE YOU SIGNED.
IT'S BEEN SO NICE BEING BACK IN CATTERICK WITH YOU THESE TWO WEEKS. JUST LIKE OLD TIMES.
I'VE NOT GOT NIGHT HOSPITAL TONIGHT, DO YOU WANT TO DO SOMETHING?
Ooh! SHALL WE GO AND LOOK AT YOUR NEW FLAT, SUSAN?
NO. I'VE MANAGED NOT TO SEE IT YET, LET'S KEEP IT THAT WAY. WE'LL GO FOR A LUXURY LADIES' DINNER.
IT'S TWO FOR ONE PIE NIGHT AT O'NEILLS. THIRD-RATE FARE AT FIRST-RATE PRICES!
AND I JUST HAD MY EATING BOOTS RE-HEELED!

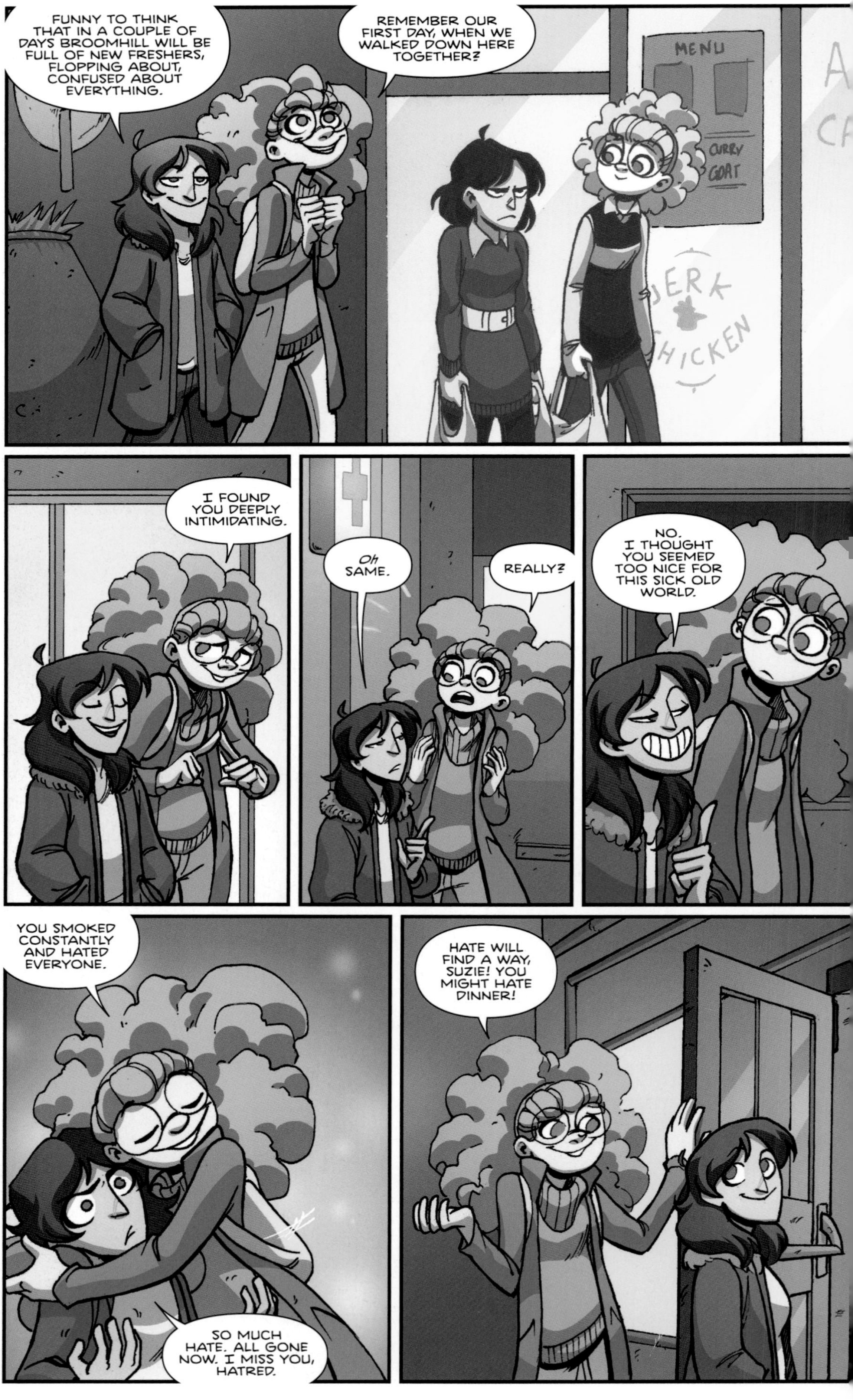
FUNNY TO THINK THAT IN A COUPLE OF DAYS BROOMHILL WILL BE FULL OF NEW FRESHERS, FLOPPING ABOUT, CONFUSED ABOUT EVERYTHING.
REMEMBER OUR FIRST DAY, WHEN WE WALKED DOWN HERE TOGETHER?
MENU
CURRY GOAT
JERK CHICKEN
I FOUND YOU DEEPLY INTIMIDATING.
Oh SAME.
REALLY?
NO. I THOUGHT YOU SEEMED TOO NICE FOR THIS SICK OLD WORLD.
YOU SMOKED CONSTANTLY AND HATED EVERYONE.
SO MUCH HATE. ALL GONE NOW. I MISS YOU, HATRED.
HATE WILL FIND A WAY, SUZIE! YOU MIGHT HATE DINNER!

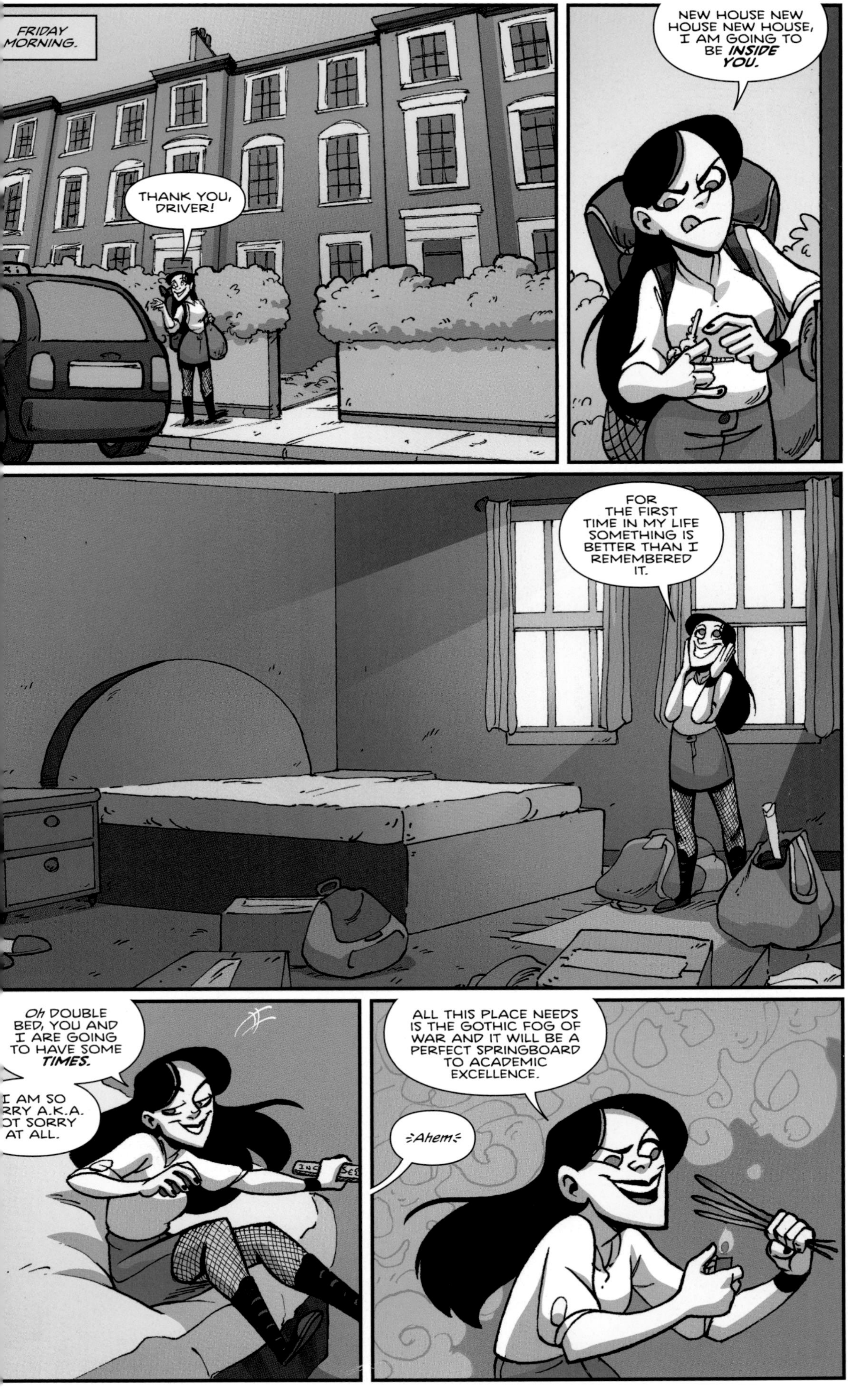
FRIDAY MORNING.
THANK YOU, DRIVER!
NEW HOUSE NEW HOUSE NEW HOUSE, I AM GOING TO BE ***INSIDE YOU.***
FOR THE FIRST TIME IN MY LIFE SOMETHING IS BETTER THAN I REMEMBERED IT.
Oh DOUBLE BED, YOU AND I ARE GOING TO HAVE SOME ***TIMES.***
I AM SO
RRY A.K.A.
OT SORRY
AT ALL.
ALL THIS PLACE NEEDS IS THE GOTHIC FOG OF WAR AND IT WILL BE A PERFECT SPRINGBOARD TO ACADEMIC EXCELLENCE.
Ahem

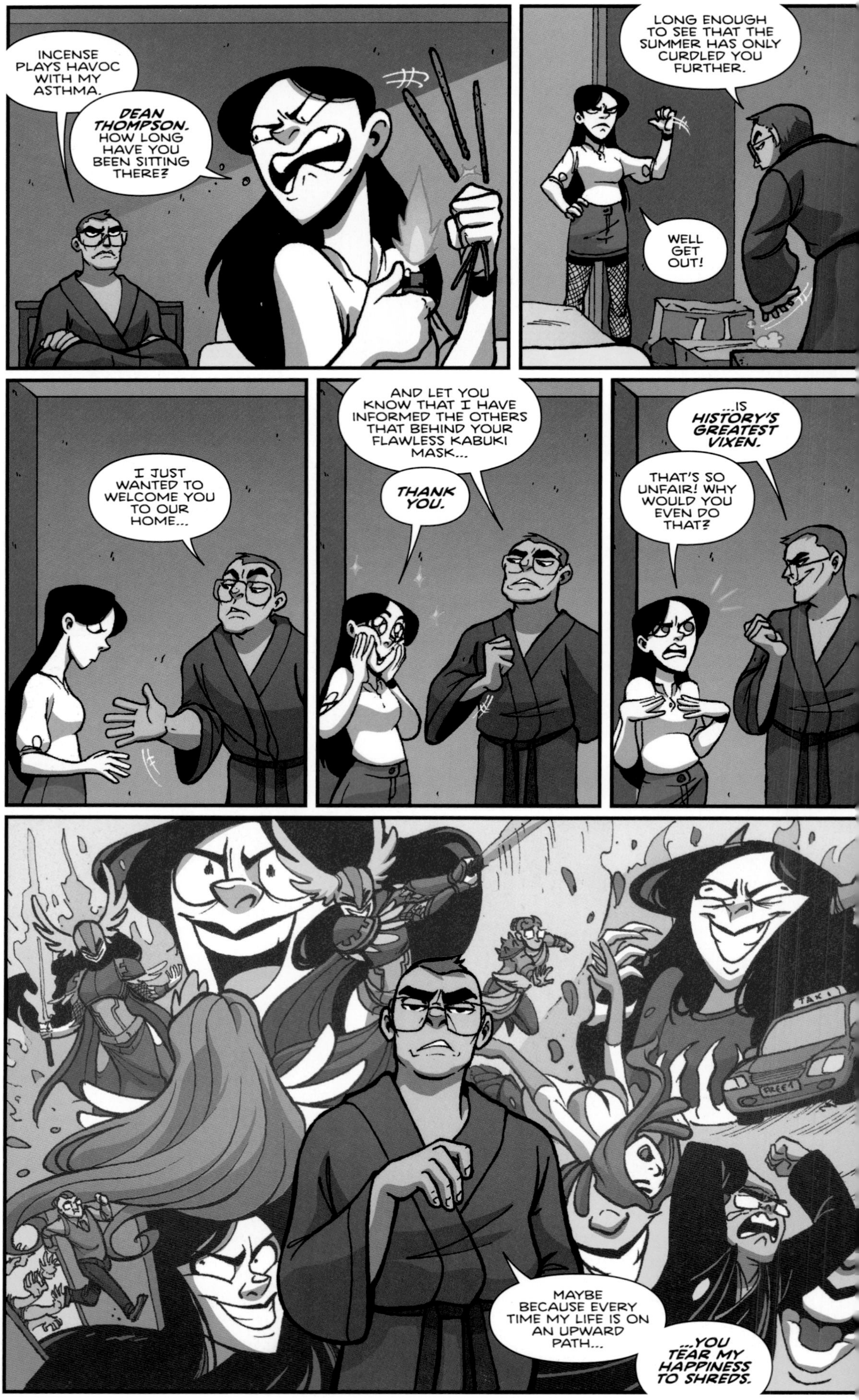
INCENSE PLAYS HAVOC WITH MY ASTHMA.
DEAN THOMPSON. HOW LONG HAVE YOU BEEN SITTING THERE?
LONG ENOUGH TO SEE THAT THE SUMMER HAS ONLY CURDLED YOU FURTHER.
WELL GET OUT!
I JUST WANTED TO WELCOME YOU TO OUR HOME...
AND LET YOU KNOW THAT I HAVE INFORMED THE OTHERS THAT BEHIND YOUR FLAWLESS KABUKI MASK...
THANK YOU.
...IS HISTORY'S GREATEST VIXEN.
THAT'S SO UNFAIR! WHY WOULD YOU EVEN DO THAT?
TAXI
MAYBE BECAUSE EVERY TIME MY LIFE IS ON AN UPWARD PATH...
...YOU TEAR MY HAPPINESS TO SHREDS.

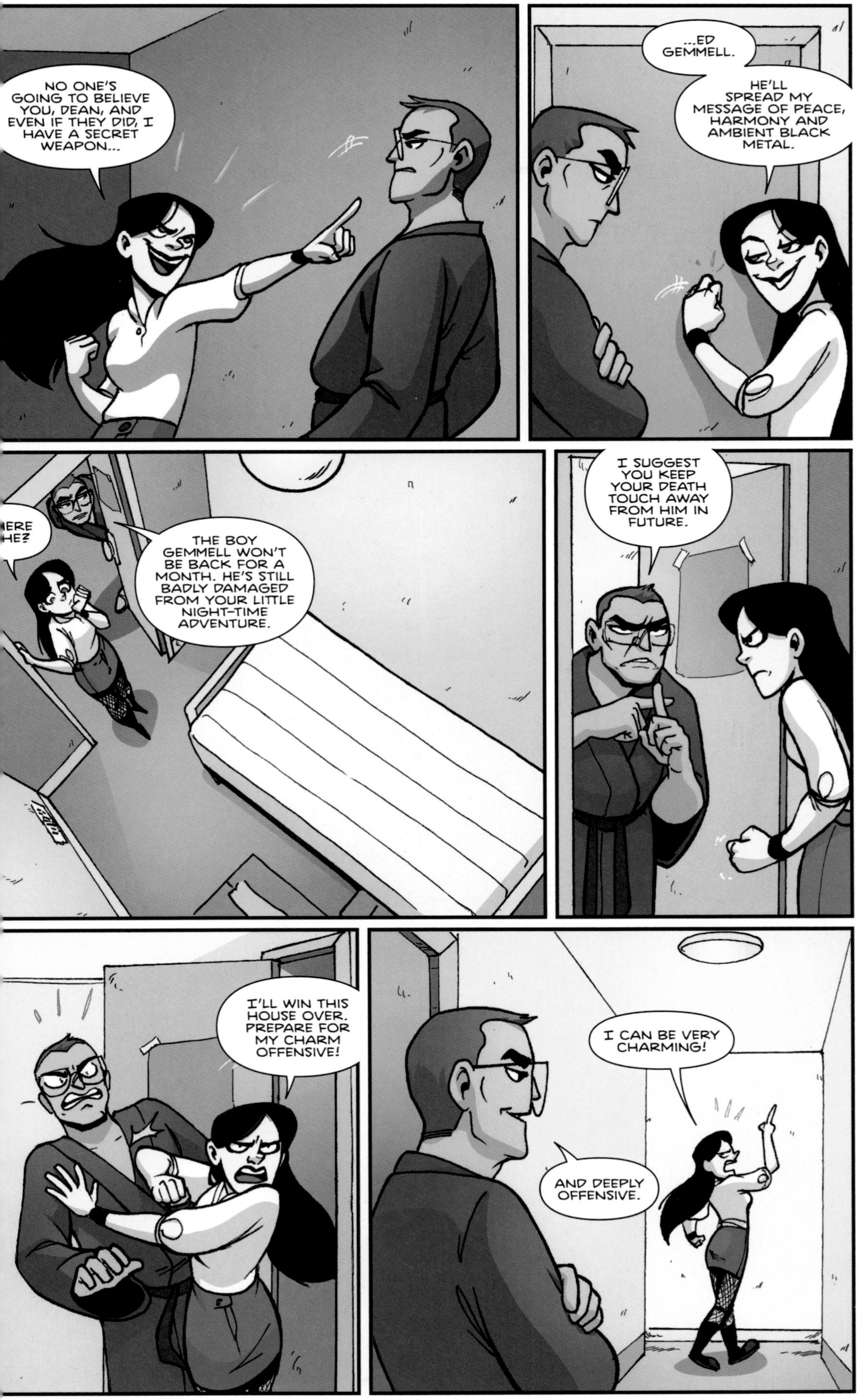
NO ONE'S GOING TO BELIEVE YOU, DEAN, AND EVEN IF THEY DID, I HAVE A SECRET WEAPON...
...ED GEMMELL.
HE'LL SPREAD MY MESSAGE OF PEACE, HARMONY AND AMBIENT BLACK METAL.
THE BOY GEMMELL WON'T BE BACK FOR A MONTH. HE'S STILL BADLY DAMAGED FROM YOUR LITTLE NIGHT-TIME ADVENTURE.
I SUGGEST YOU KEEP YOUR DEATH TOUCH AWAY FROM HIM IN FUTURE.
I'LL WIN THIS HOUSE OVER. PREPARE FOR MY CHARM OFFENSIVE!
I CAN BE VERY CHARMING!
AND DEEPLY OFFENSIVE.

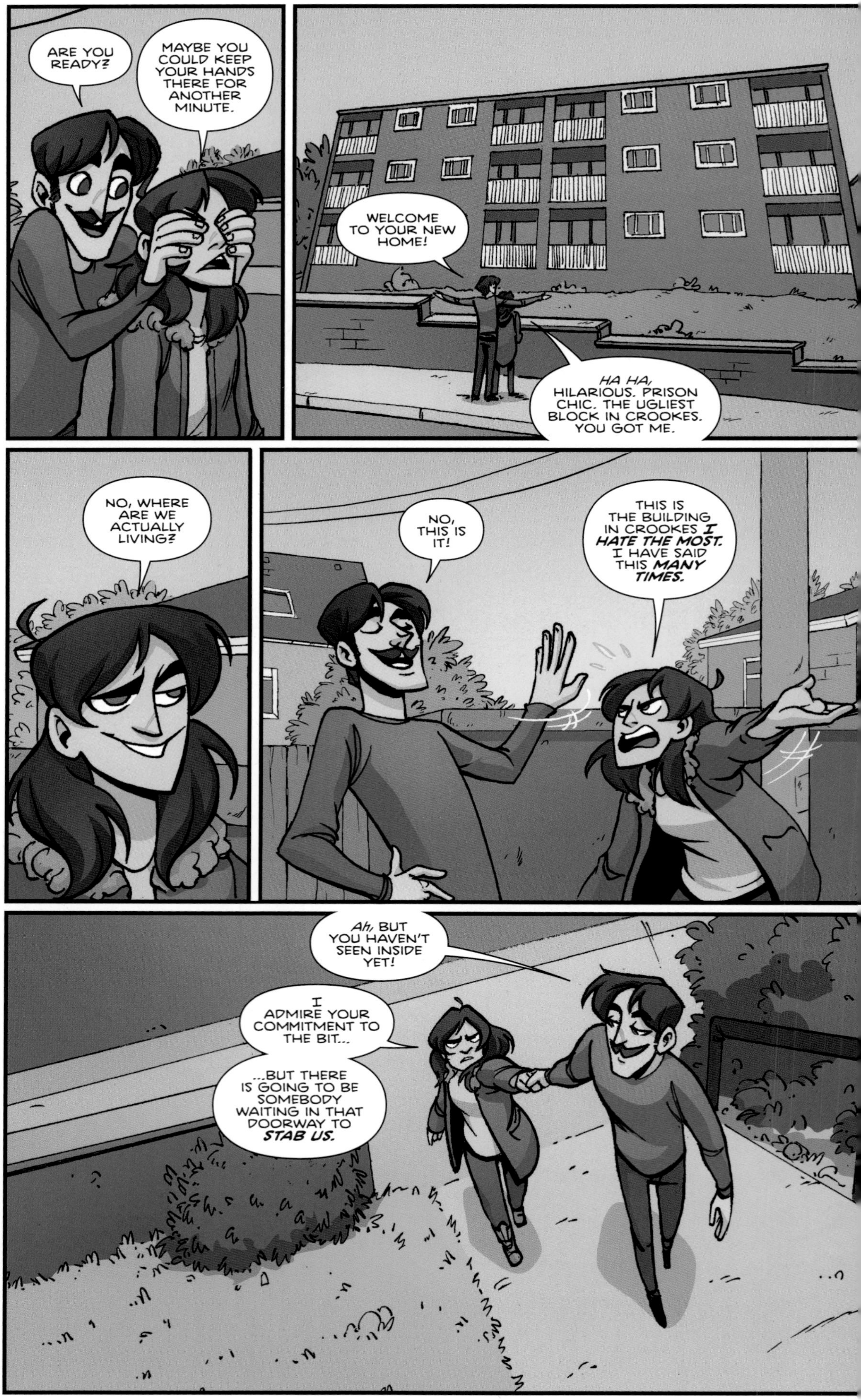
ARE YOU READY?
MAYBE YOU COULD KEEP YOUR HANDS THERE FOR ANOTHER MINUTE.
WELCOME TO YOUR NEW HOME!
HA HA, HILARIOUS. PRISON CHIC. THE UGLIEST BLOCK IN CROOKES. YOU GOT ME.
NO, WHERE ARE WE ACTUALLY LIVING?
NO, THIS IS IT!
THIS IS THE BUILDING IN CROOKES ***I HATE THE MOST.*** I HAVE SAID THIS ***MANY TIMES.***
Ah, BUT YOU HAVEN'T SEEN INSIDE YET!
I ADMIRE YOUR COMMITMENT TO THE BIT...
...BUT THERE IS GOING TO BE SOMEBODY WAITING IN THAT DOORWAY TO ***STAB US.***

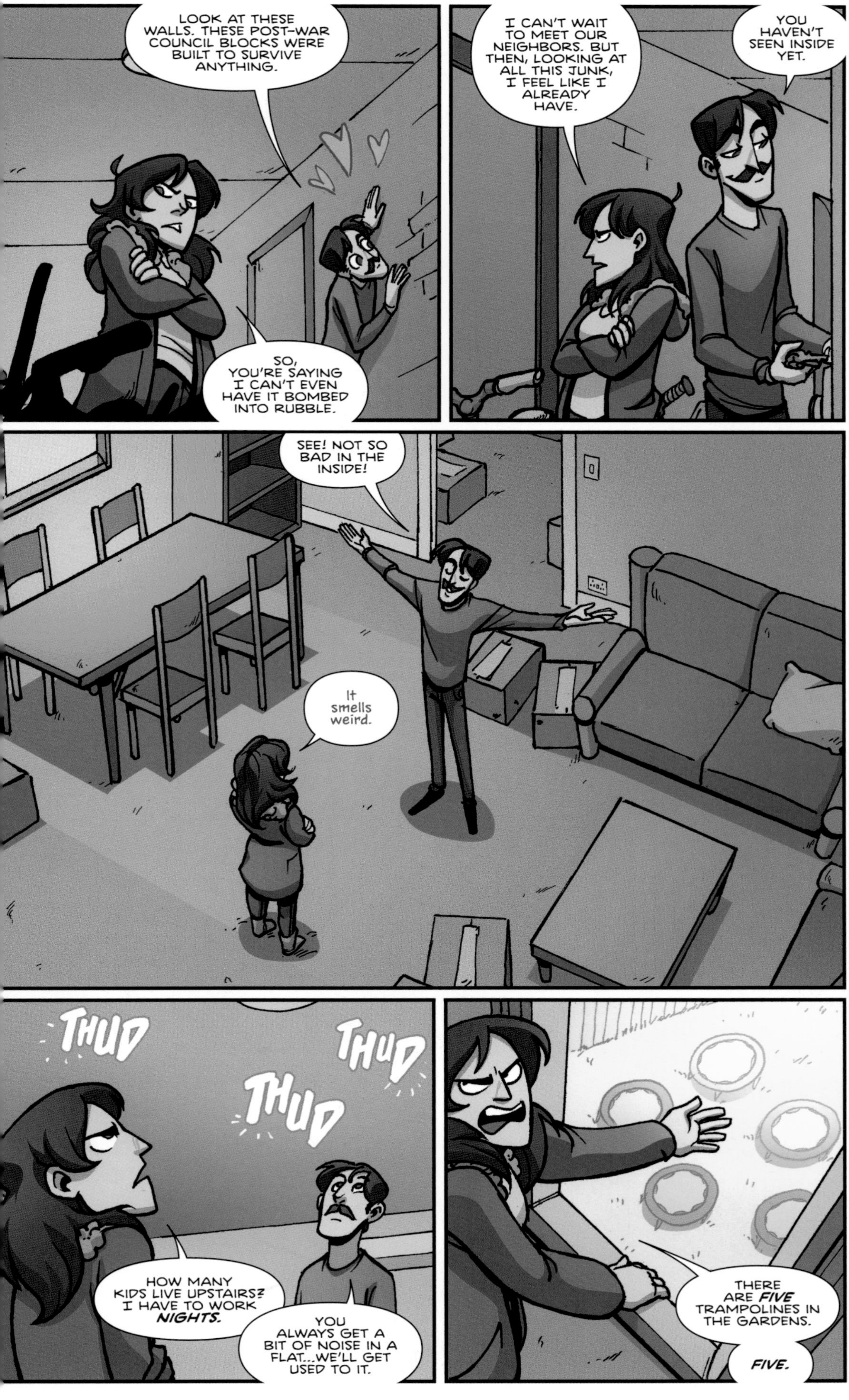
LOOK AT THESE WALLS. THESE POST-WAR COUNCIL BLOCKS WERE BUILT TO SURVIVE ANYTHING.
SO, YOU'RE SAYING I CAN'T EVEN HAVE IT BOMBED INTO RUBBLE.
I CAN'T WAIT TO MEET OUR NEIGHBORS. BUT THEN, LOOKING AT ALL THIS JUNK, I FEEL LIKE I ALREADY HAVE.
YOU HAVEN'T SEEN INSIDE YET.
SEE! NOT SO BAD IN THE INSIDE!
It smells weird.
THUD
THUD
THUD
HOW MANY KIDS LIVE UPSTAIRS? I HAVE TO WORK *NIGHTS.*
YOU ALWAYS GET A BIT OF NOISE IN A FLAT...WE'LL GET USED TO IT.
THERE ARE *FIVE* TRAMPOLINES IN THE GARDENS.
FIVE.

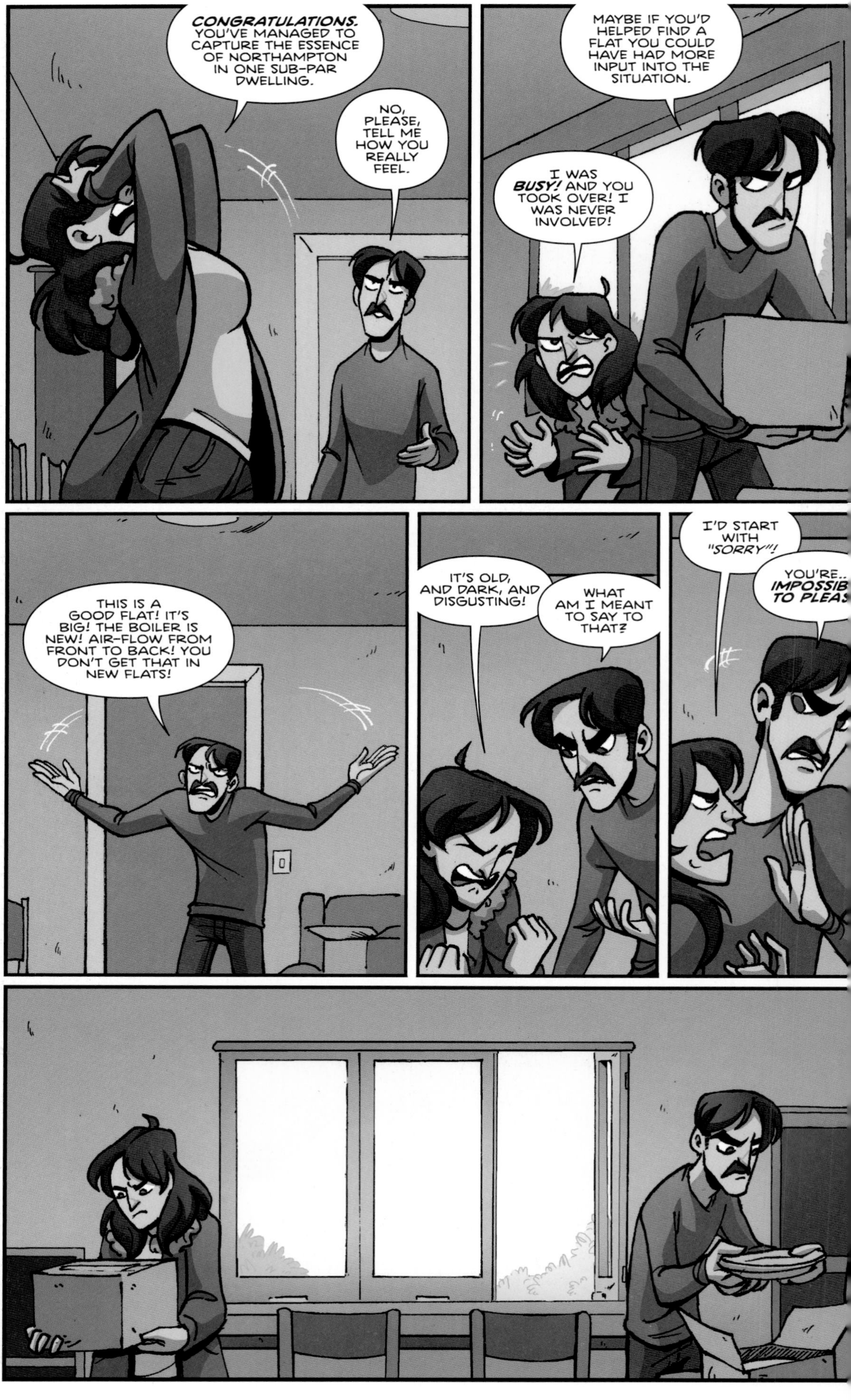
CONGRATULATIONS. YOU'VE MANAGED TO CAPTURE THE ESSENCE OF NORTHAMPTON IN ONE SUB-PAR DWELLING.
NO, PLEASE, TELL ME HOW YOU REALLY FEEL.
MAYBE IF YOU'D HELPED FIND A FLAT YOU COULD HAVE HAD MORE INPUT INTO THE SITUATION.
I WAS BUSY! AND YOU TOOK OVER! I WAS NEVER INVOLVED!
THIS IS A GOOD FLAT! IT'S BIG! THE BOILER IS NEW! AIR-FLOW FROM FRONT TO BACK! YOU DON'T GET THAT IN NEW FLATS!
IT'S OLD, AND DARK, AND DISGUSTING!
WHAT AM I MEANT TO SAY TO THAT?
I'D START WITH "SORRY"!

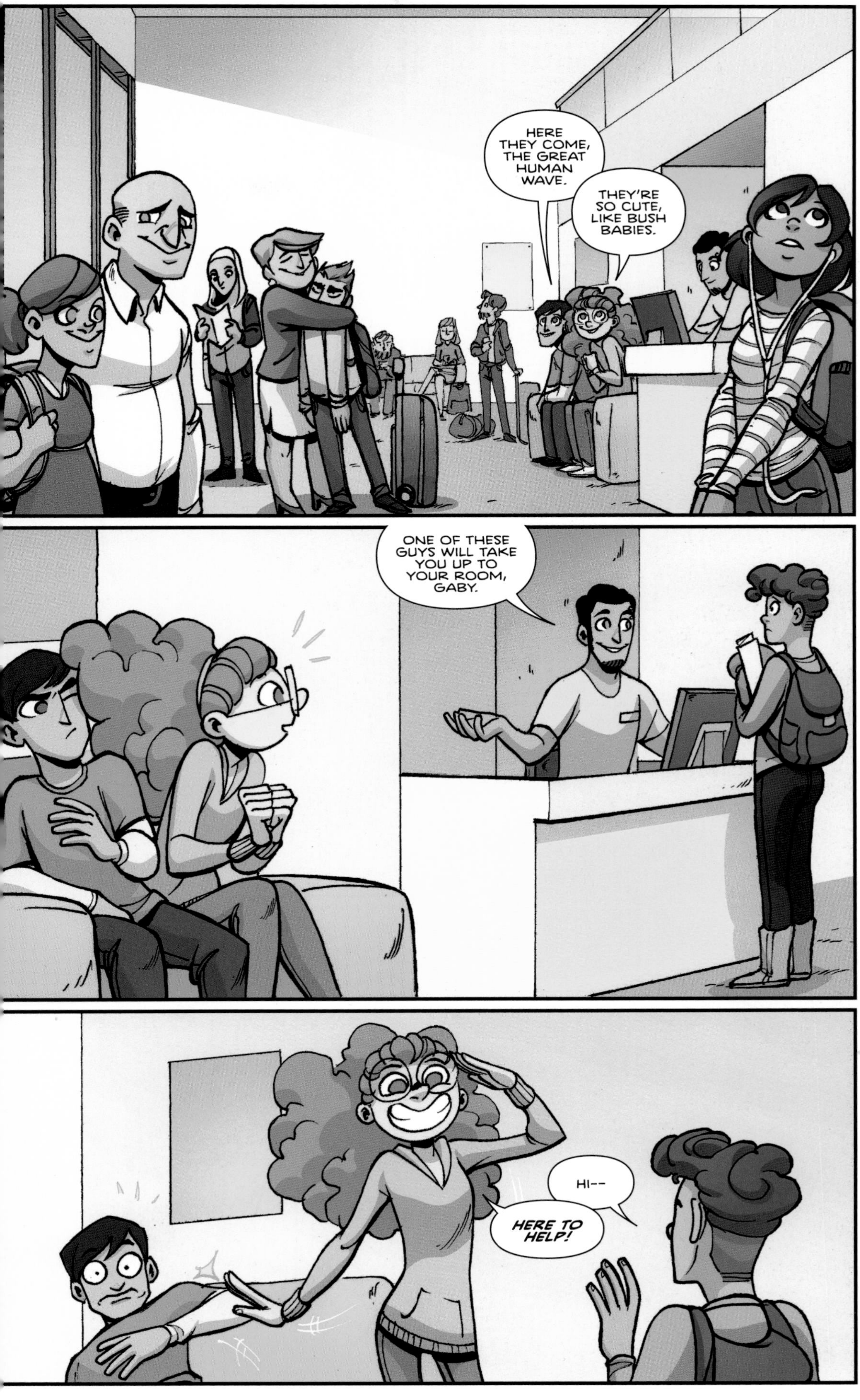
HERE THEY COME, THE GREAT HUMAN WAVE.
THEY'RE SO CUTE, LIKE BUSH BABIES.
ONE OF THESE GUYS WILL TAKE YOU UP TO YOUR ROOM, GABY.
HI--
HERE TO HELP!

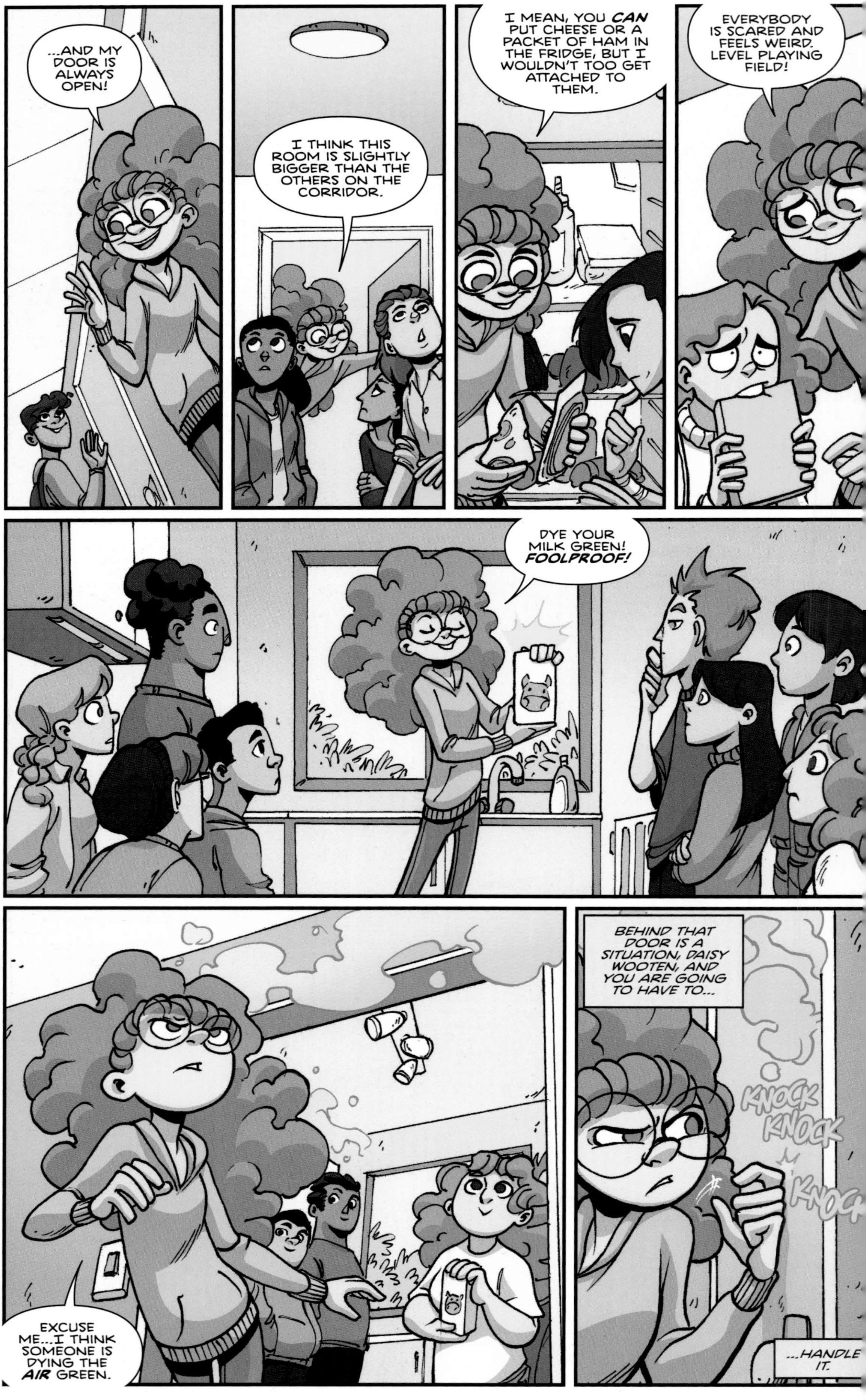
...AND MY DOOR IS ALWAYS OPEN!
I THINK THIS ROOM IS SLIGHTLY BIGGER THAN THE OTHERS ON THE CORRIDOR.
I MEAN, YOU CAN PUT CHEESE OR A PACKET OF HAM IN THE FRIDGE, BUT I WOULDN'T TOO GET ATTACHED TO THEM.
EVERYBODY IS SCARED AND FEELS WEIRD. LEVEL PLAYING FIELD!
DYE YOUR MILK GREEN! FOOLPROOF!
EXCUSE ME...I THINK SOMEONE IS DYING THE AIR GREEN.
BEHIND THAT DOOR IS A SITUATION, DAISY WOOTEN, AND YOU ARE GOING TO HAVE TO...
KNOCK KNOCK
KNOCK
...HANDLE IT.

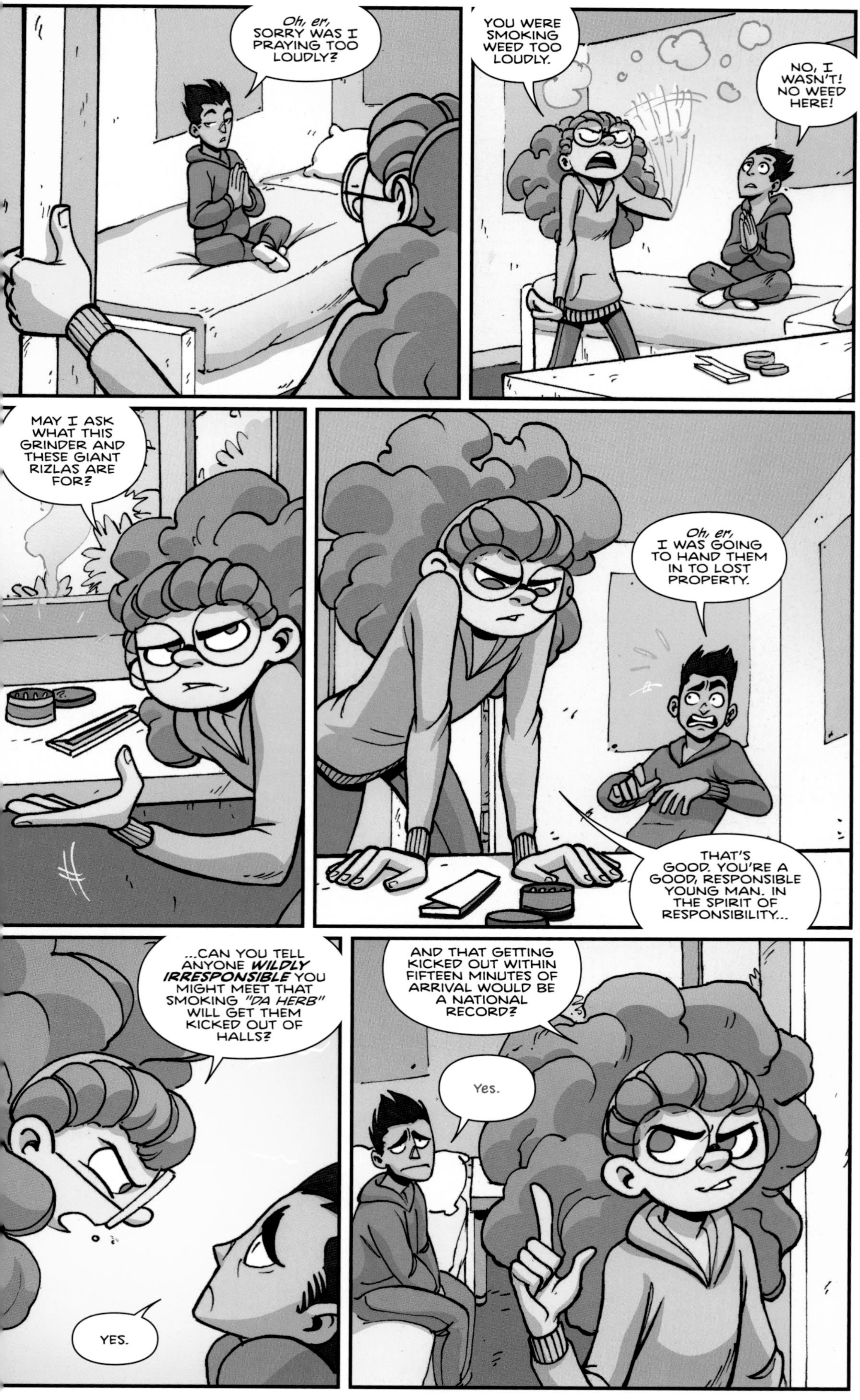
Oh, er, SORRY WAS I PRAYING TOO LOUDLY?
YOU WERE SMOKING WEED TOO LOUDLY.
NO, I WASN'T! NO WEED HERE!
MAY I ASK WHAT THIS GRINDER AND THESE GIANT RIZLAS ARE FOR?
Oh, er, I WAS GOING TO HAND THEM IN TO LOST PROPERTY.
THAT'S GOOD. YOU'RE A GOOD, RESPONSIBLE YOUNG MAN. IN THE SPIRIT OF RESPONSIBILITY...
...CAN YOU TELL ANYONE ***WILDLY IRRESPONSIBLE*** YOU MIGHT MEET THAT SMOKING *"DA HERB"* WILL GET THEM KICKED OUT OF HALLS?
YES.
AND THAT GETTING KICKED OUT WITHIN FIFTEEN MINUTES OF ARRIVAL WOULD BE A NATIONAL RECORD?
Yes.

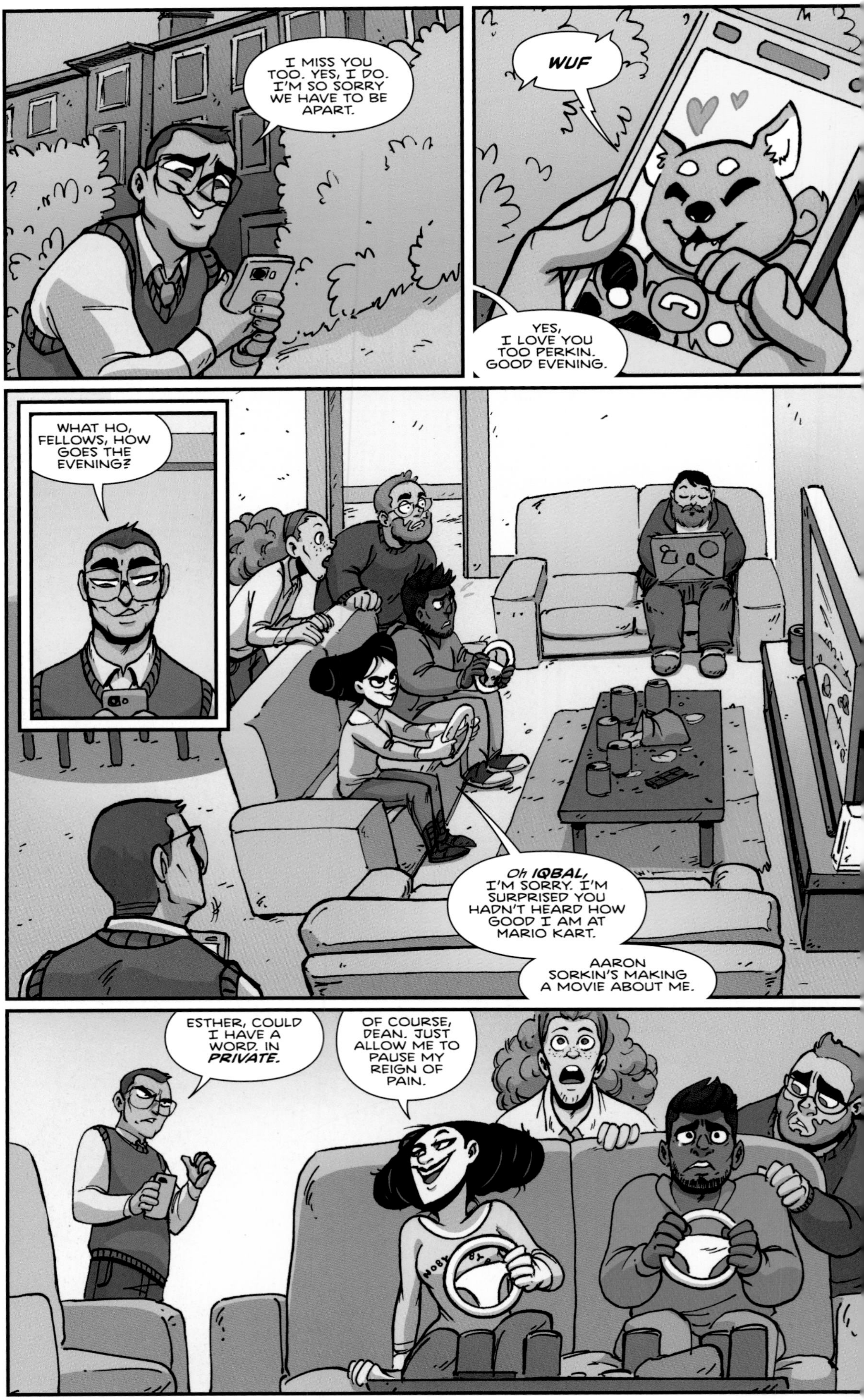
I MISS YOU TOO. YES, I DO. I'M SO SORRY WE HAVE TO BE APART.
WUF
YES, I LOVE YOU TOO PERKIN. GOOD EVENING.
WHAT HO, FELLOWS, HOW GOES THE EVENING?
Oh IQBAL, I'M SORRY. I'M SURPRISED YOU HADN'T HEARD HOW GOOD I AM AT MARIO KART.
AARON SORKIN'S MAKING A MOVIE ABOUT ME.
ESTHER, COULD I HAVE A WORD. IN PRIVATE.
OF COURSE, DEAN. JUST ALLOW ME TO PAUSE MY REIGN OF PAIN.

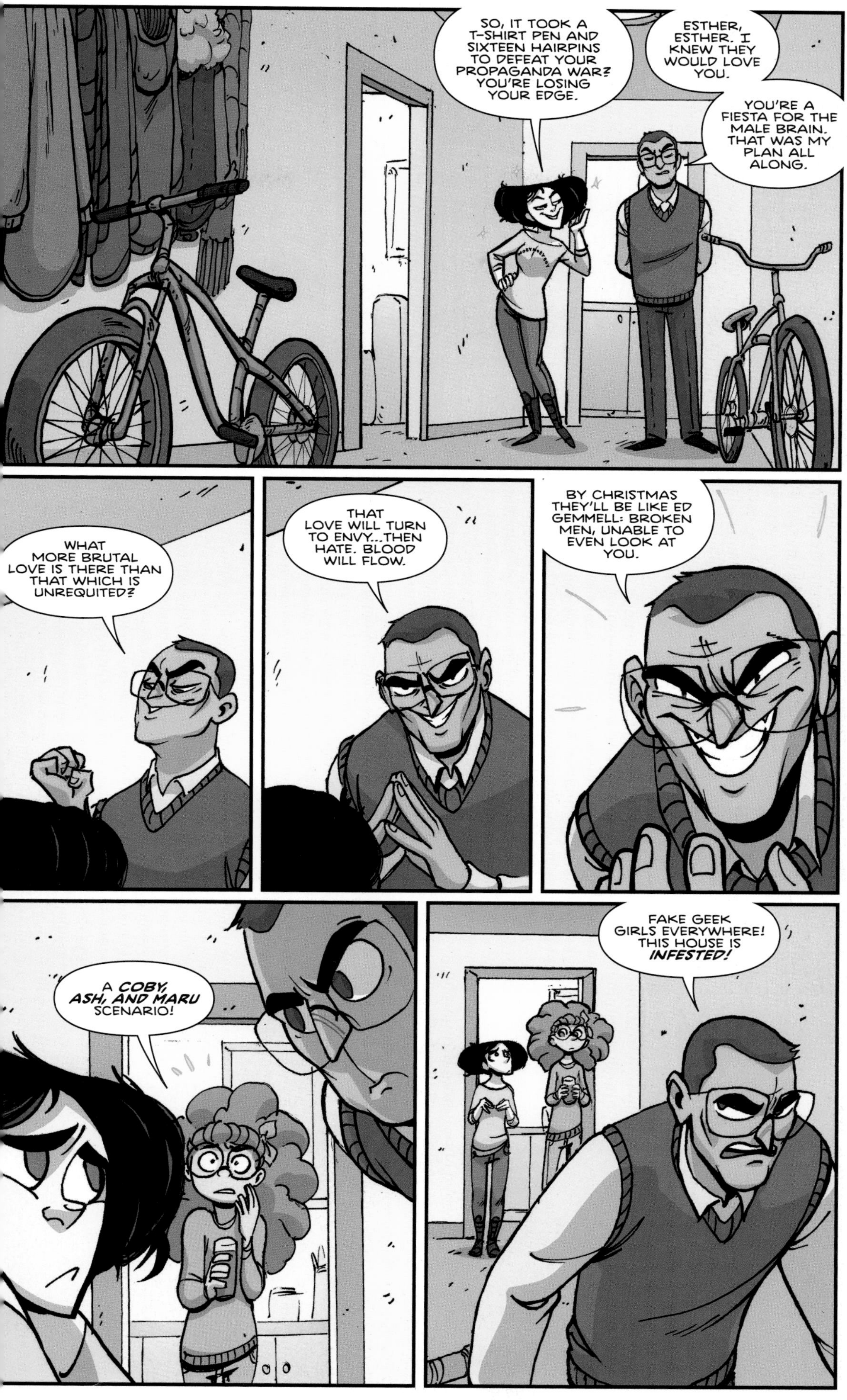
SO, IT TOOK A T-SHIRT PEN AND SIXTEEN HAIRPINS TO DEFEAT YOUR PROPAGANDA WAR? YOU'RE LOSING YOUR EDGE.
ESTHER, ESTHER. I KNEW THEY WOULD LOVE YOU.
YOU'RE A FIESTA FOR THE MALE BRAIN. THAT WAS MY PLAN ALL ALONG.
WHAT MORE BRUTAL LOVE IS THERE THAN THAT WHICH IS UNREQUITED?
THAT LOVE WILL TURN TO ENVY...THEN HATE. BLOOD WILL FLOW.
BY CHRISTMAS THEY'LL BE LIKE ED GEMMELL: BROKEN MEN, UNABLE TO EVEN LOOK AT YOU.
A *COBY, ASH, AND MARU* SCENARIO!
FAKE GEEK GIRLS EVERYWHERE! THIS HOUSE IS ***INFESTED!***

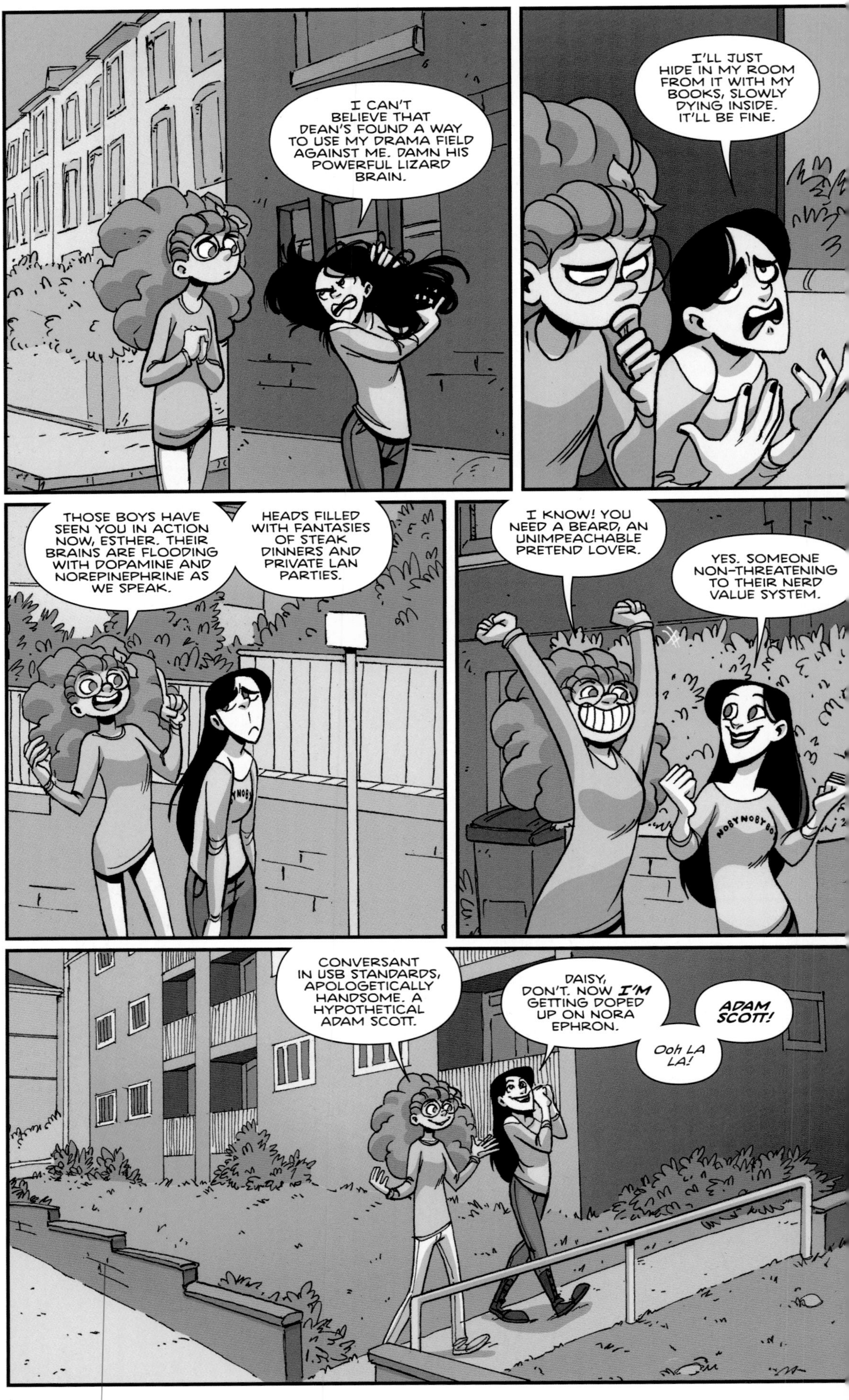
I CAN'T BELIEVE THAT DEAN'S FOUND A WAY TO USE MY DRAMA FIELD AGAINST ME. DAMN HIS POWERFUL LIZARD BRAIN.
I'LL JUST HIDE IN MY ROOM FROM IT WITH MY BOOKS, SLOWLY DYING INSIDE. IT'LL BE FINE.
THOSE BOYS HAVE SEEN YOU IN ACTION NOW, ESTHER. THEIR BRAINS ARE FLOODING WITH DOPAMINE AND NOREPINEPHRINE AS WE SPEAK.
HEADS FILLED WITH FANTASIES OF STEAK DINNERS AND PRIVATE LAN PARTIES.
I KNOW! YOU NEED A BEARD, AN UNIMPEACHABLE PRETEND LOVER.
YES. SOMEONE NON-THREATENING TO THEIR NERD VALUE SYSTEM.
CONVERSANT IN USB STANDARDS, APOLOGETICALLY HANDSOME. A HYPOTHETICAL ADAM SCOTT.
DAISY, DON'T. NOW I'M GETTING DOPED UP ON NORA EPHRON.
ADAM SCOTT!
Ooh LA LA!

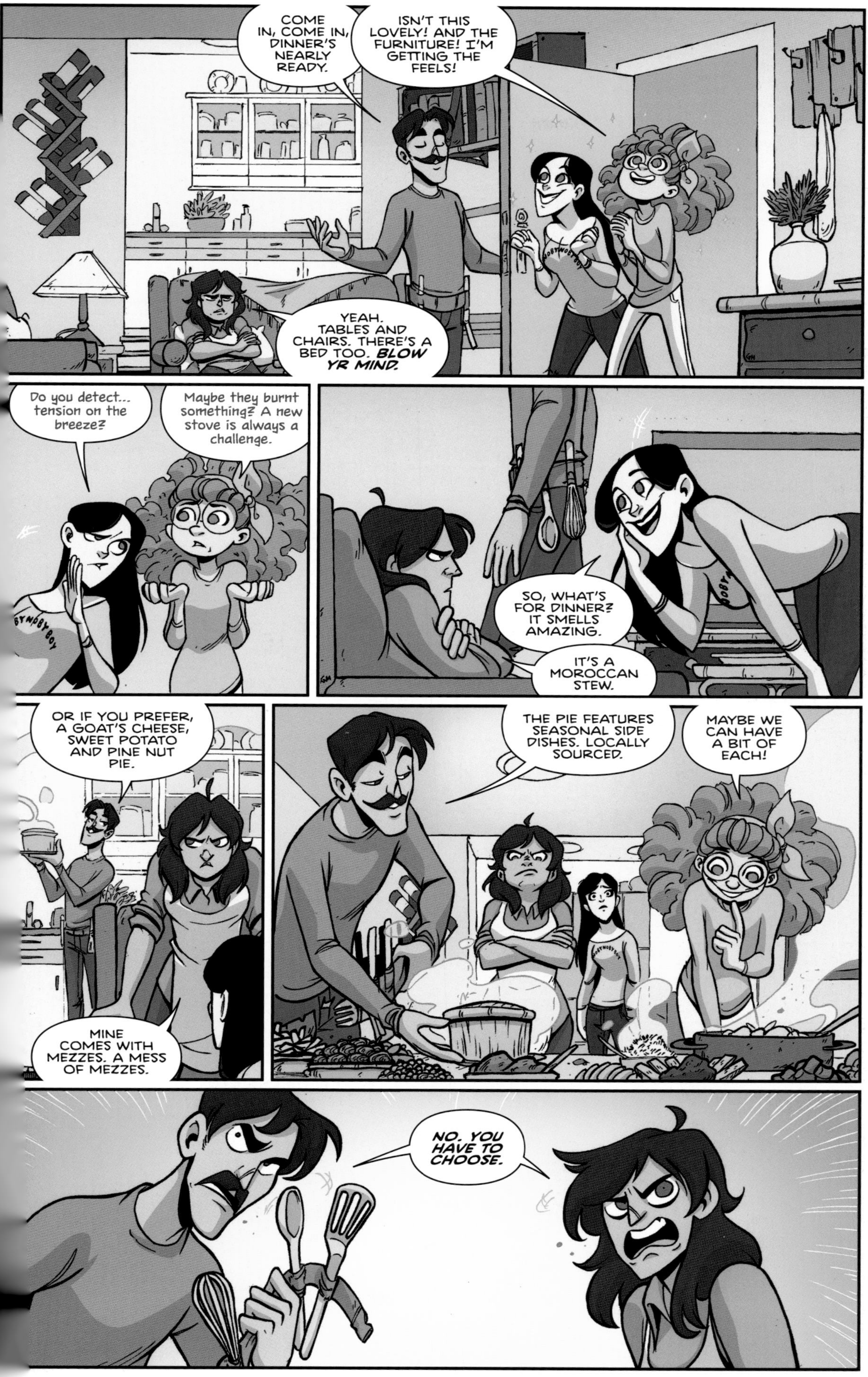
COME IN, COME IN, DINNER'S NEARLY READY.
ISN'T THIS LOVELY! AND THE FURNITURE! I'M GETTING THE FEELS!
YEAH. TABLES AND CHAIRS. THERE'S A BED TOO. BLOW YR MIND.
Do you detect... tension on the breeze?
Maybe they burnt something? A new stove is always a challenge.
SO, WHAT'S FOR DINNER? IT SMELLS AMAZING.
IT'S A MOROCCAN STEW.
OR IF YOU PREFER, A GOAT'S CHEESE, SWEET POTATO AND PINE NUT PIE.
MINE COMES WITH MEZZES. A MESS OF MEZZES.
THE PIE FEATURES SEASONAL SIDE DISHES. LOCALLY SOURCED.
MAYBE WE CAN HAVE A BIT OF EACH!
NO. YOU HAVE TO CHOOSE.

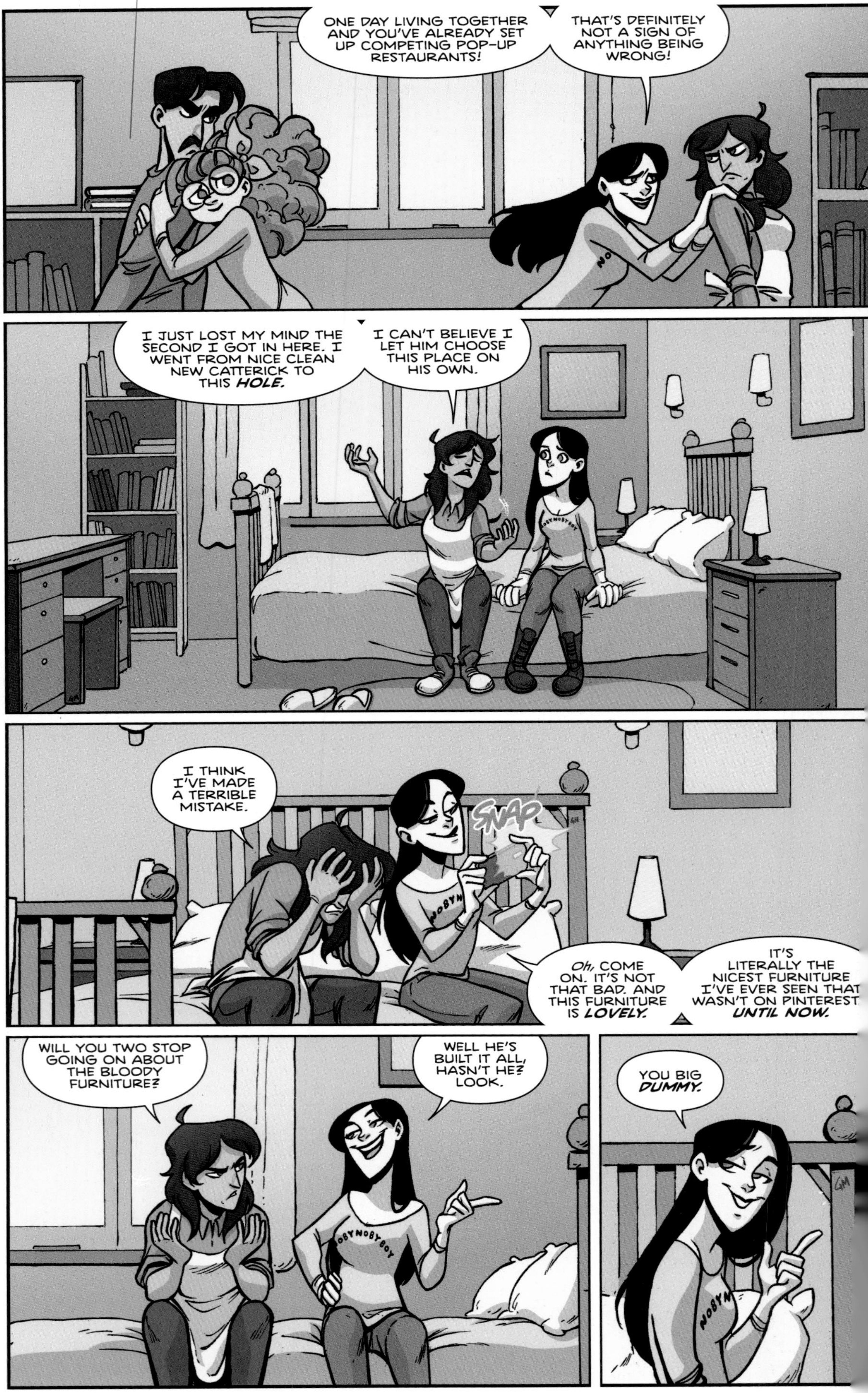
ONE DAY LIVING TOGETHER AND YOU'VE ALREADY SET UP COMPETING POP-UP RESTAURANTS!
THAT'S DEFINITELY NOT A SIGN OF ANYTHING BEING WRONG!
I JUST LOST MY MIND THE SECOND I GOT IN HERE. I WENT FROM NICE CLEAN NEW CATTERICK TO THIS *HOLE.*
I CAN'T BELIEVE I LET HIM CHOOSE THIS PLACE ON HIS OWN.
I THINK I'VE MADE A TERRIBLE MISTAKE.
SNAP
Oh, COME ON. IT'S NOT THAT BAD. AND THIS FURNITURE IS *LOVELY.*
IT'S LITERALLY THE NICEST FURNITURE I'VE EVER SEEN THAT WASN'T ON PINTEREST. *UNTIL NOW.*
WILL YOU TWO STOP GOING ON ABOUT THE BLOODY FURNITURE?
WELL HE'S BUILT IT ALL, HASN'T HE? LOOK.
YOU BIG *DUMMY.*

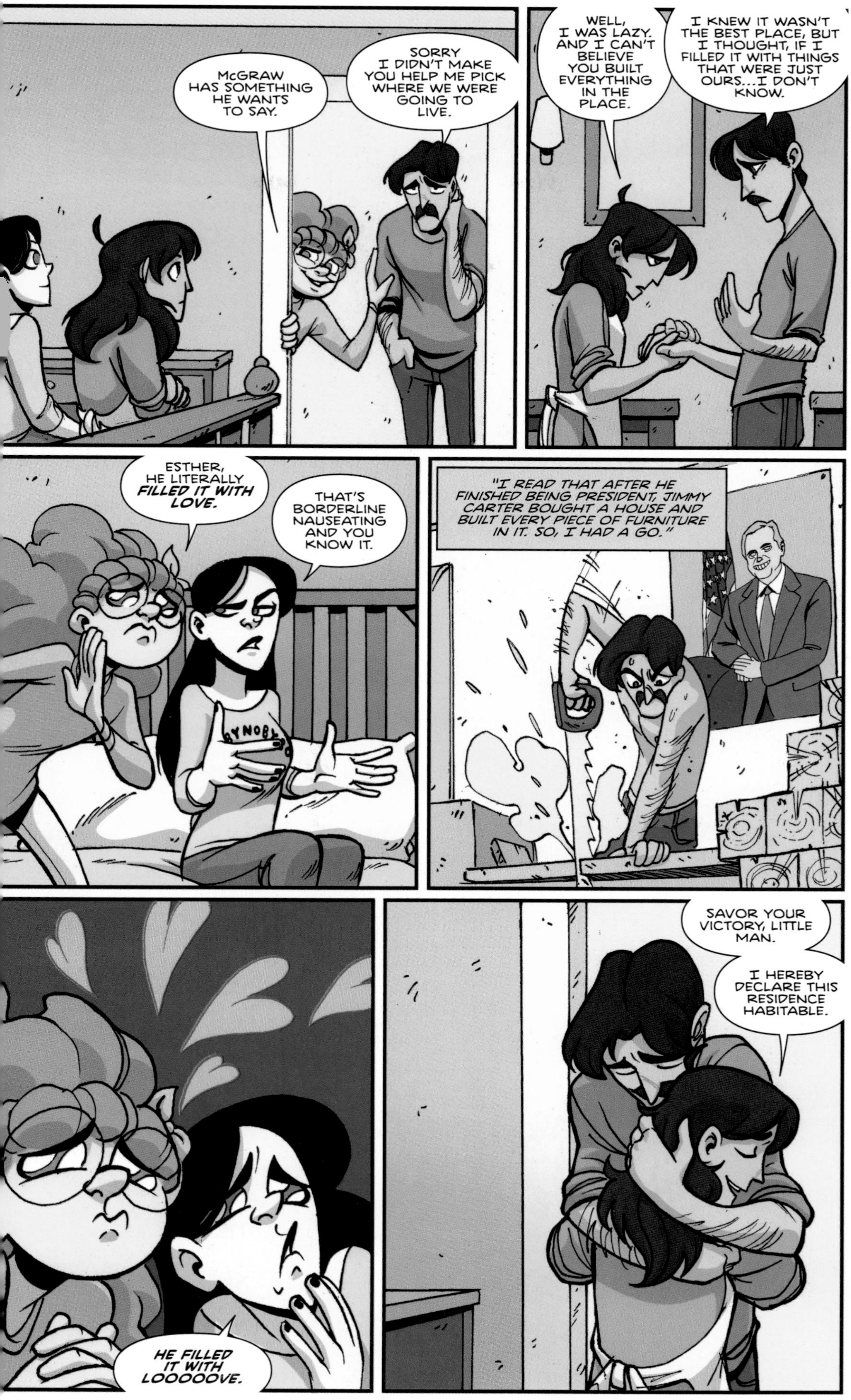
McGRAW HAS SOMETHING HE WANTS TO SAY.
SORRY I DIDN'T MAKE YOU HELP ME PICK WHERE WE WERE GOING TO LIVE.
WELL, I WAS LAZY. AND I CAN'T BELIEVE YOU BUILT EVERYTHING IN THE PLACE.
I KNEW IT WASN'T THE BEST PLACE, BUT I THOUGHT, IF I FILLED IT WITH THINGS THAT WERE JUST OURS... I DON'T KNOW.
ESTHER, HE LITERALLY FILLED IT WITH LOVE.
THAT'S BORDERLINE NAUSEATING AND YOU KNOW IT.
"I READ THAT AFTER HE FINISHED BEING PRESIDENT, JIMMY CARTER BOUGHT A HOUSE AND BUILT EVERY PIECE OF FURNITURE IN IT. SO, I HAD A GO."
HE FILLED IT WITH LOOOOOVE.
SAVOR YOUR VICTORY, LITTLE MAN.
I HEREBY DECLARE THIS RESIDENCE HABITABLE.

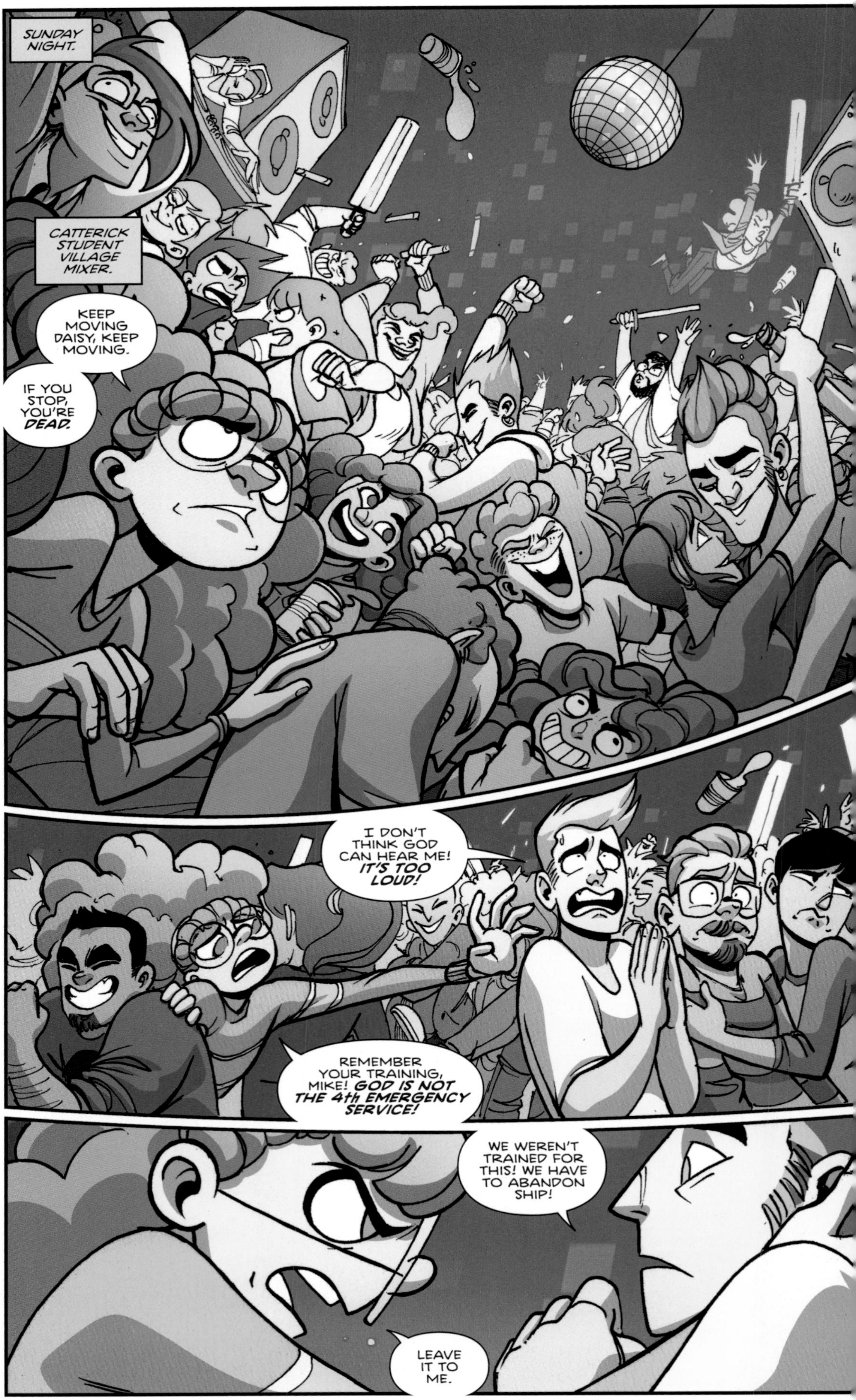
SUNDAY NIGHT.
CATTERICK STUDENT VILLAGE MIXER.
KEEP MOVING DAISY, KEEP MOVING.
IF YOU STOP, YOU'RE ***DEAD.***
I DON'T THINK GOD CAN HEAR ME! ***IT'S TOO LOUD!***
REMEMBER YOUR TRAINING, MIKE! ***GOD IS NOT THE 4th EMERGENCY SERVICE!***
WE WEREN'T TRAINED FOR THIS! WE HAVE TO ABANDON SHIP!
LEAVE IT TO ME.

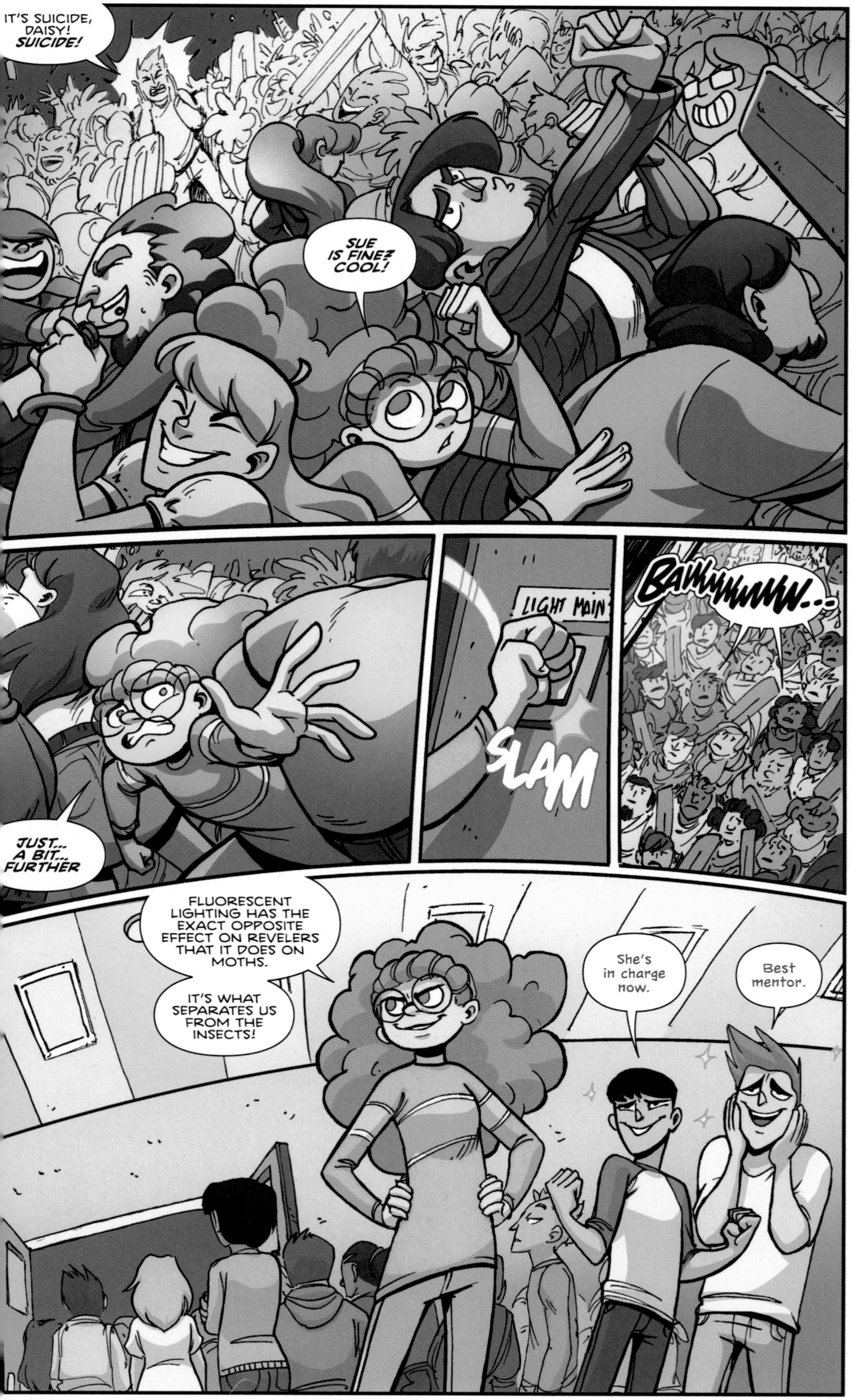
IT'S SUICIDE, DAISY! SUICIDE!
SUE IS FINE! COOL!
JUST... A BIT... FURTHER
LIGHT MAIN
SLAM
BAWWWWWW...
FLUORESCENT LIGHTING HAS THE EXACT OPPOSITE EFFECT ON REVELERS THAT IT DOES ON MOTHS.
IT'S WHAT SEPARATES US FROM THE INSECTS!
She's in charge now.
Best mentor.

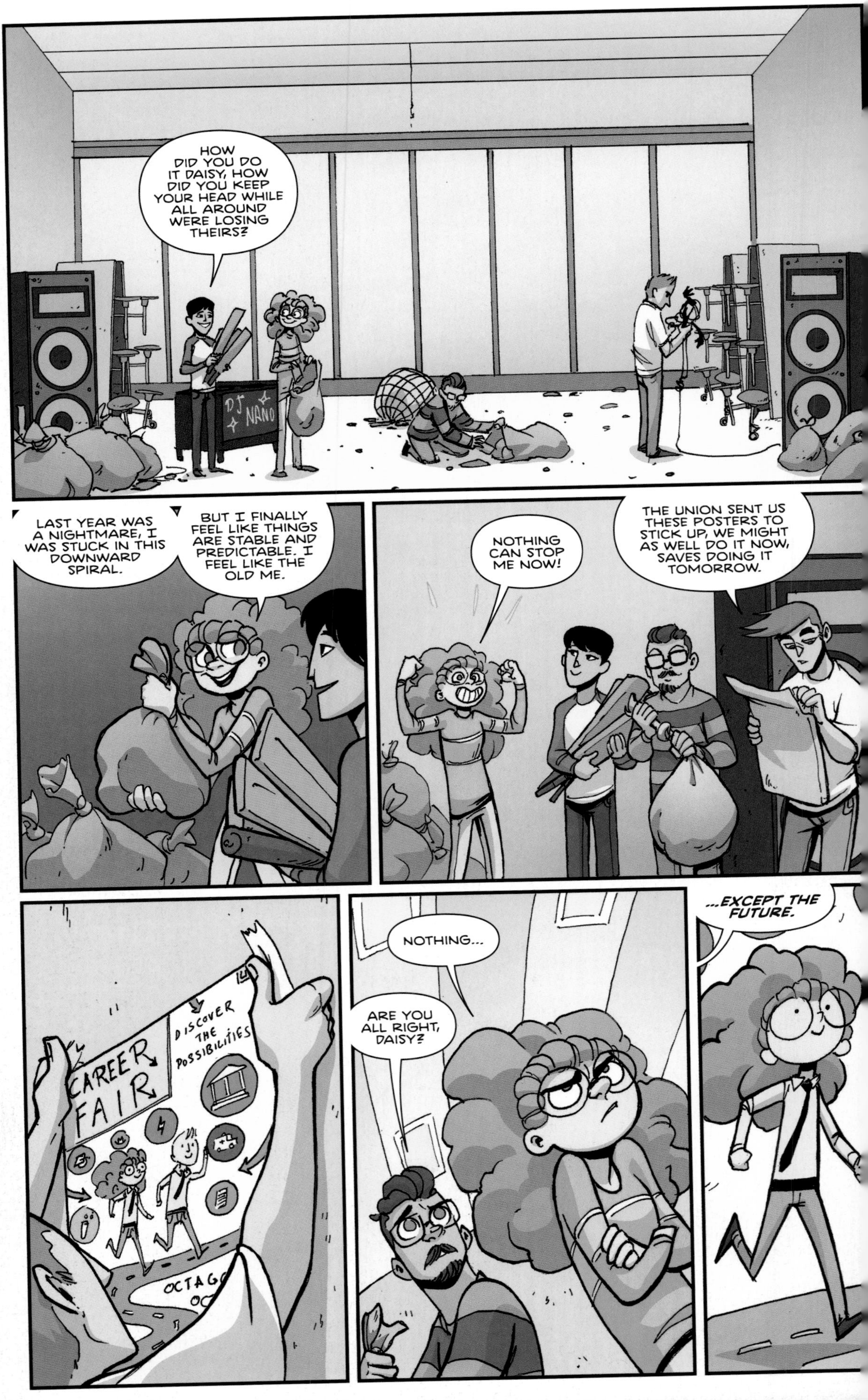
HOW DID YOU DO IT DAISY, HOW DID YOU KEEP YOUR HEAD WHILE ALL AROUND WERE LOSING THEIRS?
DJ NANO
LAST YEAR WAS A NIGHTMARE, I WAS STUCK IN THIS DOWNWARD SPIRAL.
BUT I FINALLY FEEL LIKE THINGS ARE STABLE AND PREDICTABLE. I FEEL LIKE THE OLD ME.
NOTHING CAN STOP ME NOW!
THE UNION SENT US THESE POSTERS TO STICK UP, WE MIGHT AS WELL DO IT NOW, SAVES DOING IT TOMORROW.
CAREER FAIR
DISCOVER THE POSSIBILITIES
OCTAG
NOTHING...
ARE YOU ALL RIGHT, DAISY?
...EXCEPT THE FUTURE.

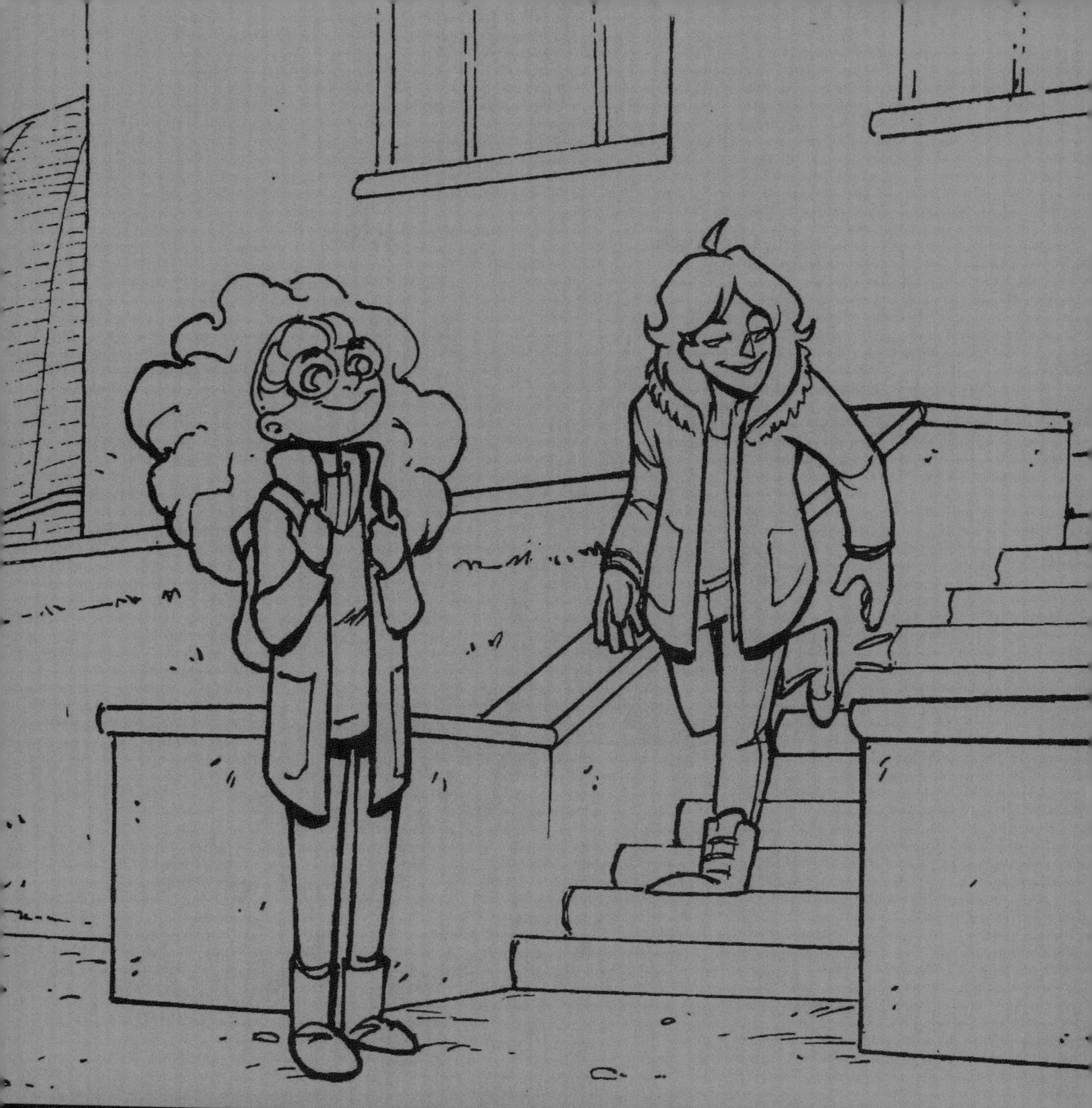

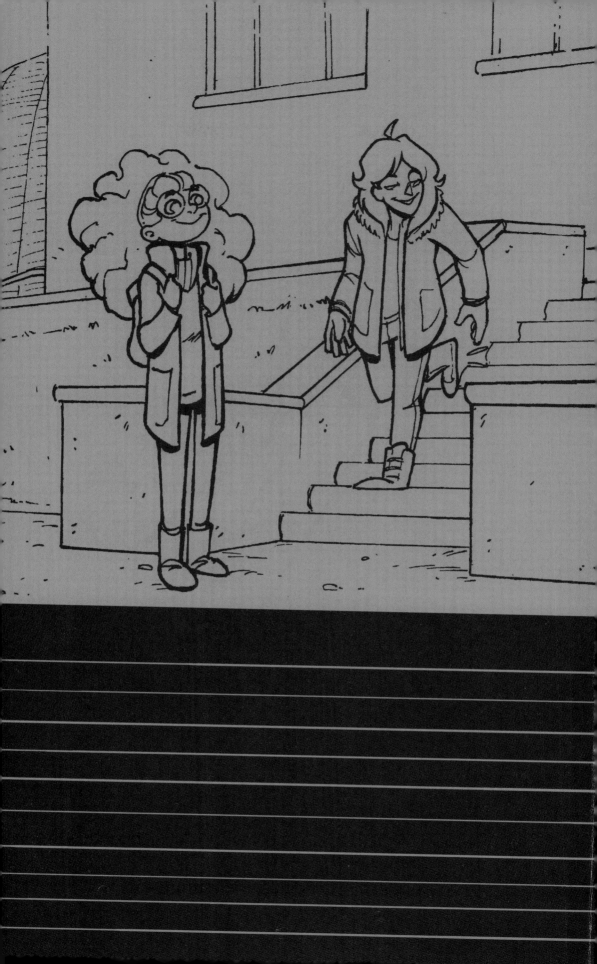

CHAPTER
THIRTY NINE

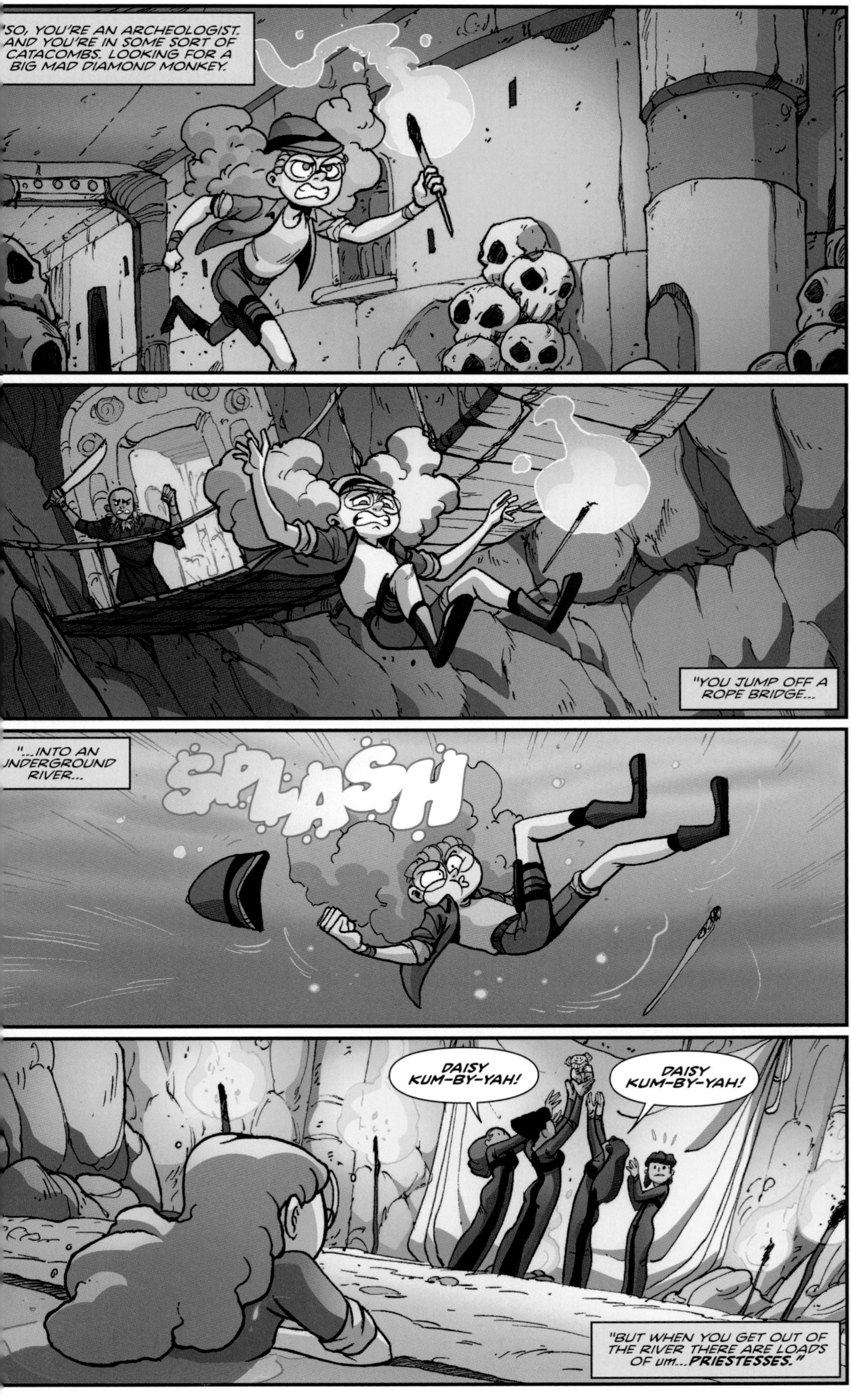
"SO, YOU'RE AN ARCHEOLOGIST. AND YOU'RE IN SOME SORT OF CATACOMBS. LOOKING FOR A BIG MAD DIAMOND MONKEY.
"YOU JUMP OFF A ROPE BRIDGE...
"...INTO AN UNDERGROUND RIVER...
SPLASH
DAISY KUM-BY-YAH!
DAISY KUM-BY-YAH!
"BUT WHEN YOU GET OUT OF THE RIVER THERE ARE LOADS OF UM... PRIESTESSES."

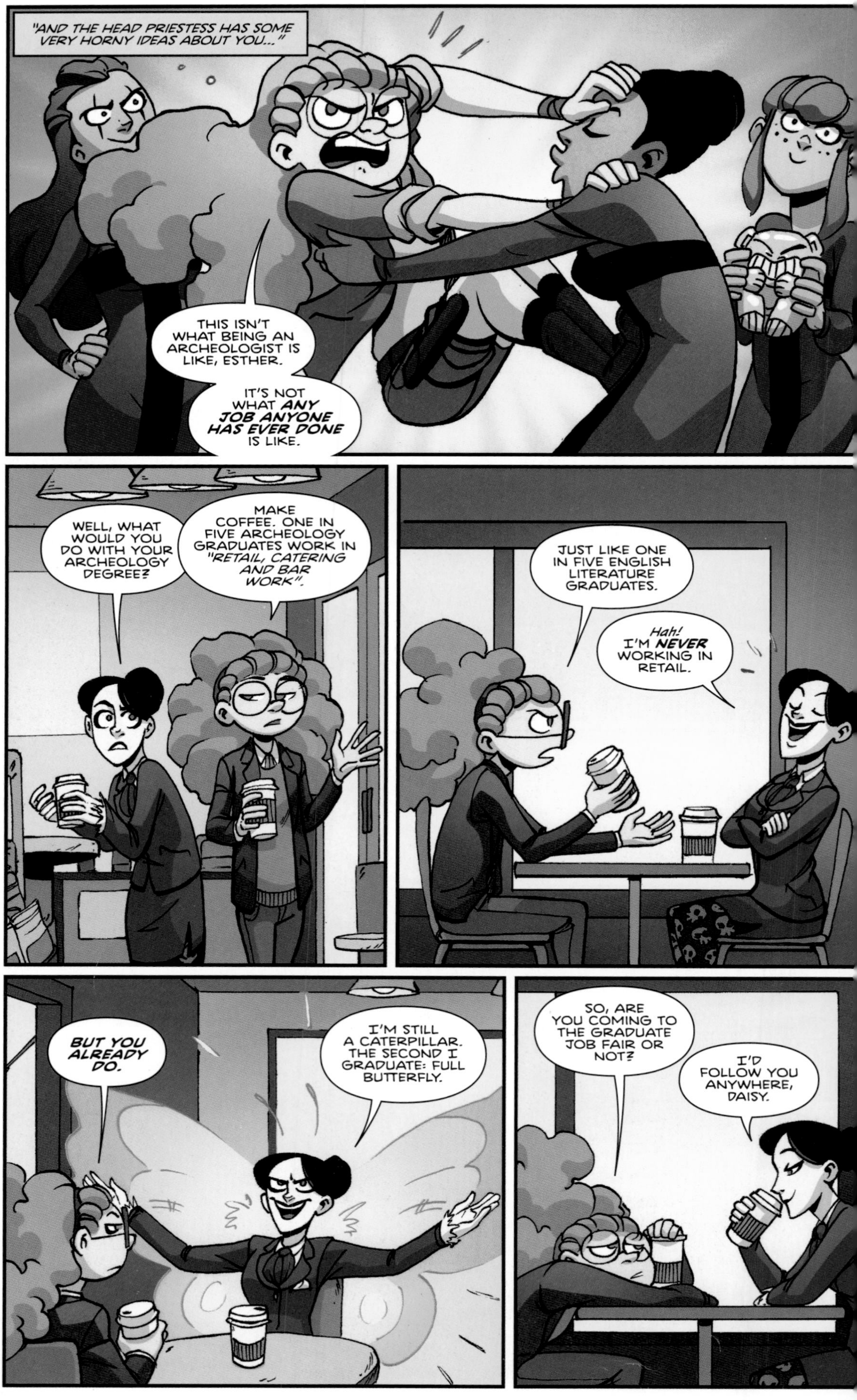
"AND THE HEAD PRIESTESS HAS SOME VERY HORNY IDEAS ABOUT YOU..."
THIS ISN'T WHAT BEING AN ARCHEOLOGIST IS LIKE, ESTHER.
IT'S NOT WHAT **ANY JOB ANYONE HAS EVER DONE** IS LIKE.
WELL, WHAT WOULD YOU DO WITH YOUR ARCHEOLOGY DEGREE?
MAKE COFFEE. ONE IN FIVE ARCHEOLOGY GRADUATES WORK IN *"RETAIL, CATERING AND BAR WORK"*.
JUST LIKE ONE IN FIVE ENGLISH LITERATURE GRADUATES.
Hah! I'M ***NEVER*** WORKING IN RETAIL.
BUT YOU ALREADY DO.
I'M STILL A CATERPILLAR. THE SECOND I GRADUATE: FULL BUTTERFLY.
SO, ARE YOU COMING TO THE GRADUATE JOB FAIR OR NOT?
I'D FOLLOW YOU ANYWHERE, DAISY.

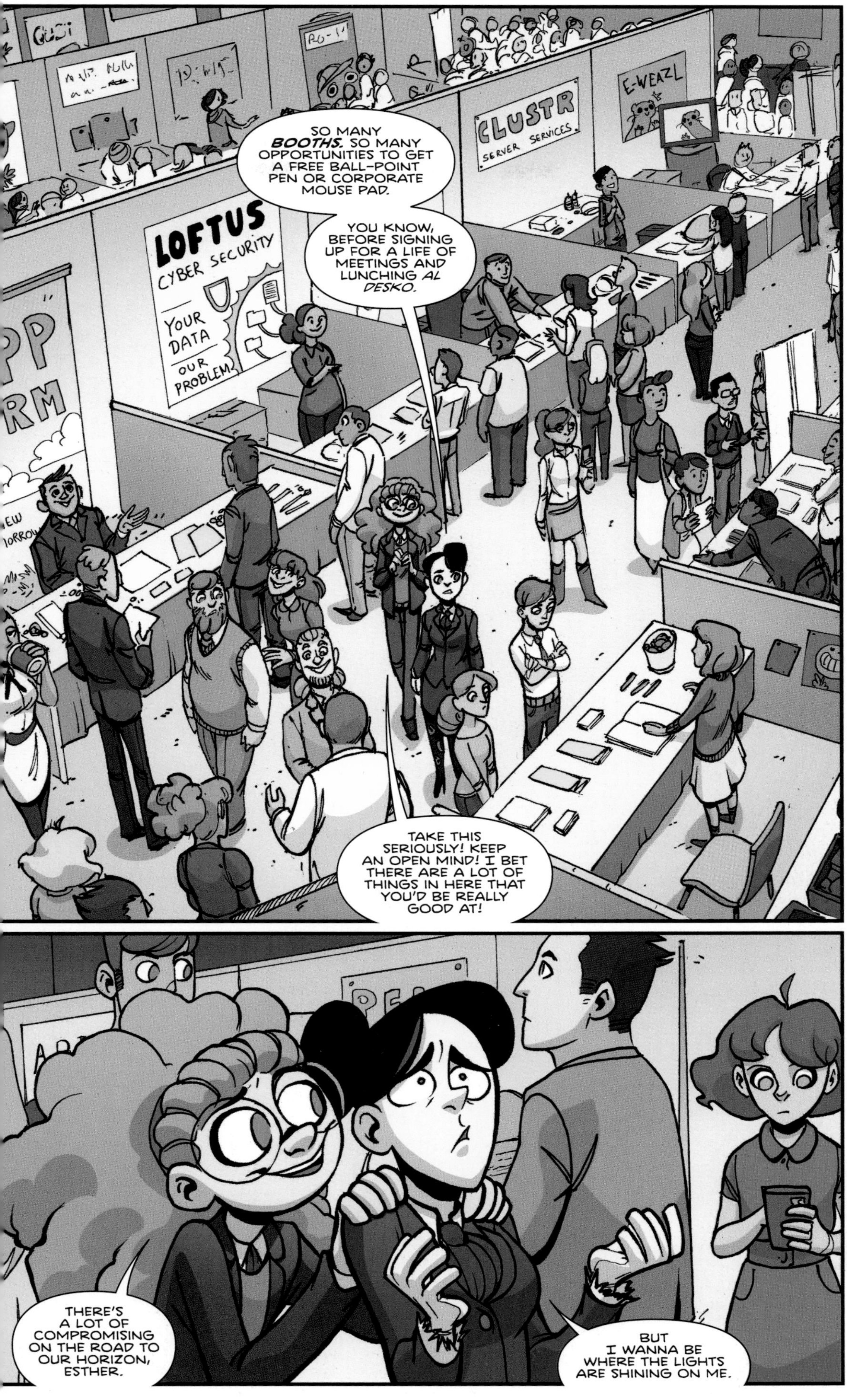
SO MANY *BOOTHS.* SO MANY OPPORTUNITIES TO GET A FREE BALL-POINT PEN OR CORPORATE MOUSE PAD.
YOU KNOW, BEFORE SIGNING UP FOR A LIFE OF MEETINGS AND LUNCHING *AL DESKO.*
CLUSTR
SERVER SERVICES
E-WEAZL
LOFTUS
CYBER SECURITY
YOUR DATA
OUR PROBLEM.
TAKE THIS SERIOUSLY! KEEP AN OPEN MIND! I BET THERE ARE A LOT OF THINGS IN HERE THAT YOU'D BE REALLY GOOD AT!
THERE'S A LOT OF COMPROMISING ON THE ROAD TO OUR HORIZON, ESTHER.
BUT I WANNA BE WHERE THE LIGHTS ARE SHINING ON ME.

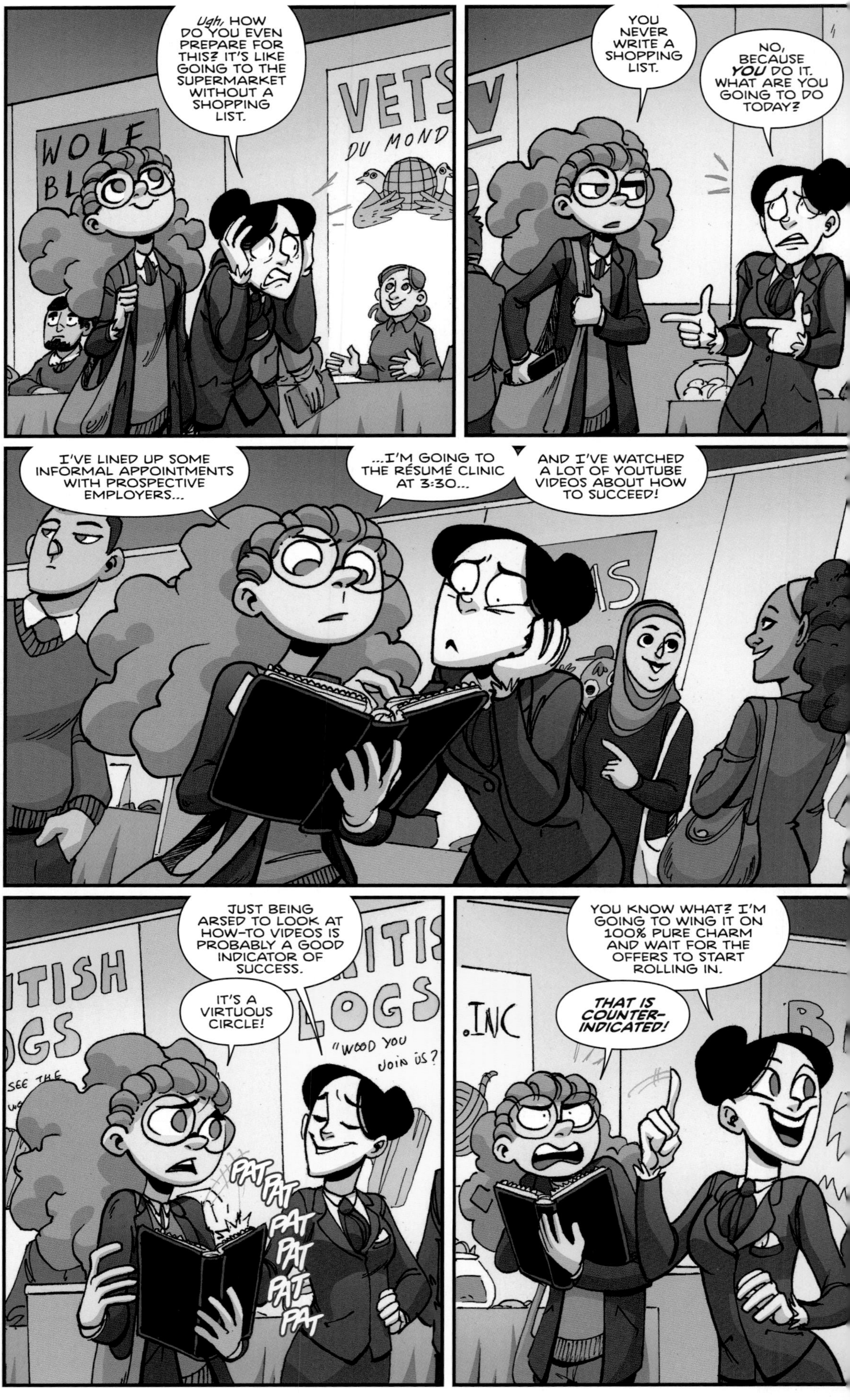
Ugh, HOW DO YOU EVEN PREPARE FOR THIS? IT'S LIKE GOING TO THE SUPERMARKET WITHOUT A SHOPPING LIST.
WOLF BL
VETS DU MOND
YOU NEVER WRITE A SHOPPING LIST.
NO, BECAUSE YOU DO IT. WHAT ARE YOU GOING TO DO TODAY?
I'VE LINED UP SOME INFORMAL APPOINTMENTS WITH PROSPECTIVE EMPLOYERS...
...I'M GOING TO THE RÉSUMÉ CLINIC AT 3:30...
AND I'VE WATCHED A LOT OF YOUTUBE VIDEOS ABOUT HOW TO SUCCEED!
JUST BEING ARSED TO LOOK AT HOW-TO VIDEOS IS PROBABLY A GOOD INDICATOR OF SUCCESS.
IT'S A VIRTUOUS CIRCLE!
"WOOD YOU JOIN US?
PAT PAT PAT PAT PAT PAT
YOU KNOW WHAT? I'M GOING TO WING IT ON 100% PURE CHARM AND WAIT FOR THE OFFERS TO START ROLLING IN.
THAT IS COUNTER-INDICATED!
.INC

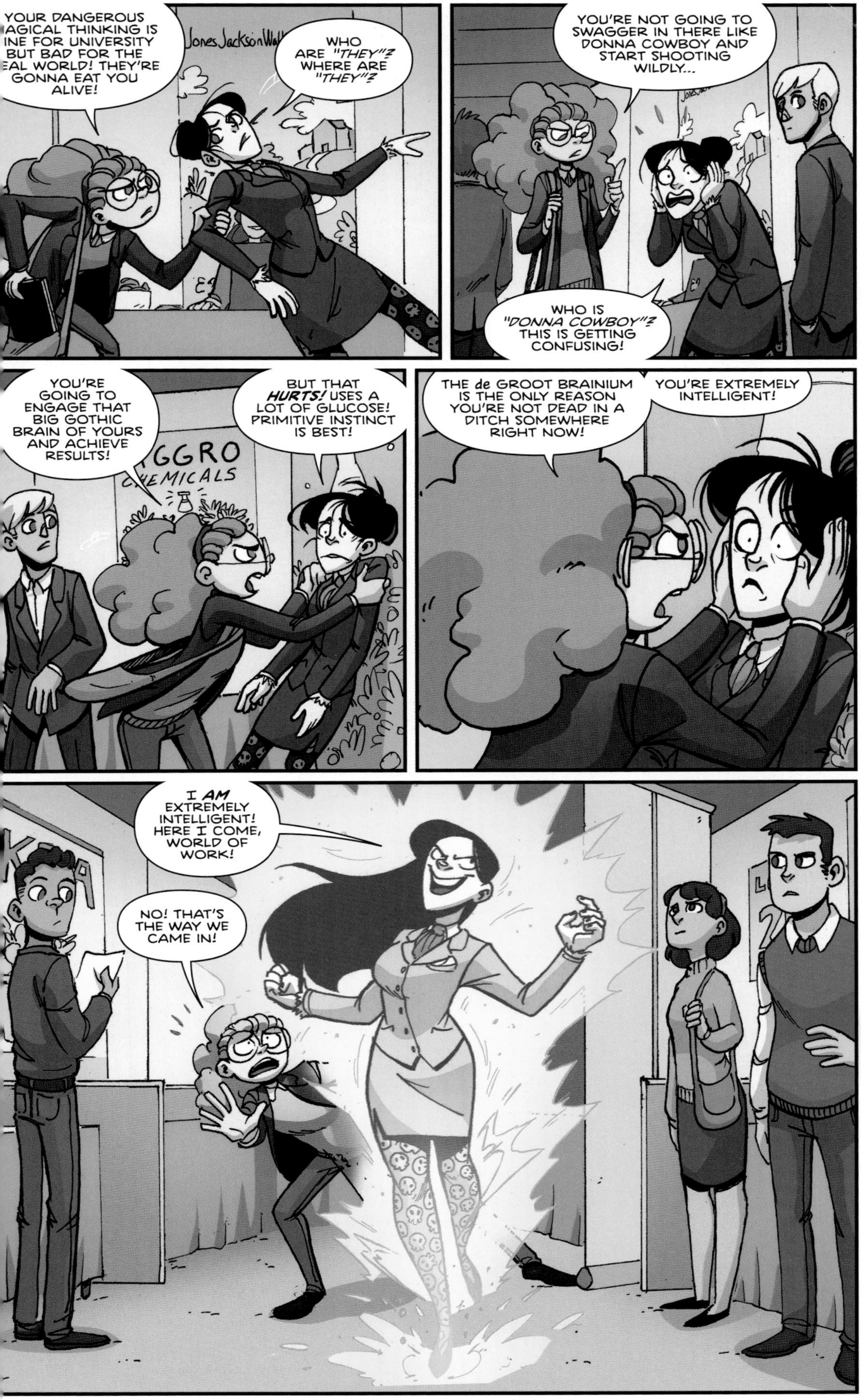
YOUR DANGEROUS AGICAL THINKING IS INE FOR UNIVERSITY BUT BAD FOR THE EAL WORLD! THEY'RE GONNA EAT YOU ALIVE!
Jones Jackson Wall
WHO ARE "THEY"? WHERE ARE "THEY"?
YOU'RE NOT GOING TO SWAGGER IN THERE LIKE DONNA COWBOY AND START SHOOTING WILDLY...
WHO IS "DONNA COWBOY"? THIS IS GETTING CONFUSING!
YOU'RE GOING TO ENGAGE THAT BIG GOTHIC BRAIN OF YOURS AND ACHIEVE RESULTS!
GGRO CHEMICALS
BUT THAT HURTS! USES A LOT OF GLUCOSE! PRIMITIVE INSTINCT IS BEST!
THE de GROOT BRAINIUM IS THE ONLY REASON YOU'RE NOT DEAD IN A DITCH SOMEWHERE RIGHT NOW!
YOU'RE EXTREMELY INTELLIGENT!
I AM EXTREMELY INTELLIGENT! HERE I COME, WORLD OF WORK!
NO! THAT'S THE WAY WE CAME IN!

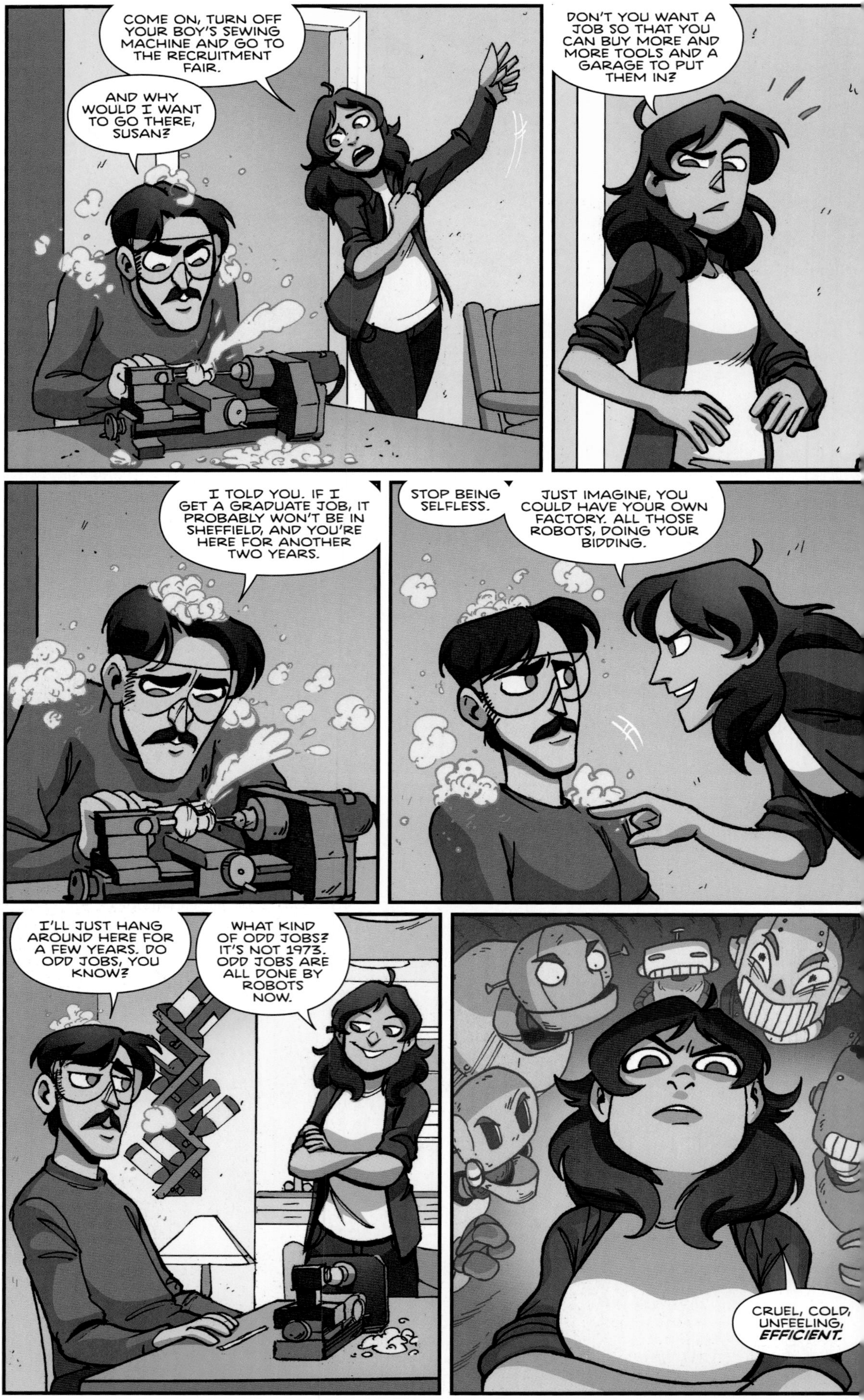
COME ON, TURN OFF YOUR BOY'S SEWING MACHINE AND GO TO THE RECRUITMENT FAIR.
AND WHY WOULD I WANT TO GO THERE, SUSAN?
DON'T YOU WANT A JOB SO THAT YOU CAN BUY MORE AND MORE TOOLS AND A GARAGE TO PUT THEM IN?
I TOLD YOU. IF I GET A GRADUATE JOB, IT PROBABLY WON'T BE IN SHEFFIELD, AND YOU'RE HERE FOR ANOTHER TWO YEARS.
STOP BEING SELFLESS.
JUST IMAGINE, YOU COULD HAVE YOUR OWN FACTORY. ALL THOSE ROBOTS, DOING YOUR BIDDING.
I'LL JUST HANG AROUND HERE FOR A FEW YEARS. DO ODD JOBS, YOU KNOW?
WHAT KIND OF ODD JOBS? IT'S NOT 1973. ODD JOBS ARE ALL DONE BY ROBOTS NOW.
CRUEL, COLD, UNFEELING, ***EFFICIENT.***

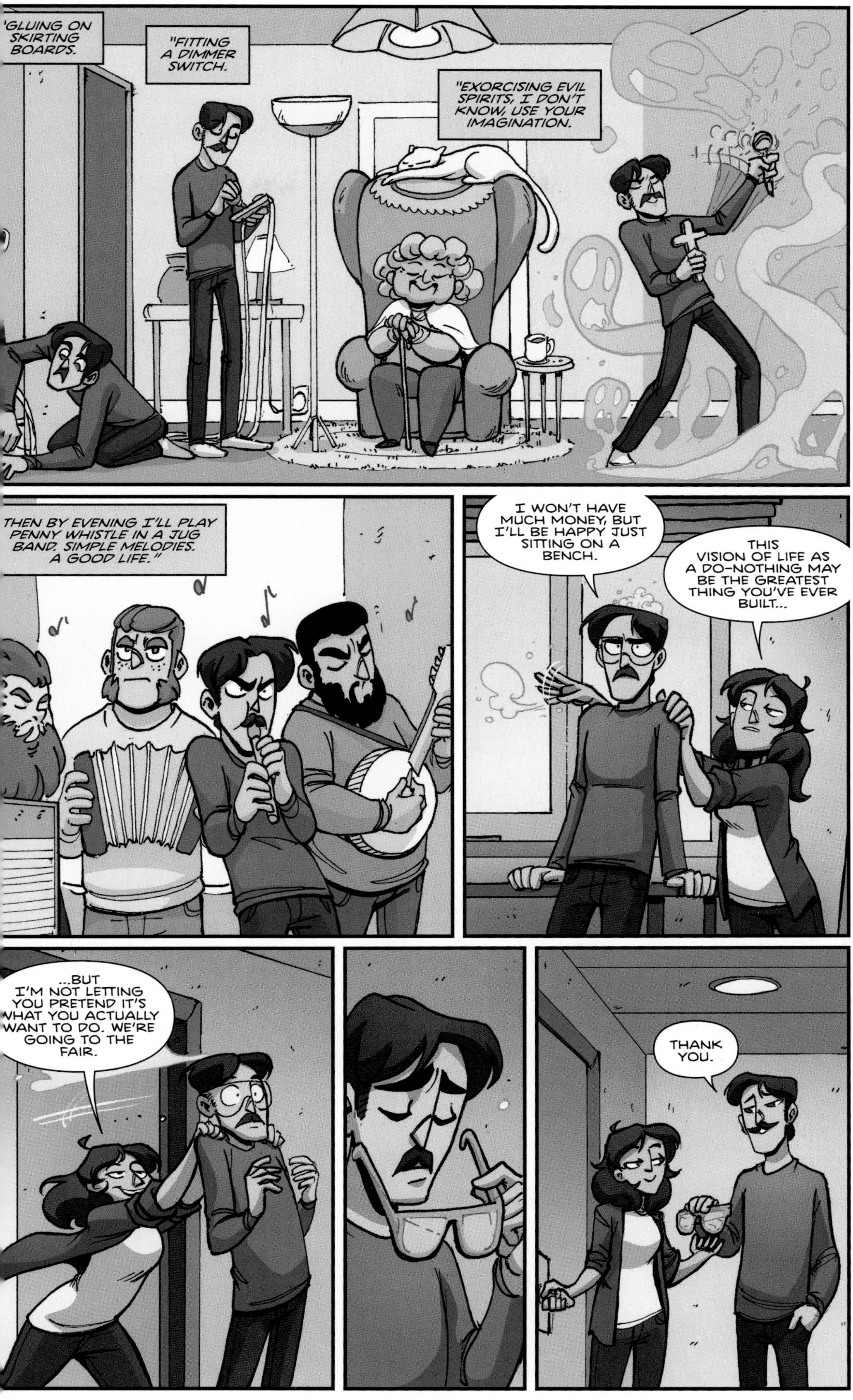

'GLUING ON SKIRTING BOARDS.
"FITTING A DIMMER SWITCH.
"EXORCISING EVIL SPIRITS, I DON'T KNOW, USE YOUR IMAGINATION.
THEN BY EVENING I'LL PLAY PENNY WHISTLE IN A JUG BAND. SIMPLE MELODIES. A GOOD LIFE."
I WON'T HAVE MUCH MONEY, BUT I'LL BE HAPPY JUST SITTING ON A BENCH.
THIS VISION OF LIFE AS A DO-NOTHING MAY BE THE GREATEST THING YOU'VE EVER BUILT...
...BUT I'M NOT LETTING YOU PRETEND IT'S WHAT YOU ACTUALLY WANT TO DO. WE'RE GOING TO THE FAIR.
THANK YOU.

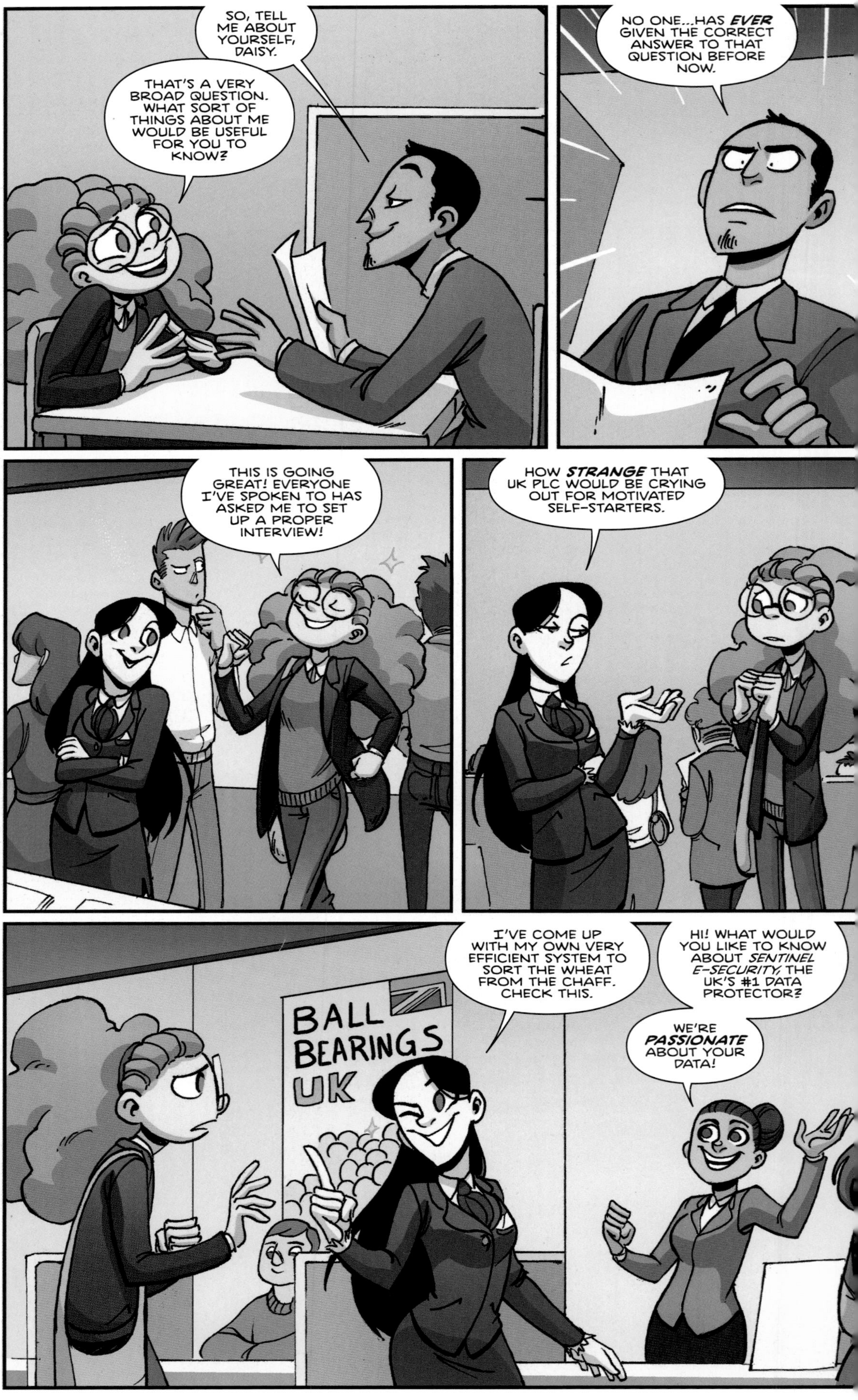
SO, TELL ME ABOUT YOURSELF, DAISY.
THAT'S A VERY BROAD QUESTION. WHAT SORT OF THINGS ABOUT ME WOULD BE USEFUL FOR YOU TO KNOW?
NO ONE...HAS EVER GIVEN THE CORRECT ANSWER TO THAT QUESTION BEFORE NOW.
THIS IS GOING GREAT! EVERYONE I'VE SPOKEN TO HAS ASKED ME TO SET UP A PROPER INTERVIEW!
HOW STRANGE THAT UK PLC WOULD BE CRYING OUT FOR MOTIVATED SELF-STARTERS.
BALL BEARINGS UK
I'VE COME UP WITH MY OWN VERY EFFICIENT SYSTEM TO SORT THE WHEAT FROM THE CHAFF. CHECK THIS.
HI! WHAT WOULD YOU LIKE TO KNOW ABOUT SENTINEL E-SECURITY, THE UK'S #1 DATA PROTECTOR?
WE'RE PASSIONATE ABOUT YOUR DATA!

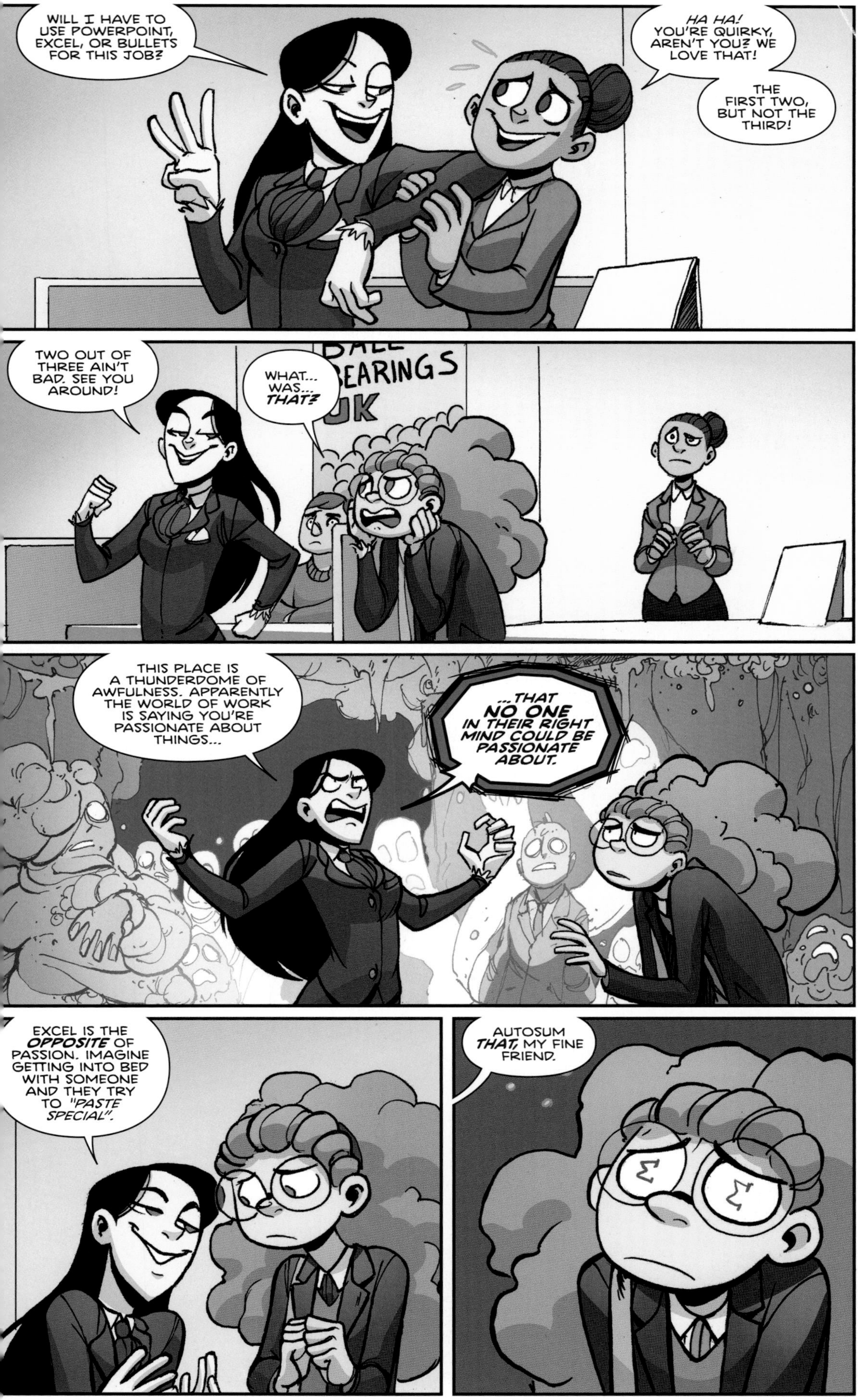
WILL I HAVE TO USE POWERPOINT, EXCEL, OR BULLETS FOR THIS JOB?
HA HA! YOU'RE QUIRKY, AREN'T YOU? WE LOVE THAT!
THE FIRST TWO, BUT NOT THE THIRD!
TWO OUT OF THREE AIN'T BAD. SEE YOU AROUND!
WHAT... WAS... THAT?
BALL BEARINGS UK
THIS PLACE IS A THUNDERDOME OF AWFULNESS. APPARENTLY THE WORLD OF WORK IS SAYING YOU'RE PASSIONATE ABOUT THINGS...
...THAT NO ONE IN THEIR RIGHT MIND COULD BE PASSIONATE ABOUT.
EXCEL IS THE OPPOSITE OF PASSION. IMAGINE GETTING INTO BED WITH SOMEONE AND THEY TRY TO "PASTE SPECIAL".
AUTOSUM THAT, MY FINE FRIEND.

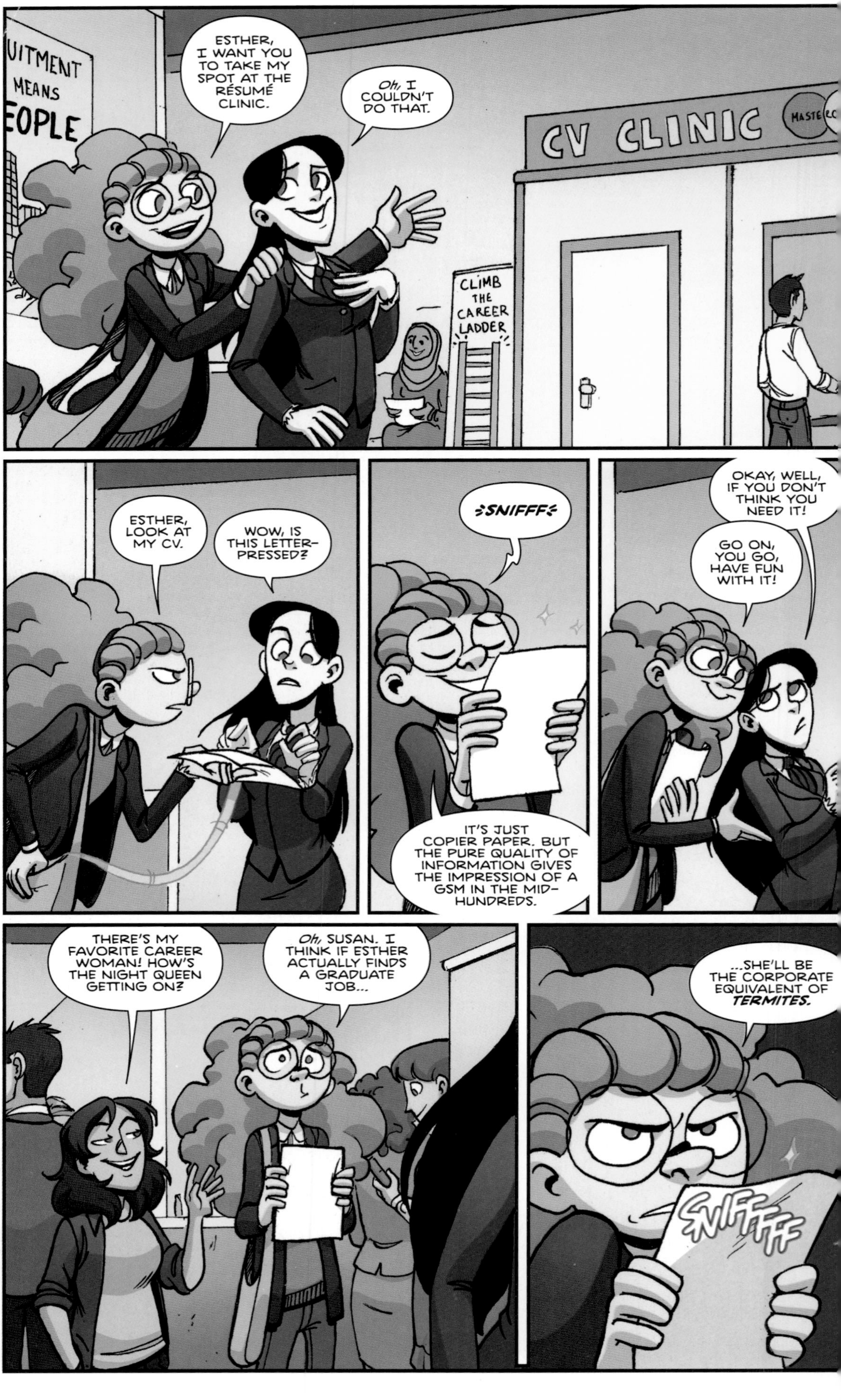
ESTHER, I WANT YOU TO TAKE MY SPOT AT THE RÉSUMÉ CLINIC.
Oh, I COULDN'T DO THAT.
CV CLINIC
CLIMB THE CAREER LADDER
ESTHER, LOOK AT MY CV.
WOW, IS THIS LETTER-PRESSED?
SNIFFF
IT'S JUST COPIER PAPER. BUT THE PURE QUALITY OF INFORMATION GIVES THE IMPRESSION OF A GSM IN THE MID-HUNDREDS.
OKAY, WELL, IF YOU DON'T THINK YOU NEED IT!
GO ON, YOU GO, HAVE FUN WITH IT!
THERE'S MY FAVORITE CAREER WOMAN! HOW'S THE NIGHT QUEEN GETTING ON?
Oh, SUSAN. I THINK IF ESTHER ACTUALLY FINDS A GRADUATE JOB...
...SHE'LL BE THE CORPORATE EQUIVALENT OF ***TERMITES.***
SNIFFFFF

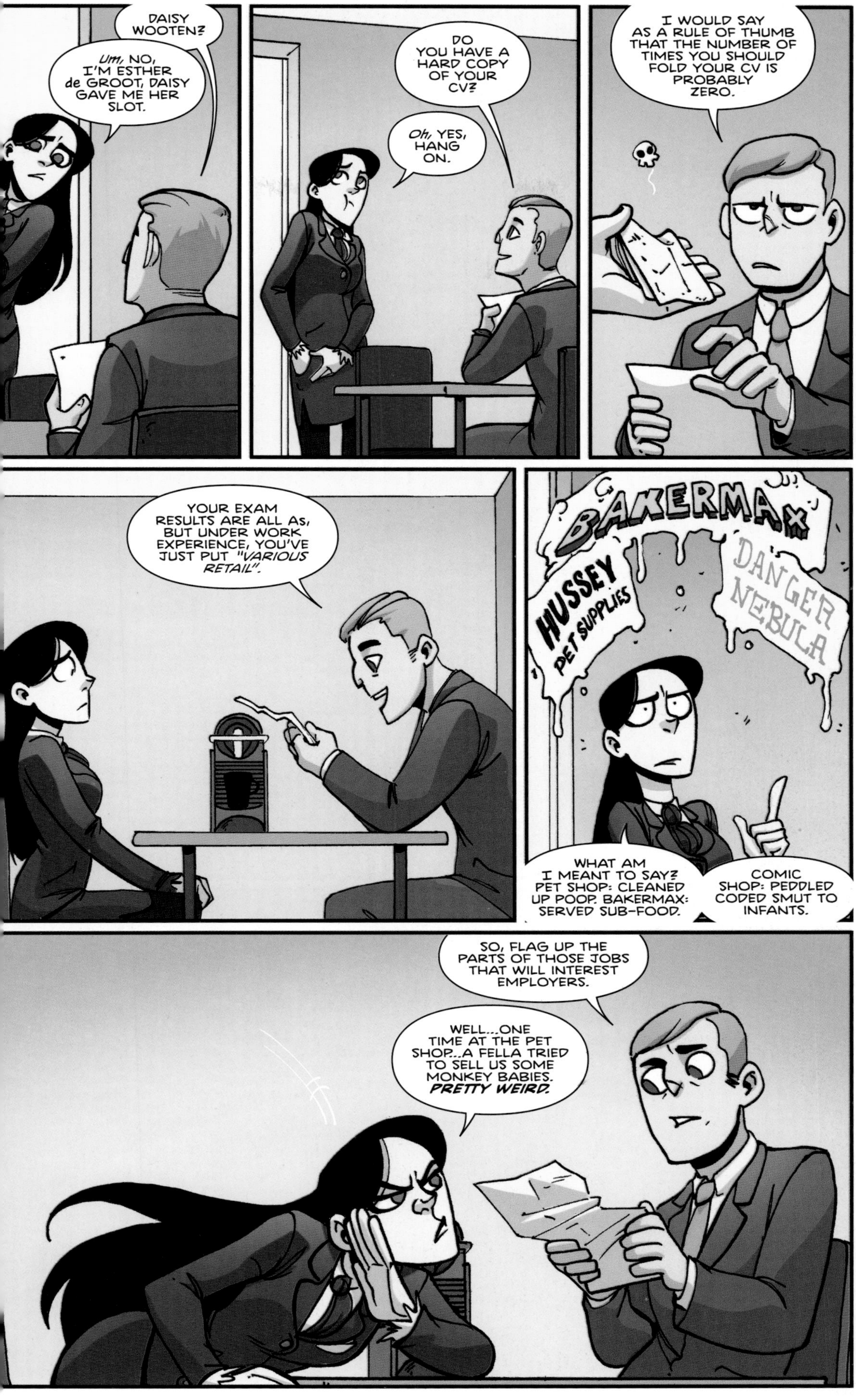
DAISY WOOTEN?
Um, NO, I'M ESTHER de GROOT, DAISY GAVE ME HER SLOT.
DO YOU HAVE A HARD COPY OF YOUR CV?
Oh, YES, HANG ON.
I WOULD SAY AS A RULE OF THUMB THAT THE NUMBER OF TIMES YOU SHOULD FOLD YOUR CV IS PROBABLY ZERO.
YOUR EXAM RESULTS ARE ALL As, BUT UNDER WORK EXPERIENCE, YOU'VE JUST PUT *"VARIOUS RETAIL"*.
BAKERMAX
HUSSEY PET SUPPLIES
DANGER NEBULA
WHAT AM I MEANT TO SAY? PET SHOP: CLEANED UP POOP. BAKERMAX: SERVED SUB-FOOD.
COMIC SHOP: PEDDLED CODED SMUT TO INFANTS.
SO, FLAG UP THE PARTS OF THOSE JOBS THAT WILL INTEREST EMPLOYERS.
WELL...ONE TIME AT THE PET SHOP...A FELLA TRIED TO SELL US SOME MONKEY BABIES. ***PRETTY WEIRD.***

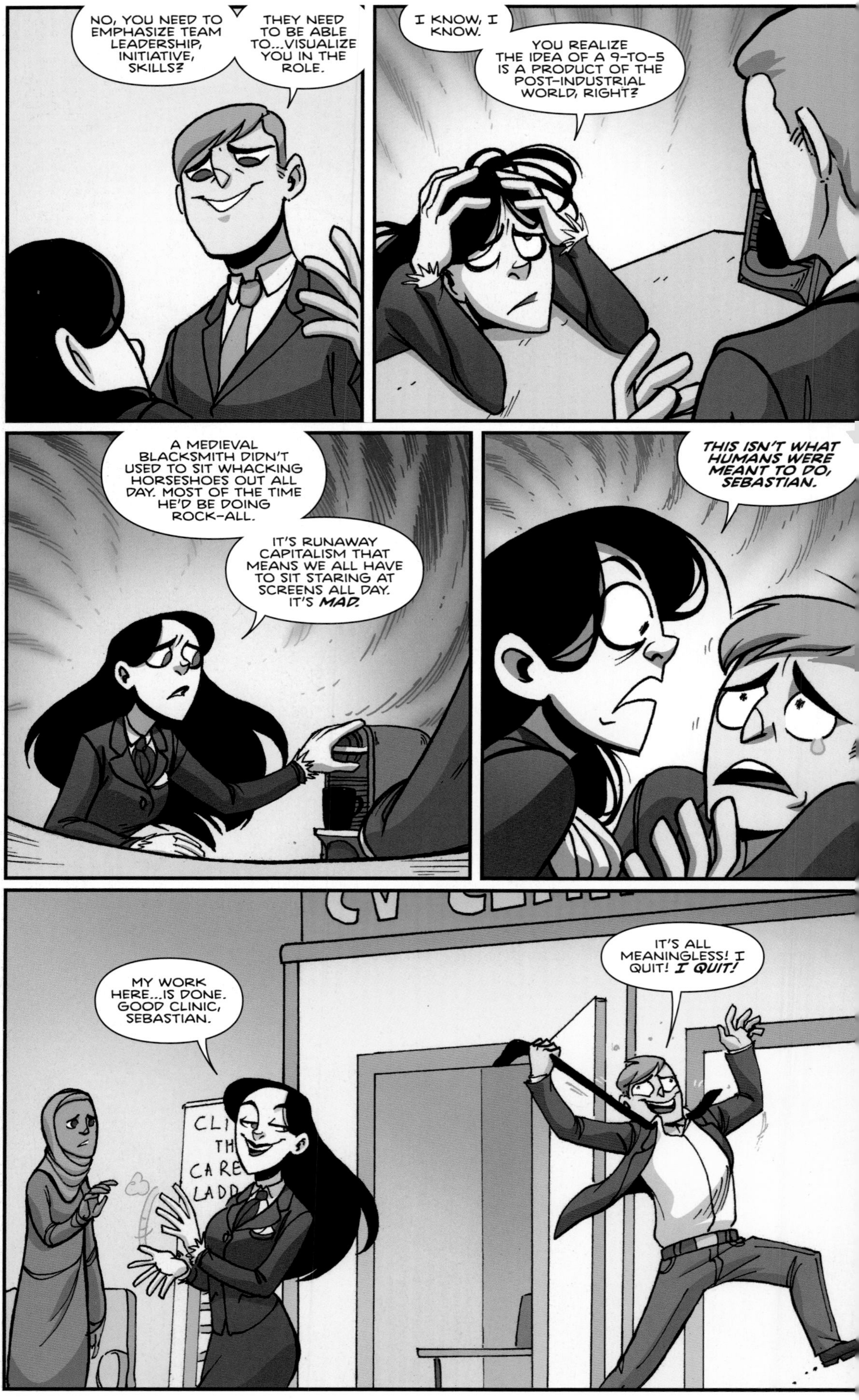
NO, YOU NEED TO EMPHASIZE TEAM LEADERSHIP, INITIATIVE, SKILLS?
THEY NEED TO BE ABLE TO...VISUALIZE YOU IN THE ROLE.
I KNOW, I KNOW.
YOU REALIZE THE IDEA OF A 9-TO-5 IS A PRODUCT OF THE POST-INDUSTRIAL WORLD, RIGHT?
A MEDIEVAL BLACKSMITH DIDN'T USED TO SIT WHACKING HORSESHOES OUT ALL DAY. MOST OF THE TIME HE'D BE DOING ROCK-ALL.
IT'S RUNAWAY CAPITALISM THAT MEANS WE ALL HAVE TO SIT STARING AT SCREENS ALL DAY. IT'S *MAD.*
THIS ISN'T WHAT HUMANS WERE MEANT TO DO, SEBASTIAN.
MY WORK HERE...IS DONE. GOOD CLINIC, SEBASTIAN.
IT'S ALL MEANINGLESS! I QUIT! *I QUIT!*

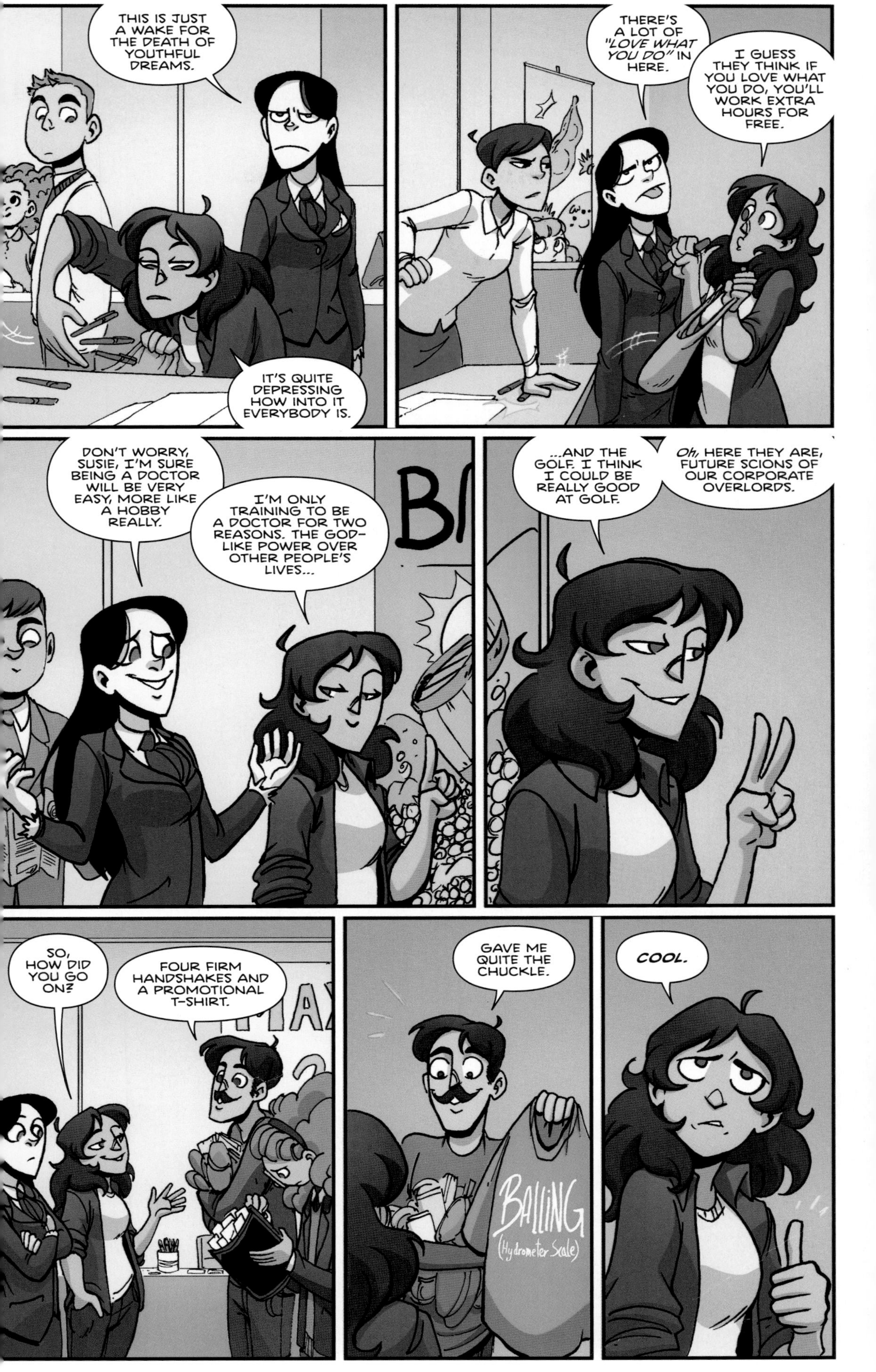
THIS IS JUST A WAKE FOR THE DEATH OF YOUTHFUL DREAMS.
IT'S QUITE DEPRESSING HOW INTO IT EVERYBODY IS.
THERE'S A LOT OF "LOVE WHAT YOU DO" IN HERE.
I GUESS THEY THINK IF YOU LOVE WHAT YOU DO, YOU'LL WORK EXTRA HOURS FOR FREE.
DON'T WORRY, SUSIE, I'M SURE BEING A DOCTOR WILL BE VERY EASY, MORE LIKE A HOBBY REALLY.
I'M ONLY TRAINING TO BE A DOCTOR FOR TWO REASONS. THE GOD-LIKE POWER OVER OTHER PEOPLE'S LIVES...
...AND THE GOLF. I THINK I COULD BE REALLY GOOD AT GOLF.
Oh, HERE THEY ARE, FUTURE SCIONS OF OUR CORPORATE OVERLORDS.
SO, HOW DID YOU GO ON?
FOUR FIRM HANDSHAKES AND A PROMOTIONAL T-SHIRT.
GAVE ME QUITE THE CHUCKLE.
BALLING
(Hydrometer Scale)
COOL.

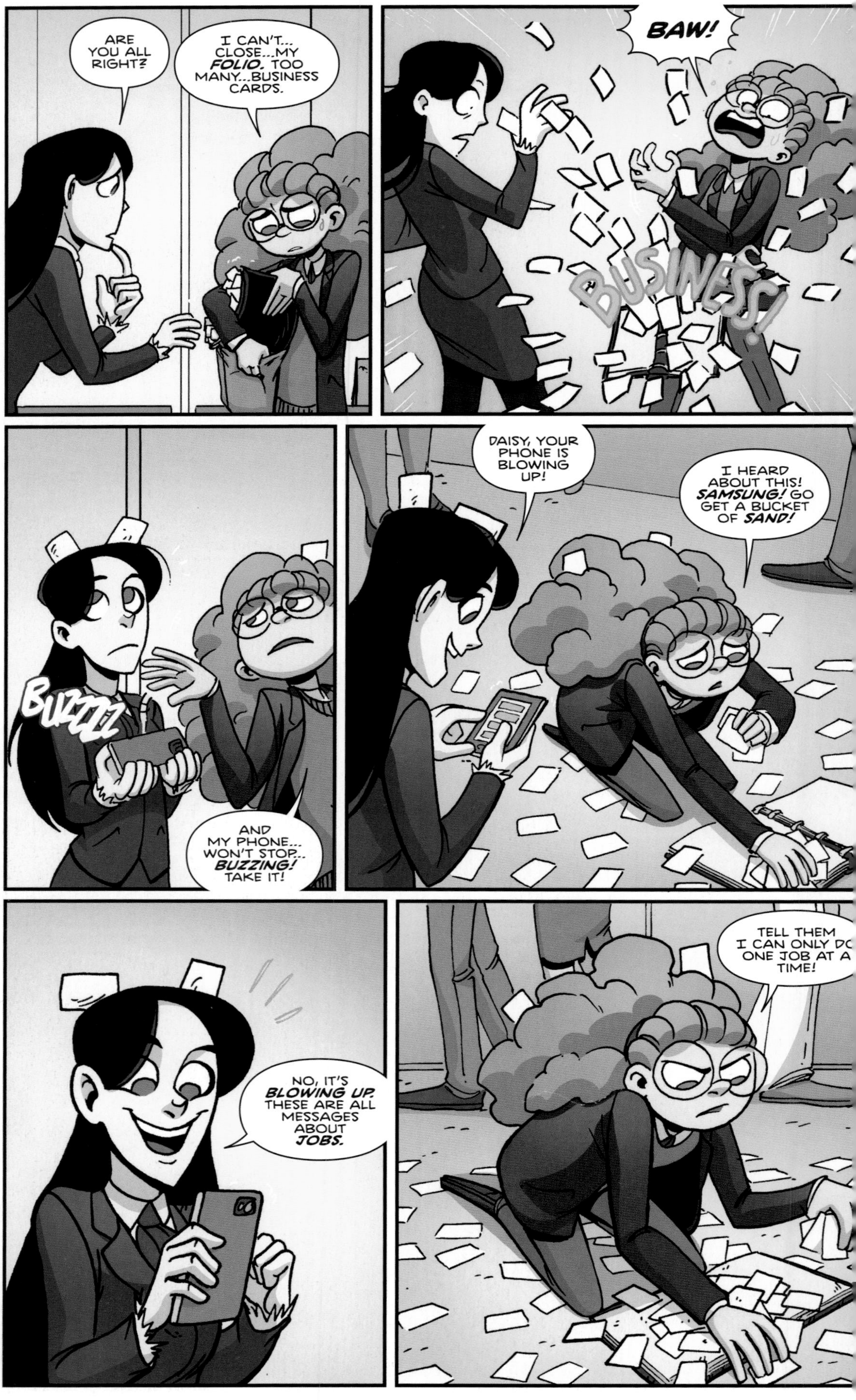

ARE YOU ALL RIGHT?
I CAN'T... CLOSE...MY *FOLIO.* TOO MANY...BUSINESS CARDS.
BAW!
BUSINESS!
BUZZZZ
AND MY PHONE... WON'T STOP... *BUZZING!* TAKE IT!
DAISY, YOUR PHONE IS BLOWING UP!
I HEARD ABOUT THIS! *SAMSUNG!* GO GET A BUCKET OF *SAND!*
NO, IT'S *BLOWING UP.* THESE ARE ALL MESSAGES ABOUT *JOBS.*
TELL THEM I CAN ONLY DO ONE JOB AT A TIME!

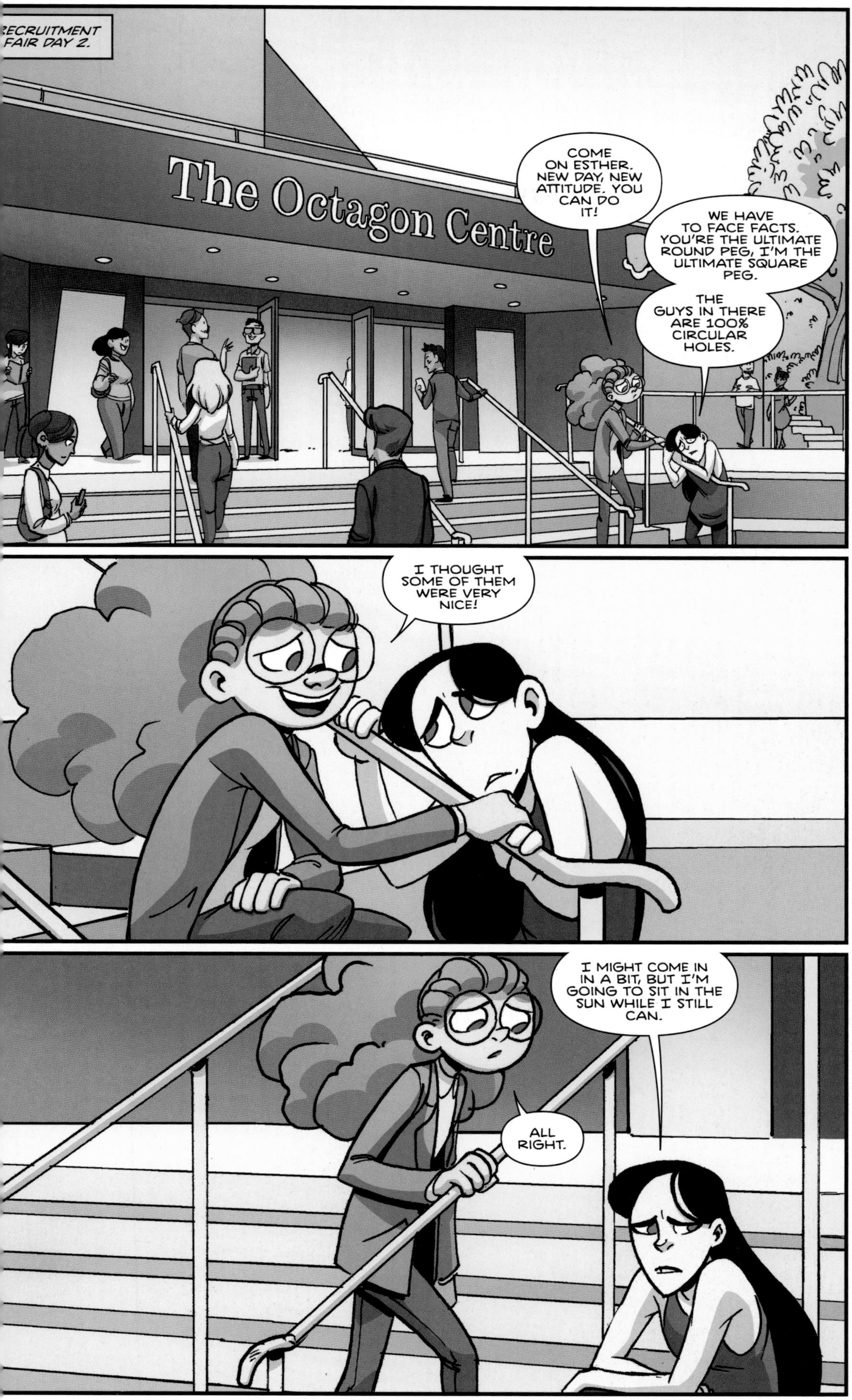
RECRUITMENT FAIR DAY 2.
The Octagon Centre
COME ON ESTHER. NEW DAY, NEW ATTITUDE. YOU CAN DO IT!
WE HAVE TO FACE FACTS. YOU'RE THE ULTIMATE ROUND PEG, I'M THE ULTIMATE SQUARE PEG.
THE GUYS IN THERE ARE 100% CIRCULAR HOLES.
I THOUGHT SOME OF THEM WERE VERY NICE!
I MIGHT COME IN IN A BIT, BUT I'M GOING TO SIT IN THE SUN WHILE I STILL CAN.
ALL RIGHT.

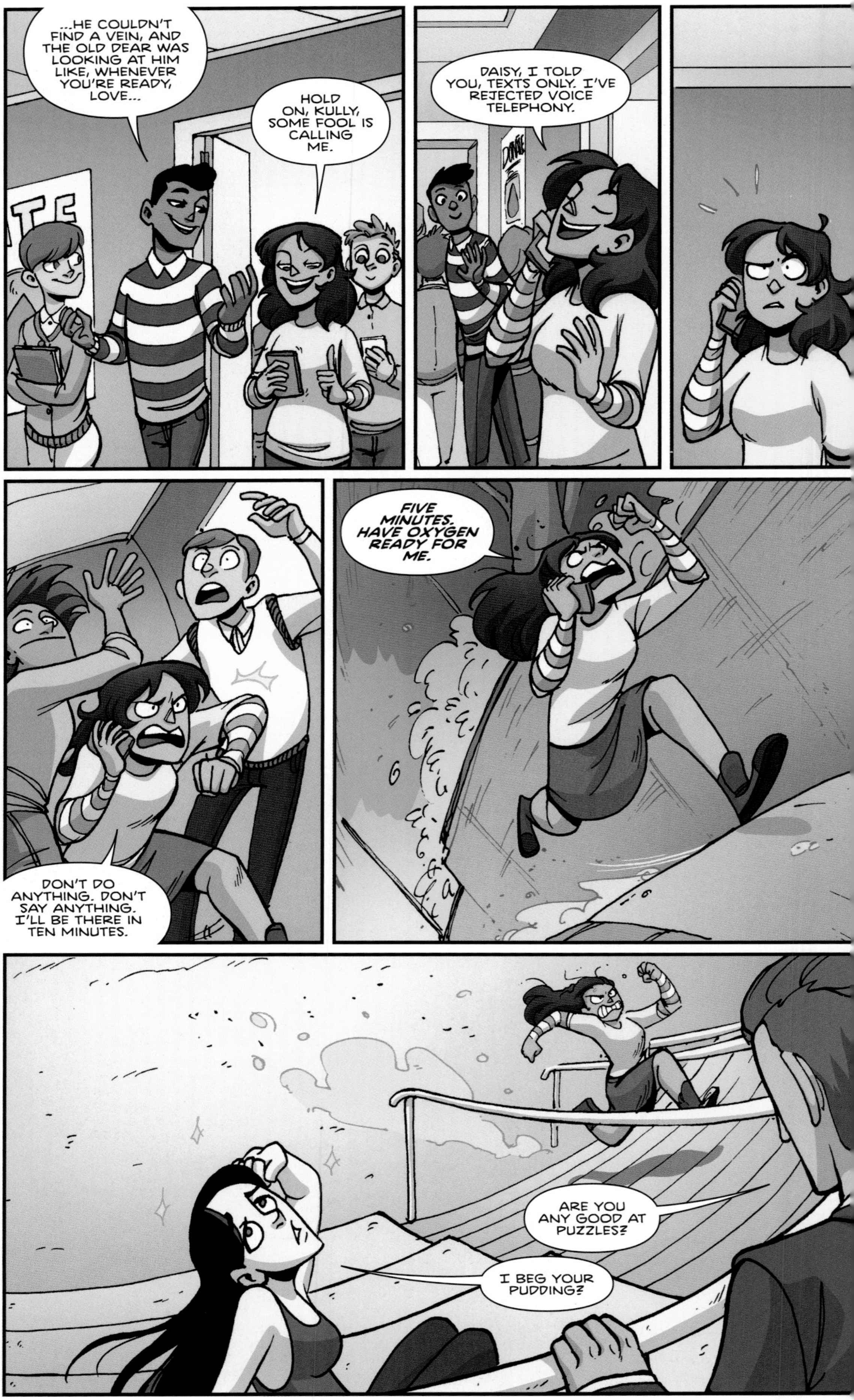
...HE COULDN'T FIND A VEIN, AND THE OLD DEAR WAS LOOKING AT HIM LIKE, WHENEVER YOU'RE READY, LOVE...
HOLD ON, KULLY, SOME FOOL IS CALLING ME.
DAISY, I TOLD YOU, TEXTS ONLY. I'VE REJECTED VOICE TELEPHONY.
DON'T DO ANYTHING. DON'T SAY ANYTHING. I'LL BE THERE IN TEN MINUTES.
FIVE MINUTES. HAVE OXYGEN READY FOR ME.
ARE YOU ANY GOOD AT PUZZLES?
I BEG YOUR PUDDING?

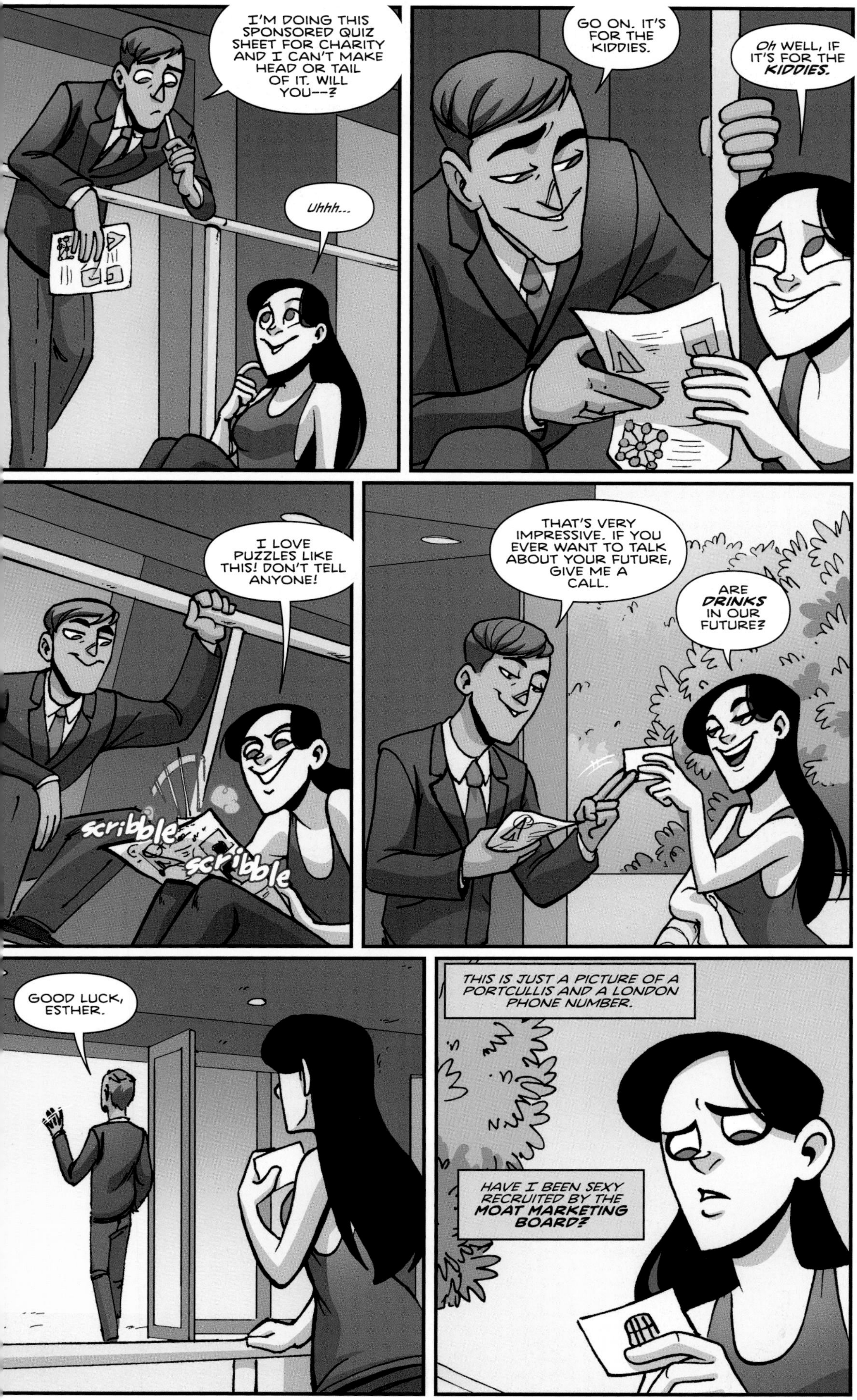

I'M DOING THIS SPONSORED QUIZ SHEET FOR CHARITY AND I CAN'T MAKE HEAD OR TAIL OF IT. WILL YOU--?
Uhhh...
GO ON. IT'S FOR THE KIDDIES.
Oh WELL, IF IT'S FOR THE ***KIDDIES.***
I LOVE PUZZLES LIKE THIS! DON'T TELL ANYONE!
scribble
scribble
THAT'S VERY IMPRESSIVE. IF YOU EVER WANT TO TALK ABOUT YOUR FUTURE, GIVE ME A CALL.
ARE ***DRINKS*** IN OUR FUTURE?
GOOD LUCK, ESTHER.
THIS IS JUST A PICTURE OF A PORTCULLIS AND A LONDON PHONE NUMBER.
*HAVE I BEEN SEXY RECRUITED BY THE **MOAT MARKETING BOARD?***

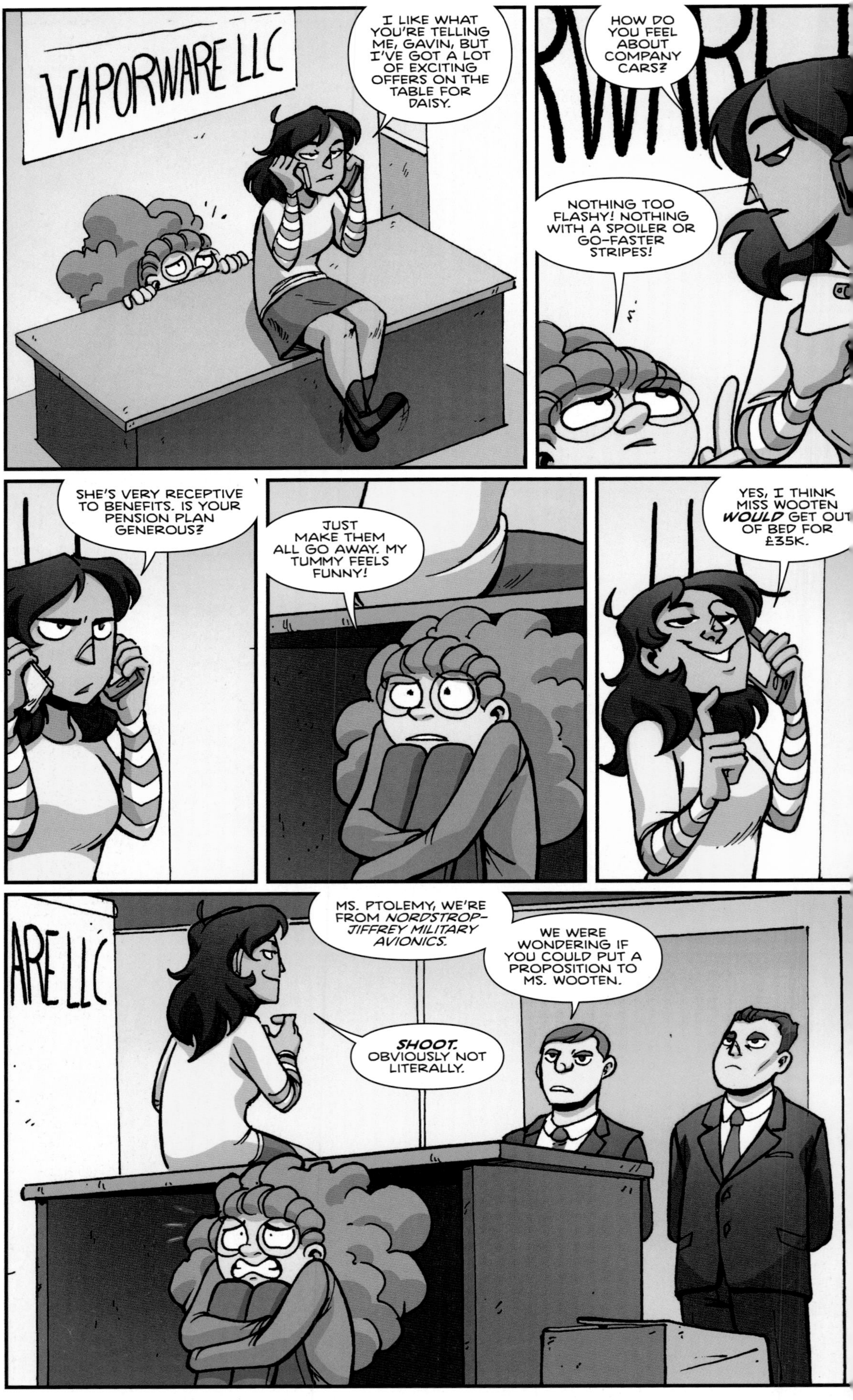
VAPORWARE LLC
I LIKE WHAT YOU'RE TELLING ME, GAVIN, BUT I'VE GOT A LOT OF EXCITING OFFERS ON THE TABLE FOR DAISY.
HOW DO YOU FEEL ABOUT COMPANY CARS?
NOTHING TOO FLASHY! NOTHING WITH A SPOILER OR GO-FASTER STRIPES!
SHE'S VERY RECEPTIVE TO BENEFITS. IS YOUR PENSION PLAN GENEROUS?
JUST MAKE THEM ALL GO AWAY. MY TUMMY FEELS FUNNY!
YES, I THINK MISS WOOTEN *WOULD* GET OUT OF BED FOR £35K.
ARE LLC
MS. PTOLEMY, WE'RE FROM *NORDSTROP-JIFFREY MILITARY AVIONICS.*
WE WERE WONDERING IF YOU COULD PUT A PROPOSITION TO MS. WOOTEN.
SHOOT. OBVIOUSLY NOT LITERALLY.

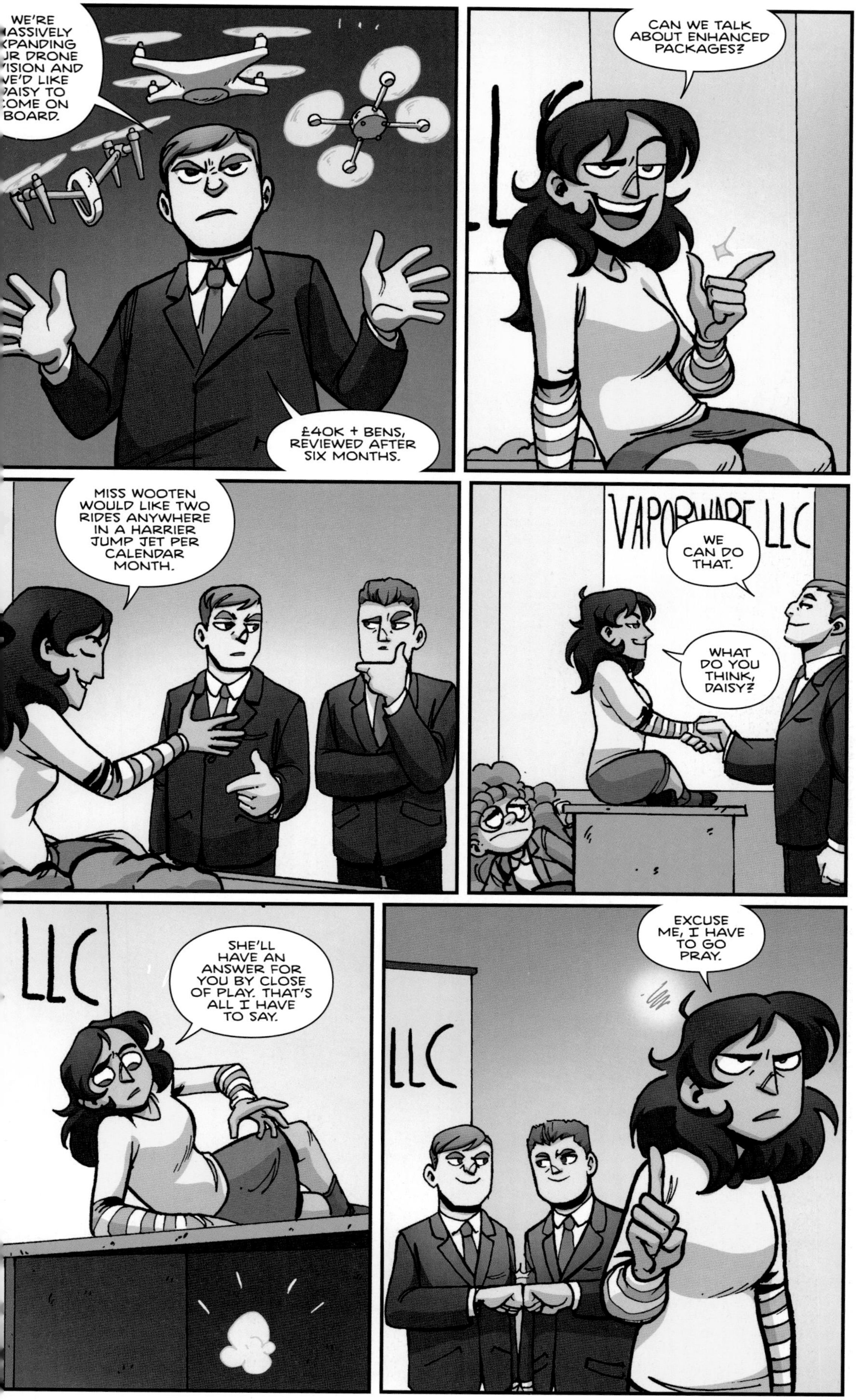

WE'RE ASSIVELY XPANDING JR DRONE IVISION AND E'D LIKE AISY TO OME ON BOARD.
£40K + BENS, REVIEWED AFTER SIX MONTHS.
CAN WE TALK ABOUT ENHANCED PACKAGES?
MISS WOOTEN WOULD LIKE TWO RIDES ANYWHERE IN A HARRIER JUMP JET PER CALENDAR MONTH.
VAPORWARE LLC
WE CAN DO THAT.
WHAT DO YOU THINK, DAISY?
LLC
SHE'LL HAVE AN ANSWER FOR YOU BY CLOSE OF PLAY. THAT'S ALL I HAVE TO SAY.
LLC
EXCUSE ME, I HAVE TO GO PRAY.

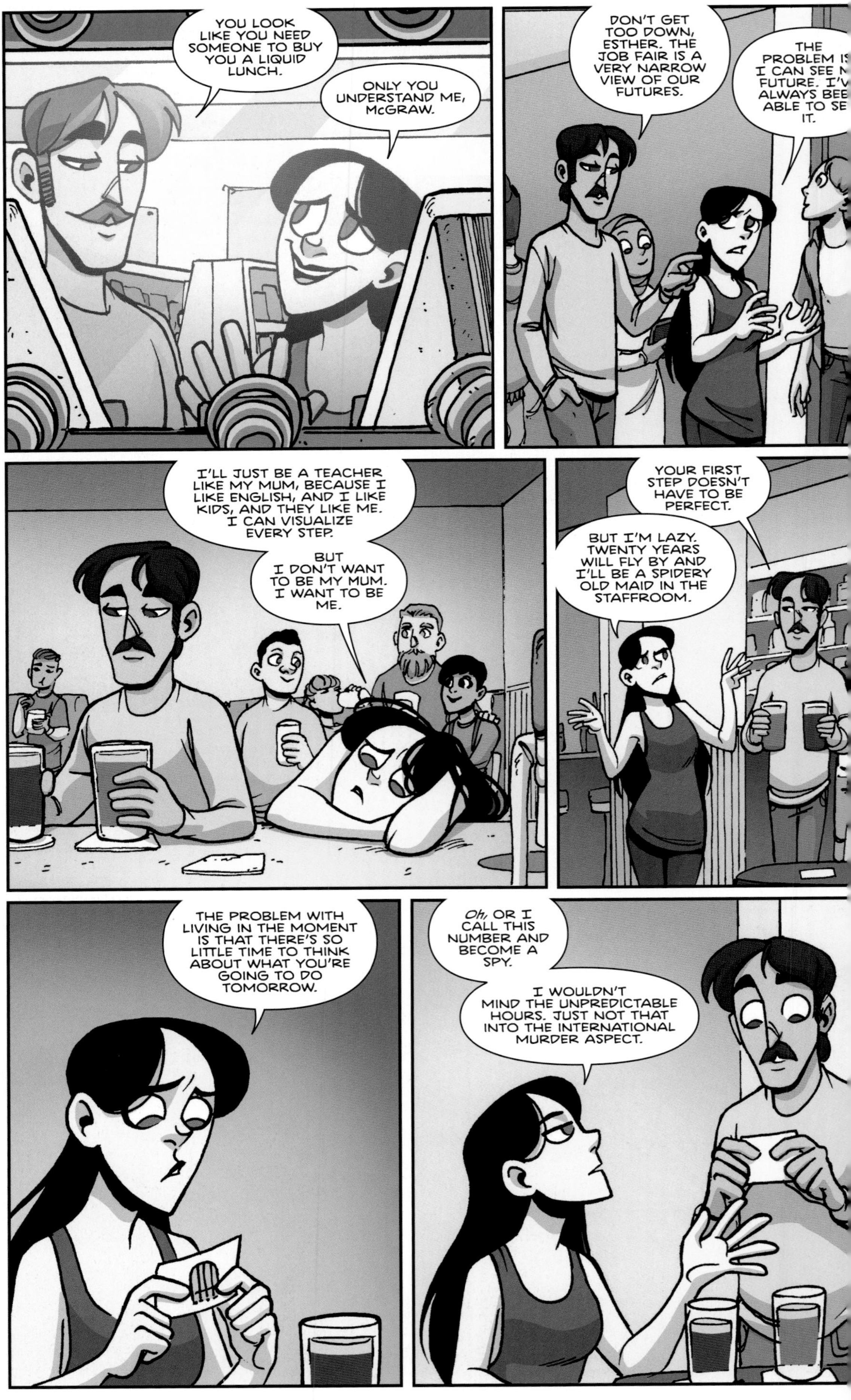
YOU LOOK LIKE YOU NEED SOMEONE TO BUY YOU A LIQUID LUNCH.
ONLY YOU UNDERSTAND ME, McGRAW.
DON'T GET TOO DOWN, ESTHER. THE JOB FAIR IS A VERY NARROW VIEW OF OUR FUTURES.
THE PROBLEM IS I CAN SEE MY FUTURE. I'VE ALWAYS BEEN ABLE TO SEE IT.
I'LL JUST BE A TEACHER LIKE MY MUM, BECAUSE I LIKE ENGLISH, AND I LIKE KIDS, AND THEY LIKE ME. I CAN VISUALIZE EVERY STEP.
BUT I DON'T WANT TO BE MY MUM. I WANT TO BE ME.
YOUR FIRST STEP DOESN'T HAVE TO BE PERFECT.
BUT I'M LAZY. TWENTY YEARS WILL FLY BY AND I'LL BE A SPIDERY OLD MAID IN THE STAFFROOM.
THE PROBLEM WITH LIVING IN THE MOMENT IS THAT THERE'S SO LITTLE TIME TO THINK ABOUT WHAT YOU'RE GOING TO DO TOMORROW.
Oh, OR I CALL THIS NUMBER AND BECOME A SPY.
I WOULDN'T MIND THE UNPREDICTABLE HOURS. JUST NOT THAT INTO THE INTERNATIONAL MURDER ASPECT.

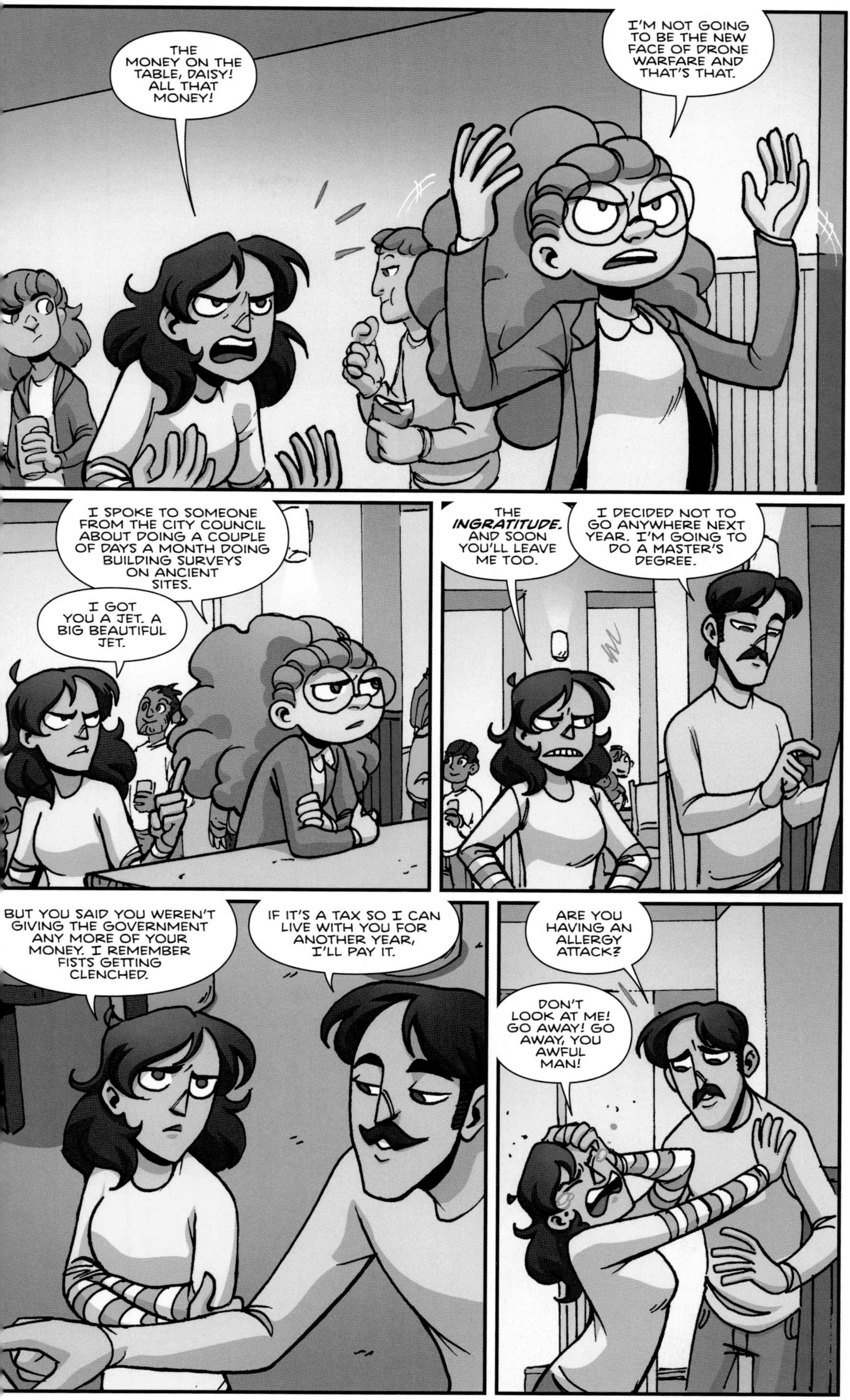
THE MONEY ON THE TABLE, DAISY! ALL THAT MONEY!
I'M NOT GOING TO BE THE NEW FACE OF DRONE WARFARE AND THAT'S THAT.
I SPOKE TO SOMEONE FROM THE CITY COUNCIL ABOUT DOING A COUPLE OF DAYS A MONTH DOING BUILDING SURVEYS ON ANCIENT SITES.
I GOT YOU A JET. A BIG BEAUTIFUL JET.
THE *INGRATITUDE.* AND SOON YOU'LL LEAVE ME TOO.
I DECIDED NOT TO GO ANYWHERE NEXT YEAR. I'M GOING TO DO A MASTER'S DEGREE.
BUT YOU SAID YOU WEREN'T GIVING THE GOVERNMENT ANY MORE OF YOUR MONEY. I REMEMBER FISTS GETTING CLENCHED.
IF IT'S A TAX SO I CAN LIVE WITH YOU FOR ANOTHER YEAR, I'LL PAY IT.
ARE YOU HAVING AN ALLERGY ATTACK?
DON'T LOOK AT ME! GO AWAY! GO AWAY, YOU AWFUL MAN!

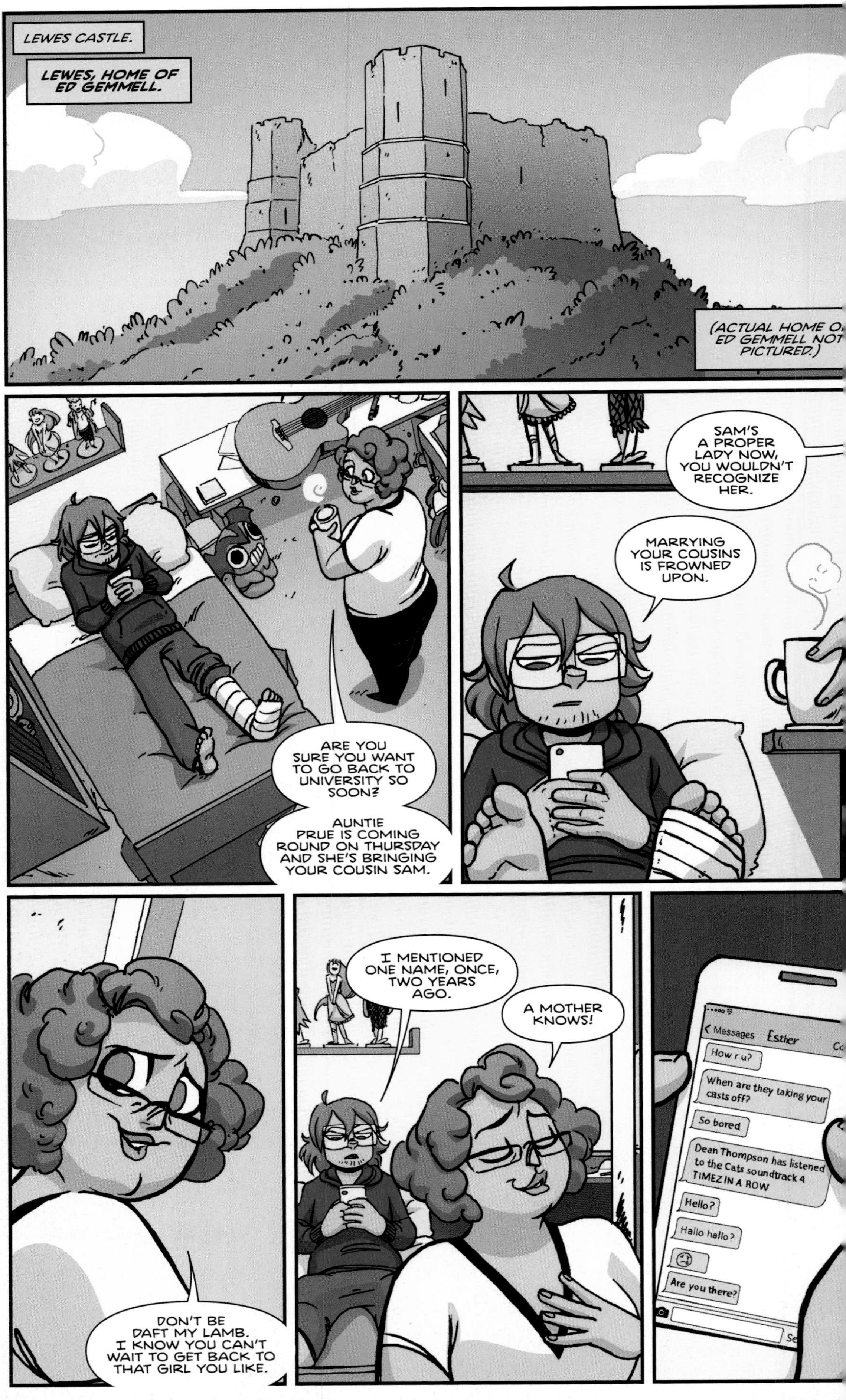
LEWES CASTLE.
LEWES, HOME OF ED GEMMELL.
(ACTUAL HOME OF ED GEMMELL NOT PICTURED.)
ARE YOU SURE YOU WANT TO GO BACK TO UNIVERSITY SO SOON?
AUNTIE PRUE IS COMING ROUND ON THURSDAY AND SHE'S BRINGING YOUR COUSIN SAM.
SAM'S A PROPER LADY NOW, YOU WOULDN'T RECOGNIZE HER.
MARRYING YOUR COUSINS IS FROWNED UPON.
DON'T BE DAFT MY LAMB. I KNOW YOU CAN'T WAIT TO GET BACK TO THAT GIRL YOU LIKE.
I MENTIONED ONE NAME, ONCE, TWO YEARS AGO.
A MOTHER KNOWS!
Messages
Esther
How r u?
When are they taking your casts off?
So bored
Dean Thompson has listened to the Cats soundtrack 4 TIMEZ IN A ROW
Hello?
Hallo hallo?
Are you there?

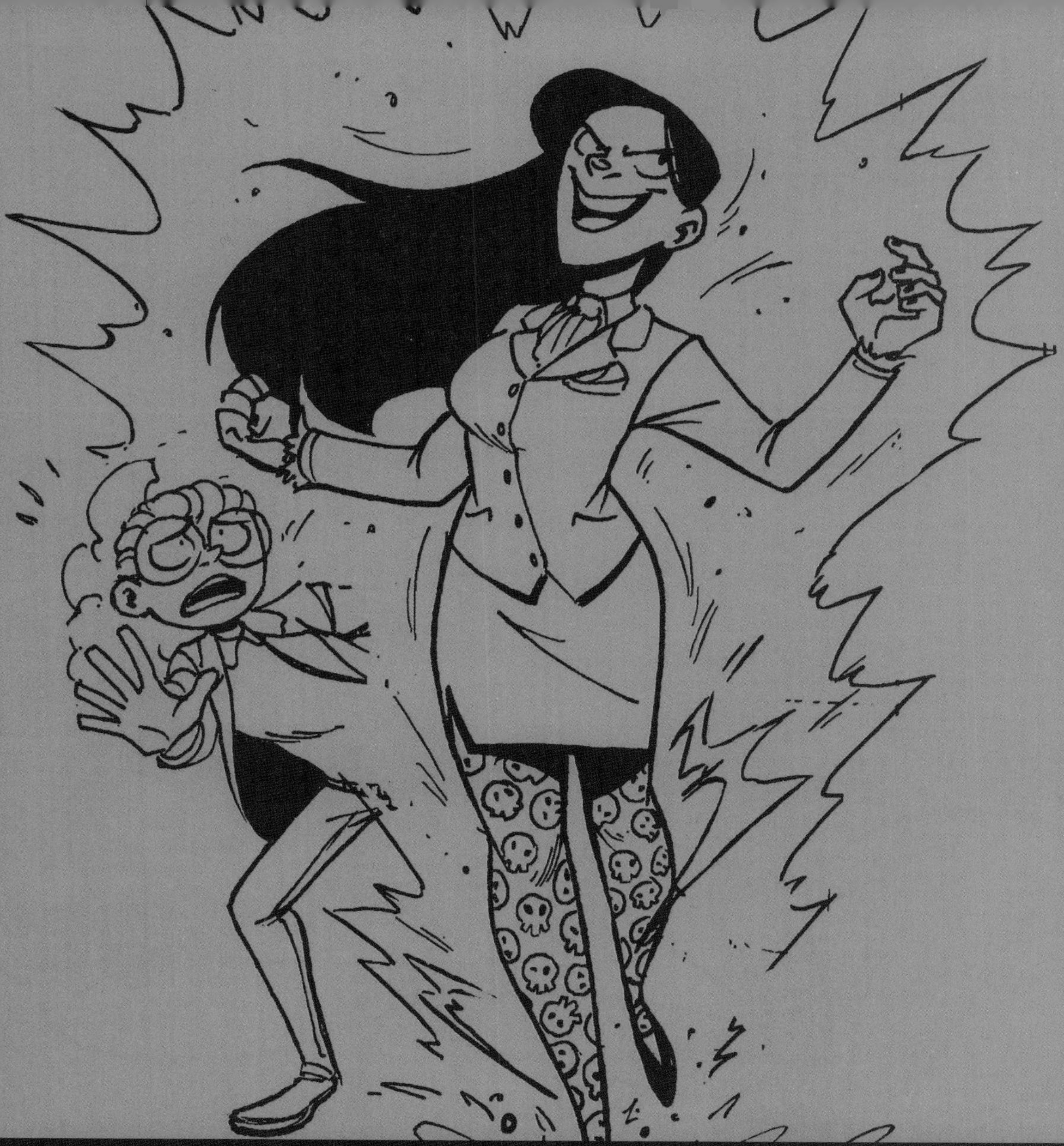

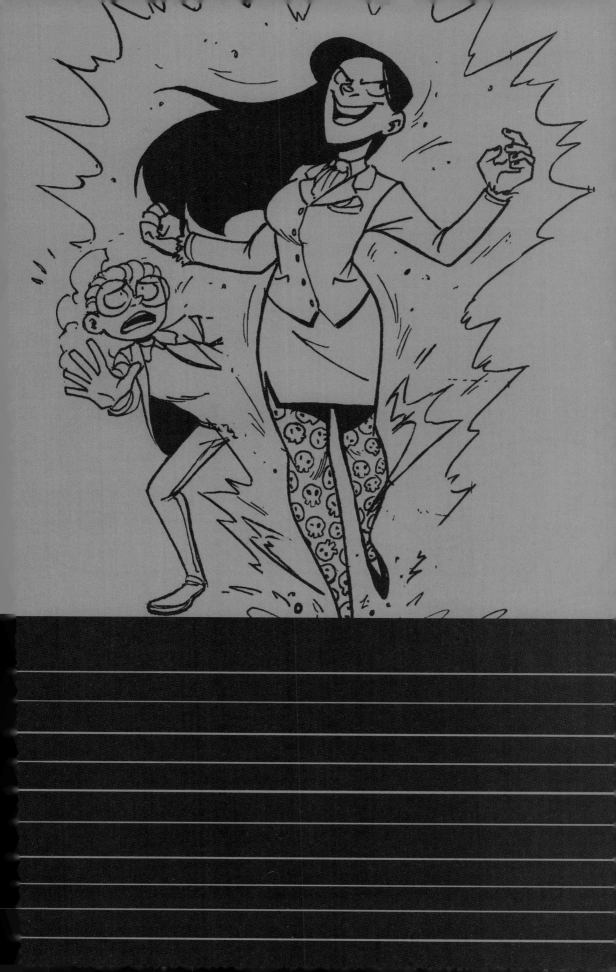

CHAPTER FORTY

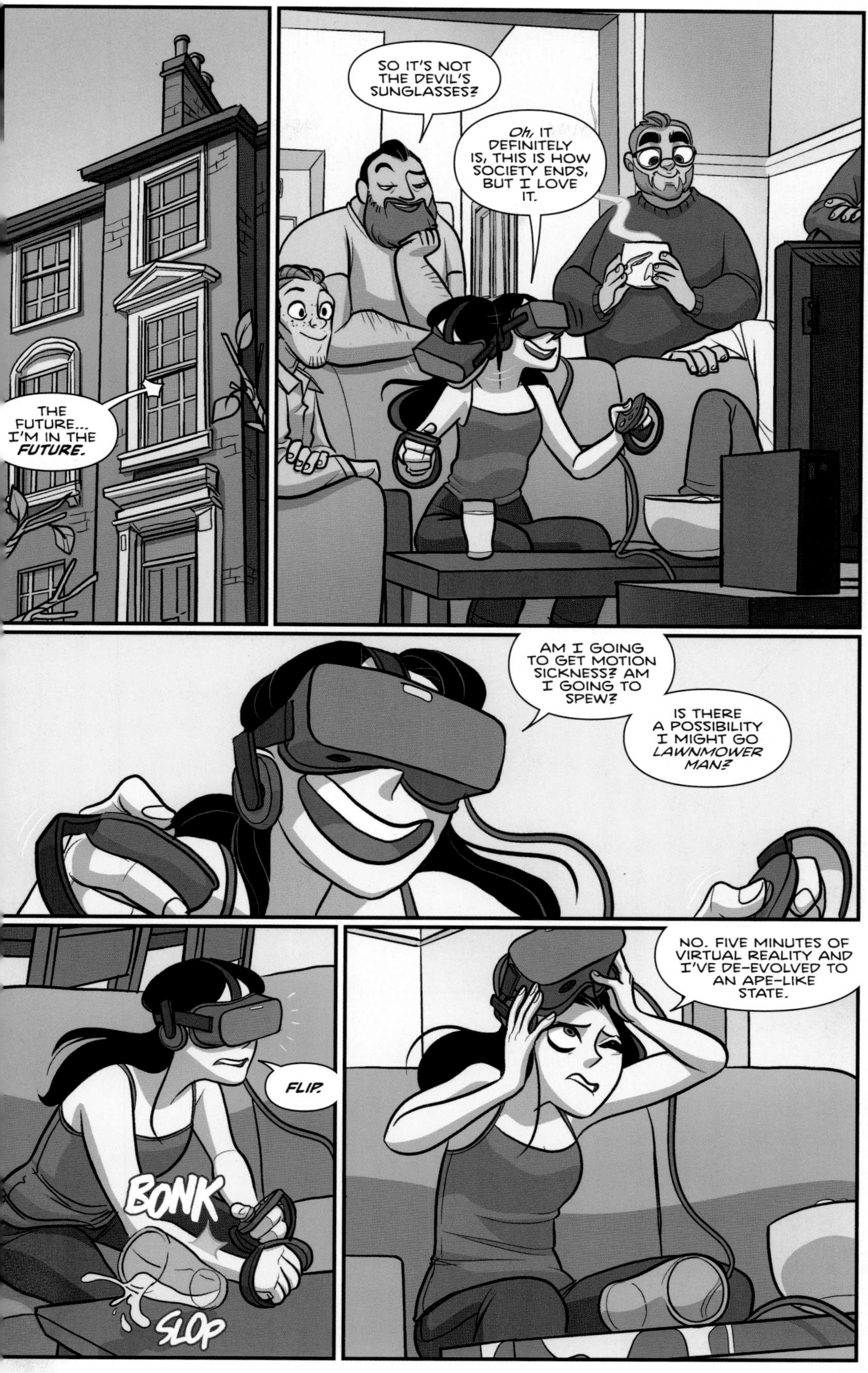
THE FUTURE... I'M IN THE *FUTURE.*
SO IT'S NOT THE DEVIL'S SUNGLASSES?
Oh, IT DEFINITELY IS, THIS IS HOW SOCIETY ENDS, BUT I LOVE IT.
AM I GOING TO GET MOTION SICKNESS? AM I GOING TO SPEW?
IS THERE A POSSIBILITY I MIGHT GO *LAWNMOWER MAN?*
FLIP?
BONK
SLOP
NO. FIVE MINUTES OF VIRTUAL REALITY AND I'VE DE-EVOLVED TO AN APE-LIKE STATE.

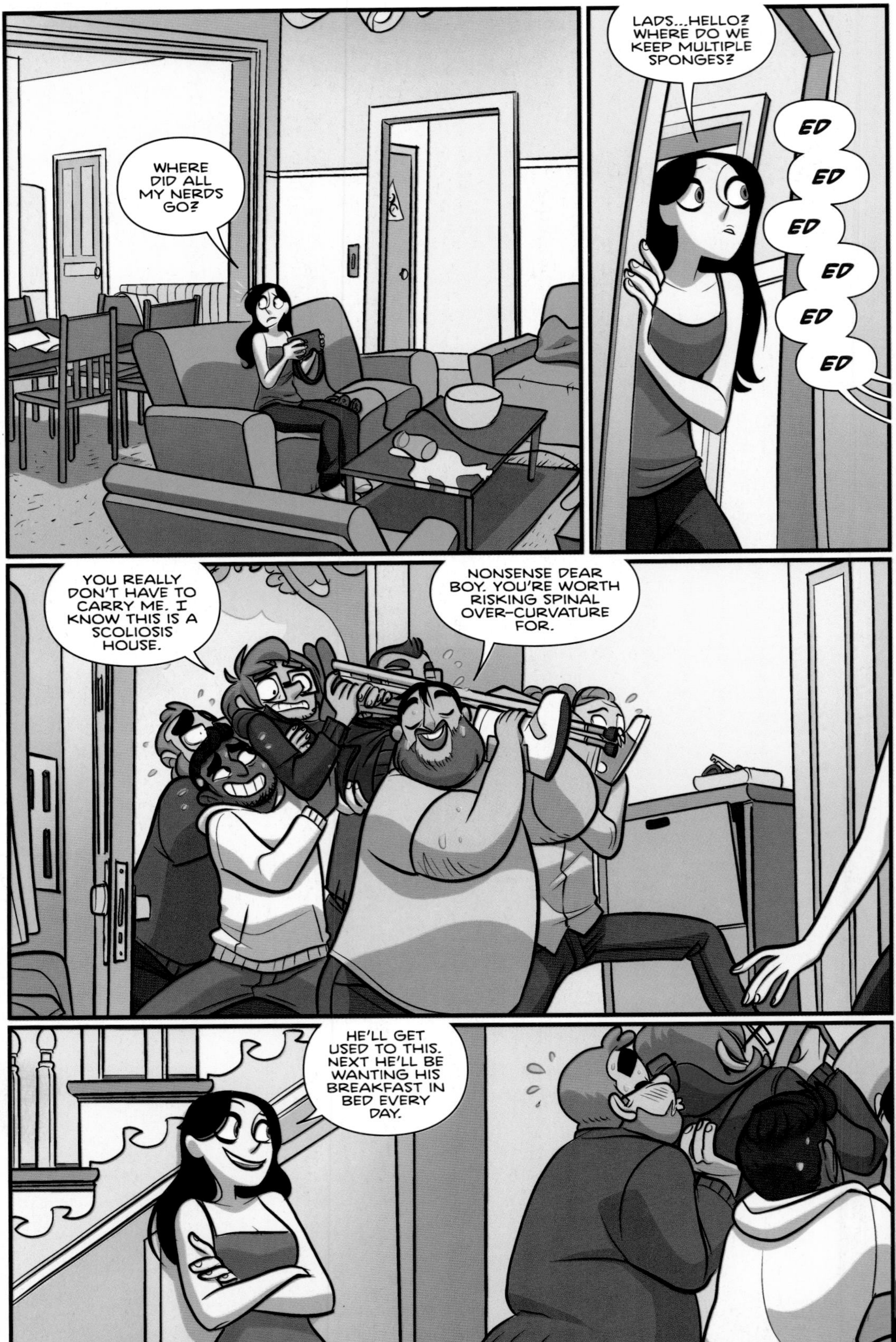
WHERE DID ALL MY NERDS GO?
LADS...HELLO? WHERE DO WE KEEP MULTIPLE SPONGES?
ED
ED
ED
ED
ED
ED
YOU REALLY DON'T HAVE TO CARRY ME. I KNOW THIS IS A SCOLIOSIS HOUSE.
NONSENSE DEAR BOY. YOU'RE WORTH RISKING SPINAL OVER-CURVATURE FOR.
HE'LL GET USED TO THIS. NEXT HE'LL BE WANTING HIS BREAKFAST IN BED EVERY DAY.

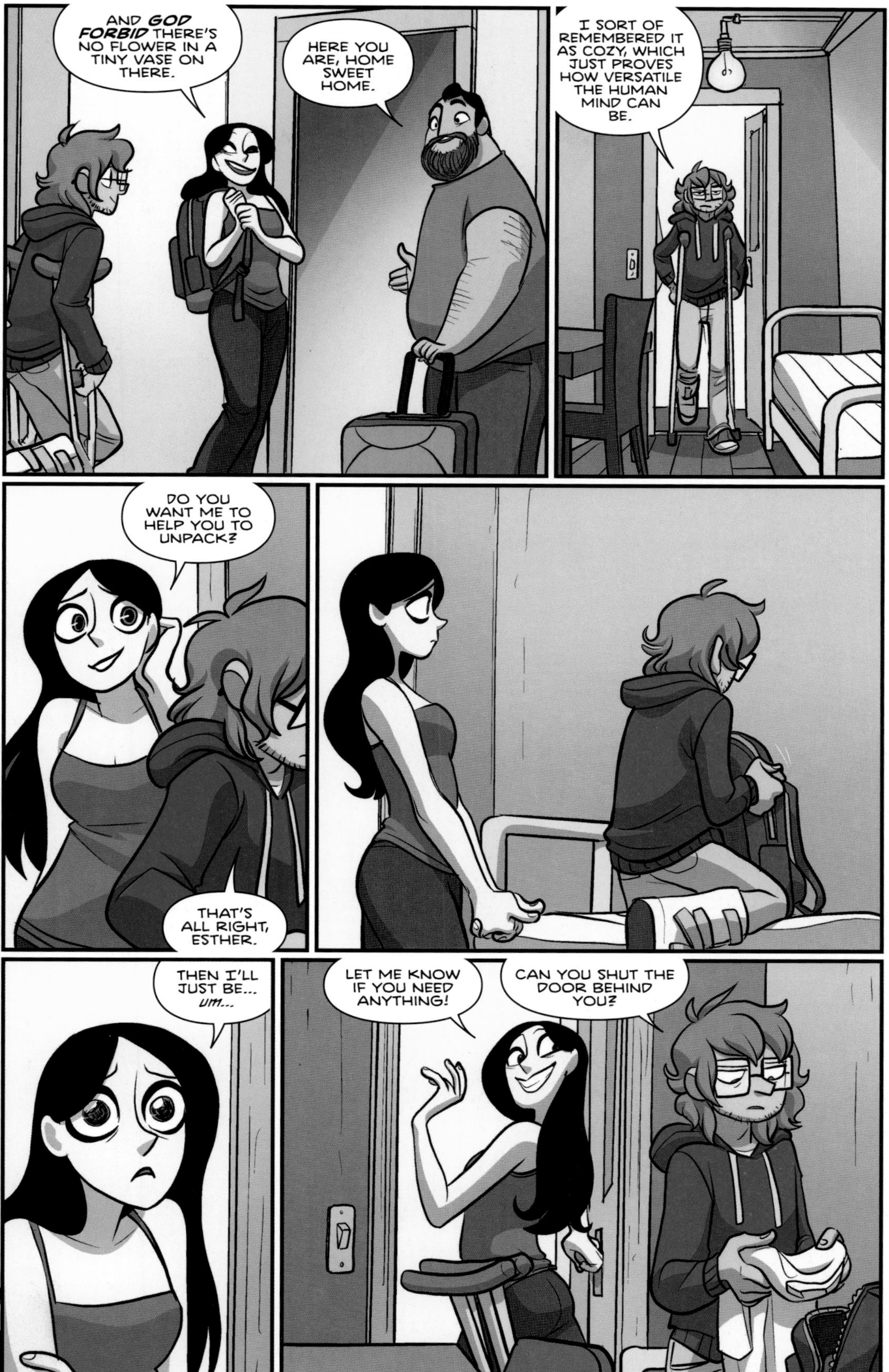
AND **GOD FORBID** THERE'S NO FLOWER IN A TINY VASE ON THERE.
HERE YOU ARE, HOME SWEET HOME.
I SORT OF REMEMBERED IT AS COZY, WHICH JUST PROVES HOW VERSATILE THE HUMAN MIND CAN BE.
DO YOU WANT ME TO HELP YOU TO UNPACK?
THAT'S ALL RIGHT, ESTHER.
THEN I'LL JUST BE... *UM...*
LET ME KNOW IF YOU NEED ANYTHING!
CAN YOU SHUT THE DOOR BEHIND YOU?

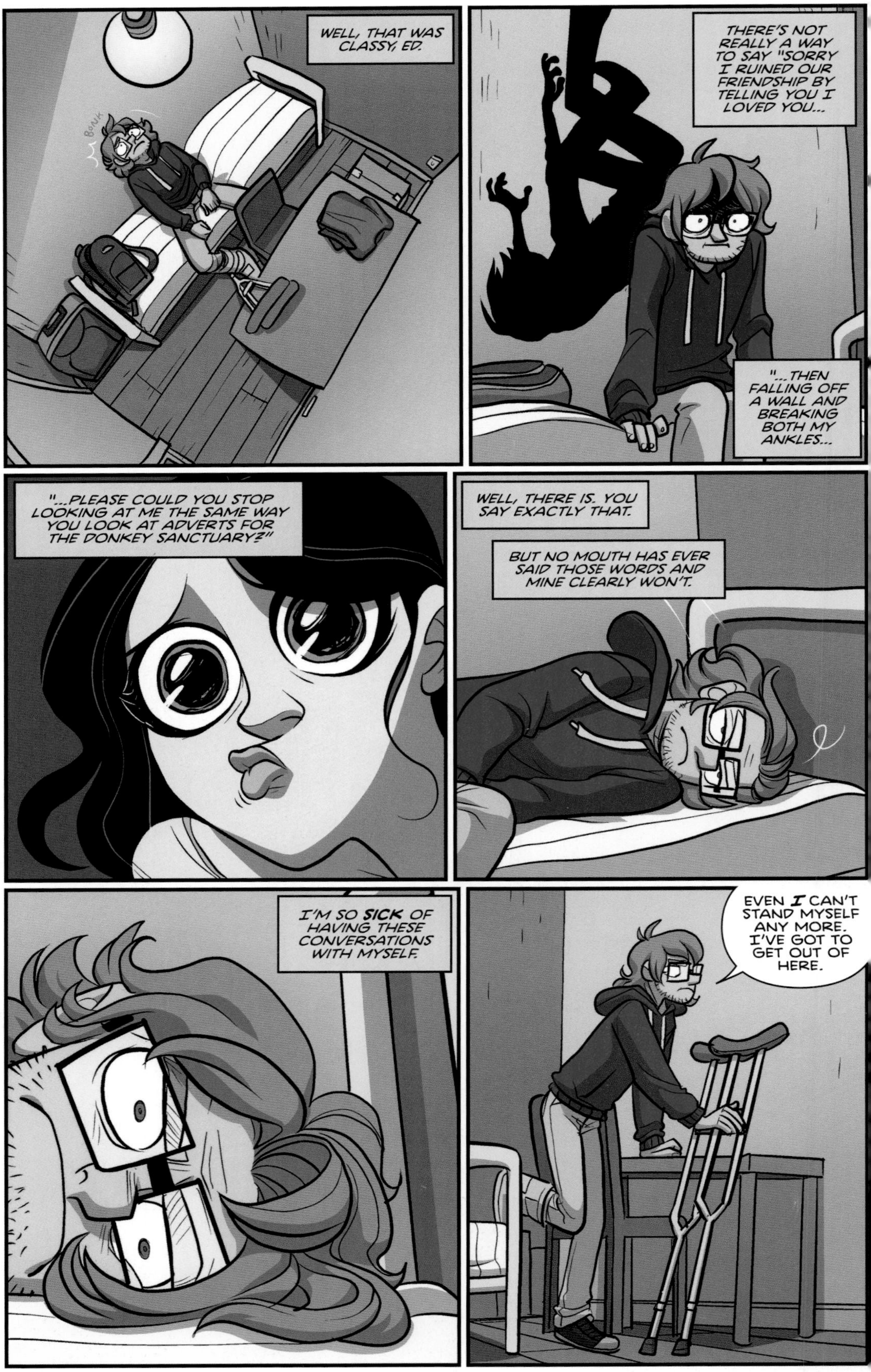
WELL, THAT WAS CLASSY, ED.
BONK
THERE'S NOT REALLY A WAY TO SAY "SORRY I RUINED OUR FRIENDSHIP BY TELLING YOU I LOVED YOU...
"...THEN FALLING OFF A WALL AND BREAKING BOTH MY ANKLES...
"...PLEASE COULD YOU STOP LOOKING AT ME THE SAME WAY YOU LOOK AT ADVERTS FOR THE DONKEY SANCTUARY?"
WELL, THERE IS. YOU SAY EXACTLY THAT.
BUT NO MOUTH HAS EVER SAID THOSE WORDS AND MINE CLEARLY WON'T.
I'M SO SICK OF HAVING THESE CONVERSATIONS WITH MYSELF.
EVEN I CAN'T STAND MYSELF ANY MORE. I'VE GOT TO GET OUT OF HERE.

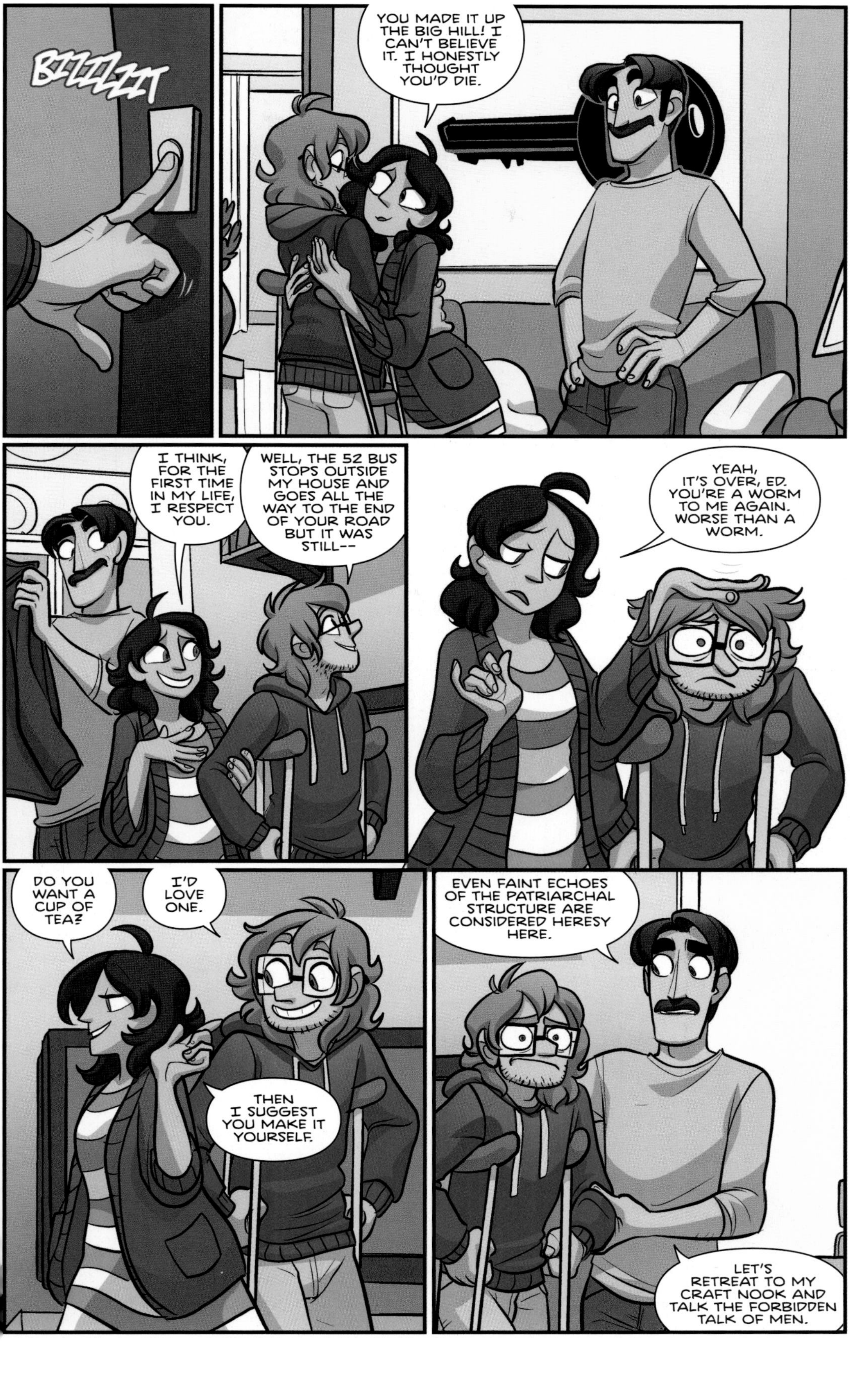
BZZZZZT
YOU MADE IT UP THE BIG HILL! I CAN'T BELIEVE IT. I HONESTLY THOUGHT YOU'D DIE.
I THINK, FOR THE FIRST TIME IN MY LIFE, I RESPECT YOU.
WELL, THE 52 BUS STOPS OUTSIDE MY HOUSE AND GOES ALL THE WAY TO THE END OF YOUR ROAD BUT IT WAS STILL--
YEAH, IT'S OVER, ED. YOU'RE A WORM TO ME AGAIN. WORSE THAN A WORM.
DO YOU WANT A CUP OF TEA?
I'D LOVE ONE.
THEN I SUGGEST YOU MAKE IT YOURSELF.
EVEN FAINT ECHOES OF THE PATRIARCHAL STRUCTURE ARE CONSIDERED HERESY HERE.
LET'S RETREAT TO MY CRAFT NOOK AND TALK THE FORBIDDEN TALK OF MEN.

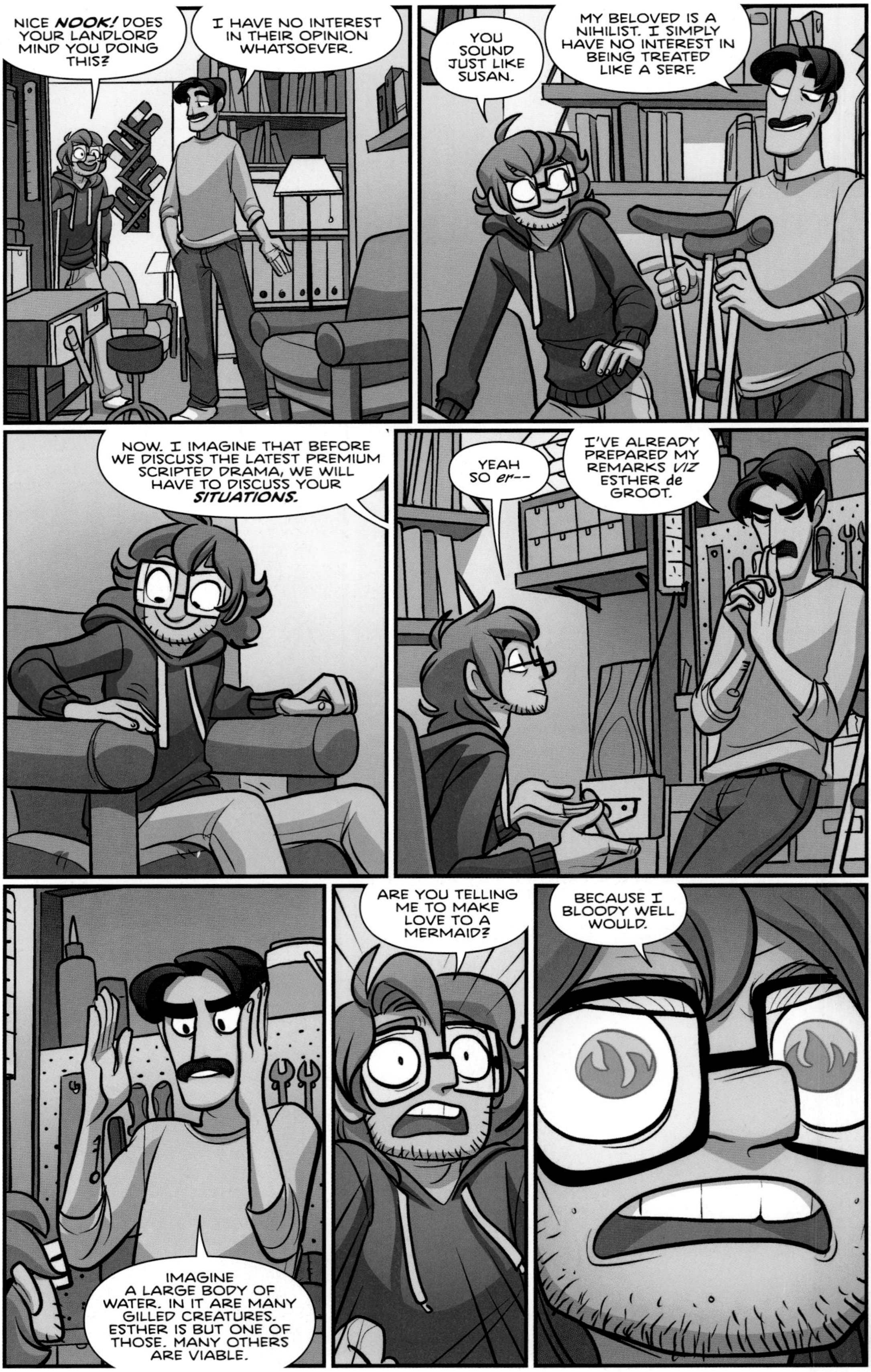
NICE **NOOK!** DOES YOUR LANDLORD MIND YOU DOING THIS?
I HAVE NO INTEREST IN THEIR OPINION WHATSOEVER.
YOU SOUND JUST LIKE SUSAN.
MY BELOVED IS A NIHILIST. I SIMPLY HAVE NO INTEREST IN BEING TREATED LIKE A SERF.
NOW. I IMAGINE THAT BEFORE WE DISCUSS THE LATEST PREMIUM SCRIPTED DRAMA, WE WILL HAVE TO DISCUSS YOUR ***SITUATIONS.***
YEAH SO *er--*
I'VE ALREADY PREPARED MY REMARKS *VIZ* ESTHER de GROOT.
IMAGINE A LARGE BODY OF WATER. IN IT ARE MANY GILLED CREATURES. ESTHER IS BUT ONE OF THOSE. MANY OTHERS ARE VIABLE.
ARE YOU TELLING ME TO MAKE LOVE TO A MERMAID?
BECAUSE I BLOODY WELL WOULD.

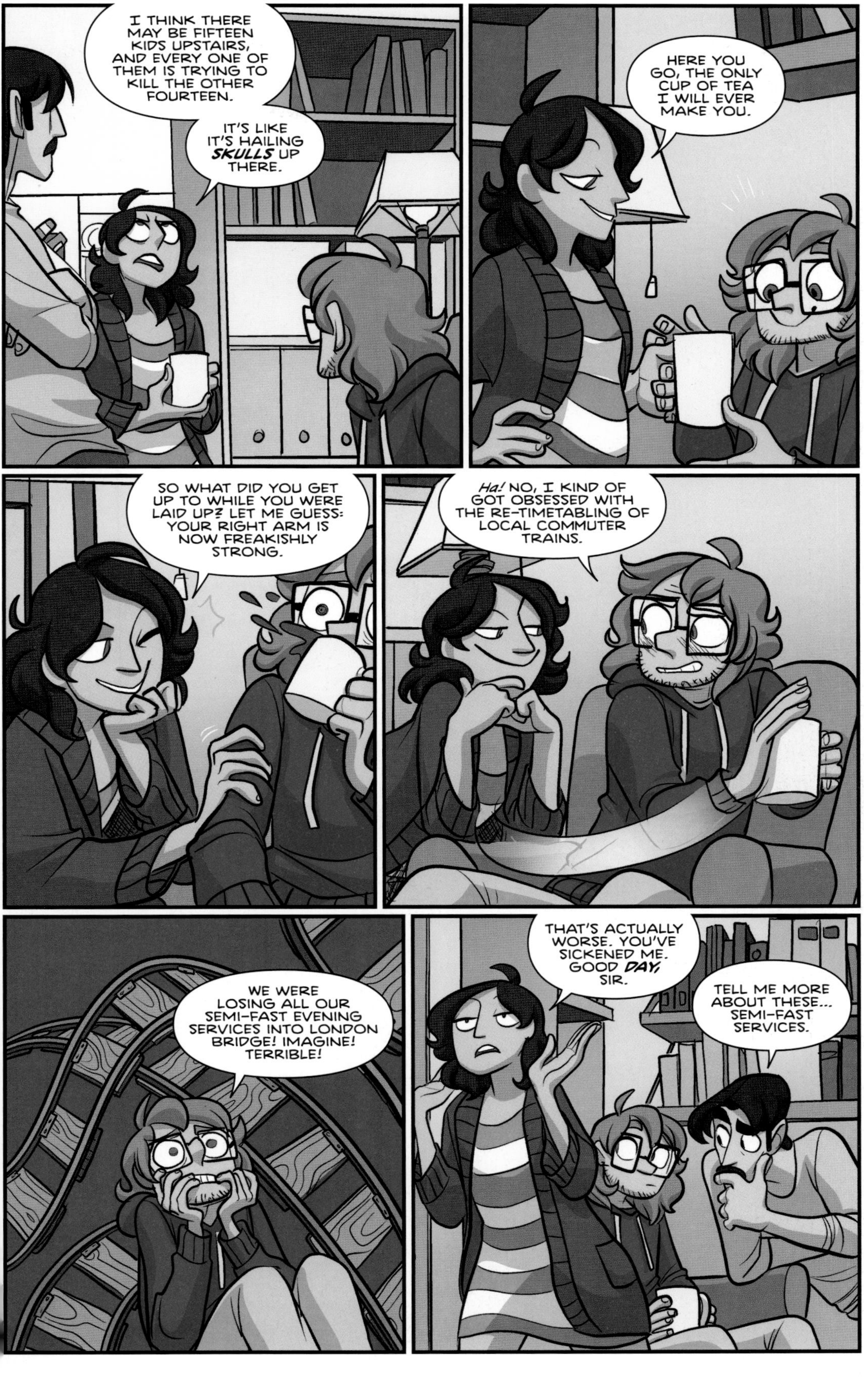
I THINK THERE MAY BE FIFTEEN KIDS UPSTAIRS, AND EVERY ONE OF THEM IS TRYING TO KILL THE OTHER FOURTEEN.
IT'S LIKE IT'S HAILING *SKULLS* UP THERE.
HERE YOU GO, THE ONLY CUP OF TEA I WILL EVER MAKE YOU.
SO WHAT DID YOU GET UP TO WHILE YOU WERE LAID UP? LET ME GUESS: YOUR RIGHT ARM IS NOW FREAKISHLY STRONG.
HA! NO, I KIND OF GOT OBSESSED WITH THE RE-TIMETABLING OF LOCAL COMMUTER TRAINS.
WE WERE LOSING ALL OUR SEMI-FAST EVENING SERVICES INTO LONDON BRIDGE! IMAGINE! TERRIBLE!
THAT'S ACTUALLY WORSE. YOU'VE SICKENED ME. GOOD *DAY,* SIR.
TELL ME MORE ABOUT THESE... SEMI-FAST SERVICES.

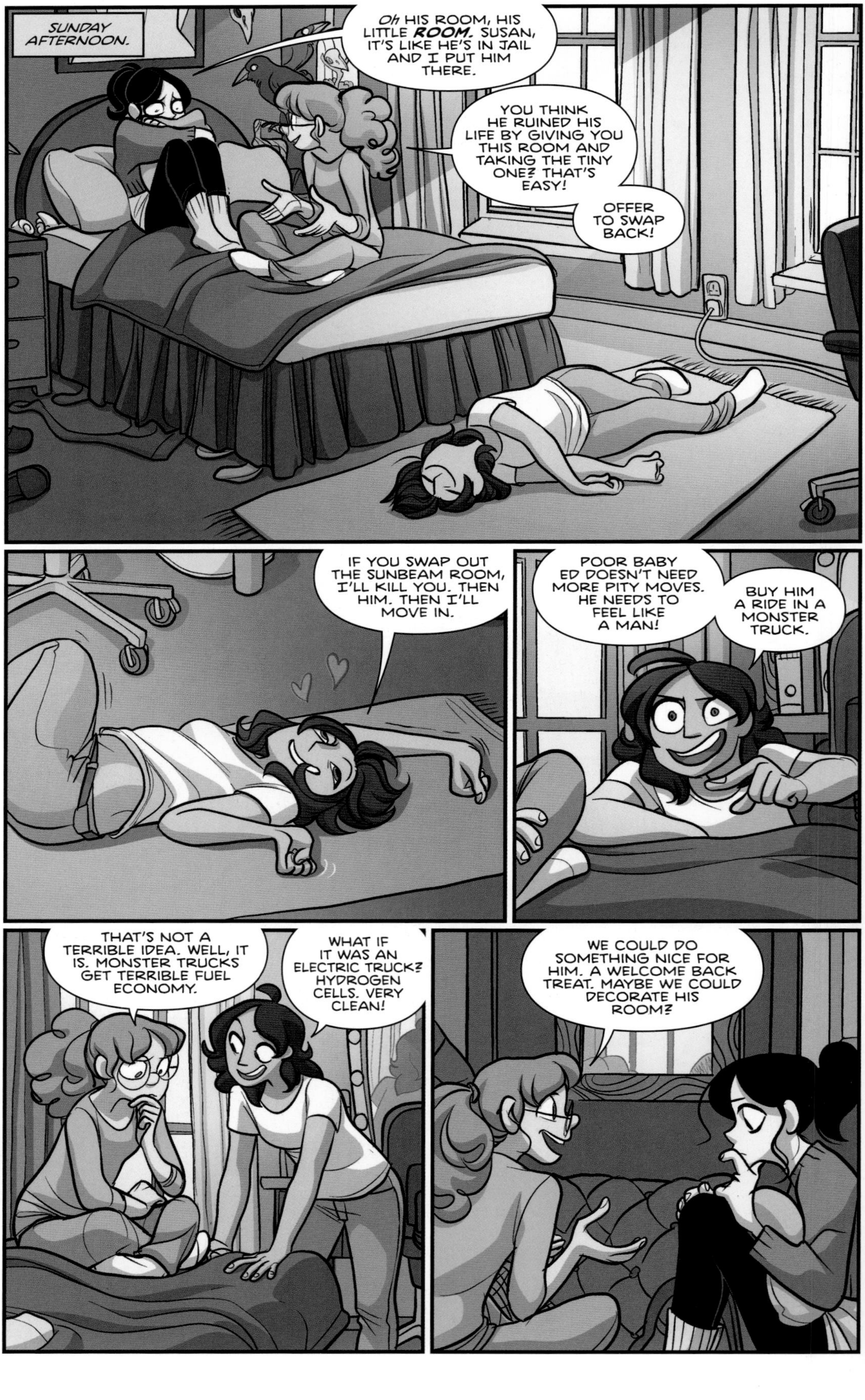
SUNDAY AFTERNOON.
Oh HIS ROOM, HIS LITTLE ROOM. SUSAN, IT'S LIKE HE'S IN JAIL AND I PUT HIM THERE.
YOU THINK HE RUINED HIS LIFE BY GIVING YOU THIS ROOM AND TAKING THE TINY ONE? THAT'S EASY!
OFFER TO SWAP BACK!
IF YOU SWAP OUT THE SUNBEAM ROOM, I'LL KILL YOU. THEN HIM. THEN I'LL MOVE IN.
POOR BABY ED DOESN'T NEED MORE PITY MOVES. HE NEEDS TO FEEL LIKE A MAN!
BUY HIM A RIDE IN A MONSTER TRUCK.
THAT'S NOT A TERRIBLE IDEA. WELL, IT IS. MONSTER TRUCKS GET TERRIBLE FUEL ECONOMY.
WHAT IF IT WAS AN ELECTRIC TRUCK? HYDROGEN CELLS. VERY CLEAN!
WE COULD DO SOMETHING NICE FOR HIM. A WELCOME BACK TREAT. MAYBE WE COULD DECORATE HIS ROOM?

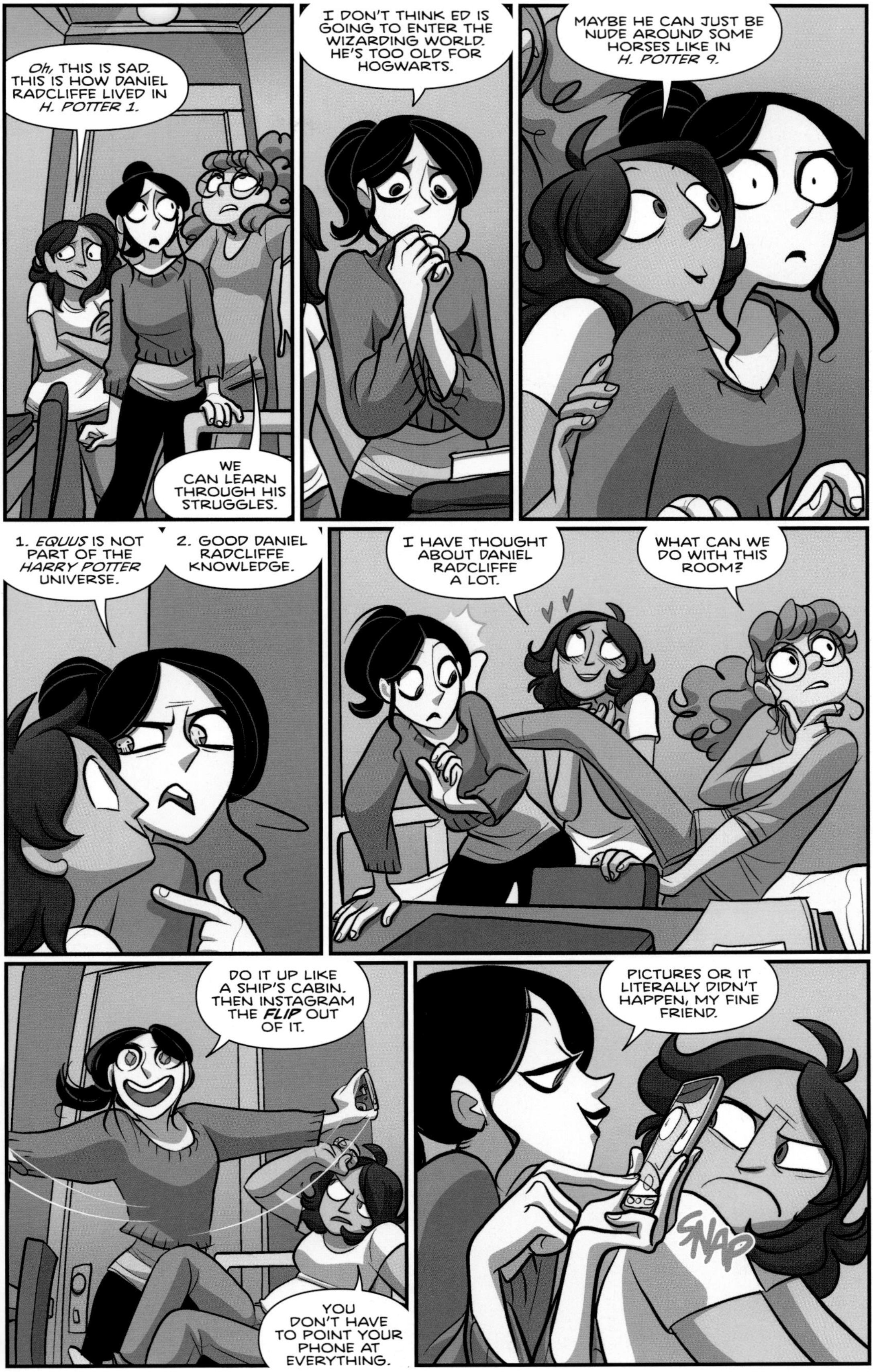

Oh, THIS IS SAD. THIS IS HOW DANIEL RADCLIFFE LIVED IN *H. POTTER 1.*
WE CAN LEARN THROUGH HIS STRUGGLES.
I DON'T THINK ED IS GOING TO ENTER THE WIZARDING WORLD. HE'S TOO OLD FOR HOGWARTS.
MAYBE HE CAN JUST BE NUDE AROUND SOME HORSES LIKE IN *H. POTTER 9.*
1. *EQUUS* IS NOT PART OF THE *HARRY POTTER* UNIVERSE.
2. GOOD DANIEL RADCLIFFE KNOWLEDGE.
I HAVE THOUGHT ABOUT DANIEL RADCLIFFE A LOT.
WHAT CAN WE DO WITH THIS ROOM?
DO IT UP LIKE A SHIP'S CABIN. THEN INSTAGRAM THE ***FLIP*** OUT OF IT.
YOU DON'T HAVE TO POINT YOUR PHONE AT EVERYTHING.
PICTURES OR IT LITERALLY DIDN'T HAPPEN, MY FINE FRIEND.
SNAP

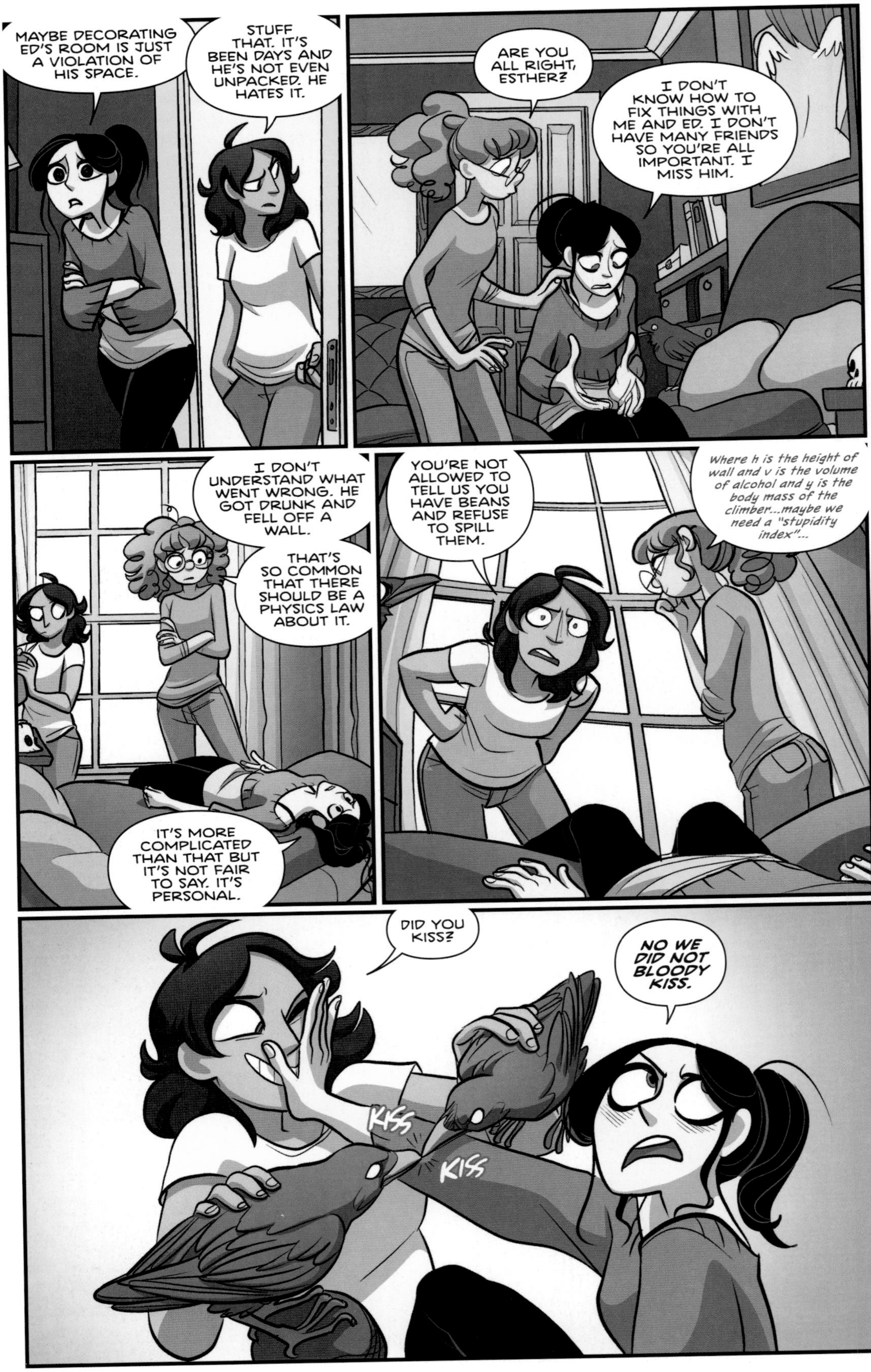
MAYBE DECORATING ED'S ROOM IS JUST A VIOLATION OF HIS SPACE.
STUFF THAT. IT'S BEEN DAYS AND HE'S NOT EVEN UNPACKED. HE HATES IT.
ARE YOU ALL RIGHT, ESTHER?
I DON'T KNOW HOW TO FIX THINGS WITH ME AND ED. I DON'T HAVE MANY FRIENDS SO YOU'RE ALL IMPORTANT. I MISS HIM.
I DON'T UNDERSTAND WHAT WENT WRONG. HE GOT DRUNK AND FELL OFF A WALL.
THAT'S SO COMMON THAT THERE SHOULD BE A PHYSICS LAW ABOUT IT.
IT'S MORE COMPLICATED THAN THAT BUT IT'S NOT FAIR TO SAY. IT'S PERSONAL.
YOU'RE NOT ALLOWED TO TELL US YOU HAVE BEANS AND REFUSE TO SPILL THEM.
Where h is the height of wall and v is the volume of alcohol and y is the body mass of the climber...maybe we need a "stupidity index"...
DID YOU KISS?
KISS
KISS
NO WE DID NOT BLOODY KISS.

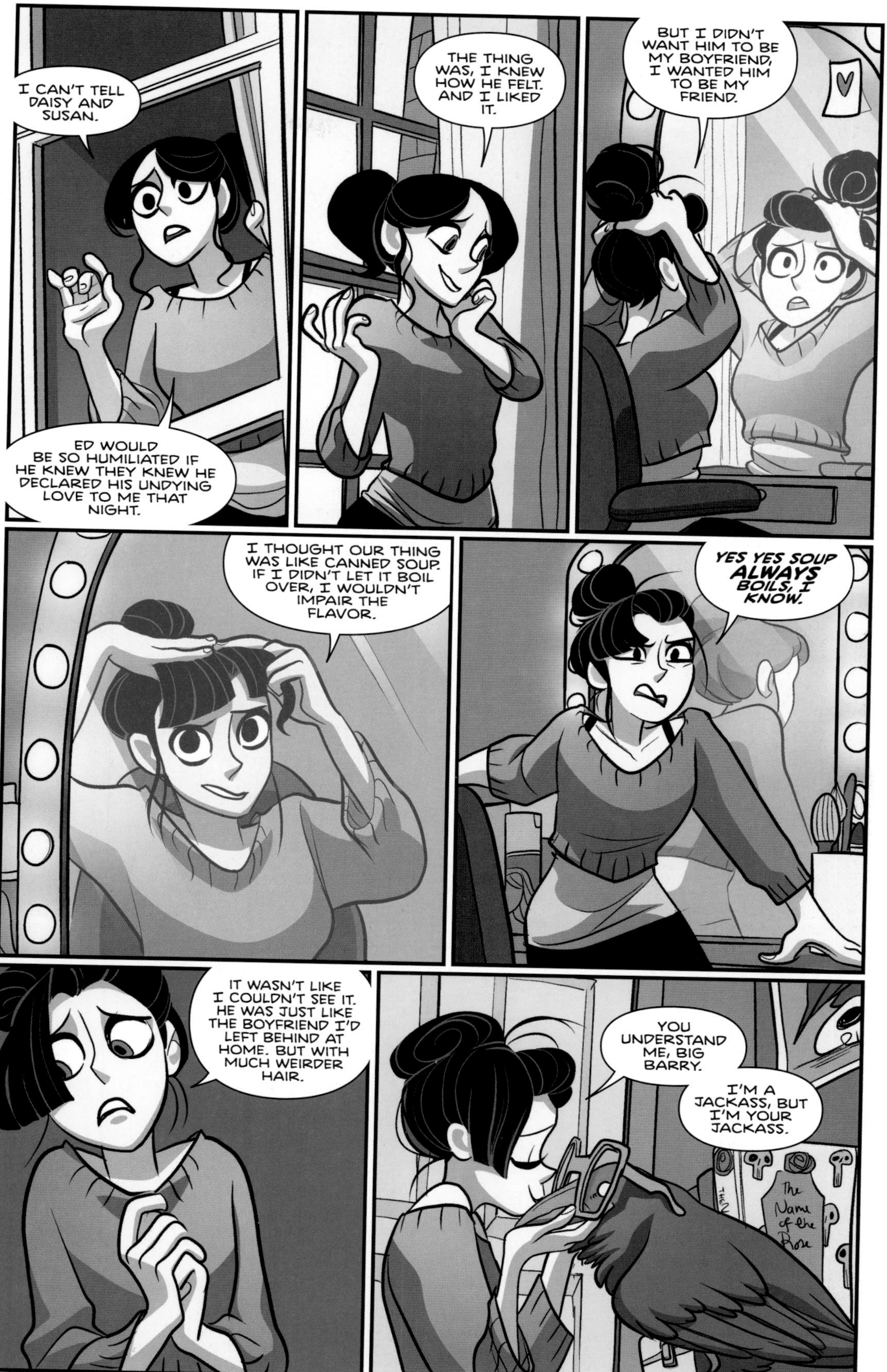
I CAN'T TELL DAISY AND SUSAN.
ED WOULD BE SO HUMILIATED IF HE KNEW THEY KNEW HE DECLARED HIS UNDYING LOVE TO ME THAT NIGHT.
THE THING WAS, I KNEW HOW HE FELT. AND I LIKED IT.
BUT I DIDN'T WANT HIM TO BE MY BOYFRIEND, I WANTED HIM TO BE MY FRIEND.
I THOUGHT OUR THING WAS LIKE CANNED SOUP. IF I DIDN'T LET IT BOIL OVER, I WOULDN'T IMPAIR THE FLAVOR.
YES YES SOUP ALWAYS BOILS, I KNOW.
IT WASN'T LIKE I COULDN'T SEE IT. HE WAS JUST LIKE THE BOYFRIEND I'D LEFT BEHIND AT HOME. BUT WITH MUCH WEIRDER HAIR.
YOU UNDERSTAND ME, BIG BARRY.
I'M A JACKASS, BUT I'M YOUR JACKASS.
The Name of the Rose

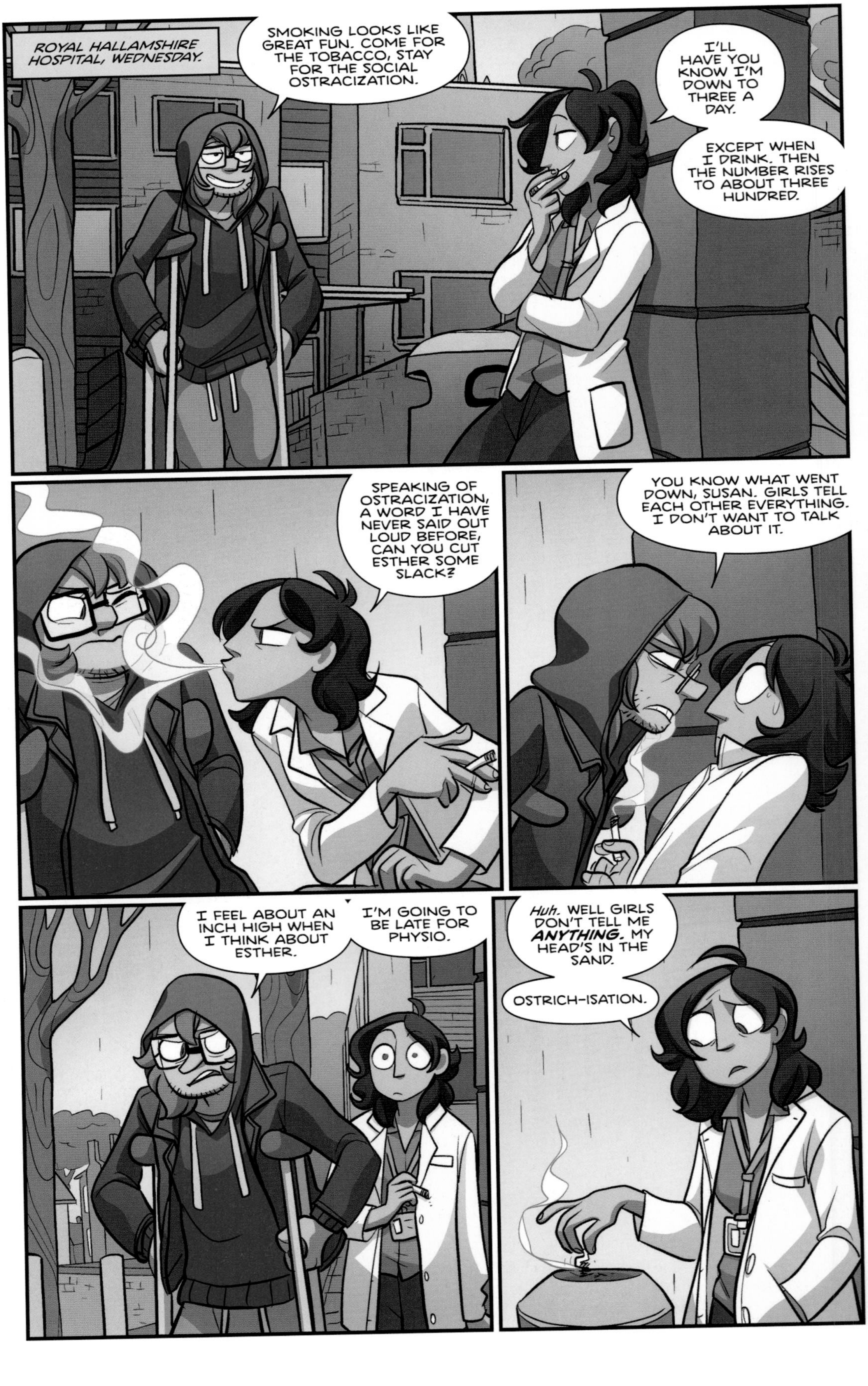
ROYAL HALLAMSHIRE HOSPITAL, WEDNESDAY.
SMOKING LOOKS LIKE GREAT FUN. COME FOR THE TOBACCO, STAY FOR THE SOCIAL OSTRACIZATION.
I'LL HAVE YOU KNOW I'M DOWN TO THREE A DAY.
EXCEPT WHEN I DRINK. THEN THE NUMBER RISES TO ABOUT THREE HUNDRED.
SPEAKING OF OSTRACIZATION, A WORD I HAVE NEVER SAID OUT LOUD BEFORE, CAN YOU CUT ESTHER SOME SLACK?
YOU KNOW WHAT WENT DOWN, SUSAN. GIRLS TELL EACH OTHER EVERYTHING. I DON'T WANT TO TALK ABOUT IT.
I FEEL ABOUT AN INCH HIGH WHEN I THINK ABOUT ESTHER.
I'M GOING TO BE LATE FOR PHYSIO.
Huh. WELL GIRLS DON'T TELL ME ***ANYTHING.*** MY HEAD'S IN THE SAND.
OSTRICH-ISATION.

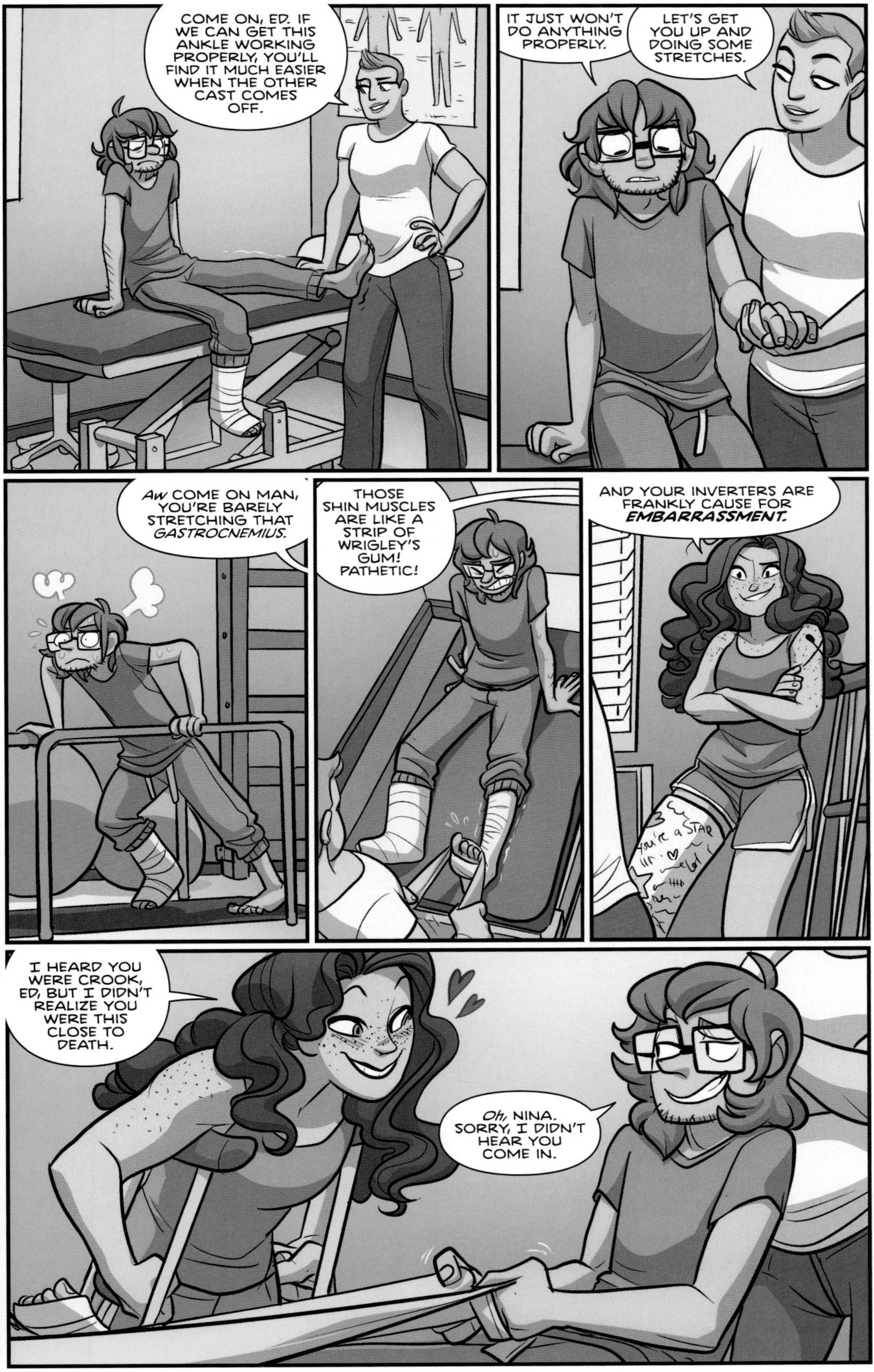
COME ON, ED. IF WE CAN GET THIS ANKLE WORKING PROPERLY, YOU'LL FIND IT MUCH EASIER WHEN THE OTHER CAST COMES OFF.
IT JUST WON'T DO ANYTHING PROPERLY.
LET'S GET YOU UP AND DOING SOME STRETCHES.
AW COME ON MAN, YOU'RE BARELY STRETCHING THAT *GASTROCNEMIUS.*
THOSE SHIN MUSCLES ARE LIKE A STRIP OF WRIGLEY'S GUM! PATHETIC!
AND YOUR INVERTERS ARE FRANKLY CAUSE FOR ***EMBARRASSMENT.***
You're a STAR
I HEARD YOU WERE CROOK, ED, BUT I DIDN'T REALIZE YOU WERE THIS CLOSE TO DEATH.
OH, NINA. SORRY, I DIDN'T HEAR YOU COME IN.

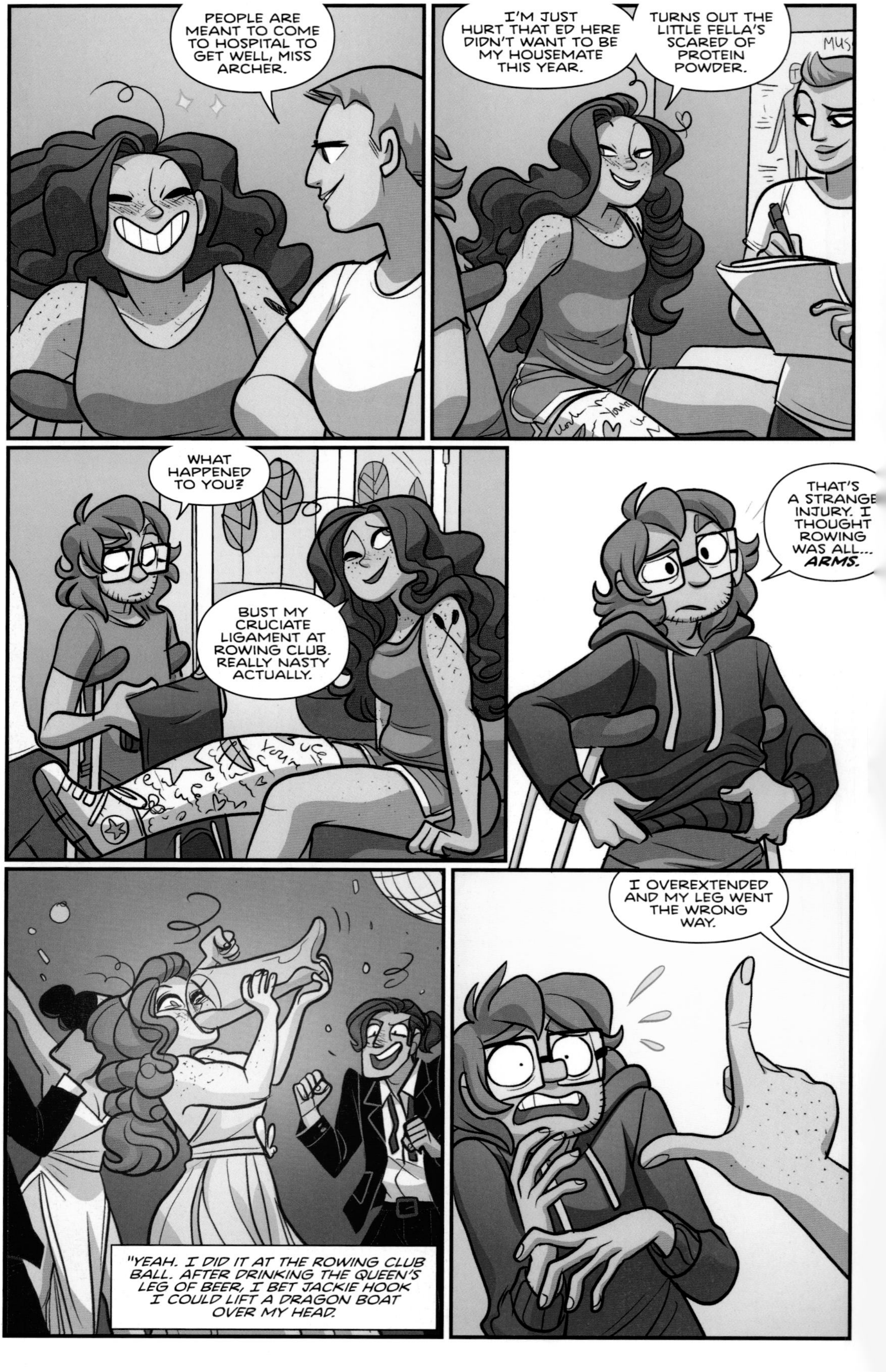
PEOPLE ARE MEANT TO COME TO HOSPITAL TO GET WELL, MISS ARCHER.
I'M JUST HURT THAT ED HERE DIDN'T WANT TO BE MY HOUSEMATE THIS YEAR.
TURNS OUT THE LITTLE FELLA'S SCARED OF PROTEIN POWDER.
WHAT HAPPENED TO YOU?
BUST MY CRUCIATE LIGAMENT AT ROWING CLUB. REALLY NASTY ACTUALLY.
THAT'S A STRANGE INJURY. I THOUGHT ROWING WAS ALL... ARMS.
"YEAH. I DID IT AT THE ROWING CLUB BALL. AFTER DRINKING THE QUEEN'S LEG OF BEER, I BET JACKIE HOOK I COULD LIFT A DRAGON BOAT OVER MY HEAD.
I OVEREXTENDED AND MY LEG WENT THE WRONG WAY.

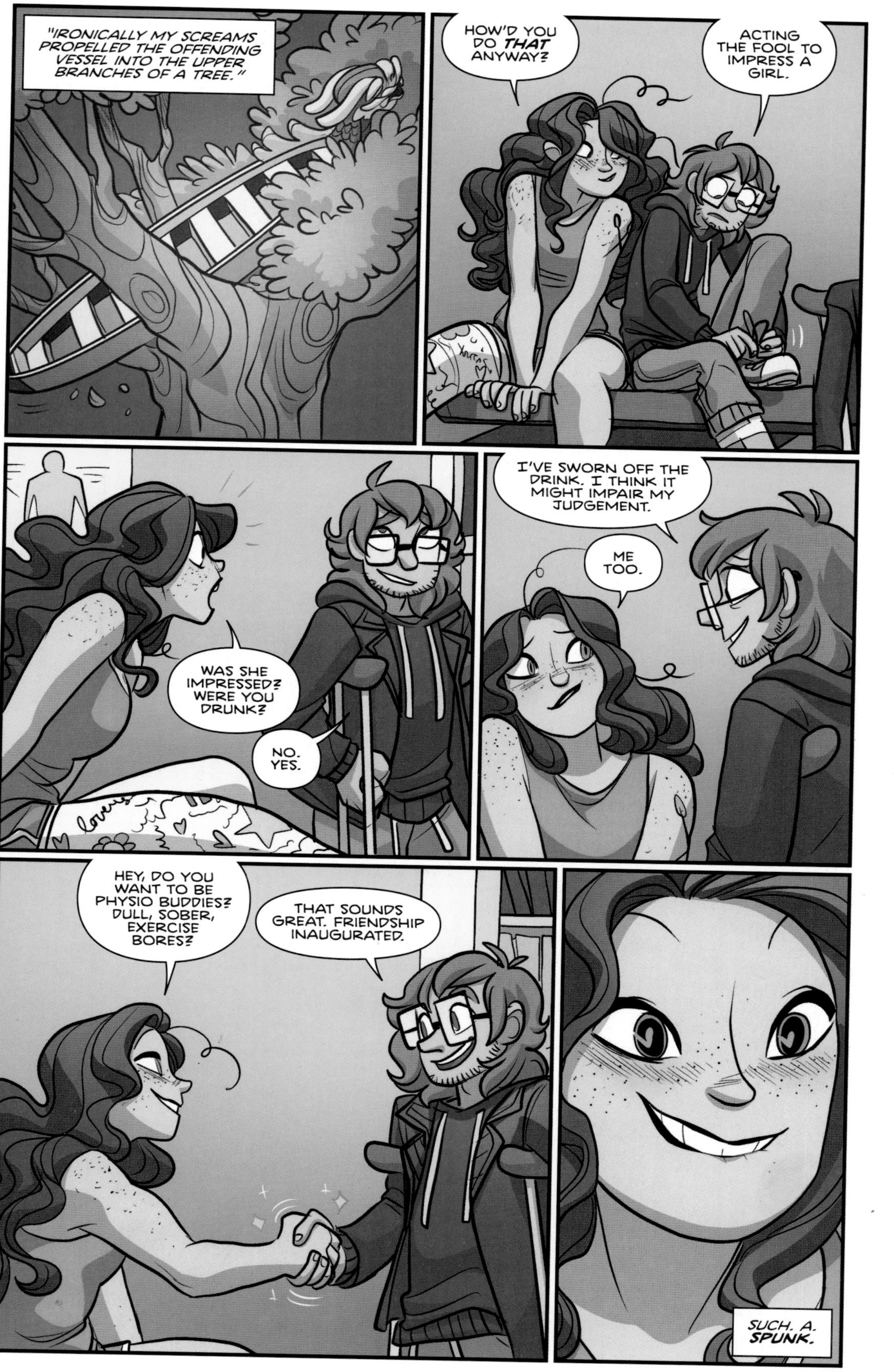
"IRONICALLY MY SCREAMS PROPELLED THE OFFENDING VESSEL INTO THE UPPER BRANCHES OF A TREE."
HOW'D YOU DO *THAT* ANYWAY?
ACTING THE FOOL TO IMPRESS A GIRL.
WAS SHE IMPRESSED? WERE YOU DRUNK?
NO. YES.
I'VE SWORN OFF THE DRINK. I THINK IT MIGHT IMPAIR MY JUDGEMENT.
ME TOO.
HEY, DO YOU WANT TO BE PHYSIO BUDDIES? DULL, SOBER, EXERCISE BORES?
THAT SOUNDS GREAT. FRIENDSHIP INAUGURATED.
SUCH. A. **SPUNK.**

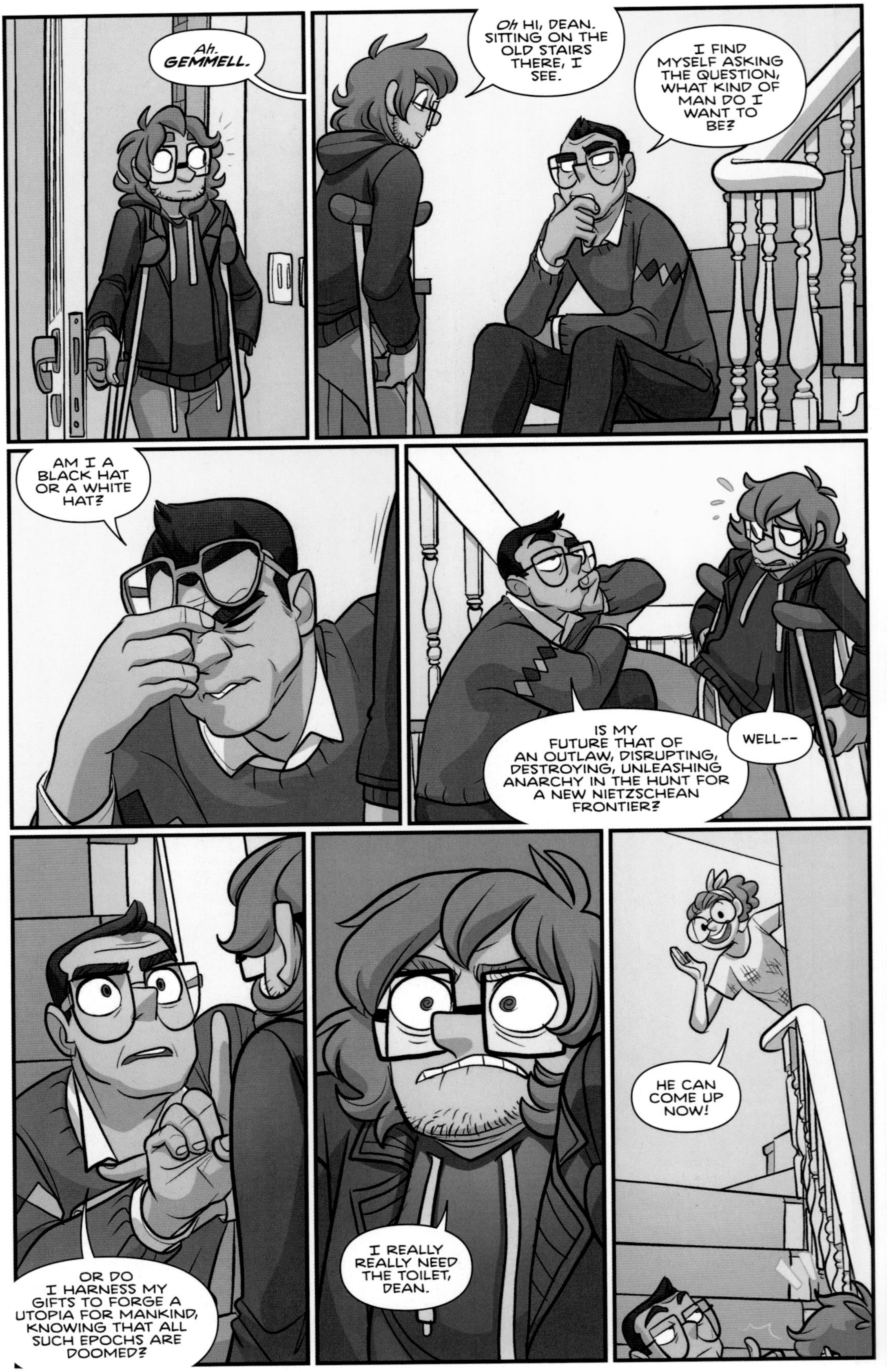

Ah. GEMMELL.
Oh HI, DEAN. SITTING ON THE OLD STAIRS THERE, I SEE.
I FIND MYSELF ASKING THE QUESTION, WHAT KIND OF MAN DO I WANT TO BE?
AM I A BLACK HAT OR A WHITE HAT?
IS MY FUTURE THAT OF AN OUTLAW, DISRUPTING, DESTROYING, UNLEASHING ANARCHY IN THE HUNT FOR A NEW NIETZSCHEAN FRONTIER?
WELL--
OR DO I HARNESS MY GIFTS TO FORGE A UTOPIA FOR MANKIND, KNOWING THAT ALL SUCH EPOCHS ARE DOOMED?
I REALLY REALLY NEED THE TOILET, DEAN.
HE CAN COME UP NOW!

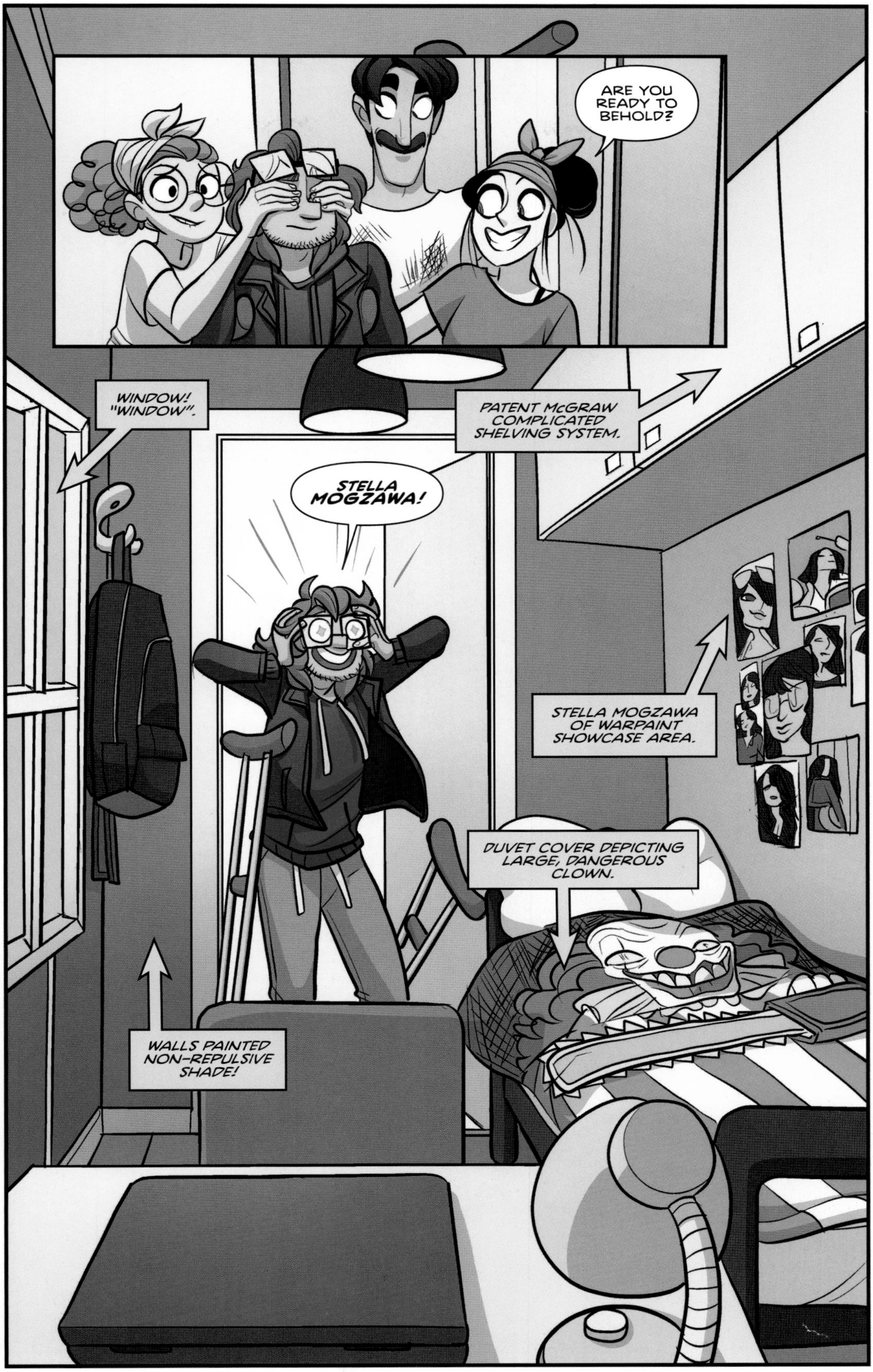

ARE YOU READY TO BEHOLD?
WINDOW! "WINDOW".
PATENT McGRAW COMPLICATED SHELVING SYSTEM.
STELLA MOGZAWA!
STELLA MOGZAWA OF WARPAINT SHOWCASE AREA.
DUVET COVER DEPICTING LARGE, DANGEROUS CLOWN.
WALLS PAINTED NON-REPULSIVE SHADE!

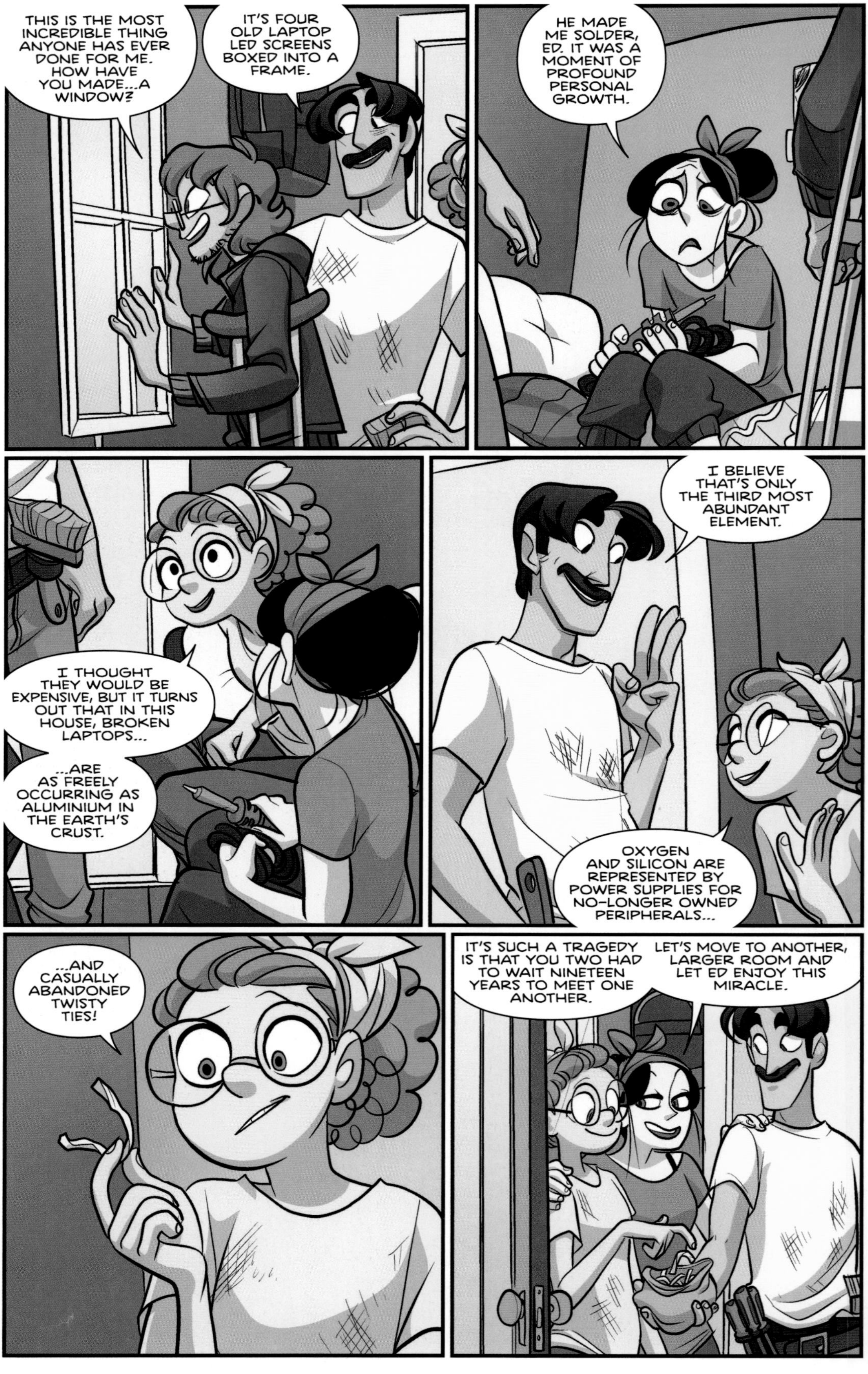
THIS IS THE MOST INCREDIBLE THING ANYONE HAS EVER DONE FOR ME. HOW HAVE YOU MADE...A WINDOW?
IT'S FOUR OLD LAPTOP LED SCREENS BOXED INTO A FRAME.
HE MADE ME SOLDER, ED. IT WAS A MOMENT OF PROFOUND PERSONAL GROWTH.
I THOUGHT THEY WOULD BE EXPENSIVE, BUT IT TURNS OUT THAT IN THIS HOUSE, BROKEN LAPTOPS...
...ARE AS FREELY OCCURRING AS ALUMINIUM IN THE EARTH'S CRUST.
I BELIEVE THAT'S ONLY THE THIRD MOST ABUNDANT ELEMENT.
OXYGEN AND SILICON ARE REPRESENTED BY POWER SUPPLIES FOR NO-LONGER OWNED PERIPHERALS...
...AND CASUALLY ABANDONED TWISTY TIES!
IT'S SUCH A TRAGEDY IS THAT YOU TWO HAD TO WAIT NINETEEN YEARS TO MEET ONE ANOTHER.
LET'S MOVE TO ANOTHER, LARGER ROOM AND LET ED ENJOY THIS MIRACLE.

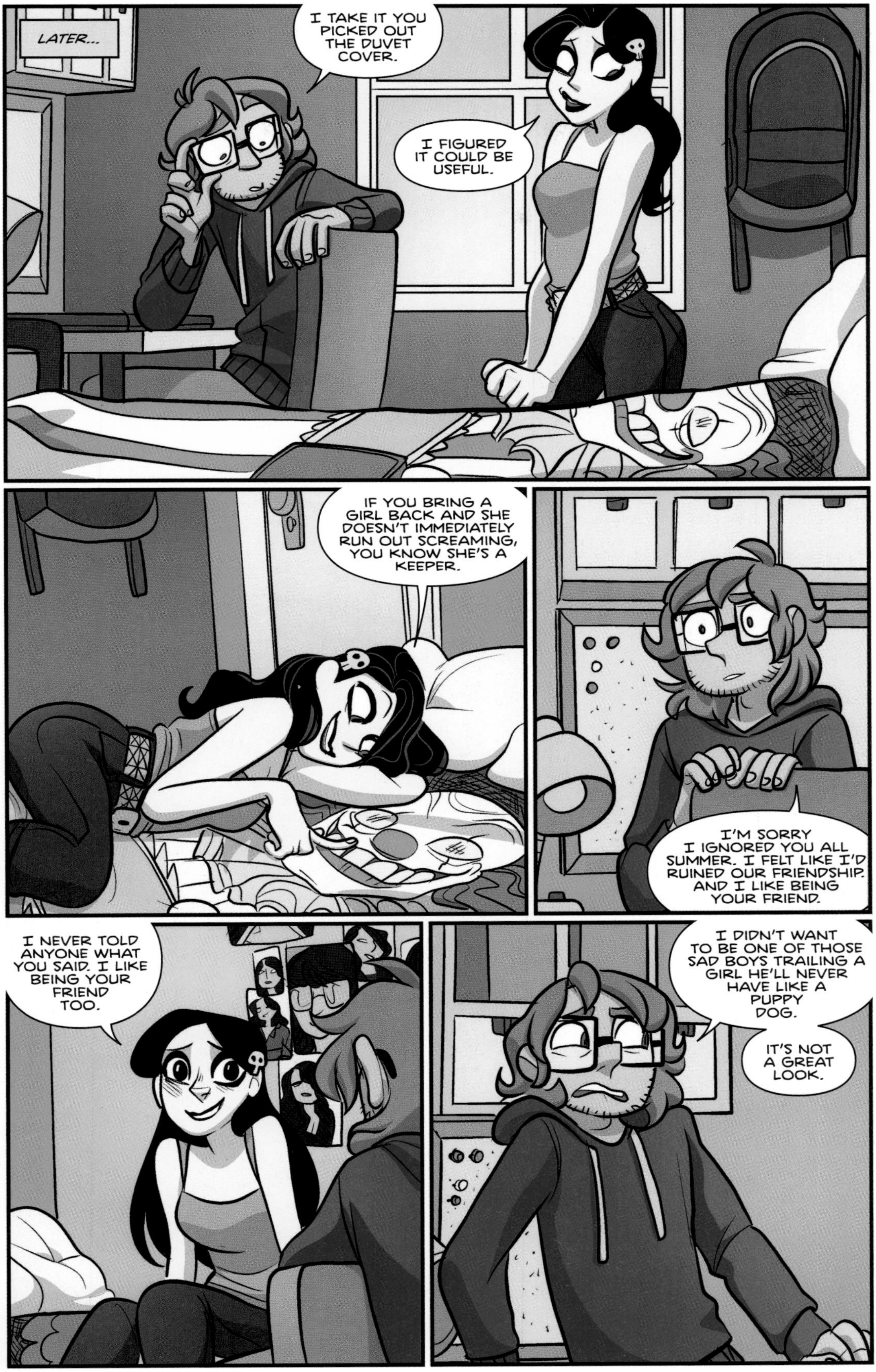
LATER...
I TAKE IT YOU PICKED OUT THE DUVET COVER.
I FIGURED IT COULD BE USEFUL.
IF YOU BRING A GIRL BACK AND SHE DOESN'T IMMEDIATELY RUN OUT SCREAMING, YOU KNOW SHE'S A KEEPER.
I'M SORRY I IGNORED YOU ALL SUMMER. I FELT LIKE I'D RUINED OUR FRIENDSHIP. AND I LIKE BEING YOUR FRIEND.
I NEVER TOLD ANYONE WHAT YOU SAID. I LIKE BEING YOUR FRIEND TOO.
I DIDN'T WANT TO BE ONE OF THOSE SAD BOYS TRAILING A GIRL HE'LL NEVER HAVE LIKE A PUPPY DOG.
IT'S NOT A GREAT LOOK.

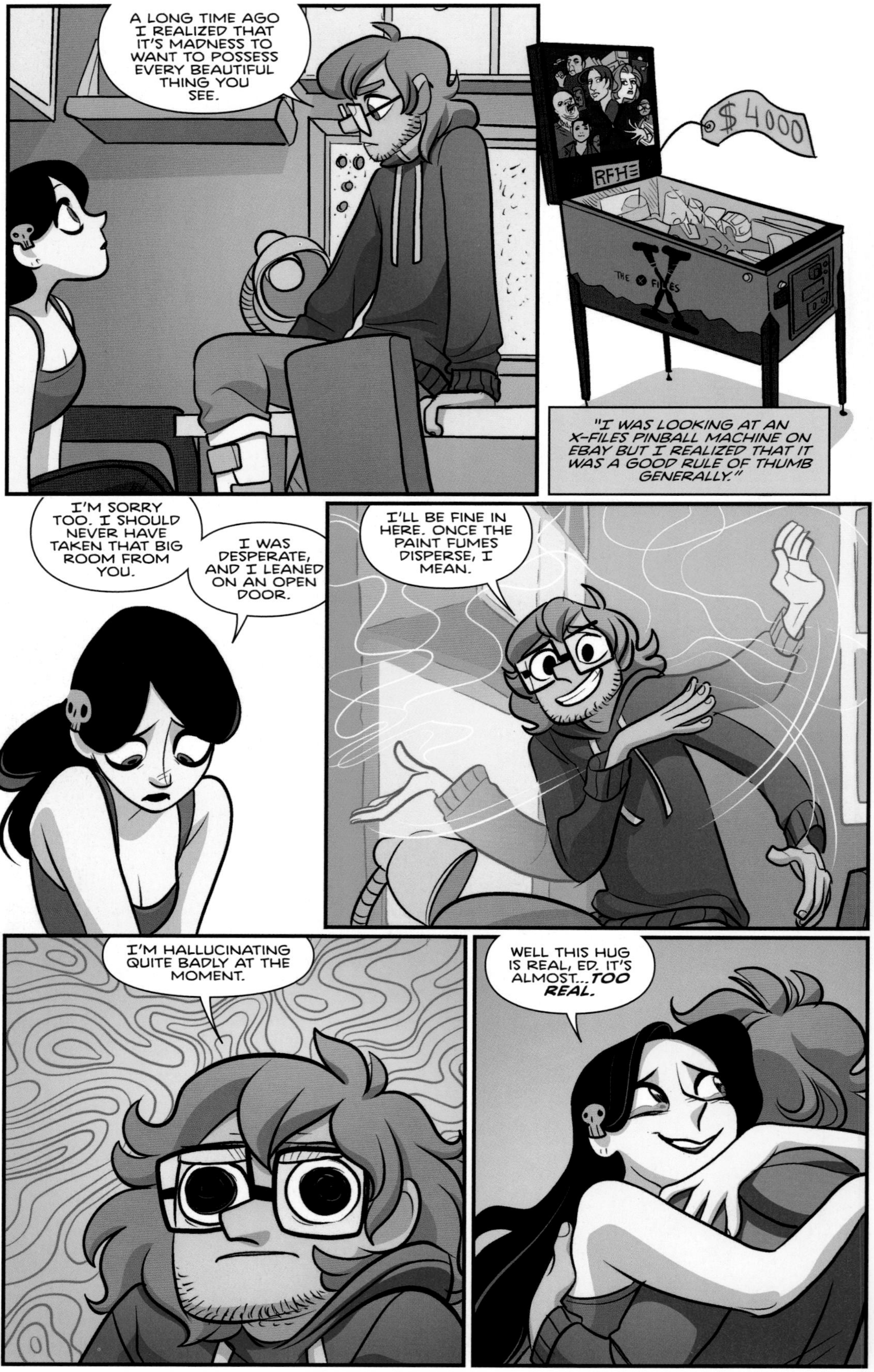
A LONG TIME AGO I REALIZED THAT IT'S MADNESS TO WANT TO POSSESS EVERY BEAUTIFUL THING YOU SEE.
$4000
"I WAS LOOKING AT AN X-FILES PINBALL MACHINE ON EBAY BUT I REALIZED THAT IT WAS A GOOD RULE OF THUMB GENERALLY."
I'M SORRY TOO. I SHOULD NEVER HAVE TAKEN THAT BIG ROOM FROM YOU.
I WAS DESPERATE, AND I LEANED ON AN OPEN DOOR.
I'LL BE FINE IN HERE. ONCE THE PAINT FUMES DISPERSE, I MEAN.
I'M HALLUCINATING QUITE BADLY AT THE MOMENT.
WELL THIS HUG IS REAL, ED. IT'S ALMOST... TOO REAL.

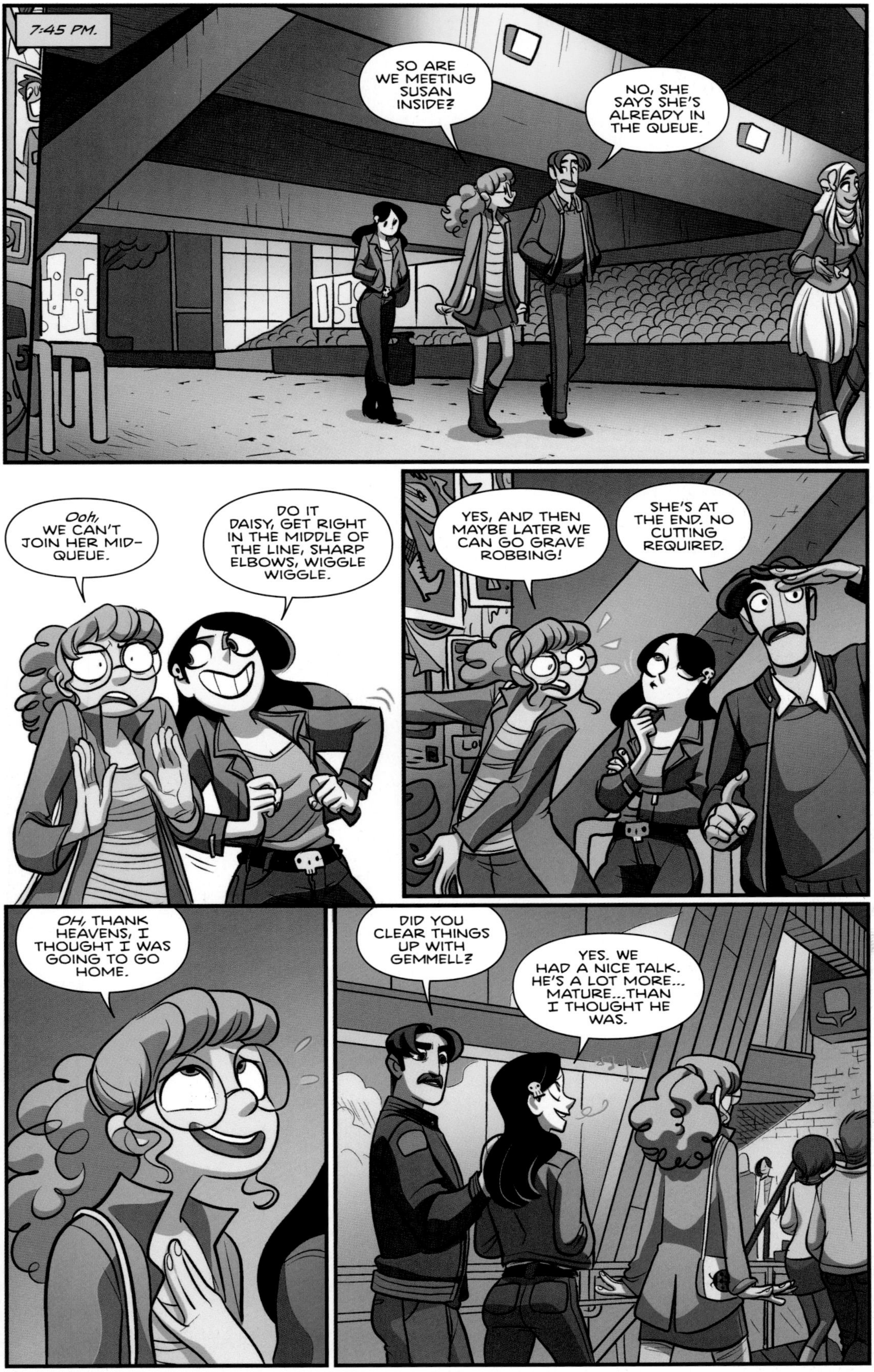
7:45 PM.
SO ARE WE MEETING SUSAN INSIDE?
NO, SHE SAYS SHE'S ALREADY IN THE QUEUE.
Ooh, WE CAN'T JOIN HER MID-QUEUE.
DO IT DAISY, GET RIGHT IN THE MIDDLE OF THE LINE, SHARP ELBOWS, WIGGLE WIGGLE.
YES, AND THEN MAYBE LATER WE CAN GO GRAVE ROBBING!
SHE'S AT THE END. NO CUTTING REQUIRED.
OH, THANK HEAVENS, I THOUGHT I WAS GOING TO GO HOME.
DID YOU CLEAR THINGS UP WITH GEMMELL?
YES. WE HAD A NICE TALK. HE'S A LOT MORE... MATURE...THAN I THOUGHT HE WAS.

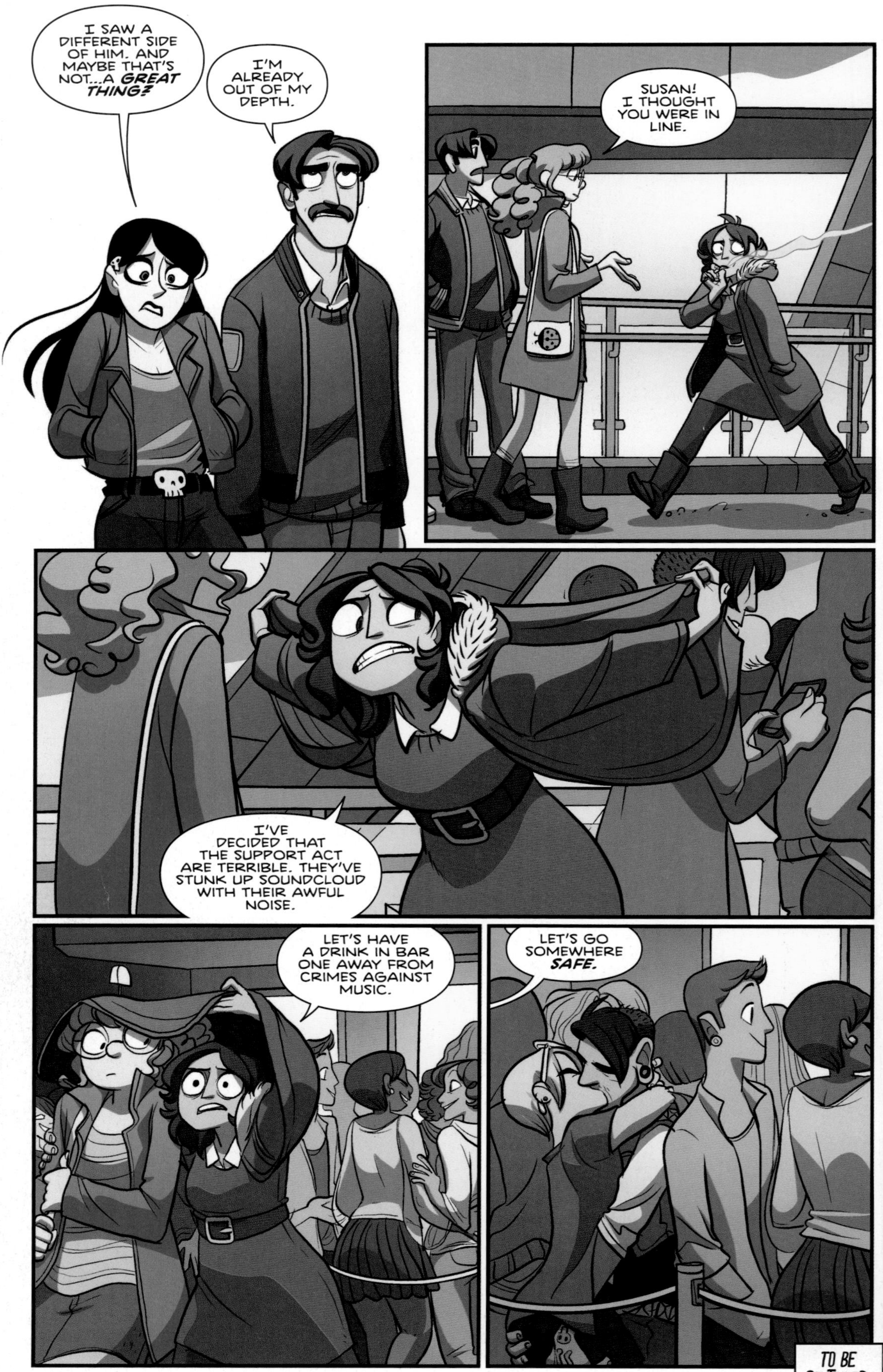
I SAW A DIFFERENT SIDE OF HIM. AND MAYBE THAT'S NOT...A GREAT THING?
I'M ALREADY OUT OF MY DEPTH.
SUSAN! I THOUGHT YOU WERE IN LINE.
I'VE DECIDED THAT THE SUPPORT ACT ARE TERRIBLE. THEY'VE STUNK UP SOUNDCLOUD WITH THEIR AWFUL NOISE.
LET'S HAVE A DRINK IN BAR ONE AWAY FROM CRIMES AGAINST MUSIC.
LET'S GO SOMEWHERE SAFE.
TO BE CONTINUED...

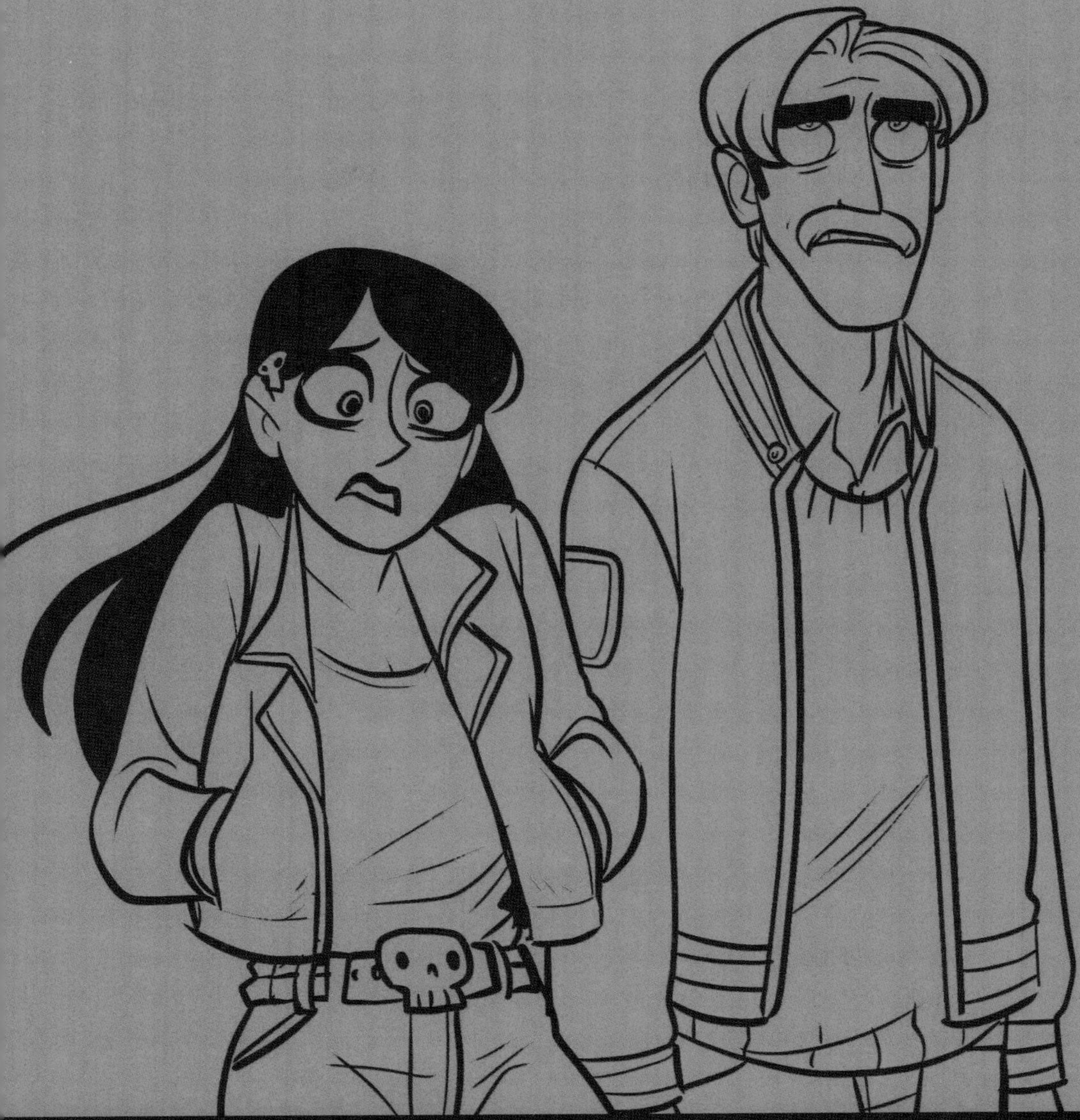

[redacted]

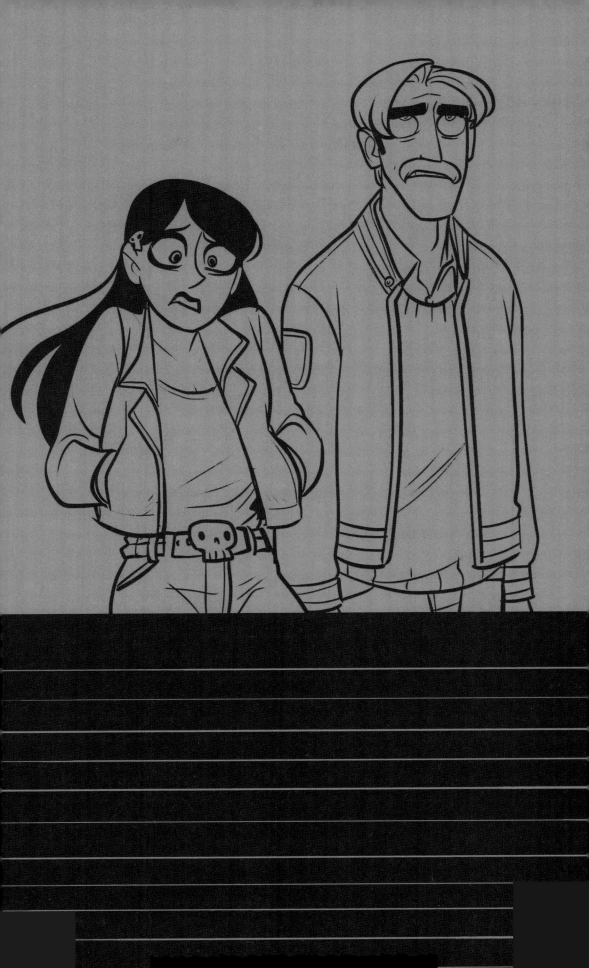

COVER GALLERY

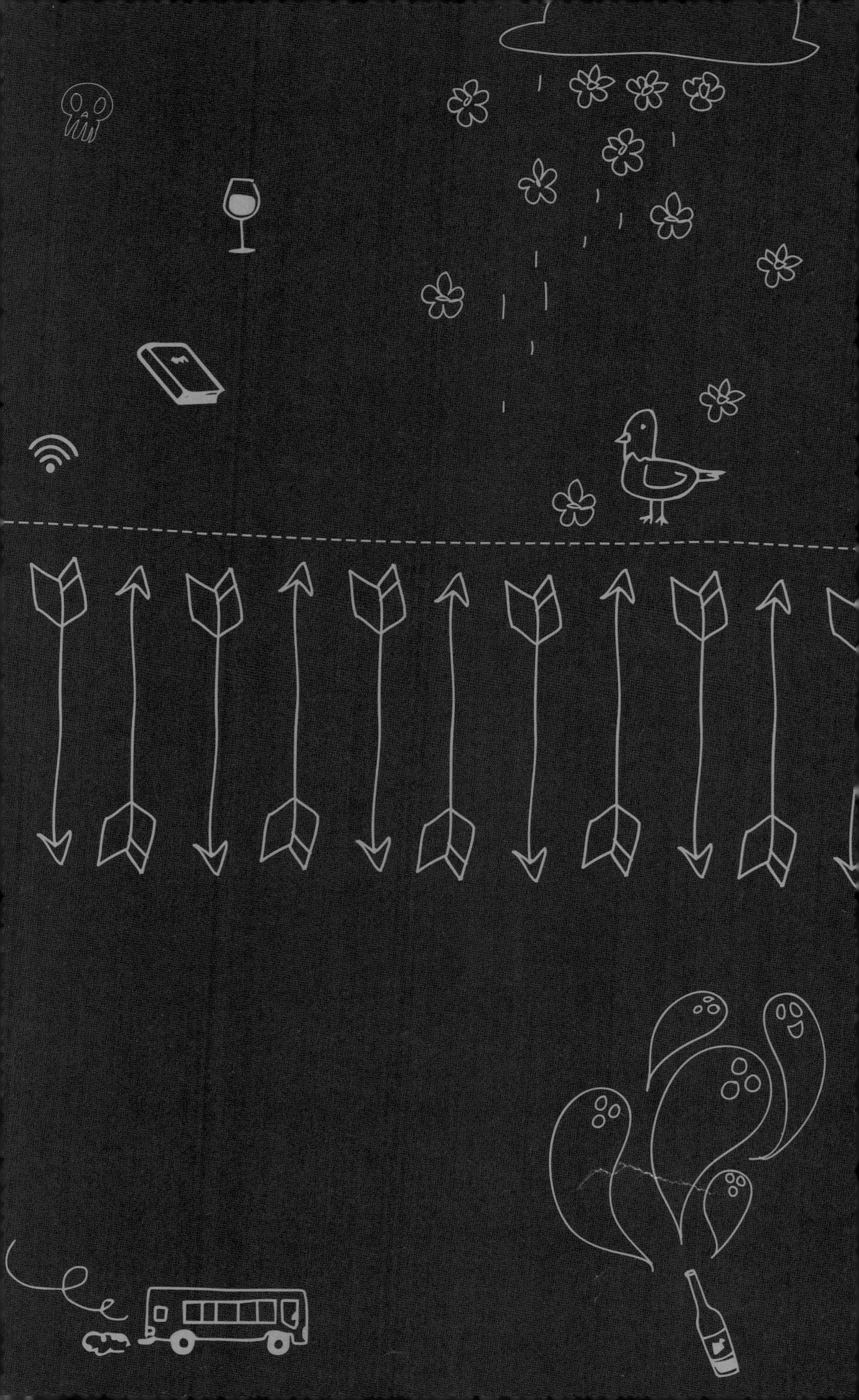

ISSUE #37 COVER
MAX SARIN

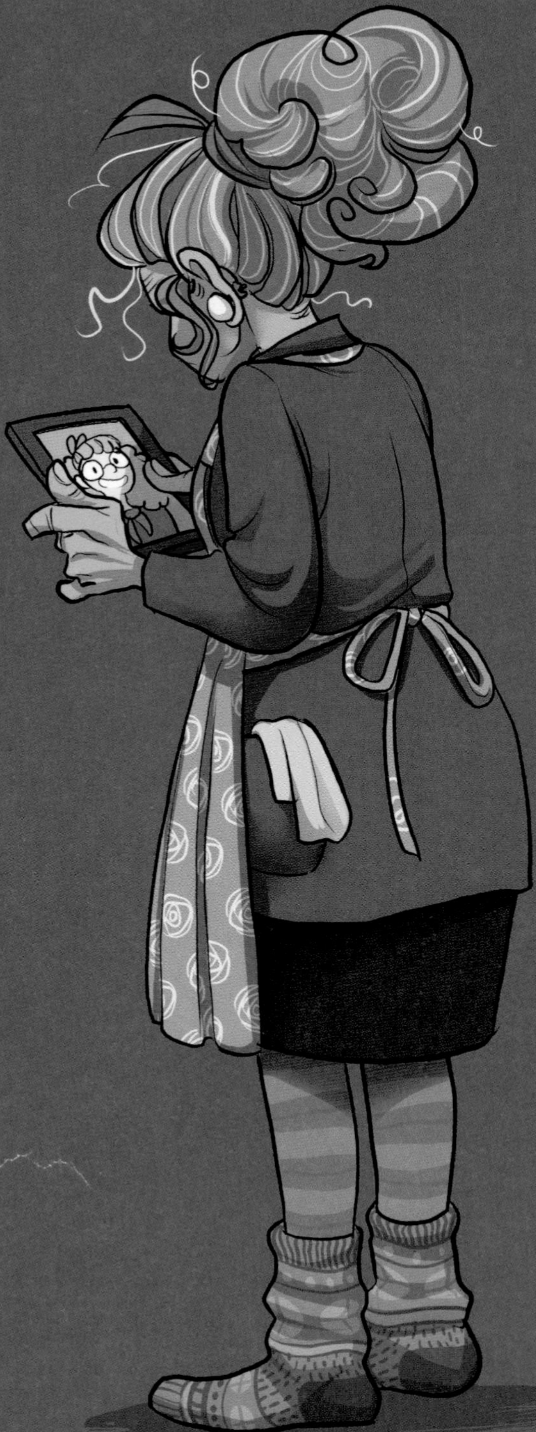

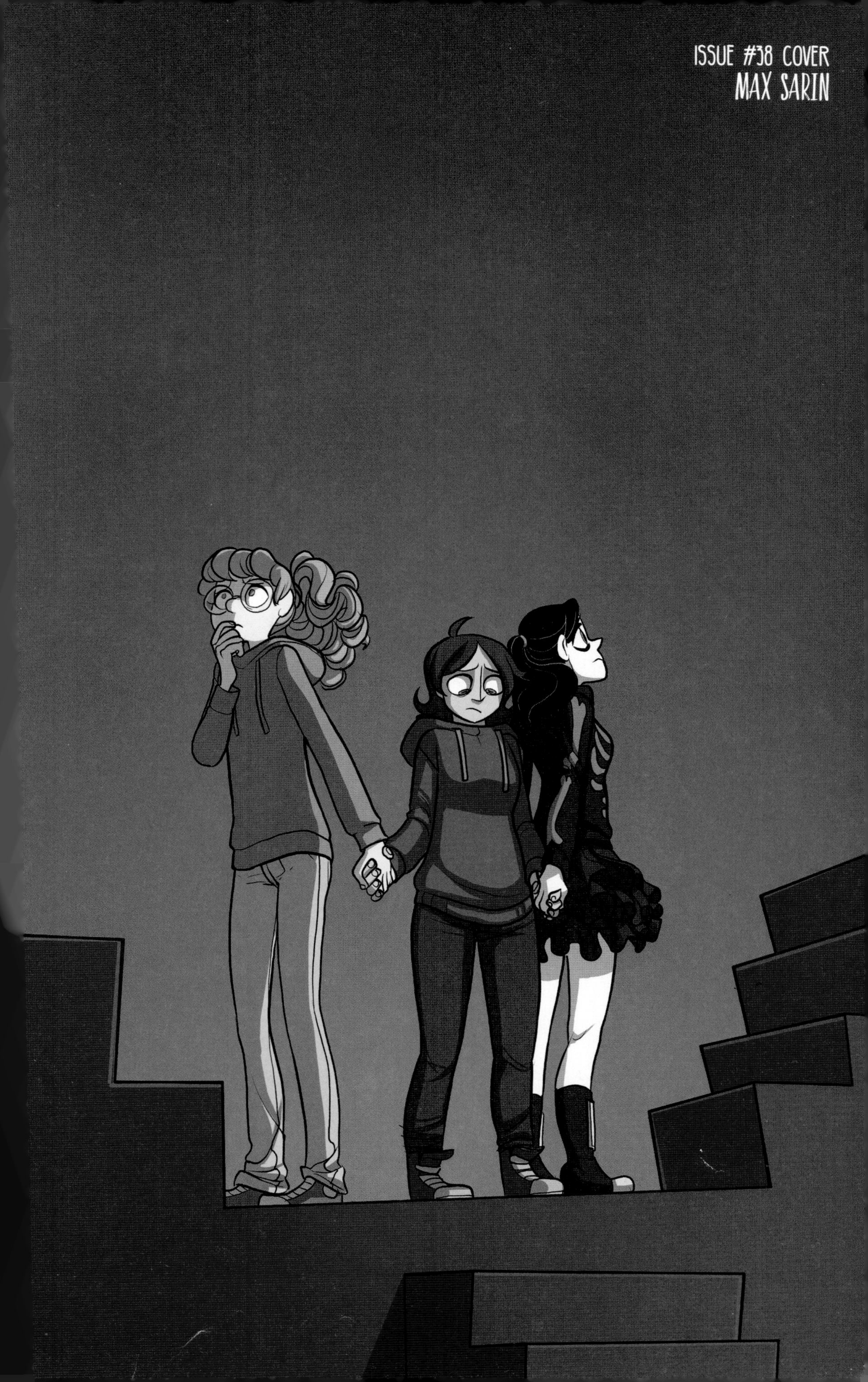

ISSUE #38 COVER
MAX SARIN

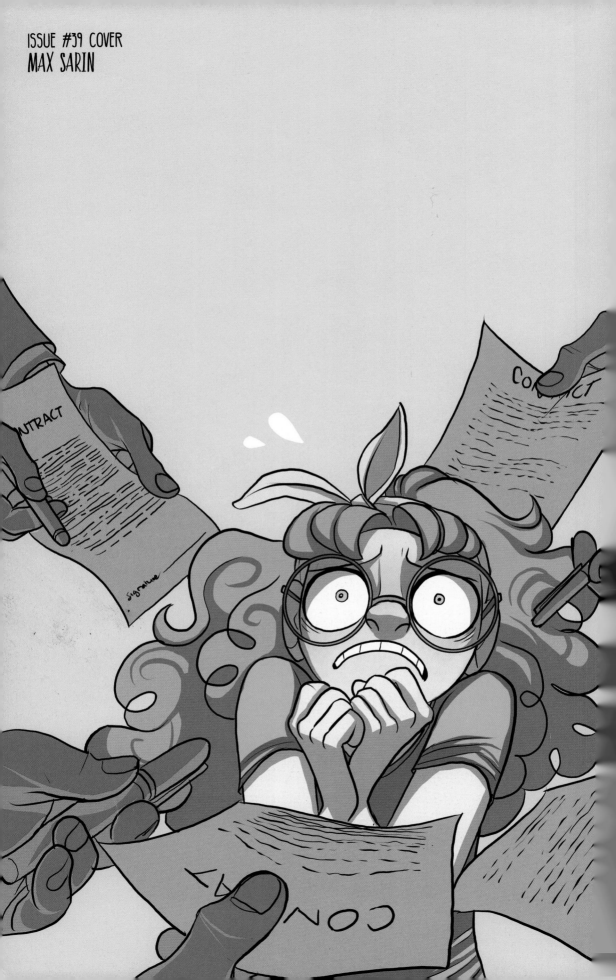

ISSUE #39 COVER
MAX SARIN

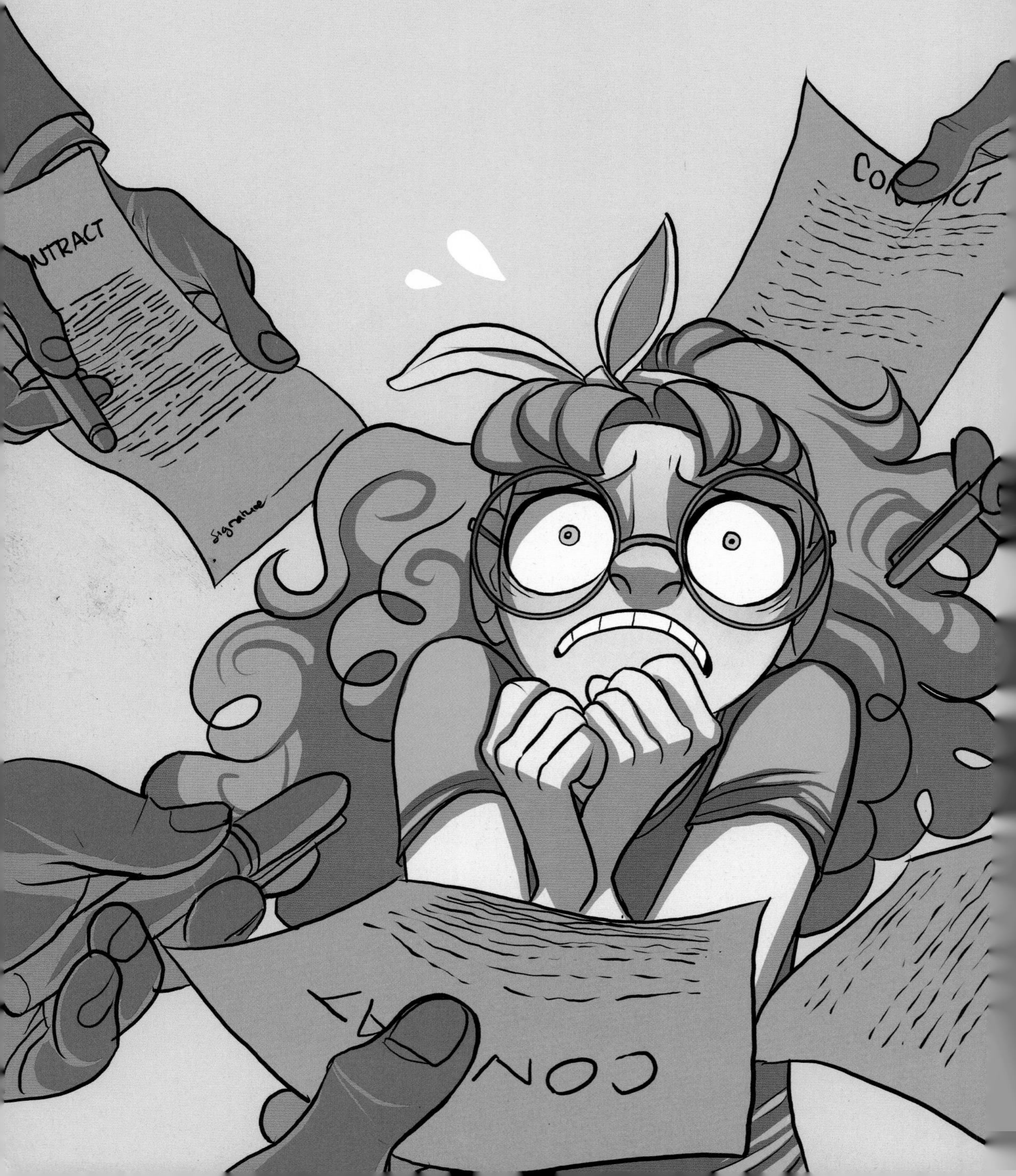

ISSUE #10 COVER
MAX SARIN

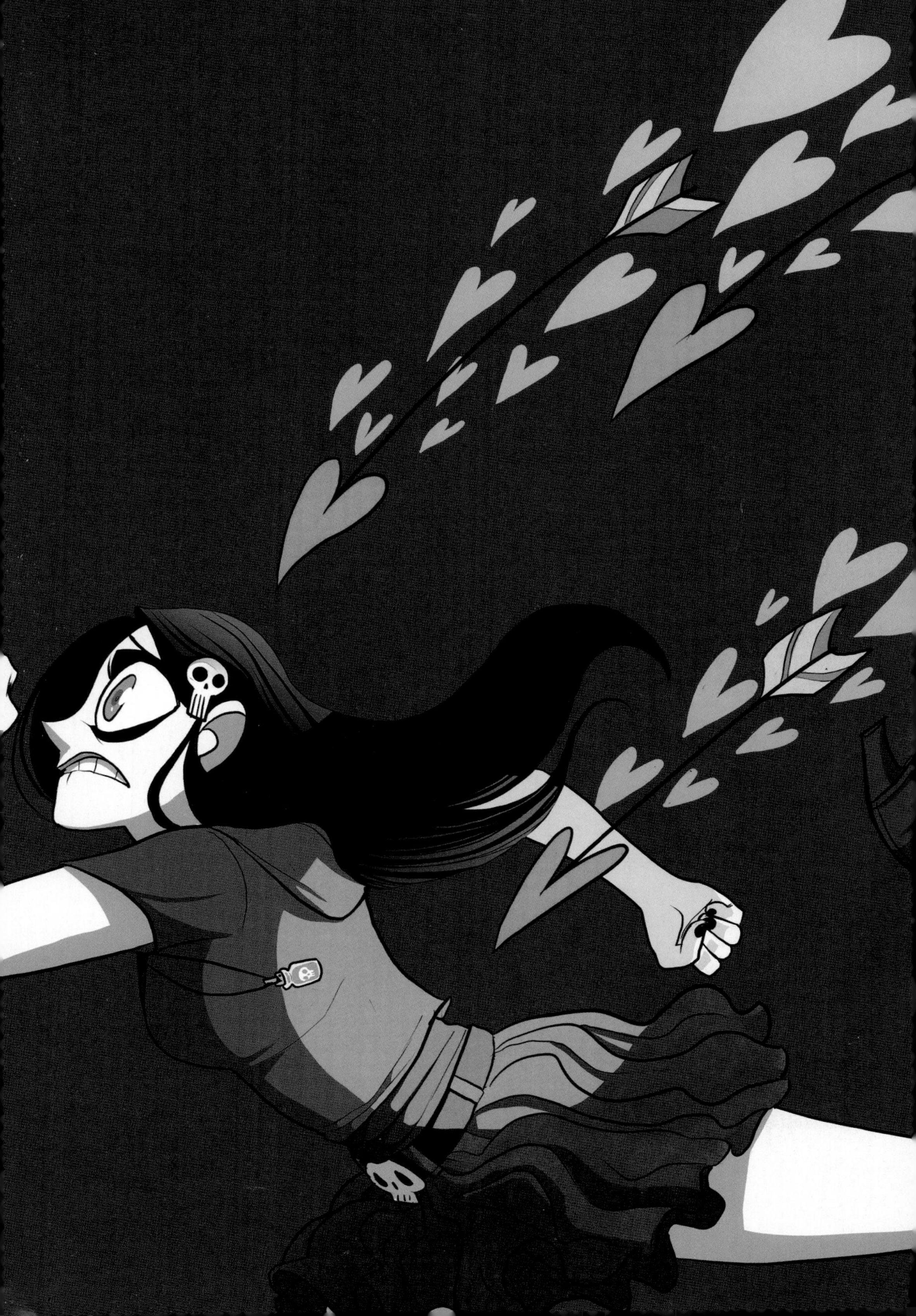

CHARACTER DESIGNS BY JOHN ALLISON

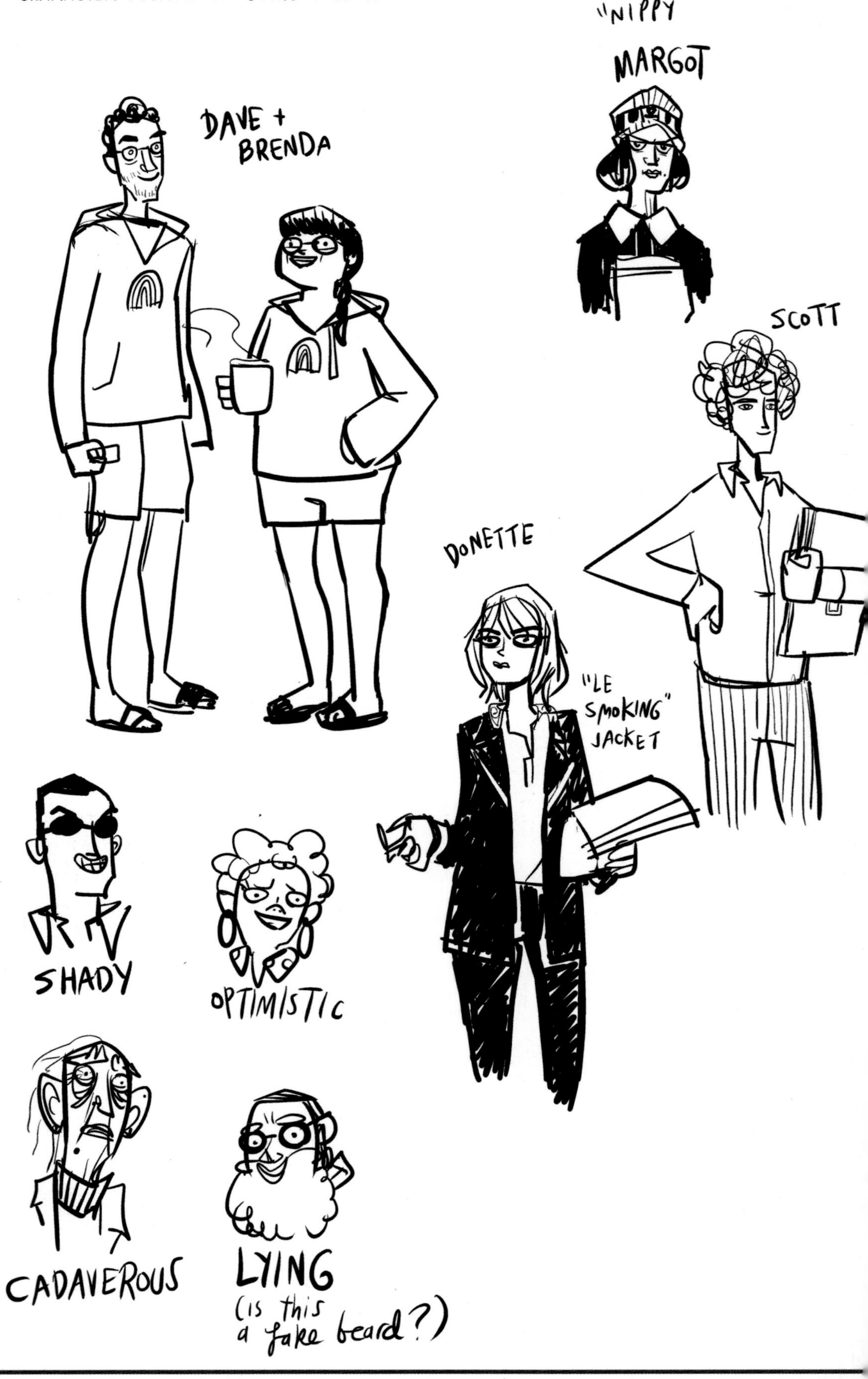
"NIPPY"
MARGOT
DAVE + BRENDA
SCOTT
DONETTE
"LE SMOKING" JACKET
SHADY
OPTIMISTIC
CADAVEROUS
LYING
(is this a fake beard?)

SKETCHES BY JULIA MADRIGAL

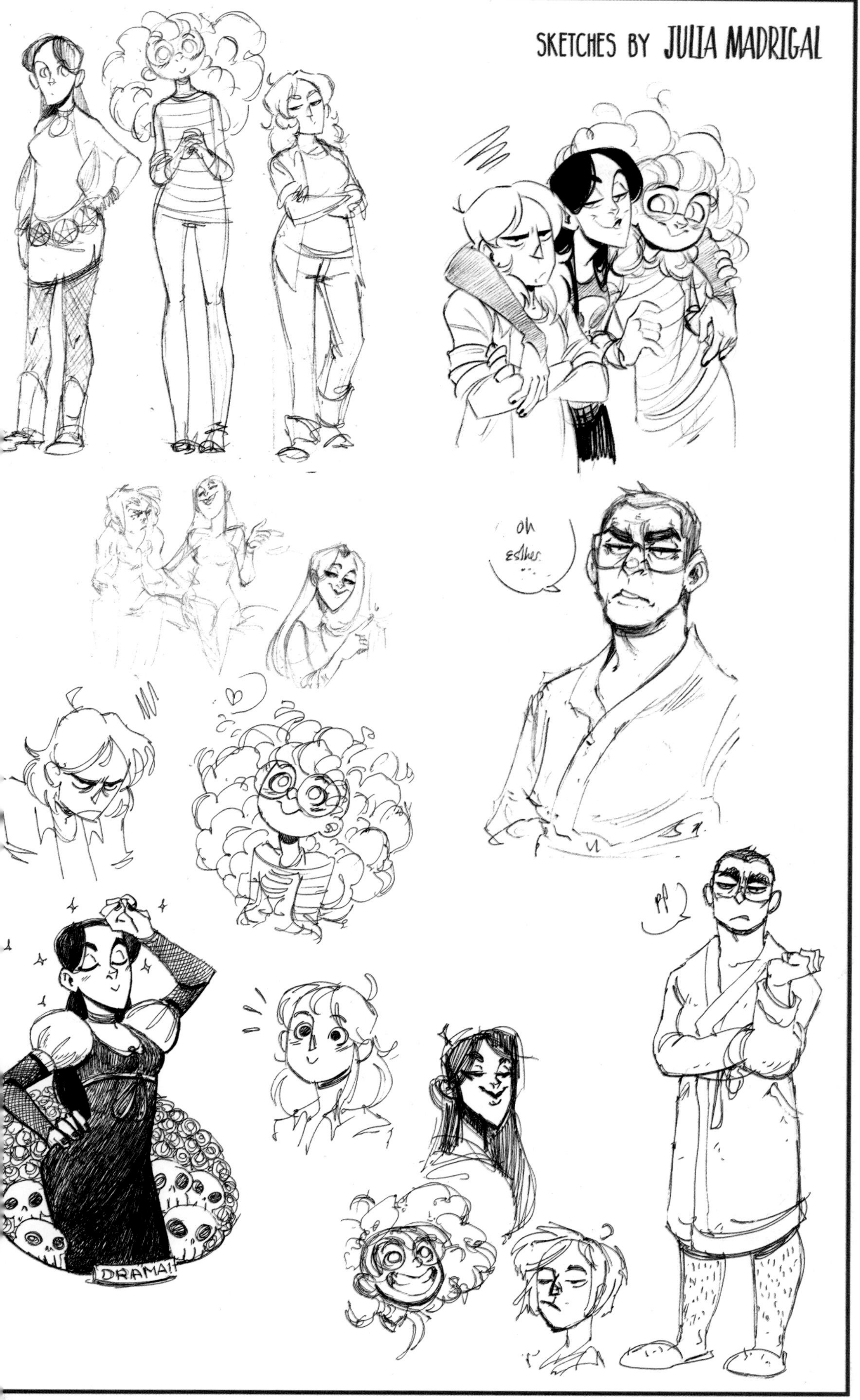

oh
esther.
DRAMA!

SKETCHES AND DESIGNS BY MAX SARIN

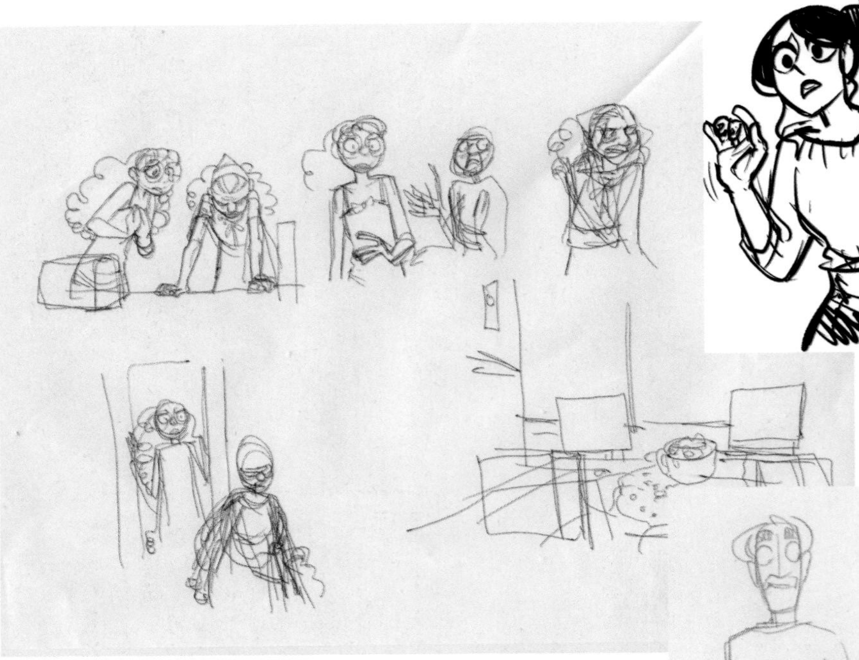

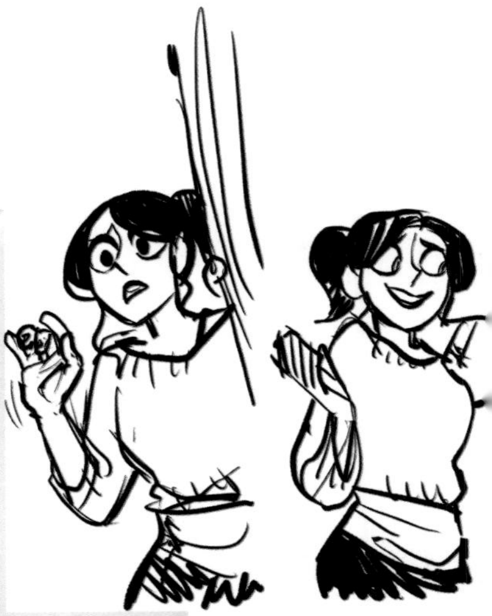

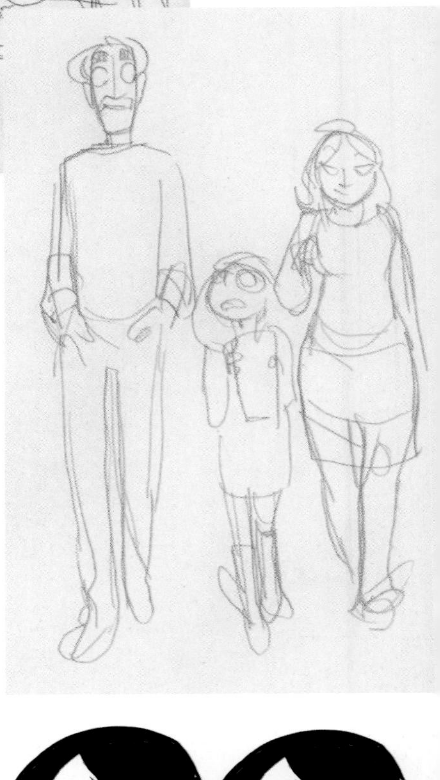

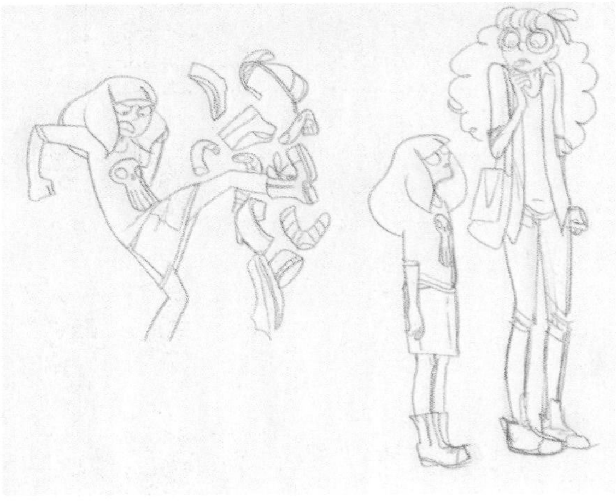

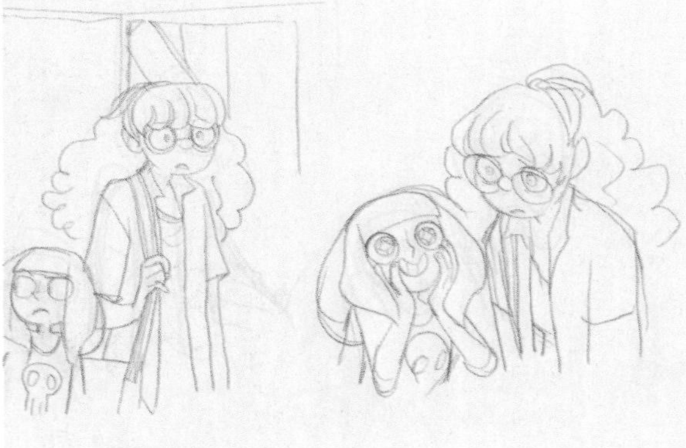

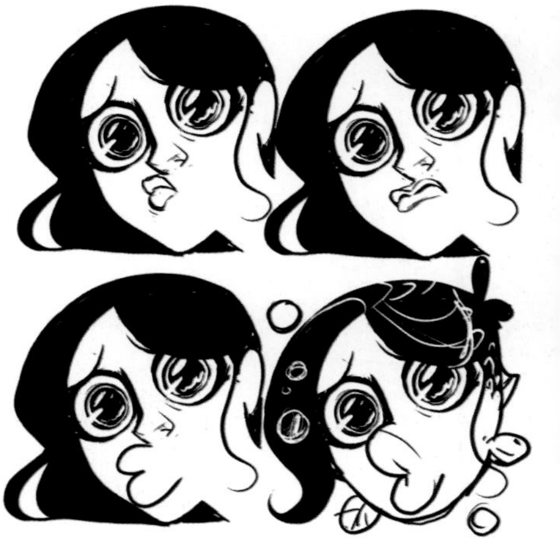

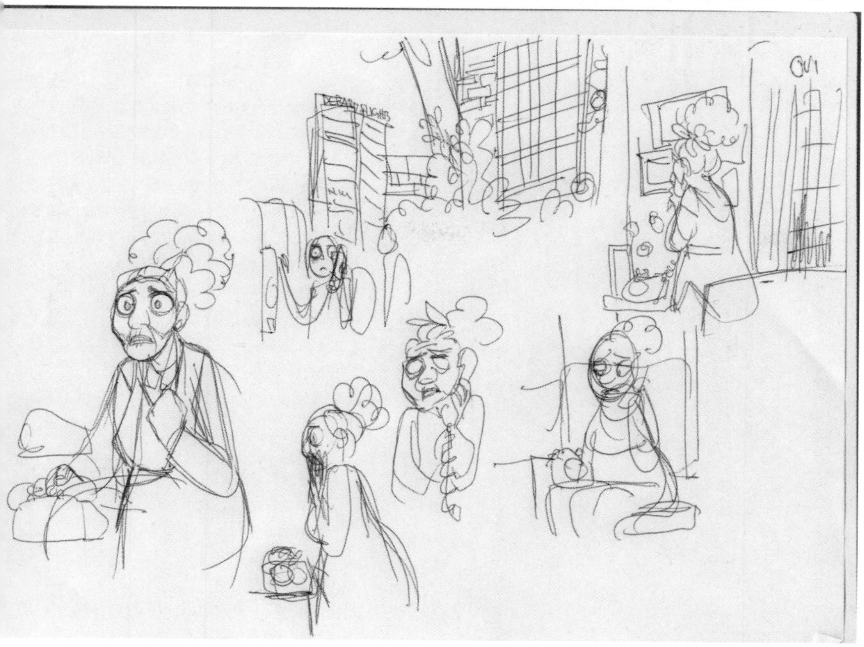

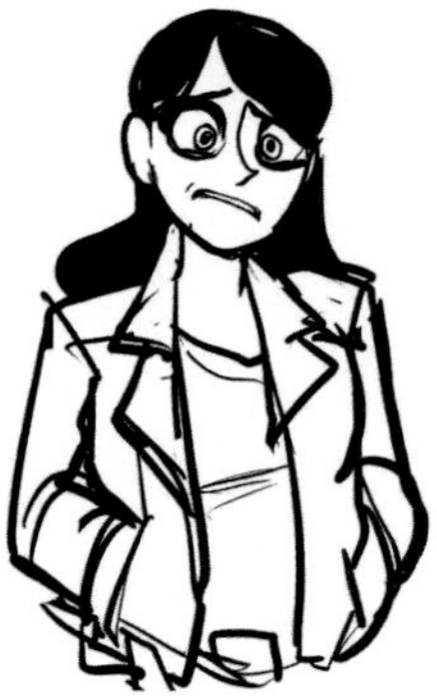

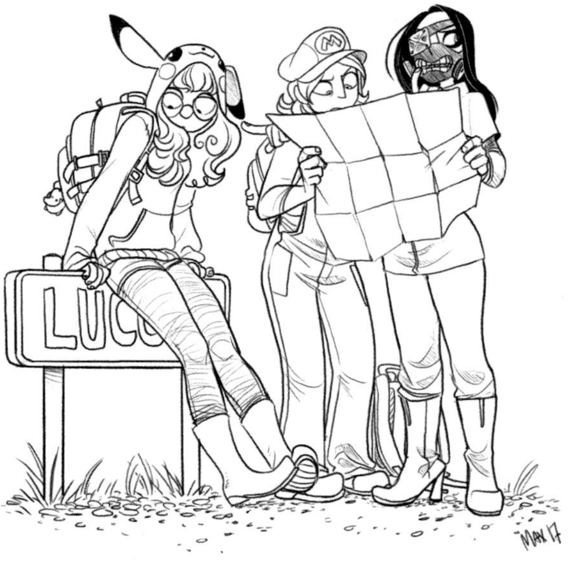
LUCC

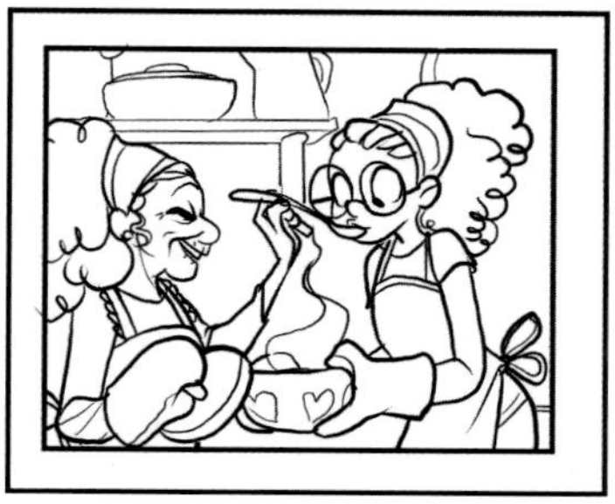

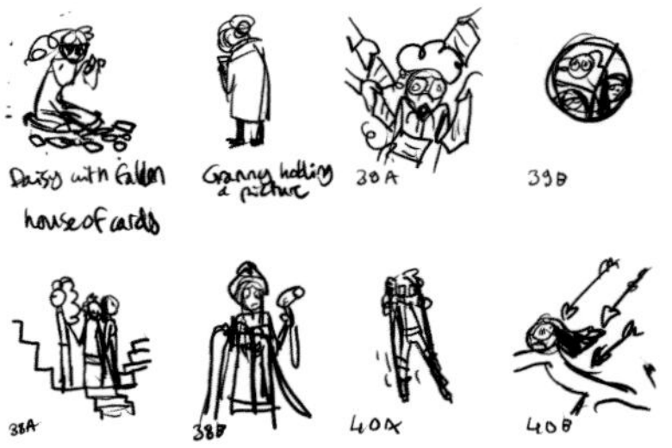
Daisy with fallen house of cards
Granny holding a picture
38A
39B
38A
38B
40A
40B

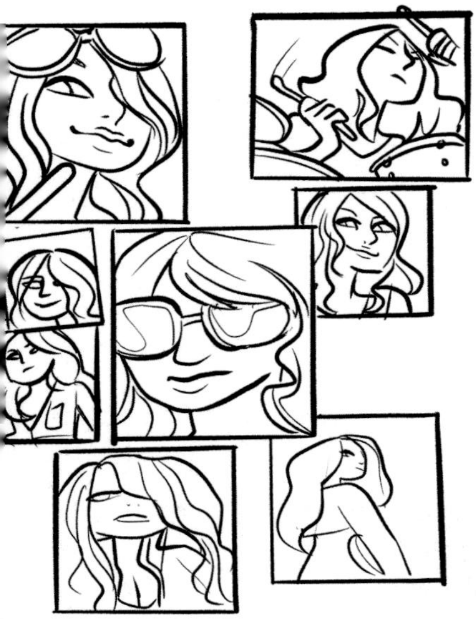

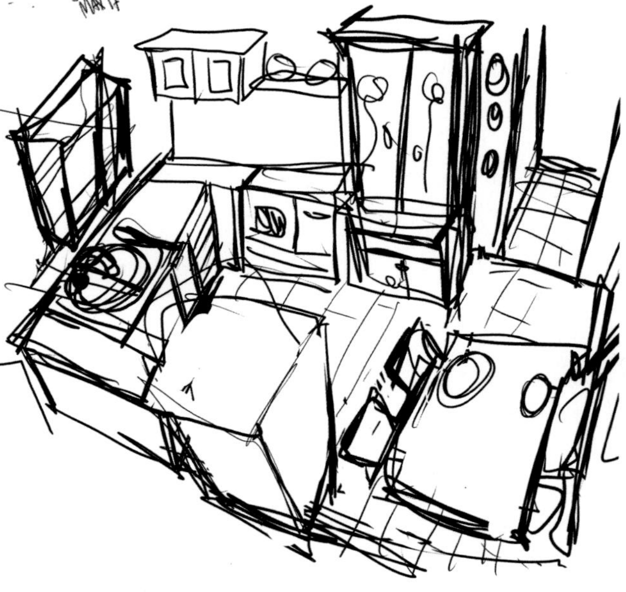

DISCOVER
ALL THE HITS

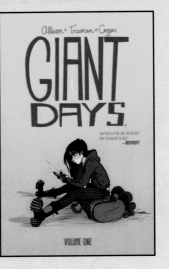